STERLING'S SOJOURN

Ted Gary

Acknowledgments

I would like to thank my wife, Carol, for her support as I worked on this story and for creating the book cover. I would also like to thank Evan Ziegenfus and Becca Wierwille for their excellent editorial suggestions.

One

FLOATING ON A thermal three thousand feet above the ground, I ruffled my wings and watched the Burke brothers carry their yard equipment down the sidewalk. Sterling held an edger over his shoulder while his brother, Hoyt, pushed their lawn mower. Sterling was lost in thought, calculating. He and Hoyt only needed to mow eight more lawns until he would have the money to buy the advanced programming kit he had been saving for.

Ten blocks from home, a glint in the grass parking strip caught Sterling's eye. He stopped, backtracked two steps, and peered into the grass. He could not find what caused the sparkle, so he walked back a few more steps and inched his way forward again. His eyes scanned the strip, moving back and forth like a flashlight searching the dark. He saw a glimmer at last and set the edger down, getting onto his hands and knees to comb through the grass with his fingers. He snagged a beautiful gold chain that held a delicate gold cross. Sterling stood up and pulled the necklace over his palm. He turned the cross over and noticed the initials M. M. engraved below an imprint that read 24K.

Hoyt, who had continued pushing the mower down the sidewalk, hollered over his shoulder, "Let's go. I want to shoot some hoops before dinner."

Sterling picked up the edger and jogged to his brother. "And I want to work on my submarine. But look at this." He twirled the necklace around his finger. "Bet it's worth real money. It'll help me buy my programming kit."

Hoyt grabbed the necklace mid-twirl. While he examined the cross, a high-school-age girl walked up. She looked at Hoyt, then at Sterling, and back again.

The boys were identical fifteen-year-old twins. Each had a hint of dark fuzz tinting his upper lip, black hair that just touched his ears, and brown eyes. A thin scar that started at the corner of Sterling's right eye and extended to his ear was the easiest way to distinguish the two. However, those who paid close attention noticed Hoyt was heavier than Sterling; ten pounds of muscle sculpted his body.

The girl wore a baggy, faded red T-shirt—stained with clashing magenta, crimson, and purple paint spatters—along with her black shorts and silver sandals studded with red and silver cut glass buttons. She reached out her hand. "Thank goodness you found it. I lost it earlier this morning and have been looking everywhere. This is my third pass down this street."

As Sterling snatched the necklace from Hoyt, he asked the girl, "What's it worth to you?"

She reached for the cross. "It was a birthday present from my grandma."

"Is there a reward?"

She frowned. "A reward? It's mine." Turning the cross over, she added, "These are my—"

Sterling pulled the cross back and said, "There must be a reward. What about a finder's fee?"

"It has my initials. Please give it back."

"Twenty bucks. It will go toward a good cause, an educational one. I'll use the money to buy a programming kit."

Her cheeks flushed, and she said, "I don't have any money with me."

"Twenty bucks seems like a fair finder's fee for such a high-quality necklace. Twenty-four karat gold. I bet the chain alone cost well over twenty bucks."

"I said I don't have money with me."

Sterling shrugged. "Too bad. Looks like I'll have to take it downtown to Lucky's Pawn. I bet I'll get more than twenty bucks. Or I can take it to Kahn's Jewelers. Their ad says they buy gold."

"I can't believe it! How can you be so greedy?"

Hoyt stepped between Sterling and the girl. He faced his brother and insisted that he give it back.

"Stay out of it," Sterling said, brushing Hoyt aside. "I need the money."

Hoyt tensed up like he was going to punch Sterling, but instead he pulled out his wallet and shoved a twenty-dollar bill into Sterling's hand. "Here's your finder's fee."

Sterling took the money and handed the necklace to Hoyt, who immediately turned to the girl and handed it to her. "Sorry about that," Hoyt said. "He's not usually such a jerk. Sometimes, one of his nerdy projects sucks him into darkness like a black hole."

Hoyt turned back toward Sterling, shook his head, and walked back to the mower.

The girl stormed off in the opposite direction.

As I circled overhead, I could see how angry she was, and her thoughts were even worse. I piffed her a thought, like a nudge, to remember that the Master had said, "But I say to you, love your enemies, bless those who curse you, do good to those who hate you, and pray for those who spitefully use you and persecute you." Piffs are flashes of thought that seem to come out of nowhere, often unrelated to what a person is thinking. But they are divine inspiration, seeds of truth planted subtlety. I send them to those seeking the beyond. People often miss them, and they may choose to ignore them, but I keep sending them. I was pleased when the girl, Laurel, responded to my piff and prayed for Sterling.

Sterling plugged in his earbuds, picked up the edger, and resumed walking home. He wondered if he should have given the necklace back. Maybe Hoyt was right about him being too focused on his projects.

WHILE STERLING AMBLED down the sidewalk, unconcerned about catching up with his brother, I landed on a tree branch one block from his house and waited for him to walk beneath my perch. To get through to Sterling, I had taken the form of an ordinary mourning dove. I did not have bright colors, and I did not vocalize, besides soft calls any normal dove would make. But, since I am always truthful, I must admit I flew with greater passion than any normal dove, and occasionally could not resist diving and spinning at high speeds.

As Sterling approached, listening to music and scheming about how he could make more money, I gave him something different to think about. I materialized a gold chain, one with a cross, and held it in my beak. It was identical to the one Laurel's grandmother had given to her. The initials on Laurel's necklace were M.M. because her grandparents called her by her given name, Meryl. Everyone else called her Laurel—Laurel Mercury.

I swooped above Sterling with the necklace and dive-bombed him. My claws knocked his Mariner's baseball cap to the parking strip.

He dove to the ground, grabbed his hat, and pulled it back over his head for protection. After a moment of lying there, he peeked through his fingers and looked for his attacker.

I stood three feet in front of him, and he saw the gold chain hanging from my beak. I tilted my head and stared at him with a penetrating eye.

Sterling was at a loss for what to do. He was not sure if he should stare back, play dead, run, or chase me away. He lay there frozen, buying time to think. I held my ground. I was not even a foot long from bill to tail, but my hooked beak was sharp, and I had already proved my willingness to attack. Without letting go of the chain, I puffed up my throat and made a cooing sound.

Sterling took the bait. He sprung onto his hands and knees and lunged for the chain. I was ready, and I was quick. I hopped three feet back, out of his reach. He rose and jumped forward again. Once more, I dodged him and moved farther away. Staring at him sideways, I dared him to try it again. This time, he steadied himself on all fours and slowly prowled toward me, like a cat on the hunt. His determined eyes were locked onto mine.

Sterling attempted to put me at ease by making his own cooing sound. I dropped the chain and answered him. As we cooed back and forth, he edged his way forward. He was very careful, but I knew his next move. I picked up the chain in my beak and retreated two quick hops.

Sterling pounced forward. He missed yet again, but he could not suppress the start of a smile. I twirled the necklace until it wrapped around my neck, and I took a bow. Sterling's smile grew into a full grin. I was enjoying our encounter as much as he was, and I broke character—I smiled back at him with my beak, very unlike an ordinary dove. Sterling puzzled at my smile, exactly as I intended. I wanted to leave an inviting image in his mind, one he would not forget. One that would intrigue him forever.

At that, I flew straight up, my wings whistling through the air with the chain glittering in the sunlight, and I circled a hundred feet above him. Executing two tight loops to unwrap the chain from my neck, I soared through the air on my back, as if floating on water. After I rolled over again, I dropped the chain and let it free fall. Right as it was about to reach Sterling, I descended fast, like a peregrine falcon, and plucked it from the air.

I landed back on the ground in front of Sterling with ease and could hear his music. He was listening to one of Bruno Mars's older hits. It had a good beat, so I danced. My head, wings, and feet all moved in perfect rhythm. Sterling giggled and then broke into hilarious laughter. Then, he danced with me, our moves perfectly synchronized. He laughed so hard and his eyes watered so much he could no longer dance.

When the song ended, I took to the air once more, flying much higher this time, heading south toward the foothills. I spiraled, the chain spinning behind me like a streamer. Sterling had left the edger on the sidewalk to run after me, so I flew back and circled, bidding him to follow me. He trailed my flight until he encountered the woods that covered the hillside. He searched the underbrush, hoping to discover a path that would let him continue. But the Oregon grape and salal were too thick, so Sterling gave up the chase and returned to his edger. I tipped a wing to him and flew to the top branch of a tall cedar tree where I could watch him as he walked home.

He later wondered if what had happened was real. He doubted it. He thought he might have been lightheaded because he had not eaten lunch. But that did not explain the strange, inner warmth that had filled his body during the experience. He could not make sense of it.

When he reached home and returned the edger to the garage, he went into the kitchen for lunch. He made himself two sandwiches, each with layers of mayo, butter, cheddar, Monterey jack, and provolone cheese. After grilling the sandwiches, he trimmed the crust at the edges. All the while, he wondered if he had been hallucinating earlier.

Sterling took his sandwiches to his room and set his plate on the wide desk that held his computers, manuals, and unfinished projects. He used Google to search for "birds Pacific Northwest" and scrolled through the images. There I was, a picture of the form I had adopted for my work with him, a mourning dove that looked exactly like me. Sterling wondered why he didn't pull out his phone and take a video or at least get a picture. That would have proved if I was real or not. While chewing the last bite of his sandwich, he concluded that his imagination, working overtime due to hunger, had conjured up the whole incident. He opened a computer programming book and tried to concentrate on how to write loops in Python. But he could not completely banish our encounter from his mind.

My rendezvous with Sterling was not a hallucination. I am the first to admit manifestations from the higher world are uncommon. But they are not impossible, as Sterling thought. As the Holy Spirit, I occasionally take on a physical form, a manifestation, depending on what I need to accomplish. Besides looking like a dove, I have been the wind, an earthquake, and fire. Fire always gets people's attention. Once, I was even an ass—yes, like a donkey. When the unseen world manifests itself in the material world, important events happen, and so I write about it, as am doing now, to help people see the invisible kingdom and realize what exists beyond.

Two

DURING THE PAST month, Sterling had spent most of his spare time working on a small submarine, specifically an underwater-remote-operated-vehicle, that he named UROV. He had ordered the plans and materials on the internet and built it himself, following each instruction carefully, double-checking, often triple-checking, each step. Sterling excelled in math and science and loved working on technical projects like UROV because they challenged him and rewarded him with a sense of accomplishment. Academically, Sterling aspired to be exceptional. He worked hard to be admired at the science club, and, whether or not he realized it, he ultimately wanted to win Pete's approval. Pete was not a teacher or a classmate. Pete was Sterling's father, and he insisted that Sterling and Hoyt never call him Dad, or Papa, or anything of the sort. They were to use first names only.

As Sterling finished constructing UROV, he hoped to use it to inspect the underside of boats moored in the nearby Port Angeles Boat Basin. A good friend of Sterling's family, Dirk McCleod, who also happened to be his dad's business partner, kept his boat down in the marina and had told Sterling boat owners often paid hundreds of dollars every couple of years to have their boats lifted out of the water for inspection. Usually, the inspections did not find any problems, and the entire operation could seem like a waste of money.

That was when Sterling's eyes lit up with a plan. He figured he could charge fifty dollars and use UROV to take detailed videos of everything below a boat's waterline. His service would save boat owners both time and money, while putting extra cash in his own pocket.

When UROV was finally ready for its test voyage, Sterling got permission to try it on Dirk's boat, *Leverage*. Pete agreed to drive Sterling and UROV to the Boat Basin on the way to one of his meetings. During the drive, Pete peered into the box Sterling held in his lap and tried to make sense of the technical gear. He cleared his throat and said, "Tell me again about this thing you built."

"Oh, it's a remotely controlled underwater drone that records video with a high-resolution camera," Sterling answered curtly.

"Uh huh. What's with all the cables?"

"One's an extension cord to power the controller, and the other connects the controller to the drone so I can steer it and watch the video while it's underwater."

"So, it's not radio controlled? Like a flying drone?"

"Well, radio signals wouldn't be able to reach the drone while it's submerged. That's what the yellow cable is for."

"Right. I mean, of course." Pete shifted awkwardly in his seat. "That makes sense."

Sterling feared he could not hide his grin, so he looked out his window.

"How much did it cost?" Pete asked.

Sterling knew the exact cost—he paid $395 for everything. But he also knew how tight his dad was with money, so he tried to play it cool. "I think it was around three hundred," he said.

Pete did not respond.

Sterling waited for a reaction, anything, but the car was quiet. When he could not take the silence any longer, he added, "I needed to buy it. It's important . . . for the science club."

Pete reoriented his hands on the steering wheel. "Sounds like a lot of money for a toy."

"Yeah, but it's mostly for business. Dirk thinks I can scan the hulls of boats while they're in the water. Look for damage or too many barnacles. Stuff like that."

"You think you'll make a profit from it?"

"That's the plan. Dirk thinks people will pay at least fifty bucks, and it should only take me about half an hour for each boat."

"I see." Pete smiled. "You'd better jump on that."

After Pete parked at the marina, he and Sterling walked down to the gate at the docks. Pete entered the combination on the keypad while Sterling held the box with UROV and looked out over the water. The smell of salt in the air reminded him of the many times he and his brother had gone fishing with Pete and Dirk and of the times they went cruising in the Strait of Juan de Fuca. Those were wonderful memories.

With the gate open, Sterling and Pete proceeded down the pier to Dirk's boat, where Sterling knelt and began setting up his submarine. He plugged the power cord into the shore-power outlet and watched as the status lights on UROV's handheld controller came to life. Pete glanced at his watch.

"We'll have to make this quick," he noted. "I told you about my appointment."

"Sure thing," Sterling said absently, his total attention fixed on lowering UROV gently into the water. "This won't take long . . ."

While standing on the dock, he lowered the drone into the water near *Leverage*'s bow. He tested all the functions. The controller moved UROV up, down, forward, and back, toggled the spotlight on and off, and started and stopped video recording. The controller's built-in screen displayed UROV's view in real time. An overly satisfied chuckle escaped Sterling. He climbed the three steps up to *Leverage*'s deck, all while staring at the controller. Pete followed him onto the boat, and Sterling guided the underwater unit to the stern. Pete watched over Sterling's shoulder as UROV videoed *Leverage*'s propeller. "Wow," Pete commented. "That picture looks good. It's really clear."

"It's better than I expected."

The sound of footsteps coming up the stairs at the bow interrupted their observation, and they both turned to see who it was. Dirk stepped onto the boat and greeted them warmly.

"Gentlemen," he said, taking Pete's hand in a firm handshake. "Fine weather for a maiden voyage!"

Dirk was a shorter man than average—about five-foot-seven on a good day. He parted his dark hair on the left, and it merged with his closely cropped beard. Like many Irish men, he had narrow blue eyes, a slightly upturned nose, and a prominent round chin. What drew the most attention about him was his right hand—his ring and pinkie fingers were all that remained following a gruesome commercial fishing accident. Ever the extrovert, however, Dirk managed to turn his maimed hand into his trademark, not unlike a child's dimples or a woman's perfume. His easy, engaging smile more than compensated for his off-putting hand.

Dirk's eyes fell eagerly on Sterling's controller, and he nudged Pete aside to get closer to the screen. "How's she looking?"

"This side is good, I'd say," Sterling answered, maneuvering UROV from the stern to the bow while Dirk observed next to him.

"Excellent," Dirk said. "And how about the starboard side?"

"Sterling," Pete interjected. "We need to get going, remember? I'm on a tight schedule."

"But . . ." Sterling started to object, but stopped. "Okay," he yielded. "Sorry, Dirk. Can I come by again tomorrow?"

"Well, wait a minute," Dirk said, putting his hand on Sterling's shoulder. "This shouldn't take too much longer, should it? Pete, how about Sterling wraps up his work here and I'll take him home as soon as we finish? You wouldn't mind that, would you?"

Pete looked at Sterling, who nodded. "Fine by me," Pete replied. "Just have him back by dinnertime. The boys have training tonight."

"That'll be no problem at all," Dirk said. "Should be done here in no time."

Pete turned to head back to his SUV, and Sterling resumed navigating UROV. "Okay. Let's walk around the bow." He manipulated the controls like a pro. "It's surprisingly easy to steer. I think I'll be able to record an entire boat in less than twenty minutes." The camera scanned the rest of the hull, which revealed little of interest except for a handful of barnacles that clung to the rudder.

Dirk let out a slow whistle as he watched. "I'm sure folks would pay at least a hundred dollars to see the underside of their boats."

"One hundred? You really think so? Last time you said I could charge fifty."

"Well, I'm saying a hundred now—this is a fine operation you're running. I'll put the word out around the marina."

Sterling thanked him and began coiling up the cables as UROV surfaced. "I'll email you a copy of your video so you can watch it on your computer. You could show it to the other owners too."

"Good idea. Now, hold on . . ." Dirk pointed to the water on the opposite side of the dock. "Bring that thing over here. A buddy of mine dropped his keys into the water last week. You know Techs, don't you?"

Sterling shook his head.

"Ah, well. See if you can spot those keys down there."

Sterling pulled UROV out of the water, carried it across the dock, and lowered it in on the other side. He let it descend almost to the sandy bottom, aimed its camera and light, and began searching the depths. After scanning back and forth for a few minutes, he stopped and turned the screen toward Dirk. "Those look like keys to me."

"Ho!" Dirk slapped Sterling on the back. "That they are. Can you pick them up?"

"No. I can't. I'd need a robotic arm attachment . . . which I suppose I could make." He mulled it over. "It must be possible."

"You should do that. How much would it cost?"

"I don't know. It would need to be waterproof, and I don't know what parts I would need. I'll have to do some research. It could take me at least a month to save up for the parts, and then I'd have to adapt them for underwater use."

"A month? It sounds like Pete needs to raise your allowance."

As UROV surfaced again, Sterling carefully gathered the cables and said, "That's not gonna happen. He likes to teach us the value of hard work."

"That so? Well, if you and Hoyt were my boys, I'd make sure you had the money you needed for projects like this. They're good for you—educational."

Sterling didn't know how to respond, so he nodded politely and focused on drying off his gear and packing it back into the cardboard box.

"By the way," Dirk added. "I have a surprise for you. And one for Hoyt too, next time I see him."

"Yeah?"

"That's right. You know, I was planning to wait until next week and take you two fishing—just the three of us. But if you promise to not tell Hoyt, I'll show you yours now."

"Deal." Sterling set down his box on the dock and followed Dirk back up the steps onto *Leverage.*

Dirk unlocked the cabin door and disappeared inside. When he reappeared, he handed a new salmon fishing pole and reel to Sterling.

"Oh wow," Sterling exclaimed, taking the rod and holding it in front of him like he was landing a fish, noting how it glinted in the sunlight. Having gone fishing with Dirk in the past, he knew how nice the gear was. In fact, it was almost as nice as Dirk's personal gear, which was top of the line.

"I . . . I don't know what to say. Thank you."

Dirk grinned. "'Thank you' will do just fine. I'll put the line on the reels before we go fishing. Now remember, don't tell Hoyt. I want to surprise him, too." Dirk took the pole and reel from Sterling and locked them inside the cabin.

They returned to the dock, and Sterling picked up his box of equipment. Dirk pointed to the locker next to *Leverage*, which the marina provided for each boat slip. "Why don't you keep your sub in my locker? That way, any time you get an inspection job, you can ride your bike here and get to work."

"You wouldn't mind?"

"C'mon." Dirk opened the locker's padlock, reciting the combination to Sterling as he did so. Sterling handed his box to Dirk, who secured it inside the locker.

"Thanks for letting me keep it here, Dirk. I really appreciate it."

"Hey, it's no problem. You're like family to me." He pulled his phone from his pocket to check the time. "All right. We better get you home. Wouldn't want the old man to throw a fit, now would we?" Dirk gave Sterling a sporty smack on the back.

As the two walked to Dirk's car, Sterling thought about how nice the fishing gear was. And about how kind Dirk was being. Actually, it struck Sterling as somewhat odd to get such an expensive present like that out of the blue. He looked over at Dirk, who caught his eye and smiled back at him.

He's acting so nice, even nicer than usual. But why?

Three

FRIDAY NIGHT BOOT Camp. That was what the boys called it behind Pete's back because Pete seemed to be training them for a fierce life, as if he was preparing them for war. And he trained them with military consistency—every Friday, without fail.

I had been circling the Burke household from the clouds that evening, and I tucked my wings close to my body and descended for a better view. As I drew close to the treetops, I spread my wings and glided toward the branch of a young cedar tree next to the Burkes' three-car garage. From where I landed, I had a clear view through a window into an upper room that was large and outfitted like a gym. The lights were off inside, and as I cocked my head, I noticed my reflection in the glass—my slight form, my delicate wings, my small eyes. I wondered what Sterling must have thought earlier, when he had looked into these piercing eyes. Did he see eternity in the depth of my pupils? Did he notice how they glistened with everlasting life?

My reflection vanished when the lights in the room came on. I saw the Burke boys enter through the door on the far side of the room. Pete followed behind them and closed the door. Now that everything was illuminated, I could see the equipment much better. Half the room was a training area complete with a speed bag and a heavy punching bag, both suspended from the ceiling. A Bowflex home gym and a Nautilus elliptical trainer stood in front of a side wall that was paneled with full-length mirrors. A boxing ring, each side having four parallel rows of nylon rope, like fence rails, filled the other half of the room. A red bell and a digital clock hung on the far wall next to a motivational poster that featured a buff boxer. Its caption read, "There is an 'I' in 'WIN.' There is an 'I' in 'PRIZE.' WIN the PRIZE!" The window near my branch was cracked open enough so that I could smell the aroma of pine scented cleaner from within, but it did not mask the musty odor that was probably from a forgotten pair of sweaty socks ripening under the ring's elevated floor.

Judging from the setup, two things were obvious: the Burke boys had everything necessary to transform the adolescent bodies into muscular young men, and Pete was not messing around.

Pete insisted the boys warm up with a series of stretching exercises and two minutes of jumping rope. Once they started to sweat, Pete told them to step into the ring. He pointed them to opposite corners, where Everlast boxing gloves hung by their laces. Pete clapped his hands and commanded, "Let's go! Put 'em on."

"Wait, what about our helmets?" Sterling asked.

Pete shook his head and said, "No. But use your mouth guards. I don't want any dentist bills."

"Are you serious?"

Pete ignored this as he walked over to Hoyt's corner and tied the laces on his gloves. With a stern look, he walked across the ring to Sterling's corner and did the same. "No helmets," he repeated. "Not anymore. It's a tough world, and you boys need to be even tougher."

Sterling looked over at Hoyt, hoping to see a sympathetic glance to let him know he wasn't the only one who thought boxing without helmets was crazy.

But there was something strange in Hoyt's eyes that was even more disturbing. He stared straight back at Sterling, unflinching, and was chewing on his mouth guard as he mumbled, "You're going to wish you had your helmet."

Whoa. What's gotten into him? He put in his own mouth guard with a slightly trembling glove.

Pete rang the bell, and the clock started counting down. "Five solid minutes!" he hollered.

The boys bounced into the center of the ring, each with his hands held in front of his face, defensively. They circled, waiting for the other to make the first aggressive move. Sterling stepped forward and quickly retreated. He moved in once more, and he and Hoyt both threw a couple of body punches to no effect. Hoyt withdrew and lowered his hands while he caught his breath, and Sterling followed suit.

Sterling shook his arms and glanced at his feet, but before he looked up again, Hoyt sprang forward and smashed a left cross into Sterling's unprotected face. Sterling had no time to defend himself. His head snapped back, and a spray of sweat and blood dotted the air. He twisted and fell onto his hands and knees. The metallic taste of blood covered his lips as he panted on the canvas.

"Stand up! Stand up!" Pete yelled. "Don't just lay there, fight back!"

Sterling was woozy, and he slowly shook his head to regain clear vision. Pete's shouts echoed in his head, and a thought crossed his mind, as it did on most Friday nights—*why are we doing this?*

Sterling remembered all too well. Years ago, when he and Hoyt were in the second grade, there was an incident during recess one day. A big kid, the class bully, had grabbed Sterling and tossed him face first into a mud puddle. Sterling wasn't hurt, but his pride and clothes were definitely sullied. He stood up, turned his back on the bully, and walked toward his classroom to leave the situation behind him.

But the bully was not done yet. He ran in front of Sterling and cut him off, then dared Sterling to hit him. Sterling shrugged and tried to walk around him. That was the wrong tactic, because the bully stepped directly in front of him again and slammed his hands into Sterling's shoulders. Hard. Sterling flew backward and landed on his back, and that time it hurt. Still, he did not want to fight. The bully demanded he stand up, but Sterling would not. He knew if he got up, he would only be knocked down a third time. So, he decided to stay down and wait for the bell when everyone, including the bully, would go back into the building.

The bully had tried to pull Sterling to his feet, but Sterling went limp, and the ruffian couldn't lift him. That made the much bigger kid even more aggressive, and he pounced on Sterling, meaning to punch him.

Right when he raised his fist, however, Hoyt had rushed in out of nowhere and tackled the rascal from behind. Sterling rolled out of the way as his attacker's face kissed the ground next to him, and Hoyt cannonballed onto the bully's back. Hoyt pounded the boy's ears and grabbed a handful of hair, pulling his head back and slamming his face into the dirt once more. "You touch him again and I'll take you apart." He seethed, "Don't you touch my brother. Ever."

After recess that day, Sterling had gone back to class as if nothing had happened, but with how muddy his clothes had become, his teacher sent him to the office along with a note for the school secretary to call home for clean clothes. He waited in the office, and his mother eventually brought him a pair of threadbare jeans and a shirt with sleeves two inches too short. Just the type of second-hand clothing he was used to wearing. Sterling said nothing to his mother about the bully. He just went to the restroom to change, took his dirty clothes to his mother, and went back to class.

Pete heard about the dirty clothes and that night at dinner, he asked Sterling what had happened. Sterling muttered something about having fallen into a puddle. But Hoyt, who was apparently proud of rescuing his brother, spoke up and told the entire story. Pete was horrified, and from that point on, he purposed that no son of his would take a beating lying down. He was on a mission to toughen up Sterling and make sure he could and would defend himself. The boot camps were not combative at first, but once Pete started earning more money through his real estate career, the family bought a big house, and Pete set aside the entire room above the garage for training Sterling and

Hoyt how to fight. So, the Friday Night Boot Camp began.

"Stand up!" Pete shouted again. "Hit him!"

Sterling was regaining some energy and struggled to his feet. He lifted his gloves to protect his face, but Hoyt was merciless. He landed a solid shot to Sterling's gut, and when Sterling doubled over, Hoyt drove another punch to his face, crumbling Sterling to the canvas. Hoyt glanced at the clock and saw there were almost two minutes remaining. He looked at Sterling and shook his head slightly, as if to say, "Just stay down."

"C'mon! Get up!"

Sterling stared at Pete in disbelief, desperately hoping for him to call off the beating. Sterling's eyes wandered to the ceiling, and he moved his head from side to side, making sure everything still worked. Somewhat to his surprise, it did. While Hoyt walked back to his corner, Sterling rolled over, forced himself up onto his hands and knees, and glanced at the clock. One minute to go.

"Let's go. Down to the last stretch!"

Sterling propped up one knee and took a deep breath.

Forty-five seconds.

He cautiously stood and braced himself with his hands on his knees.

Thirty seconds.

He teetered toward Hoyt's corner.

Ten seconds.

Hoyt was done. He put up his right glove toward Sterling to receive the victor's fist bump. Sterling looked at the clock—three seconds—and decided to throw one last punch. He surprised Hoyt with a quick uppercut that snapped Hoyt's head back like a bobble-head on a dashboard. Hoyt reeled backward and staggered into the ropes.

The bell rang.

Sterling looked over at Pete, hoping to hear congratulations for his last-second comeback. But Pete didn't acknowledge the feat.

"That's all, boys," he said coldly. "Shake hands." With that, he untied their gloves and hung them from the ropes. He quietly left the gym and went downstairs to the house.

At first, Sterling and Hoyt did not speak. They only exchanged glares as they caught their breath and leaned against their corners of the ring.

Sterling wiped his face with a towel and broke the silence. "What was that all about? I thought we agreed to take it easy. Only body punches."

"Oh, did we?" Hoyt scoffed. "I guess I was thinking about that girl's necklace and forgot."

"What?"

"You should have given it back when she claimed it."

"The necklace? That's what you're so upset about?"

"And the twenty bucks." Hoyt climbed out between the ropes. "That was messed up."

"C'mon, bro. It's not a big deal," Sterling defended. "What, you want me to pay you back? Would that make you feel better?"

Hoyt sighed. "You don't get it. It's not just about the money. You can be such a jerk."

"Me? What about that left cross when I wasn't ready? If you ever hit me like that again, you'll be on your own for math homework, and you can kiss playing football goodbye. Remember what Pete said about your GPA?"

"All right, all right." Hoyt eased up. "Next week, I'll let you knock me around. I might even play dead, so you can't miss."

The boys went downstairs into the house. Sterling went into the bathroom to wash his face, and he saw more than dried blood. His right eye was swollen half shut, and the skin around his scar shone green and purple. He winced as he gently touched his eye and washed the blood from his face. But then a plan struck him, and he looked at himself in the mirror again.

After he cleaned up and put on fresh clothes, he walked into the kitchen and waited for his mom. His mother, unlike Pete, insisted he and Hoyt call her Mom and not by her first name, Anne. When she ran into Sterling by the refrigerator, she nearly screamed. "Oh my . . ." She gently put a hand on each side of Sterling's face. "What on earth happened?"

"Boxing," Sterling answered pitifully. "Pete wouldn't let us wear our helmets, and Hoyt landed a lucky punch."

"That's it," she snapped. "I've always hated that stupid boxing. It's over. Never again." She stormed out of the kitchen toward Pete's den, yanked the door open, and slammed it shut behind her.

Sterling smiled to himself, having successfully landed a last-second uppercut to Pete. He opened the fridge, pulled out fixings for a sandwich, and happily made a late-night snack, confident that his sparring days were over. He took his sandwich to his room to research underwater robotic arms and listen to a favorite playlist. The Bruno Mars song we danced to cycled through, and my grinning face came back to his mind. He stopped chewing his sandwich for a moment and gazed out the window into the dusk. For a second, I thought he spotted me off in the trees. But then he shook his head and laughed to himself about his dove hallucination.

For Sterling, life was good. Sometimes strange, but good. He even seemed to think the black eye was worth it.

Four

THE NEXT MORNING, Sterling woke up to his mom knocking on his bedroom door and calling to him. "Sterling?" She knocked again. "You need to get up. Your dad is taking us all out to a special lunch. He wants to leave in thirty minutes."

Sterling groggily stirred in bed.

"We're going to Canaan's Kitchen," his mother added.

Sterling wanted to sleep at least another hour, but Canaan's Kitchen was his mother's new favorite restaurant—Sterling had overheard her commending it to Pete on numerous occasions since Christmas. Now, he figured Pete was using it as a peace offering to atone for upsetting her the night prior. Sterling pulled the sheets over his head and reevaluated the worth of the black eye. It was not so great if it prompted an early lunch on a Saturday morning.

Still, Sterling got himself out of bed, washed up, and dressed with five minutes to spare. When he walked into the kitchen, he found Hoyt drinking a glass of water and his mom putting a coffee cup into the dishwasher. She was more than ready to go, as evidenced by her outfit, which was carefully chosen, as usual. She wore a white blouse tucked into perfectly creased black slacks, stylish black tennis shoes, and a red button-up sweater that perfectly matched her nails was draped over her shoulders. A black ponytail emerged from the gap between her white baseball cap's back panel and its adjustable strap. Beyond the choices of her wardrobe, both sons favored their mother's appearance—dark brown eyes, Mediterranean complexion, a slender physique.

"My eye is more colorful today," Sterling commented, walking to the counter.

His mom turned to him and gasped. "It sure is," she said, stepping closer. "Does it hurt?"

"Only if I touch it."

"Do you want me to put makeup on it? I can make it almost unnoticeable."

Sterling hesitated. "Uh, no thanks. That would be weird."

"I dunno." Hoyt snickered. "I think it would look cute."

At the sound of the garage door opening, the boys and their mom gathered their things and walked to the driveway to join Pete. He was waiting in his British-racing green Range Rover HSE, and once everyone was in and buckled, they were off.

The drive to Canaan's Kitchen was a short one, and in five minutes, they parked in front of the restaurant. Cedar trees on both sides and behind the restaurant towered like sentries. Sunlight streamed through the swaying branches and dappled the area with shadows. To the right of the parking lot, less than thirty yards away, a twenty-foot curtain of water from Canaan's Creek crashed into a churning pool. Water poured from the pool into a granite chute and was channeled off into the Strait of Juan de Fuca, a mile away. The breeze carried mist from the waterfall to the restaurant, where it speckled the windows with fog-like droplets.

The Burkes exited their car and stood still, surveying the scene. Quartz embedded in the restaurant's granite walls sparkled in the sunlight. Moss and grass carpeted the roof. Flower boxes underlined the windows, and ivy covered the front of each. The ivy had intertwined to form a fabric of greens and shadows that contrasted with the red and white begonias planted in the boxes.

"My goodness," Pete remarked brightly. "What is this place? Where are the Hobbits?"

Anne stood next to Pete and wrapped her arms around him. "Everything about Canaan's Kitchen makes me feel like I'm a little girl again. I'm not sure why. It must remind me of the fantasy stories I loved to read as a kid."

Oblivious to their parents' chatter, Sterling and Hoyt put their phones in their pockets and hopped across the stepping stones to the front door. Sterling held the door open and looked back at his parents, who were still marveling at the scenery. He coughed into his fist to hurry them along.

But Canaan's Kitchen customers never hurried. In fact, the first thing any real aficionado would do after stepping into the dining room was inhale mindfully. A symphony of aromas filled the air. Cinnamon from the rolls and apple pies, full-bodied coffee, and lemon fragrance from the ice water complemented each other like instruments in an orchestra. Regulars savored the sights and sounds—the thunk of thick porcelain mugs returning to the table, the clink of knives and forks on plates, the satisfied chatter. And the servers always greeted them by name and took a few seconds to smile into their eyes. Those who savored the complete experience were likely to return. Those who rushed through their meals rarely came back, perhaps because they were afraid of what they might be forced to face if they ever slowed their frenzied lives.

The host greeted Anne. "Good to see you again, Mrs. Burke. It looks like you brought the family this time!"

Anne nodded and smiled. "That's right. I finally convinced them to come with me."

"Well, I'm glad you did. Your favorite table by the window just opened up. Would you like it?"

"That will be perfect."

Anne pointed her family toward a well-lit table that was covered with a white linen tablecloth and surrounded by four wooden chairs. The boys sat across from each other, as did their parents. Arranging their menus in front of them, the host said, "Your server, Bethany, will be with you shortly. In the meantime, I'll bring a basket of our olive bread and a cruet of olive oil. We made them fresh this morning."

Looking over a Canaan's Kitchen menu evoked anticipation, like unwrapping a present or reading a handwritten card from a friend. The lunch menu always included two soup and sandwich combinations and three daily specials: typically a vegetarian dish, a pasta dish, and a fish or light meat dish. Although, occasionally, a single entrée did double duty—such as a vegetarian pasta—but never on a Saturday.

The host returned with two porcelain oil dipping dishes. He set one on the corner between Pete and Hoyt and one between Anne and Sterling. He placed a basket full of sliced olive bread in the center of the table and poured the olive oil into the porcelain dishes. Steam from the fresh bread rose gently into the air and danced in the window's light.

Bethany arrived and introduced herself as their server, and she asked if they had questions about the menu. Pete raised his hand.

"First off," he said, "this bread is mouthwatering. Top restaurants can't compete with it. I could make an entire meal of this bread alone. What's your secret?"

"Well, some details really are secret, but for lunch, our baker starts baking the bread at ten thirty. He puts the dough into a covered, pre-heated dutch oven for thirty minutes, then he removes the cover and bakes it for fifteen more minutes until the loaf turns golden brown. After that, he lets it cool for fifteen minutes, and we serve it warm. Like your bread here." She gestured to the basket on the table. "It just cooled enough for me to serve it."

Pete nodded. "That's a suspiciously straightforward process for such a masterpiece. There must be something special you're not telling me. And what about this olive oil? Do you make it here as well?"

"We do. We make it every day using a fifty-fifty blend of green and black olives. Both are organic, and the black ones are tree-ripened.

After washing and rinsing them in cold water, we crush them into a paste. Once that's finished, we cold-press them to separate the oil."

Pete dipped another slice of bread into the oil as he listened. "Amazing. Each bite dissolves in my mouth. It's like a trip to Italy. Where on earth do you get your ingredients?"

Bethany grinned and rested her hands behind her back. "That's part of the secret. Let's just say we have a special relationship with our supplier. So," she added, looking at the rest of the family, "have you decided what you would like to eat?"

Sterling ordered a ham and provolone sandwich on nine-grain bread, and he asked them to trim off the crust. Hoyt ordered a smokehouse BBQ chicken sandwich on whole wheat. Both requested Cokes to drink. Pete asked for the spaghetti with Pacific blue mussels and crushed tomatoes, and Anne ordered a grilled portobello mushroom on a bed of wild rice with a cup of Mediterranean white bean soup on the side. Bethany commended their choices and promptly left to place their orders in the kitchen.

While the family waited for their food and relished what remained of the warm olive bread, something caught Sterling's eye outside their window. A mourning dove swooped by the restaurant and settled on an old cedar fence by the waterfall in the distance. Sterling was reminded of our encounter and wondered if the bird on the fence was me.

"Hey, Mom," he asked, "do you still volunteer at the Audubon Society?"

"Every Wednesday morning. Why?"

"Well, I saw a bird the other day, and it looked a lot like a dove. But . . . it was acting weird."

"Weird how?"

Sterling was not sure how much of his experience he could tell without sounding crazy. "It dive-bombed me and knocked my hat off."

"Really? That is strange."

"Yeah, and that's not all. It was also flying really high and fast, and it could spin and loop around. Have your ever seen something like that?"

"All right, funny guy. Don't tease your poor mother just because she likes bird watching."

"No, no, I'm serious," Sterling emphasized. "I really saw a dove do those things. Isn't that weird?"

"Well, first off, doves don't attack. They don't dive-bomb like raptors. Second, the sort of acrobatics you're describing aren't characteristic of their flight, and they don't fly very high, either—forty feet, sixty tops. Is it possible you saw a different bird?"

"I don't think so. It was definitely a mourning dove."

"Hmm. I'm not sure what to tell you. Maybe that knock on your head had something to do with what you think you saw."

Sterling wondered about that. But before he could answer, Bethany brought their lunches to the table, and a satisfying meal quickly replaced the conversation.

Thirty minutes later, the Burkes finished eating and leaned back in their chairs in unscripted unison. Bethany stopped by to refill their drinks, and Pete repeated his praise for the food. He added, "I'm sorry, but I must ask again—how do you get such fresh ingredients?"

Bethany smiled politely. "Like I said, we have a very special relationship with our supplier."

At a nearby table, another girl had come from the kitchen and was clearing the leftover dishes and utensils. When she noticed Sterling and Hoyt with their parents, she did a double take. She continued wiping down the dirty table and subtly observed the Burkes to see which boy had the scar. Once she determined it was Sterling, she gathered the last of the dirty dishes and rushed them into the back.

A few minutes later, she emerged again, carrying four forks and a fresh slice of apple pie topped with a generous scoop of vanilla ice cream. She delivered the pie and forks to the Burkes' table, setting everything down in front of Sterling. As Sterling looked up puzzling at her, she said, "Compliments of the house. Feel free to share it with your family, assuming they will pay a fair price." She pulled her gold necklace out from her collar so that Sterling's eyes fixed on it, and she turned and left for the kitchen.

While the gesture was meant for Sterling, even I felt the sting. It seemed to me like Laurel might have skipped what the Master said about loving your enemies and went straight to the apostle's words in the book of Romans: "If your enemy is hungry, feed him; if he is thirsty, give him a drink; for in so doing, you will heap coals of fire upon his head." Laurel was clearly trying to bring fire to Sterling. But she did not understand the true meaning of those words. The coals of fire are not meant to harm one's enemies—they are considered a gift, allowing them to return home with the means to kindle a warming fire. But Sterling's coals would prove to be a little too hot.

Before anyone could inquire who the girl was or why she brought out the dessert, Sterling lifted the pie and asked, "Who wants some?"

Hoyt and Pete each picked up a fork and took a bite.

Anne was not so quick to move on. "Sterling," she asked, "do you know that girl from school?"

Sterling quickly shoveled another bite into his mouth so that he could not answer. Anne waited as he took much too long to chew and finally swallow. She continued to look at him. "Well?"

He kept quiet.

"What did she mean by a fair price?"

Sterling caught Hoyt smiling and nudged him with his foot under the table. "Yeah, I kind of know her," Sterling mumbled. "She didn't really mean anything. It's nothing."

"Nothing?"

Hoyt's smirk had become obvious to the whole table.

Anne turned to him. "Hoyt, do you know that girl? What's going on?"

"Not much. Well, maybe there is something. Sterling found her necklace yesterday and demanded a finder's fee to return it."

Anne jabbed Sterling's shoulder. "You didn't!"

"It was a fair fee." Sterling shrugged, sinking into his chair.

Pete let out a pained sigh as Anne asked, "How much?"

"It wasn't much compared to the value of—"

"Sterling." Pete tapped on the table. "How much?"

"Twenty bucks."

"Outrageous!" Anne exclaimed. "I am ashamed of you."

"But it was worth much—"

"No." Anne cut him off. "I don't want to hear another word about it right now. Your father will discuss it with you after we get home."

Bethany approached the table again, timidly, well aware of the tension between Sterling and his parents. She asked if she could get them anything else, but Pete shook his head. As she delivered the check and wished them a good day, Pete touched her arm and asked her to wait. He pulled two twenty-dollar bills from his wallet. "One is for you. And will you please make sure the young lady who brought us the pie gets the other one?"

"Of course," she replied. "Thank you very much." She waved one bill and added, "I'll make sure she gets this."

The Burkes got up from the table and walked out to their car, and Pete pulled Sterling aside. "You owe me twenty bucks, and we're going to have words when we get home."

WHEN THE BURKES arrived home, Pete parked in the garage. Everyone unbuckled, but Pete told Sterling to stay put. As Anne and Hoyt quickly gathered their things and left the car, Pete pointed to the front passenger seat and told Sterling to move up. Sterling slid into his mother's seat and found it was still warm, and he feared it was about to get much warmer. He folded his arms across his chest and stared vacantly ahead through the windshield, dreading his likely punishment. Was it going to be grounding? Having his electronics confiscated? Losing his allowance? Or, heaven forbid, a combination of all three.

Pete turned and stared at him with hardened eyes. "You disappointed your mother and me. The way you treated that girl is absolutely unacceptable. What were you thinking?"

"I thought she would be glad to give me a small reward, but she didn't have any money with her. Hoyt came to her rescue and paid the twenty bucks. That's why he punched me so hard last night."

"Sounds like you had it coming."

"I know. I didn't sleep much last night, and it wasn't because of my eye. I totally blew it. I wish I had given her the necklace back."

"So why didn't you?"

Sterling leaned back in his seat and took a deep breath. "Yesterday, I had been thinking all morning about saving money. I really need an advanced programming kit, and they're not cheap. I guess I was stressed because I'm running out of time."

"Running out of time? For what?"

"Mr. Keller said that if I can complete four projects before school starts in the fall, he'll consider appointing me president of the science club. Can you imagine? I would be the youngest president ever. So, when I saw that necklace, I figured I could sell it for forty or fifty dollars. And when the girl wanted it back, it felt like I was losing money that was already in my pocket. Twenty bucks seemed like a reasonable compromise." He looked up at Pete. "You don't have to tell me how stupid it was. I already know."

"You're right," Pete said. "It was foolish." He rubbed his chin and paused. "I need you to explain something to me. Why did you tell your mom I wouldn't let you wear a helmet? I thought boxing was something between us men. You knew how much it would upset her."

"Yeah, I did. I told her because I hate sparring with Hoyt. He can kick my butt anytime he wants. We all know it, too. It's never a fair fight. Either Hoyt whoops me, or he takes it easy because I threaten to stop helping him with his math homework. I'm not Hoyt, and I won't ever fight like him. I told you I hate it, but you didn't listen. That's why I figured Mom would make you stop if I ratted you out about the helmets."

"Well, she did," Pete replied, shaking his head. "She made me promise we won't do it anymore, so you don't need to worry about boxing, for now. I'm not giving up on you boys, though. There are plenty of other ways to keep you in shape and toughen you up. I suppose that's a conversation for another time. But something has to be done about this business with the necklace. You deserve a severe punishment. I was going to cut off your allowance for the rest of the summer, but it sounds like you've learned your lesson. So, I am going to give you a break. Here's the deal—you owe me twenty bucks, and I want you to apologize to that girl. It needs to be a face-to-face apology, and it needs to happen by the end of the day Monday. Otherwise, your allowance is gone until school starts. Any questions?"

Sterling was quiet. He finally mumbled just loud enough to be heard, "Sounds fair."

"All right then," Pete said, and he went into the house and left Sterling in the car.

In the garage's solitude, Sterling faced a serious dilemma. He was not sure which would be worse, losing his allowance for the rest of the summer or being horribly embarrassed by meeting up again with that girl.

Five

STERLING WANTED TO put the apology behind him as soon as possible. He didn't even bother to go in the house after talking with Pete. He pulled his mountain bike out of the garage, put his helmet on, and started pedaling the four miles back to Canaan's Kitchen. The ride was flat until he turned south and the climb up to the foothills began. He downshifted to the smallest chainring in front to climb the last mile, and his legs pumped hard like pistons.

It took Sterling ten more minutes to reach the restaurant, where he leaned his bike against a cedar tree and hung his helmet on his bike's handlebars. He stared across the parking lot at the front door, took a deep breath, and forced himself to go inside. Within, a cloud of aromas greeted him once again, but this time, it had little effect on him. His appetite was gone. He scanned the dining room for the necklace girl. He saw other staff members who he recognized from lunch, but not the one he needed to find. He did, however, see his family's waitress from earlier, Bethany. He got her attention and waved her over. As she approached, Sterling lightly ran his fingertips over his swollen scar and felt it twitch. He already dreaded his situation, and he hated the necklace more than anything.

He tried to smile. "My family and I were in here earlier. You were our server."

"Yeah, I remember. Twins, right?"

"That's us. So, a girl who works here gave us a free slice of pie. Could I speak with her, please?"

"Hmm." Bethany raised an eyebrow. "I'm not sure who you mean. We have several girls who work here. Could you describe her?"

Sterling remembered Pete gave Bethany a twenty-dollar bill to pass along to the girl. She knew exactly who he was looking for and was just giving him a hard time. He thought about walking out the door, but he decided instead to play along and get the thing over with.

"I think she is about my age," he said. "Could be a little older. She's of average height, slender. She has dark curly hair, brown eyes, long fingers with short nails. Oh, and she wears a cross on a gold chain around her neck."

"Is she cute?"

"What?"

"You heard me. Is she cute?"

"Could be if she ever smiled. But I haven't seen her smile."

"I'm sorry. Did you say she's cute, or not? It's a simple *yes* or *no* question."

He sighed and looked down at his shoes. "Yes, she's cute." Sterling had put it lightly. She was more than cute and anticipating apologizing to her made him feel foolish, like the time two years before when he learned he wore his T-shirt inside-out for an entire school day.

Bethany chuckled. "Glad you think so. She's my cousin. When I gave her the twenty, she told me all about the necklace you nearly stole from her. And about the pie."

"Look, I just need to apologize. In person. Then I'll be out of here."

"Why? Because you think she's cute? Or is it something else? I saw the look your dad and mom gave you. I'll bet they're making you do it. Right?"

"Well, yeah, but does that matter?"

She smirked. "Actually, it does. To me. It tells me you don't really want to apologize. It's probably meaningless to you."

"All I'm asking for is to talk to her for two minutes."

"And if you don't? What happens then? Will you get into more trouble?"

"Give me a break. Can't you tell her I'm here to say I'm sorry?" He squared his shoulders. "It's a simple *yes* or *no* question."

"Even if I agreed to, it wouldn't matter. She left for the day."

"What's her name?"

"Forget it. She wants nothing to do with you."

"Gee, thanks for all your help, Bethany," Sterling grumbled. "I won't give up."

"All right then. Come back tomorrow. After ten."

Sterling shook his head as he left the restaurant and walked back to his bike. He was sure Bethany was having a great time messing with him and thought both girls were probably in the back at that very moment, having a good laugh.

SUNDAY MORNING FOUND Port Angeles buried under a thin layer of fog, as was common in the summertime. The haze blew in from the Strait of Juan de Fuca and typically burned off by noon. Around nine o'clock, Sterling finally convinced himself to crawl out of bed after lying there awake for an hour. He dressed, made himself breakfast, put four five-dollar bills next to the coffeemaker, where he knew Pete would see them, and jotted a simple note that read, "Pete, here's your money."

The next step was to return to Canaan's Kitchen, but Sterling found other things to keep him distracted instead. He went upstairs and cleaned his room for the first time in six months, and it was spotless when he finished with it. A maid could not have done any better. He took a step back and admired his work. But the looming task of returning to Canaan's Kitchen evaporated his contentment, as the sun had done to the morning fog.

Sterling considered going for a long bike ride along the Olympic

Discovery Trail, and afterward telling Pete that he delivered the apology. It was tempting. However, knowing how much Pete enjoyed Canaan's Kitchen, Sterling figured his dad was likely to return to the restaurant, and if he did, he might see the girl and ask about the apology. He decided to put the bike ride off for another day and instead took a pen and a piece of paper from a pad on his desk and put both into his pocket in case he needed to leave a note for the girl. He took his bike and helmet from the garage and pedaled, once again, up to Canaan's Kitchen.

When he reached the restaurant, he coasted to a stop in the parking lot and noticed something unexpected. The lot was empty. Not a single car. He pedaled over to the entrance and saw the unlit *Open* sign hanging in the window and a dark dining room beyond. On the front door, he spotted another sign that listed the restaurant's hours—open from seven in the morning until nine at night every day, *except* Sunday. It was closed on Sunday. Bethany had landed a punch, and it was a sucker punch at that. As Sterling blushed, he imagined that Bethany and her cousin would laugh about this clever prank for weeks.

When he turned his bike around to leave, Sterling saw a man sitting on a nearby wooden bench halfway between the restaurant and the waterfall, and the person seemed to watch him. The man beckoned Sterling with a friendly wave.

Sterling rode over, and as he pulled closer, he could see the man was older than he first thought, and his skin looked tough and weathered. His short black beard contrasted with his gray hair, which a barber had probably not touched for many months. He wore a light blue denim work shirt under a pair of dark blue bib overalls—that looked almost new. Mud had crusted around the bottom of his boots. His smile created crow's feet at the edges of his eyes, and deep lines curved at the sides of his mouth. Sterling thought he might be a farmer.

"I'm John, Bethany's uncle. Yesterday, I overheard Bethany tell Laurel she wanted you to come by today after ten. I came by in case you showed up."

Sterling wasn't sure why the man would come to the restaurant to wait for him, and he hesitated to respond. He worried the man was planning to lecture about him asking for a reward, which was the last thing Sterling wanted to hear. Still, he took a risk and hopped off his bike. He approached John and extended his hand.

"I'm Sterling," he said, shaking John's calloused hand. "I need to talk to a girl who works here. To apologize."

"Glad to hear that. Laurel told me about the necklace. She felt terrible about losing it, and she was real upset about not having the money to get it back from you."

"I know. I shouldn't have asked for a finder's fee."

"We all do things we regret."

The empathy in John's voice and the acceptance in his eyes were pleasant surprises to Sterling, and he felt himself relax. Plus, it helped that he learned the girl's name—Laurel.

"Will she be here tomorrow?" Sterling asked.

"Yes."

"Okay, and you said you're Bethany's uncle?"

John nodded.

Remembering Bethany had said she and Laurel were cousins, Sterling asked, "Are you Laurel's dad?"

"No. I'm her uncle, too, just like I'm Bethany's uncle."

"Oh. Would you give her a message for me?"

"Be happy to."

"Would you tell her I am sorry about the necklace and the money and that I would feel better if I could apologize in person? Tell her I'll meet her anywhere and anytime that works for her." Sterling pulled the pen and paper from his pocket and scribbled a note against his thigh. He handed the paper to John and said, "Here's my name and phone number. She can call or text if she wants."

"I'll see that she gets it," John said, looking over the note. "But don't get your hopes up. I'll be surprised if she contacts you. She should, but don't be disappointed if she doesn't. She has a hard time dealing with these sorts of thing. If you really want to tell her you're sorry, come back tomorrow after lunchtime."

"What's one more trip over here?" Sterling walked back to his bike and propped it up. "You know, as long as we are talking about apologies, I deserve an apology from Bethany. She embarrassed me and tricked me into coming here today."

"That was wrong of her," John admitted. "She has recently begun her metamorphosis, so old things like that will happen."

"Wait, what do you mean, 'metamorphosis?'"

"Well, she started to change from her old self to her new self. It's a bit awkward for her right now, since she's between old behaviors and new ones, but she'll grow into it. I'll suggest she talk to you."

John read the note again, folded it, and stuffed it into his shirt pocket. He stood. "Nice to meet you, Sterling. I hope to see you again." He waved and turned, where he headed for an old barn that stood next to the falls. The building was made of cedar planks, and the siding looked like it had taken decades of beating from the elements. John opened the door, went inside, and shut the door again behind him.

I had watched Sterling's conversation with John from high in the branches of a nearby tree, and as Sterling hopped on his bike to ride home, I swooped down in front of him and flew toward the barn. He watched me land at a birdhouse mounted above the barn door. He stared after me for a moment, and I dearly wanted him to come closer. But instead of investigating, he simply continued on his bike. Other things seemed to occupy his thoughts.

There would be other opportunities.

Six

HAVING RETURNED FROM another failed mission, Sterling stowed his bike in the garage and went into the kitchen to lift his spirits. He made two tuna salad sandwiches, each with a layer of Ritz crackers between the tuna salad and the top piece of bread. He stacked the sandwiches and four Double Stuf Oreo cookies on a plate, poured a tall glass of milk, and took his lunch to the table, where he mulled over his attempts to resolve the great necklace caper. Based on the serious effort he had made to apologize to Laurel—riding his bike to the restaurant twice and leaving a message with her uncle—he wondered if Pete would let him off the hook. Probably not. Pete had often said that *results*, not effort, counted. Effort was expected, but without results, effort was a waste of time and energy.

Sterling dunked the last Oreo in his milk, drained what was left in the glass with a gulp, and wiped his mouth with the back of his hand. He put his dishes in the dishwasher and went upstairs. As he passed Hoyt's room, he heard music playing and knocked on the door. Hoyt called him in, and Sterling found his brother spinning a basketball on his pointer finger.

"Hey. Where have you been?" Hoyt asked, propelling the ball again with his freehand. "I was looking for you about an hour ago."

Sterling had told Hoyt earlier about the punishment he was trying to avoid and how Bethany had toyed with him the first time he tried to apologize. Hoyt recapped his second attempt and mentioned meeting John. "At least I learned her name this time," Sterling concluded. "It's Laurel, and I hope she'll at least text me."

"Sounds like a weak plan," Hoyt replied. "Are you just going to cross your fingers and hope she contacts you?"

"No. If she doesn't, my allowance is toast. Do you have any idea how long it would take me to save enough money for the programming kit?"

"I dunno. How long?"

"Honestly, I don't even want to think about it," Sterling replied, his mind still on losing his allowance. "If I don't hear from her today, I'll to go to the restaurant tomorrow and put an end to all this."

"Uh huh. And what if she's not there? Like, what if her uncle was wrong about her schedule?"

A chill crawled down Sterling's back. He had not considered that possibility.

"Do you have a backup plan?" Hoyt added. When he saw Sterling's shoulders slump, he knew Sterling did not. "Did you at least ask the old guy to tell you her last name?"

Sterling shook his head. "Didn't cross my mind."

"You know, for an Einstein, you can be as dumb as dirt. Or maybe the thought of talking with a cute girl has turned your brain to mush."

Sterling slapped the basketball off Hoyt's finger. "Thanks. For nothing. Now, give me a few minutes to think."

"Relax," Hoyt said, leaning back on his bed. "If she doesn't contact you, try again at the restaurant tomorrow and ask them for her number and her last name."

"No, you were right the first time. I need to find out her last name sooner rather than later so I can contact her." Sterling paced the room. "If I don't, I'll cut it too close to Pete's deadline and run the risk of having this whole situation blow up in my face. I won't have the money for the programming kit, and the summer will have been worthless.

Next year at school will be ruined. I won't get into a top college, and I'll probably spend the rest of my life mowing lawns, all because of twenty bucks and a waitress."

"Okay, that's a little dramatic, even for you," Hoyt commented as got up to collect his basketball. "Let's figure this out. How about you call Mr. Purvis and ask him for this girl's contact information? After all, you kissed up to him all last year. I can still hear it. 'Mr. Purvis, everyone on student council thinks you are a great assistant principal.' I wanted to puke."

Sterling pinched his bottom lip and considered the idea. "No, that won't work. I'm sure he can't give out private information like that. There must be some policy against it."

"Hmm. You're probably right. Schools have policies against everything. Looks like your allowance is goodbye. Welcome back, poverty."

"No. I'll think of something. I have to."

"Oh, and by the way," Hoyt said as he spun his basketball on his finger again. "Mom is still sore about the boxing helmets. I wouldn't want to be Pete right now."

"I guess lunch at Canaan's Kitchen didn't change her mind."

"Nope. She told me that boxing is over. For good."

This was at least some good news for Sterling. As he walked to his bedroom to consider other options for finding Laurel's last name, he smiled about the end of boot camp. But by the time he reached his desk, it was back to business. Although he was sure Mr. Purvis would not help him, perhaps there was someone else at school who would. He considered his homeroom teacher and his academic adviser, and then he decided on Mr. Keller—the science club sponsor.

Sterling and Mr. Keller had developed an easy bond, almost like they were friends. But the only way Sterling knew how to contact him was through his school email address, and he doubted that Mr. Keller checked it often during the summer. Besides, Sterling thought it would be better to ask him in person, so he searched the internet for Mr.

Keller's address and discovered he lived only five miles east, toward Sequim.

Sterling punched the address into his phone and a few minutes later was bolting out of the driveway on his bike, pedaling hard and fast to the Olympic Discovery Trail. He followed his GPS directions and eventually veered off the trail and into a neighborhood of modest single-story houses. Three blocks later, he pulled up to the destination and spotted Mr. Keller bent over, working under the hood of an old shiny blue car that was halfway in and halfway out of the garage.

Sterling laid his bike down on the sidewalk and called out to him, "Is that you, Mr. K.?"

Mr. Keller jerked up and bumped his head on the underside of the car hood. As he turned toward Sterling, he rubbed the back of his head and squinted. "Oh, Sterling. Nice to see you." He pulled a rag from the back pocket of his coveralls and wiped the grease from his hands. "You caught me working on my baby."

"Good to see you too. Cool car! Is it yours?"

"Yep, it's my pride and joy. I've spent nearly all my free time over the past two years working on it. Just about every evening and weekend, and summers too. I'm almost done.

"Wow. It looks like new."

"Thanks. It better look like new—I spent all my spare money on it, and then some."

"What kind of car is it?"

"It's a 1967 Pontiac GTO, one of the first muscle cars," Mr. Keller answered, stuffing the rag back into his pocket. "Many people think it is the best-looking GTO ever, and I agree. Because of that, they're hard to come by. I bought mine from an elderly friend in Port Townsend who had begun to restore it when his wife got sick. Unfortunately, his wife passed away, and by then he had lost interest in the car. So, he sold it to me for a fraction of its value. Now, over twenty thousand dollars and a ton of labor later, it's back in showroom condition."

Sterling circled the car as he listened. He nodded at the license plate. "67 GOAT. Greatest of All Time. That's cool."

Mr. Keller laughed and said, "Back then, Goat was slang for GTO. I wanted to add the letters *H* and *O* to the plate for 'high output,' but that had too many letters. So, I settled for *67 GOAT*, and I even requested it two years ago, because I didn't want anyone else to claim it. Sure, I've been paying for the license since then to keep it current, but I think it was well worth it."

Sterling continued to admire the exterior and interior from different angles. He stuck his head through the open driver's window. "What's this thing between the two front seats?"

"Good eye. That's a Hurst dual-gate shifter, often referred to as a *His* and *Hers* shifter. For normal driving, people use the left side, the *Hers* side. But if you want to race, you can use the right side, the *His* side. '67 was the first year Pontiac offered that kind of shifter as an option."

"Cool. Are you planning to street race it when you're done?" Sterling teased.

"Well, if I am, it won't be in this part of town. Everyone in this neighborhood knows it's my car." Mr. Keller glanced down his street and winked. "Speaking of which, what brings you out here? Do you have a friend in the area?"

"Actually, Mr. K., I came here looking for you. I have a favor to ask."

"Sure. What's up?"

"The other day, I found a necklace that belongs to a girl about my age. I know her first name, but don't know her last name or address, and I'm trying to contact her. Is there any way you could log in to the school's database and look her up for me?"

Mr. Keller frowned. "Sorry, Sterling, but I can't help you there. You're right that I could look her up, but I couldn't give the information to you. The district has strict policies about that. I wish I could help."

"No worries, I get it. I wouldn't want you to get in trouble. By the way, I wanted to tell you I built a remote control submarine, and I bought that Raspberry Pi you suggested. I just completed a project with it and am hustling to finish a couple more by the time school starts."

Mr. Keller had introduced the science club to Raspberry Pis, which are small computers—about the size of a deck of cards—designed for students and those dabbling in programming to develop their skills. Users can connect all kinds of hardware to a Pi, and it's powerful enough to program robots, weather stations, and underwater exploration drones.

"That's great," Mr. Keller replied. "I'm glad you're making good use of your summer break. You know, when I was your age, we didn't have inexpensive computers, so a lot of us tech guys spent our time souping our cars up and racing them instead."

"That sounds pretty fun, too." Sterling was suddenly painfully aware that he couldn't yet drive, and even if he could, he didn't have a car. But he stuffed that feeling down and added, "I'm saving up now for the advanced programming kit you mentioned. But . . . I guess we'll see how the rest of the summer goes."

Mr. Keller smiled. "Well, I hope that works out for you. There's still plenty of time before the fall."

"That's true." Sterling nodded. "Hey, I need to get back. Glad I caught you, though. Maybe the next time I see you, you'll be driving your goat to school."

"I'm planning to, but only during nice weather. It was good to see you, Sterling. Take care."

During the ride back to his house, Sterling anxiously pondered how he might discover Laurel's last name. Time was running out, and unless Laurel worked tomorrow, he would lose his allowance and, with it, the chance of becoming the youngest science club president ever. *Talk about the greatest of all time*, Sterling thought. But his plan to use Mr. Keller for help had fallen apart.

Or had it?

A new idea struck Sterling, perhaps out of desperation, and the more he considered it, the more it seemed like his best shot. Sure, Mr. Keller couldn't help him directly, but he might be able to help him *indirectly*. The idea was simple—Sterling would hijack Mr. Keller's school account and use it to get the information he needed. He realized it was a long shot, and it was risky. If he got caught, Mr. K. would probably kick him out of the science club. But then again, how could anyone possibly catch him? Besides, he wouldn't actually steal anything. He knew Mr. Keller's email address and assumed the email address would also be his default username. If that was true, the only thing missing was the password.

Sterling pedaled faster, as his mind raced with possibilities. He remembered that during a club meeting, Mr. Keller had mentioned he was single and did not have any kids. So, names of immediate family members were not likely candidates for the password. That put *67 GOAT* at the top of Sterling's list.

After returning his bike to the garage, Sterling trotted up to the computer in his bedroom and searched for the school district's website. The teachers' login page appeared in the search results, and its link took him to a legal warning that said unauthorized users would be prosecuted to the full extent of the law. Sterling paused, but not long enough to reconsider his plan. He checked the box that said he had read the warning and was an authorized user. I wish Sterling would have heeded that small voice in his head that was telling him to stop, but he pushed ahead anyway.

Sterling entered Mr. Keller's email address as the user ID. Staring at the entry field for the password, he leaned back in his chair, made an educated guess, and typed *67goat* into the password field. He rubbed his hands together, blew on them for good luck, hit the enter key. The screen loaded, and a message popped up that read, "*The user ID and password combination are not valid. After three unsuccessful login attempts, the account will be locked and an administrator will be notified.*"

Only two more chances. Sterling stuck with the email address as the username. This time, he opted for a stronger password, one that included uppercase and lowercase letters and a special character. He entered *67-Goat*, crossed his fingers, and hit the enter key. The failed login message appeared again. Sterling let out an exasperated sigh and gave himself a quick pep talk.

One last chance. He pressed his clammy hands together and considered praying, but he thought that might be hypocritical. I agreed. We rarely answer prayers that might make someone think *we* exist to serve *them*, instead of the other way around. We're not a genie in a bottle that performs magic tricks.

He typed *67-Goat-HO* as the password, closed his eyes, and hit enter. A moment later, he peeked through slits between his eyelids, almost too afraid to watch. He saw a blur of motion on the screen as the web page loaded. He could barely believe it—he was in! He had access to the student database for the entire school district and hoped the apology business was almost behind him. He could practically feel the new programming kit resting in his hands.

Sterling easily navigated the user interface and clicked on *Students* and then *Search*. He typed "Laurel" in the first name field and clicked search. Immediately, seven students were pulled from the records, but there was one major problem. The oldest Laurel was twelve.

At first, Sterling was calm and tried spelling Laurel several other ways in the search bar, in case she was buried in the records under an unusual spelling. But that generated no more results. It was no use—she was simply not in the system.

Sterling scratched his head as he logged out and got up from his computer. So much for his clever idea. Everything now hinged on who he would find at Canaan's Kitchen tomorrow, and with his luck, Bethany, not Laurel, would be the one working. She could amuse herself and mock him again before suggesting he come back on Tuesday. He would plead with Pete and explain how hard he tried to apologize, but Pete would cut off his allowance, and the summer would be a waste. Sterling ran his sweaty hands through his hair and tried to think of another way.

Maybe Hoyt would loan him some money.

Seven

THAT MONDAY MORNING, when Sterling got out of the shower, he wiped the steam from the mirror and leaned forward to study the peach fuzz on his upper lip, hoping it had somehow darkened and grown long enough that it needed to be shaved. This was a daily ritual, but so far, the need for a razor was somewhere in the future, and the confidence that might be granted by a mustache or the ability to grow one was unrealized.

He would have to face Laurel, nonetheless. He hoped to see her this time, but worried she would not be at work, or worse, that she would refuse to talk to him. After eating a bowl of granola for breakfast, Sterling rode to Canaan's Kitchen for the third time in as many days and rehearsed his apology along the way. But the simple phrase, 'I'm sorry,' tasted like backwash to him, so he stopped rehearsing the words and visualized apologizing with courage.

When he reached the restaurant, the parking lot was half full with cars and the red neon *Open* sign was lit, both of which encouraged Sterling to proceed. He leaned his bike against a flower box out front and pulled the door handle at the entrance. Immediately, the aroma of cinnamon rolls wafted like a warm breeze past him and into the parking lot beyond. At the tables, people enjoyed their breakfast chatter and drank coffee from cozy mugs.

Sterling spotted Bethany ringing up a customer at the cash register. She looked over at him and smiled. When he approached, she said, "You're back. Sorry about yesterday—I forgot it was Sunday."

"No problem. I enjoy coming over here every day. There's nothing else I'd rather do with my free time. Now, could you help me? I need to speak with the manager."

"The manager?" She continued to smile. "That won't be necessary. I can help you."

Sterling shook his head. "I'm not sure you can, actually. Besides, I don't want to talk with you until your metamorphosis—or whatever it is—has taken place. All I know is if it's a change, it's got to be an improvement. In the meantime, I'll speak with the manager." As Bethany began to answer, Sterling's eyes scanned the room over her shoulder, and he walked past her to find someone who seemed managerial.

Bethany caught up and stopped him. "All right, already. Will you just chill? I'll see if she's here. Just stay here. Maniac . . ." Bethany pushed her way through the swinging doors that separated the dining area from the kitchen. Sterling peered through the window where the cooks staged food under heat lamps. He saw a couple of workers, but not Laurel.

Bethany returned and said, "The manager made a run to the bank. Laurel is here, but she is too busy to see you now."

"When is she off? I can come back then. What's another trip? I bet I can ride here with my eyes closed by now."

"Four thirty. But she said she can talk with you during her lunch break at one o'clock. Come back then, and she'll meet you outside."

"Is this another one of your famous 'come back laters?'"

"No, she told me she would meet you. For real."

Sterling agreed to meet her then. Out in the parking lot, he realized he had quite a bit of time to spare, and he didn't feel like sitting on a bench all morning or pedaling all the way home and back. To make the best use of his time, he figured he could ride over to Pete's office,

48

which was only several blocks away, and say hello. With the apology lined up, he would recount to Pete his sincere attempts to get ahold of Laurel over the past three days and attempt to negotiate a time extension—just in case.

PETE'S OFFICE WAS only a five-minute ride from Canaan's Kitchen. It was located in a two-story building that Pete co-owned with his partner, Dirk, and they rented out units to other businesses. Three retailers occupied the first floor—a dry cleaner, a jeweler, and a take-and-bake pizza shop. Ten executive office suites filled the top floor, two of which were used by Pete and Dirk. The rest were rented by an attorney, a financial planner, three different insurance brokers, and three remote workers. Each suite shared a break room, restrooms, and a common reception area, including a receptionist who answered the phone for all ten businesses.

Sterling always felt a little strange to visit the complex, as if they were too nice to be real. He could never forget the days when Pete ran his business out of their cramped apartment across town. Those days were difficult, and Sterling wished he could forget about them.

Sterling rolled into the lot and saw Dirk loading a cardboard file box into the trunk of his Tesla, alongside several similar boxes. Pete's SUV was nowhere to be found. Sterling waited until Dirk looked up, having learned from startling Mr. K. the day before.

"Morning," Dirk called to him. "What brings you to the office?"

"I'm looking for Pete. Is he around?"

"He left an hour ago for an appointment. Said he wouldn't be back today. Something you need?"

"No, it's no big deal. I had a question for him, but I'll see him at home later." Sterling's thoughts snapped back to when he was on Dirk's boat and saw that over-the-top gift Dirk had shown him. He added, "And I haven't said a word to Hoyt about the fishing poles."

There was something about the way Dirk responded to Sterling's comment, either his peculiar expression or how he shifted from foot to foot, that made Sterling suspect something had changed since he had held the new salmon pole in his hands only three days earlier. Dirk seemed agitated, and he swallowed as if searching for the right words. "That reminds me, Sterling," he said firmly, "there's something we must discuss, and it's fortunate you stopped by. I needed to get a hold of you or Hoyt about my lawn. I recently got a new tenant for my warehouse west of town, and filling the space was very important to me. The tenant's brother is starting a yard care business, and the tenant agreed to rent on the condition that I also hire his brother to do my yard. It's a full yard care service, not just the lawns and weeding. He can prune my trees and shrubs and maintain the sprinkler system. You have to understand, I hardly had a choice in the matter."

Sterling nodded slowly, but wasn't sure what Dirk was getting at. "So . . . after school starts, you're going with a different yard service?"

"Not exactly. I don't need you and Hoyt to do my lawn anymore. The new service starts next week. I really hate to do this because you and Hoyt are almost like sons to me. And I hate the saying, 'It's not personal. It is only business,' but in this case it's true." Dirk pulled out his wallet and thumbed through a thick wad of money. He took out two crisp one-hundred-dollar bills and handed them to Sterling. "Think of this as a severance package." Dirk forced a smile, but it masked a subtle sneer that puzzled Sterling. It almost seemed to him that Dirk enjoyed firing Hoyt and him.

Dirk patted Sterling on the shoulder and told him not to take it too hard. With that, he got into his car and drove away.

Sterling rubbed the two bills together. He did not know what to think. Dirk's warmth from a few days ago had cooled to ice. The summer was taking a bizarre turn. A week earlier, Sterling was full of hope—earning money for his projects and for Hoyt's football camp had looked easy. Now they needed to find another yard job to replace Dirk's. Between that and the threat of losing his allowance, Sterling wondered if he had offended the universe and brought some type of curse upon himself. It was a puzzling thought, but in his defense, he was missing important pieces to life's puzzle.

IN HIS SHAKEN state, Sterling bet he wouldn't have enough money for his programming kit anyway, so he decided to squander a few bucks on a good lunch. He returned to Canaan's Kitchen at half past noon and ordered a smokehouse BBQ chicken sandwich on wheat, no crust, with cheddar, provolone, lettuce, tomato, mayo, mustard, fries, and a Coke. All to go.

Ten minutes later, Bethany handed him a paper sack and said, "Twelve-fifty-three, including tax."

He handed her a ten and a five and said, "Keep the change." He exited with his lunch and walked his bike to the bench, where he had met John on Sunday. He sat down and carefully peered into the bag, almost suspecting something to jump out at him. To his relief, the order was perfect.

I perched upon the birdhouse at the barn and watched Sterling from a distance. He didn't notice me, so I sounded made two oowoo woo calls to get his attention. He gazed up and squinted. We locked eyes for a moment, and neither of us would look away, as if was a contest. Eventually, Sterling lost. *Huh*, he thought. *Looks like that bird from my dream.*

His consideration of me was immediately driven away by Laurel walking from the restaurant, and he practically choked on his BBQ sandwich at the sight. She came over to Sterling, who stood up to meet her. She wore a forest green baseball cap and matching polo shirt—both embroidered with Canaan's Kitchen's logo—black jeans and black tennis shoes. Even in her work uniform, she looked great. Sterling hoped he wouldn't say anything to embarrass himself. She extended her hand, stole a glance at his bruised scar, and said, "Hey, I'm Laurel. Laurel Mercury. What's your name?"

"Sterling Burke."

Laurel paused. "You look familiar. I think I know you from school. Do I?"

"I'm not sure." Sterling was certain he wouldn't have forgotten her. He searched his memory and tried to recall her, but Laurel beat him to it and snapped her fingers.

"Oh wow, that's it. It was fourth grade. I used to see you in the free-lunch line. You would wear that one shirt that was too small and jeans with holes in the *knees all the time*. That was you."

"I don't think so," Sterling answered, but she was exactly right. He could keep memories of the poor years buried for a while, but then something would dredge them up—the bland smell of instant coffee, the snap of a mousetrap, the tightness of an empty stomach, or an innocent comment like Laurel's. They would rise to the surface and reek like kelp sunbaked on the beach after a high tide—a salty, rotting, and putrid stench. Sterling tried to weigh them down with Nikes, designer jeans, and feigned indifference, but he knew they could resurface at any moment. It still stung when they did.

"Yeah," Laurel added. "And you hardly ever smiled."

Sterling looked down at his shoes and said, "Must have been a favorite set of clothes." He thought back to grade school and recalled seeing a young girl whom could have only been Laurel. He said, "Might have been a different kid, though."

"No, it was you all right. I remember those dimples."

A half-smile escaped Sterling, but he tried to play it cool. He changed the subject. "Look, I appreciate you coming out here to talk with me, but I don't want to take up your entire break. I just need to apologize. What I did the other day with your necklace was wrong. I should have returned it like a normal person. I'm not always a jerk like that."

Laurel's expression softened. "The free pie I delivered to your table wasn't very nice, either. I wanted to give you a hard time in front of your family. I'm sorry."

"No, no. I deserved it—the hard time, not the pie. But the pie was great." Sterling chuckled as he rubbed his arm with his hand. "So, uh . . . are we cool?"

The silence waiting for Laurel's reply felt much longer and more painful to Sterling than it actually was. "Yeah. We're cool. Thanks for the apology," Laurel answered at last. "Nice bike, by the way." She gestured toward the bench. "I have one almost like it. Mine is blue."

"Awesome. Maybe I'll see it around sometime." As Sterling stood there, admiring Laurel in the dappled midday light beneath the cedars, a wild thought struck him. It surprised him that he said out loud. "Hey, do you think I could get your number?"

With an expression of mock astonishment, Laurel replied, "My number?"

"You know, in case I get hungry for some more of that pie. I'll even pay for it."

"Well, if it's for ordering food, the restaurant's number is on the website," she joked. "But just in case their line is busy, I'll give you my number." She recited her phone number, and Sterling entered it into his contact list. She said, "I better get back to work now. But text me, so I'll have your number, okay?"

Sterling promised he would, and as she said goodbye, Laurel's perfect white smile nearly sparkled beneath her brown and piercing eyes. Sterling watched her return to the restaurant and hoped she would give him a chance to get to know her. Yes, she was unbelievably cute, but there was something that attracted him to her, almost an aura.

Sterling finished his lunch in peace, having finally delivered the apology. The weight of losing his allowance was off his shoulders, and all he had left to do was let Pete know the job was done. After that, he could break the news to Hoyt about Dirk's yard, but Sterling was feeling much better about it now. *How hard is it to find another yard or two?* Sterling wondered. *I'll buy that advanced programming kit in a few weeks, and then I'll start saving for UROV's robotic arm. Piece of cake.*

Eight

BECAUSE STERLING'S PARENTS were both realtors, they had designed and decorated their house to a tee. It checked every box of desirable features. Street appeal? Check. Three-car garage? Check. Spacious kitchen with an island and granite countertops, four bedrooms, en suite master bath, den, private back yard with shaded deck? All checked. The list ran on.

Sterling had grown accustomed to his family's impressive home and paid no attention to its features as he walked his bike into the garage, parked it against the wall, and pushed the button to close the garage door. With the garage door shut, the room was dark, save for the light that crept in through the small windows on the side. Sterling passed between his parent's Range Rover and BMW, heading for the kitchen, when he noticed a shadow in his dad's SUV. To his surprise, it was Pete, sitting in the driver's seat in the dark with his hands on the wheel and his forehead resting between them. Sterling pulled the passenger door open.

"Pete, I did it," he announced proudly. "I apologized."

Pete slowly sat up and turned toward Sterling. The stippled texture of the steering wheel imprinted small dents on his forehead, like a golf ball had rolled across it. All color had drained from his face, and his eyes were vacant.

"I apologized," Sterling repeated. "Remember? The necklace." He noticed that Pete's knuckles were white from clenching the steering wheel.

"Fine," Pete mumbled. "That's fine."

"Pete? Are you okay?"

His dad took a deep breath. "No. Nothing is okay."

"What happened?"

Pete groaned and put his head back onto the steering wheel. "Go inside. I need a few minutes."

Sterling shrunk back a step from the car door and closed it gently. He had never seen Pete like that. His dad was always upbeat, so optimistic that Sterling sometimes wondered if Pete's endless enthusiasm crossed the line into phoniness. Sterling went inside the house to find his mom and see if he could get some answers.

The kitchen was empty, and the house was quiet. He searched her craft room and then upstairs, but there was no sign of her. The sound of a door slamming shut downstairs got Sterling's attention, and as he turned around in the hallway, he bumped into his mom.

"What's going on?" he asked her.

But before she could answer, Pete hollered from downstairs for a meeting in the living room. Anne and Sterling hurried down and found Pete sitting in the shadows, away from the streaks of sunlight that spilled through the partially open drapes. He sat upright in his armchair, his elbows resting on the wide oak armrests. He had pushed the matching footstool away, and his feet were firmly on the floor. Hoyt came straggling into the room behind Anne and Sterling.

Pete pointed the three of them toward the eight-foot-long sofa. Anne sat between the boys, and they each watched Pete uneasily. For nearly a minute, he did not speak, but held his hands together and focused his eyes on the bookshelf across the room, brooding.

Anne could not bear to wait any longer for an explanation, so she asked, "What's this all about? You're scaring me. Is something wrong?"

Pete's eyes turned to his wife, and he answered, "Something has happened that concerns all of us. You know that as a rule, I've always kept my business and our family matters separate. Business has been good for this family, but I leave it at the office. Now, I'm realizing how much the two are bound together. How much they can impact each other."

"Pete," Anne blurted. "What happened?"

Pete shook his head. "Dirk betrayed me. Really, he betrayed *us*. Earlier today, he met me at our new development and handed me overdue tax notices from the county. The thing is, I gave Dirk the money for those taxes months ago, but now it's gone. Dirk swindled me. He stole the money and somehow covered his tracks. Now, he's terminated our partnership, and we're each going our separate ways. But that's not the worst of it." He held up several papers. "These letters Dirk gave me detail every penny of unpaid property taxes, including accrued interest and penalties. Unless the full balance is paid by the deadline, the county will seize my commercial properties to cover the debt. The amount I owe is . . . over \$550,000. And I must pay it in ninety days, or I lose everything I've worked for." Pete slumped into his chair and buried his face in his hands.

Anne slowly stood and walked over to her husband. She sat on the armrest and hugged Pete against her side. He put his arm around her waist and looked up at her with gratitude. Hoyt and Sterling sat like mannequins on the sofa, unable to move under the weight of Pete's news. They struggled to understand the impact it would have on their lives.

Then Pete addressed them. "You boys must understand. I owe an extraordinary debt. I'll be honest with you. I'm not sure where that money is going to come from. At the very least, we'll all have to do a lot of belt-tightening in the weeks to come. I'll make a plan for us to get through this—don't you worry about that. But in the meantime, we'll do everything possible to cut back on spending—cancel the club membership, cancel the yard service, sell a building or two before the foreclosure auction. I'll work harder than ever, twice as hard, and we'll each need to play our part to make this work. As a matter of fact . . ." Pete took his arm from Anne and stood up. "I'm going to the office. I need to get started. Every day counts." He walked to the window and flung open the drapes, letting light fill the room.

"Whoa, whoa, whoa," Hoyt said, making a timeout signal with his hands. "What about Dirk? Isn't *he* the one who owes *us* the money? Why is this our problem?"

"I don't have the time or money for a legal battle that I would likely lose," Pete asserted. "It would be my word against his, and that's not good enough to win a lawsuit."

"We're going to let him get away with this? No way. We need to stand up to him! Make him pay!"

"No, Hoyt. Let it be." With that, he walked out of the room, and Anne followed him to the den, where they closed the door to discuss the situation further.

Sterling raised an eyebrow and said to Hoyt, "I'd like to know what they're talking about in there. There must be more to the story. I . . . I can't believe Dirk would do this to us. Can you?"

Hoyt shook his head. "It doesn't make any sense. Dirk's been good to us. Well, I thought he had been. And I can't figure out why Pete won't fight it."

"Right. Something doesn't add up."

The boys sat in silence as they realized the consequences of the situation. Like Pete said, the coming storm would rock each of them. Sure, they could drop the club membership, the yard service and maybe the cable TV package, but those cutbacks would be like bailing out a sinking ship with a teacup. In order to survive, they would need to drop much, much more. New clothes for the upcoming school year—gone. Allowances—gone. Programming kit—gone. Football camp—gone. Sterling guessed he and Hoyt would get stuck maintaining their yard for free.

"Whatever's going on," Hoyt said, "I know I won't get to the bottom of it sitting here. I can't think straight unless I'm moving. I'll be out shooting hoops if you want to talk."

After Hoyt left, Sterling remained alone on the sofa, still trying to wrap his mind around the turn of events. He replayed Pete's monologue in his mind again and again, hoping to make sense of it. He pondered the situation from every angle, but felt like he was missing key pieces to an enormous and complex puzzle. He thought about the humbling apology he delivered to Laurel and how worried he had been about keeping his allowance. Now it was lost anyway.

Sterling went to his room and laid on his bed to think of another way around it. He and Hoyt might be able to do things to keep some money flowing in. They could get additional yard jobs to take up the allowance slack until the fall, when lawns and weeds stop growing. It wasn't much, but something was better than nothing. As he considered that, he had another idea. *Maybe Dirk will back off. Maybe I can convince him to change his mind.*

Nine

STERLING COULD NOT push Dirk out of his mind. There must be an alternate explanation for the wrongs Pete claimed Dirk had done to him. Certainly, this entire mess was a big misunderstanding, and Pete must have missed something. Sterling bet that if he and Hoyt rode over to Dirk's house and listened to his side of the story, he would answer a lot of their questions and maybe clear up the entire situation. Sterling went to Hoyt's room and knocked, but there was no answer. So, he decided to go to Dirk's by himself. As he entered the garage to get his bike, he heard Hoyt bouncing a basketball on the driveway outside.

Sterling joined Hoyt and said, "All right, I know what we need to do."

Hoyt passed the ball hard to him and said, "Unless it involves blowing up Dirk's Tesla or something, I'm not interested. He's got to pay." It seemed like moving around hadn't cleared Hoyt's mind like he had hoped. It had only cleared the way for anger to move in.

Sterling casually dribbled the ball as he answered. "I have a plan. You should hear me out."

"Here's what we do," Hoyt interrupted. "We sink his stupid boat."

"What? No, we need to focus on getting more money—for my projects and your football camp."

"He loves that boat."

"Hoyt. Forget the boat. We need money."

"Don't be a wuss. I know where he hides the key. We could sneak on board tonight. Cut a few hoses. Open the sea-cock valve. Loosen the ropes. Watch that sucker gurgle its way to the bottom."

Sterling hurled the ball against the backboard, and Hoyt caught it on the rebound. "Listen to me. We've got to prioritize. Sinking his boat gets us nothing. First, we try to get more money. If that fails, then we can look at other options."

Hoyt shrugged and dribbled his way to the edge of the driveway. He turned and swished a three-pointer. "I don't see why we can't do both."

Sterling passed the ball back to him. "Do you really think you could sink *Leverage* without getting caught? The Boat Basin has cameras at every entrance. People are at the marina at all hours, day and night. Some people even live aboard their boats. Sure, you could try to sneak around, but you would probably leave evidence somewhere. And if anything happened to Dirk or to his stuff, whose name do you think would be at the top of the suspect list?"

Hoyt studied the basketball as he tossed it from one hand to the other. "Ours?"

"Bingo!"

"So, how are we going to get even?"

"That's what I'm trying to tell you. We may not *have* to get even. You might want revenge, but it's not what you need. You need money for football and for clothes."

"Maybe," Hoyt admitted, passing the ball the Sterling.

"No, I'm right about this." Sterling thought back to the fishing poles Dirk had bought for them and added, "This whole thing with Pete and Dirk must be a misunderstanding, and if we talk to Dirk, we could maybe set things straight. Probably even avoid this mess altogether. There must be a reasonable explanation."

"I don't know. Pete was certain."

"Look, how long has Dirk known us? He wouldn't backstab Pete or anyone else in our family like that. And we both know how Pete can jump to a conclusion."

Hoyt nodded in agreement. "It's gotten him in trouble more than once . . . You really think Pete got this one wrong? What about those tax letters he waved around? He said he owes a ton of money."

"I heard that, too. I still think it's possible he's wrong," Sterling answered. He shot the ball toward the hoop and missed, sending the ball into the garage. Hoyt started to chase after it, but Sterling stopped him. "Leave it," he said. "Let's ride over to Dirk's right now and ask him to explain things to us."

Hoyt reluctantly said, "Well, I guess it can't hurt."

Dirk lived only a few streets from the Burkes. Both houses were in the first development Pete and Dirk completed together, years before. All the homes were on half-acre lots, except for Dirk's—his was on a full acre. Only Dirk's mailbox and driveway entrance could be seen from the street. His enormous, six-bedroom house was tucked away out of sight behind the driveway's gentle, tree-lined curve. Sterling and Hoyt pedaled down to the house, as they had done many times, and saw three unfamiliar cars parked in front of the garage. Sterling wondered if they should come back later when Dirk would be alone, but Hoyt insisted they move ahead. They left their bikes by the garage and walked to the front door.

As Sterling raised his hand to knock, he noticed the door was ajar. He and Hoyt looked at each other, unsure of whether they should enter the house. But Sterling talked Hoyt out of it and rang the doorbell instead. They waited. After a moment, Sterling rang it again.

When no one answered, Hoyt decided it was his turn. He pushed the door open and motioned for Sterling to follow him. They entered the large foyer, and Hoyt called out, "Dirk, are you here? We need to talk to you."

Both boys listened for a response. They heard distant voices and muted laughter coming from the back of the house. Hoyt led Sterling carefully down the hall toward the voices, not knowing what they would find. As they reached the edge of the living room, they saw seven people standing and talking. It looked like Dirk was hosting a party. Everyone held a drink and appeared to be having a good time.

The boys stepped into the living room, and immediately a lady noticed them and stopped talking mid-sentence. The man she was speaking with followed her eyes and turned to look at the boys. Soon, each conversation halted, and six sets of puzzled eyes settled on the twins. Dirk noticed the growing quiet and had to scan the room before he spotted the boys. He saw the twins and did a double-take.

Sterling nervously cleared his throat and wanted to be anywhere but there. But it was too late to turn back.

Dirk smiled politely, set his glass on the coffee table, and extended his arms to the boys. "These are my two favorite teenagers," he announced to his guests as he walked over to Sterling and Hoyt. "I always welcome their visits. Please excuse us for a minute." He put a hand on each of the boy's shoulders and directed them out of the room. "What a nice surprise," Dirk noted smugly. "Why don't we go into my office, where my guests won't disturb us?" Dirk herded the boys across the house and into his office and closed the door.

Sterling and Hoyt crossed the lush carpet and lined themselves against the far wall.

Dirk studied the boys and took a deep breath. "Okay, first things first. How did you get in here?"

"The door was open," Hoyt answered.

"And what are you doing here?"

"Pete said you two aren't partners anymore."

"And," Sterling interjected, "he said you embezzled a lot of his money."

"Right," Hoyt continued. "We wanted to talk to you to see if that's true."

"I see." Dirk drummed his fingers on his desk and thought for a moment. "I have to tell you, the issue isn't so simple. To make things easy to understand, I'll put it this way. From the very beginning of our partnership, our contract included an automatic termination clause. Unless both of us took action to extend it, the contract was written to end automatically. I didn't extend it, and apparently, Pete missed the fine print. The situation shouldn't have surprised him. The expiration was listed there all along."

Sterling nodded. "All right, but what about the property taxes? What went wrong there?"

Dirk straightened up and pointed a defiant finger at the boys. "Hey, don't give me attitude," he barked. "Real estate finances are complex, and you don't know what you are talking about. Pete gave me that money, but we ran into unexpected costs. Surveying, site preparation, utilities, things like that. There wasn't enough money to cover those expenses and the property taxes, so the property taxes got the short straw."

"You took a hit, too?" Sterling asked. "You owe the county like Pete does?"

"Well . . ." Dirk paused, and his silence gave the boys the answer they suspected.

"No." Hoyt jumped in. "I bet he doesn't owe a dime. Looks like Pete's the one who got the short straw."

"Listen," Dirk defended, "as much as I love having people barge into my house and accuse me of wrongs I didn't commit, what's going on with Pete is very complicated, and I don't have the time to explain it right now. There is a lot of history between us that you don't know. Honestly, I hoped it wouldn't come to this. I really did. But unfortunately, Pete has made some serious mistakes, and this is what we're dealing with. I'm still hopeful the three of us can remain close— you boys and me—despite the decisions your parents have made. When it all settles down, let's go fishing again."

Sterling wondered if Dirk seriously believed he and Hoyt would forget about him wrecking their dad's business and pushing them back to the brink of poverty. *Not a chance.*

"For now," Dirk added, motioning to the door, "I really must get back to my guests. Let me show you out."

Dirk exited the office and waited for Sterling and Hoyt to follow him into the hall. Hoyt was two steps behind Dirk, and Sterling followed several seconds later. Dirk reached the front door and pulled it open.

Sterling stopped and turned to Dirk, looking him firmly in the eyes. "Why don't you do the right thing? Give the money back."

Dirk only smirked in response. He ushered the boys outside, closed the door hard behind them, and clicked the deadbolt.

Sterling and Hoyt looked at the door in disbelief. They walked over to their bikes in silence and began pedaling out of the driveway. Before they were even a block away, Sterling told Hoyt to pull over, and they stopped in the middle of the bike lane.

"He's definitely hiding something," Sterling said. "I don't trust what he said about Pete or their business."

Hoyt agreed. "Yeah, he was being really weird. Did you notice how he rushed us away from his friends? It's like he didn't want to blow his cover in front of them."

"Exactly. And he locked the front door behind us like we were total strangers. What was all that about? I thought we were practically family."

"No way." Hoyt shook his head. "Not anymore."

"What do you make of what he said about a history between him and Pete and about decisions our parents have made?"

Hoyt thought for a second. "I dunno. It could have to do with him and mom."

"What?"

"You know he has a thing for mom, right? Haven't you noticed how uncomfortable she gets around him? How she tries to avoid him?"

"Yuck!" Sterling's face shriveled up like he had just swallowed a mouthful of soap. "Dirk does *not* have a thing for her. That's disgusting." He shivered and then spit onto the sidewalk.

"I've seen what I've seen. Like last month, I was with her when she was going to drop off mail at Pete's office. That morning, Pete had told her he would be staying in the office because Dirk was going to Seattle on personal business. So, we pulled up, but Dirk's Tesla was in the parking lot. When Mom saw it, she would not even go inside the office. She handed the envelopes to me and told me to take them to Pete. I made note of it because she had just been talking about how long it had been since she was in the office and how she was looking forward to popping in to see how Pete had redecorated the place."

"That's not proof."

"You can think that, but it's good enough for me. I was there."

"Well, I'm through talking about it. There are probably more important things going on here, anyway." Sterling reached into his pocket and pulled out his phone. "Look at this." He showed Hoyt a picture of a sticky note.

"What's that?" Hoyt asked.

"Did you see the router on the shelf in his office? I took a quick picture on the way out. Hopefully, it is clear enough for us to read it." He enlarged the photo. "It must be the password to get onto his Wi-Fi network. It also shows the router's make and model."

Hoyt looked up at Sterling blankly, "What good is that? We have our own Wi-Fi."

"No, it's not for us to use like that. As I said, Dirk's hiding something, and I want to know what it is. If we can get onto his network, we might be able to access his computer, read his files, and figure out what's going on. Maybe even hijack his accounts and get Pete's money back."

"Whoa. What? Are you crazy?"

Sterling stared back at Hoyt with unusual determination in his eyes.

"Wait, don't answer that," Hoyt added. "I can already see that you are."

Ten

THE BOYS PARKED their bikes in the garage back home, and Hoyt picked up his basketball. "Hey," he said, "how about a game of HORSE? We can make a plan while we shoot. I think better when I'm moving around. And you can start." He passed the ball to Sterling.

"No thanks. I always lose."

"Okay, I'll make you a deal—if I make a shot, you can move five feet closer for your shot. If you make a shot, I'll step five feet back."

"And no left-handed shots?"

"No left-handed shots. But as fair warning, I'm still going to win."

Sterling dribbled the ball into the driveway, lined up a twenty-footer, and swished it.

"All right! Lillard scores! Nice shot. Lucky, but nice." Hoyt dribbled to a spot twenty-five feet from the hoop.

Before Hoyt took aim, Sterling pulled his wallet from his pocket and said, "Oh, by the way, with all Pete's drama, I forgot to tell you I ran into Dirk at the office this morning."

"Yeah?"

"Yep." He sighed, handing one of the hundred dollar bills to Hoyt. "He fired us. Here's your severance pay. He hired somebody else to do his yard, all so he could close some real estate deal. But I'm not sure I believe that anymore."

"You're kidding, right? He fired us?"

"I'm serious. And listen to this. Last Friday, he showed me brand-new fishing gear he bought for you and me. He wouldn't let me tell you about it because he wanted to surprise you. And then he fires us? Talk about a surprise. How could he change into a completely different person so fast?"

"Maybe a vampire from Forks came over here and bit him." Hoyt laughed. He took his shot and missed. "I have an *H*." He got his own rebound and passed the ball to Sterling. "Seriously, we'll probably never know. It's definitely weird, though." Sterling missed a fifteen-footer from the corner as Hoyt asked, "Do you think Pete and Mom know anything about the sudden change in Dirk?"

"Dunno. They talked in the den for quite a while."

"Well, whatever it is, Dirk's boat is going down!"

"Bro, forget the boat. It won't keep you on the football team."

Hoyt shook his head and dribbled to a new spot as Sterling continued, "I told you. Focus on the money. We get it back and we get our lives back. Can you even imagine the look on Pete's face if we got his money back?"

"Can you imagine the look on Dirk's face when he goes down to the Boat Basin and only his antenna is above the water?"

Hoyt was about to launch a long shot when Pete walked into the driveway. He held out his hands for the ball, and Hoyt passed it to him. Pete went out past the free throw line, spun toward the basket, and swished his shot.

"Wanna play?" Hoyt asked.

"I'd like to, but your mom and I need to tell you something. Let's sit on the grass for a minute." Pete and the boys walked to the lawn, and Mrs. Burke joined them. Her eyes were red, and she carried a tissue in her hand. As she sat next to Pete, he said, "You both deserve an explanation for Dirk's surprising behavior. Earlier when I told you about our situation, I didn't want to—"

Anne sniffled and put her hand on Pete's knee, interrupting him.

"Please," she said. "I should tell them." Pete nodded, and she began to explain. "This morning, Dirk texted me to say he had a surprise for Pete. He asked me to meet him for coffee. I almost didn't go, but I was curious and thought doing something for Pete was a nice idea. So, we met at what used to be my favorite restaurant." She blew her nose. "I-I don't know how else to say this . . . Dirk asked me to divorce your dad and marry him. I didn't even answer. I just got up and walked out. For the next hour or so, I drove around, trying to process what happened and figure out why he would think I would ever consider leaving Pete."

Pete put his arm around Anne's shoulder and said, "He must have been planning it for weeks. I think he planned to ruin me, collect my money, and lavish it on your mother. He's gone crazy."

"That actually makes sense," Sterling noted. His mother gasped in horror. "No, no, not like that," he clarified. "I saw Dirk around lunchtime today. He was loading boxes from the office into his car. He told me he hired someone else to do his yard and that Hoyt and I were done."

"You're kidding!" Anne replied. "He had always cared so much about you boys."

Hoyt scoffed. "He *used* to care. Not so much anymore. He fired us."

"What would make him think you would leave Pete and marry him?" Sterling asked.

"That's what I was asking myself while I was driving around town to clear my head. Recently, Dirk had been acting odd whenever I spoke with him, so I started avoiding him. I have never encouraged him."

"Why would he want to ruin Pete? And me and Hoyt? I thought we were his friends."

"Like your dad said, I think Dirk wanted to undermine him, no matter what I decided. I don't know why he fired you. The thought of seeing you boys might have reminded him I love Pete and not him."

Pete pulled a blade of grass from the lawn and inspected it in his hands, though his thoughts were evidently elsewhere. "As long as we are all here," he said carefully, "I need to update you boys on some things."

He outlined the cost-cutting measures. Sterling expected most of them: canceling the family's athletic club membership, trading in the Beemer for an older model, hacking allowances, dropping health insurance, skipping back-to-school shopping. But he didn't see the big one coming. Pete was considering renting out the house and moving the family back into an apartment.

Hoyt's head jerked up. "Time out! You're killing me. Health insurance is required for football."

Pete pursed his lips for a moment, as if reconsidering, but he said, "We don't have the money for insurance. And we can't afford the football fees." He looked over at Sterling. "No after-school activities. Nothing that has any fees, including the science club."

That was the last straw for Sterling. He jumped to his feet. "You get to keep your Range Rover, but I can't even buy new clothes. My shoes are pinching my feet! I need new school clothes."

"Same here," Hoyt added.

Pete held up both hands. "Easy," he answered in a soft, calming voice. "The Range Rover is leased for two more years. I can't get out of it. You boys can pick up additional yard jobs. Ask your customers for references. When I was your age, I paid for my own school clothes."

"And walked to school in the snow," Hoyt grumbled. "More lawns won't be enough."

"Shop the sales. Buy at Goodwill. Make it work. Learn how the other half lives."

"No," Sterling said. "I know how the other half lives. Been there, done that. I'm not wearing someone else's used clothes. With my luck, the old owner will recognize me in his shirt on the first day of school."

"I don't want to be in this bind any more than you do," Pete explained. "I'm doing everything I can to get us out of it. I'll continue to work on our commercial properties during the day and see if I can make that new development work out. It's a long shot given our financial situation, but I have to try. I'll work evenings and weekends at the office too, and your mom's joining me. That's right—she's going back to work as a real estate agent. If we can turn a couple of quick sales, we might be able to afford a few extras. Your mom and I are giving this one hundred percent. It'll mean long hours and hardly any family time. You two will need to look after yourselves. Cook for yourselves, clean up after yourselves, do the yard. We'll leave grocery money for you. Spend it at the store, not for fast food. We're trusting you both to do your part and stay out of trouble."

"One more thing," Anne said. "Remember that real estate seminar in Seattle we discussed a while back? The one that conflicts with your birthdays? It starts next week. We already paid for the seminar and the hotel, and it's too late to cancel, so we'll be out of town for the full five days. Hopefully, it will pay for itself in teaching us how to develop more business. Like we all agreed, we'll celebrate your birthdays the following week. Okay?"

"Yeah, I remember talking about it," Hoyt said. "It's still okay. One week doesn't matter."

"Sterling?" Anne asked.

Sterling wanted to leave and blow off steam, but instead, he remained seated on the lawn. "Who cares about the birthday?" he snapped and looked at Pete. "This cost-cutting plan stinks. How is it going to fix anything? Dirk has your money, our money. Stand up to him. Get it back."

Pete stood and walked straight toward Sterling. Sterling jumped, stepped back, and crossed his arms in front of his chest to protect himself. But Pete went right past him, into the house. Anne motioned for Sterling to sit back down on the grass. After he settled, she waited for him to look over at her.

"Do you think this is easy for your father? For me?" she asked. "He feels like a complete failure. He knows he should have understood the contract. We just met with a lawyer. The contract favors Dirk. The fine print, the details that your father either did not read or did not understand, laid the groundwork. Dirk planned this from the beginning. He is cunning, and he is patient. We wouldn't win a lawsuit against him. So, try to have compassion for your father, all right? He's under enormous pressure." The boys nodded, and Anne got up and went into the house.

Sterling and Hoyt sat in silence. The reality of their hardship was sinking in. Sterling felt like everything in his world was jacked up. Less than a week ago, he was enjoying his summer break, hanging out with friends at the park, finishing UROV, thinking Dirk was their friend. Life was good. Now, he could only hope things would be better by the time school started. Maybe Pete wouldn't find a renter for the house, and they could avoid moving back into a cramped apartment. Maybe Dirk would reconsider and return the money. Maybe it wouldn't be so bad wearing last year's clothes. But he still wasn't going to buy any at Goodwill.

Hoyt interrupted the quiet. "I suppose we should look for more lawn jobs."

Sterling agreed. "Let's start tomorrow. In the meantime, we need to make a plan to get back that money Dirk stole from Pete."

"Sounds good. Want to continue our game while we talk it through?"

They returned to the driveway, where Hoyt missed a jump shot from the three-point line. He got the rebound and passed the ball to Sterling. Hoyt asked, "So, what are you thinking?"

Sterling sunk a ten-footer. "We need to know Dirk's patterns. When he's home, when he's away. We'll log his activity—coming and going. Once we know that, we can try to get into his home office."

"We're going to spy on him? From where? The woods along his driveway?" Hoyt sunk his fifteen-footer. "Better bring bug spray and a warm sleeping bag. And we'll need a good story to tell Pete about why we're never home."

"I'll install a surveillance camera to watch the front of his house."

"Right. You're going to buy one from the neighborhood spy store . .

"

"It's not that hard to set up a camera simple surveillance camera. I have the hardware, and I can download the software from the internet." Sterling clanged a foul shot off the rim. "Should take an hour or two to get it running."

"Oh. Really? You're must not be as dumb as you look."

"By the way, I look just like you, genius."

"What happens once you have it running?"

"Well, then we can connect it to Dirk's Wi-Fi and live-stream the video over his internet to a web page. It will cost us about ten dollars a month to host the page. But I don't know of a way around that, unless there's a free trial."

"Sounds boring. Probably hours and hours watching a whole lot of nothing." Hoyt swished a jump shot from the baseline.

"I can make it motion activated so it won't record unless something is happening. We can fast forward through the video every night." Sterling missed his shot and grunted, "That's an *H* for me."

Hoyt sunk a fifteen-footer. "I can think of lots of uses for something like that."

"The only thing I can't figure out is how to get power to the camera. I hope he has an outdoor outlet close by."

Hoyt said, "We'll need to know if he has an outlet before anything else, right? Tell you what, let's quit this game. You won, I lost."

"Wait, really?"

"It was really a tie, but you drew first blood, so you won." Hoyt shrugged. "It sounds like I need to scout Dirk's place for an outlet, and you need to get started on that super-duper spy camera. We'll meet back in an hour or so. What do you say?"

Sterling was ready to take matters into his own hands. "Let's do it."

Eleven

STERLING DID NOT plan to use his laptop for the surveillance camera because it was too valuable to leave outside at Dirk's, where someone might steal it. Fortunately, he could connect the camera to his Raspberry Pi computer. His gear included a camera and cable, as well as weatherproof cases for both the Pi and the camera. Sterling found instructions on the internet to install and configure the software he needed to stream live video from the camera to a web page. Once that was taken care of, he gathered everything he needed and started loading it into his backpack.

Before he finished, Hoyt burst into his room and nearly gave him a heart attack. "He scores!" Hoyt yelled and high-fived Sterling. "There's an outdoor outlet on every corner of his house. The one we want is next to the garage, behind a shrub."

"Anyone see you?"

"No. I was stealthy, like a cat. The same cars from earlier were there, and I heard people talking. But they were in the backyard. The party was still going strong."

"We need to wait until everyone is gone."

"Don't be a chicken. Let's go now."

"If anyone sees us, we're dead."

"No one will. We'll be as silent as ninjas."

Sterling looked down at his backpack and considered it. "Fine. I'm going to get an extension cord and tape. Then let's go set it up." Hoyt pumped his fist as Sterling left to gather the rest of the supplies.

On the ride over to Dirk's, the two boys talked about how good it would feel if they could bring Dirk down and get Pete's money back. Not surprisingly, their chatter faded as they pulled into Dirk's driveway.

They hid their bikes behind the fir trees in the woods that bordered Dirk's property and walked toward the house, avoiding the wide-open driveway that would leave them exposed to anyone in the front yard. Hoyt led the way, high stepping over ferns and salal plants, picking his way from tree to tree, pausing at each one to peer out and listen. As they neared the house, their steps slowed and their stops became more frequent until they hid behind a tree next to the garage.

Hoyt fished the extension cord from Sterling's backpack and crawled to the corner of the garage, where he plugged it in. He covered the cord with leaves as he snaked it back to Sterling. Sterling taped the camera under a fir branch and aimed it to capture the traffic going into and out of both the garage and the front door. He powered up the Pi and pulled out his laptop to view the video.

The page was blank. Nothing.

"It isn't working," Hoyt said, looking over Sterling's shoulder. "C'mon, I did my part."

"Quit breathing down my neck. I need to test it." Sterling pointed to his laptop. "Keep an eye on it." He dashed to the garage door and back to the tree.

Hoyt watched the screen as it lit up. "It works!"

"Shh! Not so loud. It's motion activated. I needed to trigger it to send the video."

"Duh," Hoyt muttered, "I knew that."

"One more test—the front door. Got to make sure people going in or out will trigger it."

As Sterling approached the front door and nearly reached it, he heard a dreadful sound. The deadbolt clicked. Someone was about to come outside. Sterling spun around and sprinted back to the tree. He knew they would see him, and he planned to escape through the woods.

As I watched the events unfold, I could see Sterling was in quite a mess. The couple exiting the door was bound to see him. It was then I considered that making a video of the front of Dirk's house was not wrong, per se, so I stepped in to help Sterling. I had been circling Dirk's yard from above, and I executed a spiral dive toward the ground, opening my beak just enough to make a whistling sound and get the couple's attention. They were stepping out of the door when I swooped right in front of them, startling them backward.

I slammed into the front window. The impact was as loud as a crash cymbal, but it sounded worse than it was. I had intentionally hit the window with my back, as not to break any bones. Although I was unhurt, I fell to the ground and, for a moment, lay there in a pathetic heap. To buy Sterling a bit more time to escape, I limped toward the garage door like a peg-legged sailor.

The woman spotted me and gasped. "Is it all right?"

The man with her winced as he observed me. "I'm sure it'll be fine. Come on."

Sterling had reached the woods without being seen, and I turned toward the camera, puffed out my chest, and let out a loud oowoo-woo-woo call. Then I flew away.

Sterling and Hoyt hugged the ground in the bushes until the couple's car moved down the driveway and was out of sight. "Think they saw me?" Sterling asked.

Hoyt shrugged. "They didn't seem to."

"Oh man. If they did, I'll bet they are calling Dirk right now, and the cops will be waiting for us when we get home."

"Maybe not. He might not want to involve the cops."

"True. I guess we'll know soon enough. Let's get out of here."

Sterling put his laptop into his pack, and they raced home. As they rounded the street corner and could spot their own driveway, Sterling was relieved to see there was not a patrol car parked out front. But his relief evaporated when he saw a For Rent sign in their front yard and a For Sale sign in the back window of his mother's BMW. The belt-tightening was already taking effect, and fast.

The boys rushed into Sterling's room to see if the camera was still working. Sterling opened the web page on his laptop, and he and Hoyt focused their attention on the screen. They watched the footage of my flight into the front window and how it distracted the people until Sterling escaped unseen.

"Close one," Hoyt said. "They didn't see you."

Sterling brushed Hoyt's comment aside, and he eagerly backed up the video. "Did you see that? I want to watch that bird again." They watched my perfect spiral in slow-motion, followed by my crash into the window. Sterling forwarded the video to watch me stare at the camera, puff out my chest, and coo. He paused and pointed at my image. "Have you ever seen that bird before?"

"Never," Hoyt replied. "But you're into doves right now, aren't you? Didn't you ask Mom about it the other day?"

"No, I'm not into doves. Just this one." He tapped on the screen. "It keeps turning up. It's really bugging me."

"It's just a bird. Probably not even the same one you saw before. There's a ton of them around here."

"*That* is no ordinary bird. You saw it spin. Ever seen that before?"

"No, but—"

"It stared into the camera. It knew about the camera."

"No way." Hoyt looked down at the screen again, mesmerized by my image. "That would be spooky. I can't believe it."

"I saw what I saw."

"You saw what you imagined."

"It's on the video."

"Coincidence."

The brothers left it at that. Despite Hoyt's assurance that I was a random bird, Sterling was no longer sure such an easy answer could explain me away. He tried to think of a scientific rationale for a dove that could dive-bomb and dance; he was not sure what to believe. I was becoming harder for him to forget.

Twelve

*Truth is so obscure in these times, and falsehood so established, that,
unless we love the truth, we cannot know it.*

—Blaise Pascal

STERLING HAD IMPLEMENTED the first step of his plan—
surveillance. The camera was monitoring Dirk's comings and goings
and would help the boys learn his daily routine. The next step was to
sneak inside Dirk's house and search for clues relating to Pete's
business. Because Sterling thought it would be nearly impossible for
them to pick a lock on one of Dirk's main doors, he focused his
attention on getting in through the garage. But they needed a way to
trigger the opener.

Sterling loved to geek out on tech puzzles, so he spent most of the
night searching the Internet for ways to hack garage door openers. He
found multiple resources that explained how to clone the opener's
signal. Most recommended using an instrument called a spectrum
analyzer to characterize the signal, and he could buy a basic one for
less than one hundred dollars. However, to use one, he needed to
understand obscure terms like magnitude, frequency domain,
modulation domain, and distortion. He studied the low-cost spectrum
analyzer's twenty-page Quick Start Guide and understood almost none
of the technical mumbo-jumbo. After an hour, he realized he would
need months to make sense of it. He was searching the internet for a
lock picking kit when Hoyt walked into his room to see what was going

on.

"I am trying to learn how to hack into Dirk's garage door opener," Sterling explained, "so we can get inside his house. It looks pretty hard."

"How hard?"

"Hard enough to take me three or four weeks. Maybe less, if I knew his opener's make and model. And we would need to buy some equipment."

"Expensive equipment?"

"Maybe. We can buy a cheap analyzer for under a hundred bucks, but I'm not sure it would be good enough to do the job. Good ones cost a lot more. But it's too hard. It's like brain surgery," Sterling admitted. "Plus, we would need to be near his house while he's using his remote, which is way too risky. Let me do more digging. I might be able to come up with a better idea."

"All right, but you have one day. After that"—he pounded his fist into his other hand—"we sink *Leverage*."

Sterling finally had learned to ignore Hoyt's rantings and continued discussing his plan. "I'm going to order a universal remote control, one I can program to work with nearly any garage door opener. It may save us time. If we don't need it, I can always send it back."

"Can't hurt. Let me know how much it is, and I'll pay half."

"Sounds good," Sterling said. "Hey, are you up for scouting for lawn jobs tomorrow?"

"Sure. Let's leave here at nine."

"Hmm, make that ten. We won't get any new customers by dragging them out of bed."

"Fine. Just don't be late."

Sterling promised to be on time and returned to his computer as Hoyt left the room. Although Sterling was reluctant to spend the money, he ordered a universal garage door opener—and a lock picking kit, in case his efforts to hack the garage door opener failed. The uncertainty about the next steps in their operation bothered him, but he knew landing more yard jobs would lift his spirits. He'd feel even better if he and Hoyt could get Pete's money back from Dirk.

ACROSS TOWN, LAUREL had been praying for Sterling, asking that she could help him see with eyes of faith, see his need for inner transformation. I love to answer prayers like hers, and I piffed Sterling to call her. A piff is never demanding but is only a suggestion because people's free will is incredibly important to us—their moral freedom to make their own choices, to love or to hate, to do good or to do evil.

My piff entered Sterling's mind as an image of Laurel smiling at him. He saw it and welcomed the idea of taking a break from his family's troubles. He pulled out his phone to text Laurel, but as he started to type, he froze up. His hands grew clammy, and he laid his phone on his desk. Sterling wondered why he was hesitating. After all, he *had* told her he would contact her. What did he have to lose? She already thought he was a jerk. The worst she could do was ignore him.

He wiped his hands on his pants and picked up his phone again, typing, "Hey, it's Sterling. Forgot to text you my number. Sorry. You up for a bike ride? On the ODT? Wednesday, or???" He reread the message and then sent it.

After an excruciatingly long minute, his phone chirped. Laurel had replied. "Sure. Wanna meet Wednesday at the benches by the Coho? At 10?"

"Perfect," he replied. "See you then."

Sterling slid his phone into his pocket and let out a big, contented sigh. He was relieved, and honestly, a little surprised she agreed to meet him. Energy buzzed inside him, so he stood up and wiggled his shoulders up and down like he did when we danced.

I was pleased Sterling had received my piff and acted on it. Not everyone does. Most people sense my piffs but do nothing about them, and the problem is always a stony heart. Piffs bounce off hard hearts like BBs off a Kevlar vest. Dirk was an example of that. I first piffed him when he was a sophomore in high school. The piff was a suggestion to accept a friend's invitation to a Wednesday night youth group meeting. Dirk went, but the next day in school, two of his friends teased him about *getting religion*. Dirk was embarrassed, and he did not attend another meeting, despite multiple piffs pointing him in that direction. Over the years, Dirk received more invitations to explore life in the spirit—summer camps, Easter and Christmas Eve services, deep conversations with a friend. Each time, I sent a piff to nudge him forward, but he always declined. He wanted to be one of the cool kids. Really, he was afraid of being teased. Still, I longed to reveal transforming mysteries to him. I wanted the two of us to walk through life together. But he saw no use for those things.

Instead, Dirk convinced himself that money would grant him a good life and fulfill his desires for acceptance. Gaining more money became his obsession. He told himself that his wealth would entice Anne to leave Pete. After Anne refused his proposition, I piffed Dirk, yet again, to turn around and tell Pete the truth about the property taxes. But he hated that idea, and he became more determined than ever to accumulate as much money as he could.

Sterling had no awareness of Dirk's inner life, of the true hardness of his heart. In less than a week, however, Sterling would see to its depths, and what he discovered there would astonish him.

TEN O'CLOCK THE next morning found Sterling in the garage, stuffing work gloves into his rear pocket. He had topped off the mower's gas tank and used bungee cords to strap a gas can and a gas-powered edger onto the mower's deck. He double-checked his wallet to make sure he had several ones and fives in case he needed to make change for a twenty-dollar bill. The prospects for the day looked good, and Sterling was looking forward to bringing in more money for his projects. Maybe he could buy new shoes and a new hoodie, too.

Sterling glanced at his phone and saw the time was 10:05. Hoyt was nowhere to be found, and his bike was gone. *Too bad,* Sterling thought, clicking his tongue against his teeth. *I guess I'll keep all the money from the new jobs for myself.* He pushed the mower into the driveway and was about to close the garage door when he heard a shout behind him. Sterling turned to see Hoyt braking to a stop on his bike.

"Keep it open," Hoyt hollered.

"Where have—"

"I was at Dirk's," Hoyt interrupted. He panted to catch his breath. "I went to take a picture of his garage door opener so you would have its make and model."

"In broad daylight? Did anyone see you?"

"Forget about that. Look at this." Hoyt pulled a remote control from his pocket and handed it to Sterling. "Now we can get in whenever we want."

Sterling turned it over in his hands, as if to check whether it was real. "How did you get your hands on this?"

"I was taking a picture of the main unit, and while I was still looking through the side window, Dirk walked into the garage from the house and opened the garage door. He had backed his car into the garage, and as soon as the door opened, he took off without waiting for it to close. He was already around the curve before the door had shut halfway, so I ran around to the front and slid under it. I took a close-up picture showing the make and model, but then, in a flash of brilliance, I took the remote out of his truck. It's ours as long as we need it."

"Until he wants to drive his truck and sees that it's missing."

"What? Have you ever seen him drive that thing?"

"Yes."

"Whatever. He usually drives his car, so we should be safe for a few days at least. Besides, if he can't find the remote before we put it back, he'll just assume he lost it."

"I guess it'll be all right."

"Of course it is. Don't be such a chicken."

"Well, we're committed now. But as soon as I program the universal remote to replace it, we need to return this one. Deal?"

"Yeah, yeah."

"All right. The other remote is scheduled to arrive tomorrow. By the way, your share is twenty bucks."

"Twenty bucks? You think I'm made of money?"

"No, but that's what this is for." Sterling gave a slight kick to the lawnmower next to him. "Let's get more yard jobs."

STERLING AND HOYT took turns pushing the mower through a nearby neighborhood and scouting for lawns that were shaggy but healthy. They identified a good prospect right away. Sterling mentally paced off the size of the yard and calculated the number of square feet. With the size in mind, he computed the price, added 10 percent to allow for unforeseen snags, and finally added or subtracted a couple of bucks to leave room for a reasonable tip. A calculated price at thirty dollars became thirty-three, and since paying with two twenty-dollar bills was easier than exact cash, he expected customers to fork over forty dollars flat, including a tip. Sterling ran the quote by Hoyt, who gave his full approval.

Because Hoyt was more comfortable talking with customers, he was the one to knock on the front door. Sterling stood back and off to one side so the homeowner would notice the team of two. A middle-aged woman answered the door, and Hoyt asked if she needed two capable young men to care for her yard.

"Hmm," she replied, "My husband travels on business, and he's not always home when the lawn needs cutting. How much do you boys charge?"

"Thirty-three dollars. We even have an opening and can do it right now."

The woman shook Hoyt's hand, and the boys got to work.

Sterling mowed and edged while Hoyt pulled weeds. When they finished, Hoyt walked to the front of the house and rang the bell to let the woman know. She opened the door with her purse in her hand and handed him two twenties. As Sterling had hoped, she said, "Keep the change." Both boys smiled, thanked her, and told her to expect them again next week.

Twenty minutes later, they landed their second new job. It was only three houses away from the first one, and the yard was the same size. After the boys mowed and weeded, the owner promised to pay Hoyt on Venmo. As they walked home, Hoyt checked his Venmo balance and saw that the man had sent forty dollars. "Not a bad haul," Hoyt commented, showing Sterling his phone. "I'll send you your share, plus twenty for the remote."

Back at home, they put the tools away and dealt with the most important thing in their lives at that moment—food. They rushed into the kitchen, starving as only teen-age boys could be. In their defense, it had been five hours since breakfast. While eating lunch, Sterling casually mentioned, "I can't scout for new yard jobs tomorrow morning. I have plans with a friend."

"Okay, but remember, we have two jobs in the afternoon."

"No problem," Sterling replied.

"You and Doug working on your robots?"

"No. Going bike riding."

"Didn't know Doug liked to ride."

"It's not with Doug. It's with Laurel, the necklace girl."

Hoyt stopped chewing and gave Sterling a bewildered look. "Whoa. Do you like to hurt yourself?"

"She seemed to like the idea of hanging out."

"I don't know, man," Hoyt said through a mouthful of food. "She's gonna break your heart."

Thirteen

STERLING SHOWERED AND carefully combed his hair. He leaned over the sink to get closer to the mirror and turned his face left and right. He lifted his head to examine the skin under his chin and on his neck. Thankfully, no surprise zits had popped up overnight. His bike ride with Laurel was only two hours away, and Sterling was feeling jittery. He attempted to calm himself. *It's no big deal. It's not a date. We're not going to a movie or anything. We're just two friends biking— hanging out.* But the more he thought about it, the more he wondered if they were even friends. Or if they ever could be. That line of thought made Sterling more nervous, so he settled on waiting to see.

He spent the rest of the morning killing time, researching how to program a universal remote to work with Dirk's garage door opener. An article explained how easy it was, and it seemed to be as simple as using Bluetooth to connect earbuds to a phone. The remote was supposed to be delivered that afternoon.

It promised to be a big day.

STERLING ARRIVED AT the benches next to the Coho ferry terminal exactly at ten. He leaned his bike against the back of a bench, removed his helmet, and ran his fingers through his hair before sitting on the bench to observe the strait. A westerly breeze fluttered the flags mounted above the loading ramp in front of him. A seagull perched on a nearby piling repeated its annoying squawking, as if it was scolding the world. The recently arrived ferry from Victoria was releasing passengers and vehicles, temporarily clogging the surface streets in all directions. Laurel was going to be more than a minute or two late. While he waited, Sterling tried to think of a casual line he could say to start his conversation with Laurel. Unfortunately, he was drawing a blank.

After the stragglers disembarked from the ferry and the parade of vehicles cleared out, Sterling noticed out of the corner of his eye that Laurel was riding up. He sat a little straighter and pretended he was simply observing a second seagull near his feet that was begging for a snack.

Laurel leaned her bike against the end of the bench opposite Sterling's and said, "Sorry I'm late. Got caught in the ferry traffic."

Before he could awkwardly blurt, "*I love the strait,*" she continued.

"What a fantastic morning." She sat next to him, leaned back, and closed her eyes. "Mm. Shut your eyes and smell that sea air. Listen to the gulls cackling and the waves splashing against the breakwater . . ."

Sterling was unsure whether she really expected him to do what she asked. Still, he closed his eyes for a moment and took a deep breath. When he opened them again, he looked over at Laurel. Her eyes were still shut, and she was smiling with contentment. She wore a black windbreaker, black leggings, and a purple scarf tied around her neck. She suddenly opened her eyes and caught him looking at her. Sterling noticed her brown eyes were two shades darker than her skin, which was the rich hue of coffee with a splash of cream. She held her smile and said, "You're staring."

"No, I'm just taking in the sights," Sterling replied, still facing her.

"I bet I know what you're wondering, but you're probably too considerate to ask . . .scratch that. You're not the considerate type. Maybe tongue-tied."

"What do you mean?"

"I'll just tell you. My mother is black. My father is white. They say I got the best of each of their traits."

"Oh, I wasn't thinking about that." Sterling pointed at the top of her head. "A spider is crawling on your helmet."

Laurel ripped her helmet off and waved it around like it was on fire.

"You got it. You shook it off." Sterling chuckled. "Sorry, was that inconsiderate of me to mention the spider?"

Laurel searched around her with a crazed look. "Was there really a spider?"

Sterling paused and then began laughing. He laughed so hard he snorted. "Sure was," he said, regaining his composure. "Hey, you want to ride out on the Ediz Hook?"

Laurel agreed, and as they rode side-by-side on the Olympic Discovery Trail toward the hook, Sterling told her the story of how he tried to learn her name. "I even hacked into the school's database to find it," he said. "There were three girls named Laurel, but the oldest was twelve. Do you go to the public school?"

"I'm registered there, but I take all my classes at Peninsula College."

"Really? Are you out of high school?"

"No, I'm going into my junior year. But I'm in the Running Start program. All my classes count for both high school and college."

"Cool."

"Yeah, it's pretty sweet. You should look into it. The best part is that I get to take much better art classes—drawing, painting, ceramics, even jewelry making. The ones at the high school are kind of lame."

"Huh. I wonder why I couldn't I find you in the directory. You said you're registered at the high school."

"Yes, but my real name isn't Laurel. It's Meryl."

"Is Laurel your middle name or something?"

"Or something. When my mom was pregnant with me, I was twelve days overdue, and she really wanted me to pop out. She and Dad drove to the stairs on Laurel Street. Mom hoped that if she kept climbing up and down the hundred steps there, that would get things moving. It ended up working better than she had hoped, and I was born on the second landing on her third lap. They had already agreed to name me Meryl, but after I was born, Dad started calling me Laurel—after the street with the steps. And it stuck. Now, I'm Laurel to everyone, except my grandparents."

Sterling grinned. "I guess Laurel is better than Zigzag."

"Zigzag?"

"You know, the Zigzag ramps on Oak Street—between First and Second. Your parents could have been walking there when you showed up."

"Very funny." Laurel smirked. As they turned off the ODT and onto the road to the hook, Laurel asked, "So, what's your brother's name? Zolotnik?"

"What?"

"Never mind. It's a useless fact from my jewelry class. Zolotnik is a Russian silver that can be higher grade than Sterling silver. Like how your brother was nicer to me than you were."

Sterling had pushed the necklace incident out of his mind and was not happy she hadn't done the same. "Are you ever going to put that behind you? And his name is Hoyt, by the way."

"Interesting names. What was wrong with the usual twin names like Tom and Tim, or Mark and Mike?"

"Pete—that's my dad—he wanted each of us to be his own person. To be independent. Not half of a matched set."

"That makes sense. I'd hate having a twin. If I had one, I'd do everything possible to be different."

"We're not as much alike as people assume. We're twins, not clones, you know? But we're good friends, and I enjoy having someone around to hang out with—at least most of the time."

Laurel nodded toward some rocks by the water and said, "Want to sit for a minute?"

"Sure."

They parked their bikes, and each climbed onto a boulder that provided a good view of the strait. Laurel stared out at the water, tracking a seagull as it floated on the breeze. "Wouldn't you love to fly? To see everything from a lofty perspective? To let the wind carry you?" She turned to watch the gull fly eastward until it disappeared in the distance. "Being on a sailboat might come close to it—the wind filling your sails."

Sterling nodded, but he couldn't imagine soaring on the wind. As he observed two seagulls land on the roof of the ferry, a red pilot boat near the middle of the strait caught his eye. He stood up to watch the pilot boat intercept a black container ship that was cruising up the strait from the west. A barely visible sailor on the deck of the ship dropped a rope ladder over the side seconds before the pilot boat nudged its bow against the side of the ship, perfectly matching its speed. A pilot wearing a high-visibility life jacket made a well-timed leap to the ladder and scurried topside.

Laurel said, "My uncle, John, was a pilot for many years, but now he's mostly retired. He still drives one of the pilot boats if they are short-staffed, usually once or twice a month. He loves it."

"I think being a pilot would be cool," Sterling noted. "Except for going up and down those ladders in bad weather. Driving the pilot boat would be fun, too."

"I might be able to get us a ride-along with John, sometime."

"Really? I'd like that." A skulking shadow in Sterling's peripheral vision caught his attention. He watched as a feral cat pounced at a butterfly and then disappeared behind a rock. "You know, when you were talking about Running Start earlier, I didn't realize you could do that at the beginning of high school. I thought you had to be a junior or senior. I might have applied for it if I had known. I'm going to be a sophomore in the fall."

"Well, they don't usually admit sophomores."

"But you were one last year, right?"

"That's correct. I'm on track to graduate early, too. Could be at the end of next year, but probably the following December."

"So how did you get in a year early?"

"Look at me . . . How many people of color do you see in Port Angeles?"

When Sterling realized Laurel was not asking a rhetorical question, he said, "Not many."

"Right. So, I had petitioned the program for early admission, and they liked the idea of using me as a poster student for their politically correct program. We agreed they could use my picture if they admitted me early." She turned to Sterling, flashed an exaggerated smile, and shrugged playfully. "Check out the website. This beautiful face shows up twice."

"Hey, that's a good idea," Sterling said, poking her with his elbow. "I could start in the fall, too. And the school could update their website with someone who's *really* good looking."

Ignoring his jab, she said, "It's worth a try, even with that black eye. You'll need to get three letters of recommendation from your recent teachers. And one from a youth pastor would help."

"Three letters from teachers won't be a problem, but I don't see the youth pastor thing happening."

"Well, if you get in, I can show you around. My first week there was overwhelming." She thought for a moment and added, "Better yet, I'll ask the director if he'll meet with us. He can tell you what your chances of early admission look like."

"Cool. I'd appreciate that."

"Say, are you hungry?" Laurel checked her phone for the time. "It's early, but I'm starving. I overslept and skipped breakfast."

"Yeah, I can always eat."

"Want to grab lunch at Canaan's Kitchen?"

Sterling rubbed the side of his face. "Will Bethany be there?"

"I think so."

"Is there anywhere else you'd like to go?"

"C'mon, are you afraid of Bethany? Don't worry about her. She's nice—like a sister to me . . . at times, like an overprotective sister. But, if we go there, we'll get an employee discount—half price on the food and free drinks. What do you say?"

"Sold."

Fourteen

The heart has reason, of which reason knows nothing.

—Blaise Pascal

THE PARKING LOT at Canaan's Kitchen was nearly full when Sterling and Laurel rode past it to the barn. They leaned their bikes against the old, weathered siding and walked to the restaurant. Sterling opened the door for Laurel, and she thanked him and led the way into the dining room. The cozy aromas of cinnamon and coffee and the murmur of light conversation were like a warm blanket on a chilly night.

Sterling and Laurel took a two-person table on the left side of the restaurant, near the front window. Soon after they sat down, Laurel smiled at someone over Sterling's shoulder, and he turned to see Bethany grinning from across the dining room. Sterling wondered if he had walked into a trap. There was no telling what those two girls might devise.

He picked up his menu, and Laurel watched two birds sitting on the flower box on the other side of the window. She apparently had memorized the menu.

A moment later, Bethany delivered two glasses of ice water. She looked at Laurel and said, "Nice necklace." Then she picked at the corner of Laurel's purple scarf and said, "I wondered where that went. I thought I had lost it."

"Sorry," Laurel answered. "I'll wash it tonight and put it back."

"Sterling." Bethany smiled. "Nice to see you again."

"Always a pleasure." Sterling smirked. "Are you working this Sunday? Thought I might stop in."

"No. We're closed on Sundays, as the sign out front clearly states." She turned to Laurel and asked, "What'll it be?"

"A bowl of the soup, bread, and a lemonade, please."

"Sure thing. And for you, Sterling?"

"I'll have a grilled ham and provolone on nine-grain bread and a Coke. Can you add an extra layer of cheese so that it's cheese, ham, and more cheese? And trim the crust, please."

Bethany wrote it all on her pad and took their order to the kitchen. Laurel and Sterling watched her go, and when they were alone again, their eyes met in the quiet.

Sterling felt awkward and tried to think of a good question or an intelligent comment. Slowly, a safe question formed. "Do you and your cousin live together?"

Laurel nodded. "My parents live in Alaska. They started doing that two years ago. Although right now, they are visiting my older brother in Boise."

"Why Alaska?"

"Their jobs. Dad's a guidance counselor and Mom's a tutor. They both work for a school district that covers three different villages, and each one is more than a hundred miles away from the others. Mom and Dad rotate through them, spending a week at one and then flying their bush plane to the next. As you might imagine, the places they stay in are primitive. Too primitive for me. So I stay with Bethany and her parents."

As Sterling listened, he glanced out the window and recognized the back of a man who was walking toward a familiar car. As he fixed his attention on the man, Laurel saw Sterling's expression harden and stopped her story.

"Is something the matter?" she asked.

"Huh?"

"Are you okay? You look like you've seen a ghost."

"You're not far off. You see that man opening his car door?" Sterling pointed out the window. "He used to be my dad's business partner and a good friend of mine. His name is Dirk."

Laurel spotted Dirk and watched him get into his car. "I recognize him. He's been in here a few times. I first noticed him a few weeks ago. It unsettled me."

"What happened?"

"I was meeting John here for breakfast before my shift started. We sat at this same table, and that guy and another man sat over there." She gestured to a nearby table in the corner. "They seemed nervous about something and spoke in hushed tones. But it was early, and the restaurant was quiet, so I couldn't help hearing bits of their conversation. At one point, John went into the kitchen to pick up his produce order, and I heard the other man tell Dark—"

"Dirk?"

"Sorry—Dirk. Anyway, the other man told Dirk something about how he had been fired at work and replaced by a hot-shot young guy. Dirk said he had a special job for him. That's when John came back from the kitchen and we finished our breakfast together. A couple of minutes later, the two guys left."

"You remember that from a few weeks ago?" he asked. "That's a long time."

"It stuck in my mind because the other guy flirted with me as he left. He creeped me out."

Sterling leaned back in his chair, not sure what to make of the mysterious meeting Laurel had witnessed. "And that was it?" he asked. "Did you see anything else between them? Maybe in the parking lot?"

Laurel tried to remember more. "No, I think that's all I noticed," she said. "Wait. Now that I think about it . . .when I cleared their table, I found a business card one of them had left behind. It had information written on it, and I thought one of them might come back for it, so I put it in our lost-and-found drawer."

"Is it still there?"

"That's what I'm wondering. Let me check." Laurel got up from the table and walked into the back. She returned a minute later, waving a business card in her hand.

Sterling took the card and read both sides. It was for a man named Techs Niblick, an IT consultant. His phone number and email address were printed on the front, and someone had handwritten another phone number and email address on the back. Sterling took a picture of the front and back and returned it to Laurel. "Doesn't mean much to me right now," Sterling said, "but it could come in handy later. Thanks for telling me about it."

"Sure."

Sterling's stomach growled, and he wondered why their food was taking so long.

Laurel said, "I thought I was the one starving."

"I guess we both are."

"Oh." Her eyes brightened, and she tapped on the table. "I saw Dirk again just a few days ago. It was weird."

"What happened?"

"One morning, after I started work, your mother came in. She sat at her usual table, reading a book and sipping her coffee. Then that Dirk guy showed up. I happened to watch him cross the restaurant and approach your mom. He walked up behind her and kissed the top of her head. She stiffened like a startled cat, and he took the seat across from her. But before his butt could even hit the chair, your mom snatched her purse and stood up to leave. Dirk put out his hands and tried to talk her down so she'd stay."

"And? Did she?"

"She took a second to decide, and she ended up sitting down again. Curiosity got the better of me, so I went into the kitchen to watch the rest of their interaction from the pass-through window. I could see them, but couldn't hear what they were saying. Your mom was tense.

She kept her purse in her lap and fidgeted with its clasp. Dirk talked to her for a minute or two, and she seemed to listen. That's when whatever he said must have made her mad, because she took cash from her purse, slapped it on the table, and marched out without looking back. Dirk called out to her, but she ignored him. He sat there like he was stunned. After several minutes, his server went to check on him, but Dirk waved him away. Then he put some money on the table and stormed off. That was the last time I saw him in here, except for now in the parking lot."

"When was that?"

"Hmm. Recently. Might have been Monday."

"Are you sure it was him and my mom?"

"Definitely. She comes in here a lot, and I remember her from when your family was here. Besides, she always looks so beautiful. And Dirk is easy to recognize. His hand is hard to forget." She spread her fingers out onto the table unconsciously.

"My mom told us about that conversation," Sterling said. "I know what Dirk told her."

"What?"

"That jerk asked her to leave my dad and marry him instead. Can you believe it?"

"Whoa. Well, if it makes you feel any better, she obviously hated the idea."

"That's what she told us." The truth of Dirk's betrayal was settling more and more, and Sterling's stomach tightened at the thought of it. He wondered why he didn't see through Dirk's deception sooner—the promise to promote his UROV business, and the expensive fishing poles for Hoyt and him. It was all a lie meant to buy his affection. Sterling was disgusted, and he wanted to get Pete's money back more than ever.

"So Mom didn't encourage him?" he asked.

"Not a bit."

"That's good to hear."

Bethany arrived and set their plates on the table. Sterling wasted no time digging into his sandwich, but he stopped when he looked up at Laurel. She had not touched her food yet and was praying silently with her eyes closed. When she finished, Sterling said, "Sorry. I didn't know you would pray."

"No worries."

Sterling took another bite of his sandwich and hurried to change the subject. "So, do your parent's own a house here?"

She shook her head, still chewing a bite of olive bread. "Not anymore. When they come to PA for the holidays, they stay with my Uncle John. He's dad's brother."

"He seems like a good guy. He was nice to me when I met him."

"Totally. He's my mentor."

"Oh, is he an artist like you?"

"No. He's more of a life coach."

Before Sterling could ask what she meant, Bethany returned to the table carrying a pitcher of water. She refilled Laurel's glass and picked up Sterling's to do the same. But it slipped through her fingers and fell to the table. The glass bounced, and a small geyser of water landed right in Sterling's lap, soaking his jeans. He jumped up and wiped his pants with his napkin. Laurel tossed him her napkin, and Bethany rushed off to grab a towel.

When she returned, she apologized repeatedly as Sterling tried to dry his pants.

"Were you in on this?" he asked Laurel.

"No, this is all my fault," Bethany confessed. "I am so, so sorry. Please—lunch is on the house, and don't leave a tip."

Laurel stood and suggested, "Let's go to the bench out front. Your pants should dry pretty quickly out there in the sun."

Sterling set the towel and napkins on the table and walked toward the door. Laurel followed, and they walked to the bench, which was in the shade of the nearby trees. But the air was warm, and the breeze was blowing the spray from the waterfall in the other direction. As they sat,

Sterling turned toward Laurel and asked, "Tell me the truth. Did you and Bethany plan that?"

Laurel's dark brown eyes met his, and she said, "Part of me wishes we did. The look on your face was priceless. But no, we didn't plan it. Bethany's shock was almost worse than yours, so I know it was a complete accident. She'll have to pay for our food out of her own pocket, too."

"Okay. I believe you. It was nice of her to offer a free meal, but I don't want her to have to pay for my lunch." He took out his wallet, pulled out a twenty, and handed it to Laurel. "Please give this to her. I'd give her more, but I'm low on cash. Trying to save up for new school clothes."

"Come on. I watched your family when you left the restaurant last Saturday. Nice car, nice clothes. There's no way you're hurting for money."

"We weren't then, but we are now," Sterling said. "Dirk ripped us off. Bad. Now we have to rent our house and sell my mom's car. My allowance is gone. My dad's business is torpedoed. I'll be back to wearing jeans with holes in the knees soon enough."

"That's terrible." Laurel looked down at the twenty-dollar bill in her hands. "By the way, I didn't expect you to pay for my lunch, too. That's kind, especially with what your family is going through. I always carry money with me now."

"And I am trying to become considerate," he grinned. "Besides, Hoyt and I are trying to get Pete's money back. Teach Dirk a lesson." Sterling loved the thought of it. *Justice.*

Laurel smiled and said, "Well, whatever happens, at least you'll always have that cute dimple."

Sterling blushed. "Yeah, and this scar," he said, rubbing his fingers over the red ridge at his temple.

"How did you get it?"

"Riding a neighbor kid's bike when I was seven. I didn't know how to use the brakes and ran into a barbwire fence. We didn't have insurance or money for a doctor back then. My parents patched me up with Band-Aids, but the cut opened up and left the scar. Don't you think it makes me look manly?"

Laurel laughed. "Not with that dimple."

Not far behind the bench, a squeaky wooden door drew Laurel and Sterling's attention. They saw John emerge from the barn, pushing a wheelbarrow with two buckets in it. One was filled with apples and the other with oranges. John wore a pair of faded overalls, a long-sleeved shirt, and the same boots he wore when Sterling first met him. He spotted Sterling and Laurel and nodded as he hauled the buckets to the back of the restaurant.

Sterling looked back at Laurel. "That reminds me. John mentioned something strange when we were talking the other day. He said Bethany had begun her metamorphosis. I asked him what he meant, and he talked about her changing into her new self. Do you know what that means?"

Laurel peered at her hands in her lap, thinking. She took so long to respond that Sterling wondered if she had heard his question. "Yes," she said. "Yes, I know."

"So, what is it? Some sort of makeover? Like Mom gets at the spa?"

"It's an inner thing. Nothing to do with the outside."

"Gotcha. Like core strength training. Crunches? Planks?"

"It's a spiritual thing, not physical."

"Oh." Sterling considered what Laurel said. "Sounds weird to me."

Laurel chuckled. "I'm sure it does. But it isn't. It's all about moving beyond the limits of our five senses. It's about looking past the natural world and into the spiritual, becoming a spiritual person. A person who knows God."

"Do you believe in that?"

Laurel smiled and said, "Yes, I do. More and more. John says transformation is a lifelong process, a journey. I am still getting used to it, even though I started almost a year ago."

Sterling nodded. "I guess if it works for you, you need to do it."

"It's not just for me. It could work for you, too."

"I don't know about that," Sterling replied, shaking his head. "It sounds way too far out for me."

Sterling's phone chirped with a text, and he pulled it out to see a message from Hoyt. "Shoot," Sterling said. "It's later than I thought. I'd better get going—I promised to meet up with Hoyt. We have two yard jobs to do this afternoon." He put his phone away. "This has been fun. We should do it again sometime."

"Sounds good to me."

"I'll text you."

Laurel smiled. "Sure."

"Okay. I'll see you later."

Sterling left Laurel on the bench. On his way to his bike, I flew down toward him and spiraled right in front of him. He jerked back and threw his hands up to protect his face. Laurel saw me as I soared by, and she gave me a quick wave. I turned around and flew by Sterling again, giving him more space to observe my aerobatics. After performing two tight loops, I was certain I had Sterling's attention, and I darted into an almost invisible space beside the barn. It was between the cascading waterfall and the sheer rock face behind it.

Sterling watched me disappear and expected me to come out on the other side of the waterfall. But I did not. Instead, I flew into Canaan's Garden, a place still unknown to Sterling. He looked around, trying to spot me again and make sense of my stunts, but when he could not, he got on his bike to ride home. As he worked with Hoyt that afternoon, he continued to think about me, which was exactly what I wanted.

Fifteen

THE TWO YARD jobs on Sterling and Hoyt's calendar that day came from recommendations Dirk had made to his friends in the early spring. The boys started with the front of the Hansens' yard and worked their way to the back lawn. After edging along the back deck, Hoyt noticed something attached to the shed door. He walked closer and saw that it was an envelope, addressed to the "Burke Boys." Ripping it open, he read the handwritten note, "Boys, thanks for the excellent yard care you've always provided. Mr. McCleod told us that your family is about to move out of the area. He was nice enough to suggest a new yard service, and they will start next week. Thanks again and best of luck wherever you land." Mrs. Hansen had signed it and added a smiley face.

Hoyt read the note one more time, took a step back, and then landed a violent kick to the shed's plastic door. His outburst left a big dent, but after a moment, it popped back into shape. Hoyt ran around the side of the house toward Sterling, waving the note in the air and yelling. Sterling took out his earbuds and asked what was wrong.

Hoyt thrust the note into Sterling's hands. "Read this!"

Sterling read the note and felt as if Dirk had knifed him in the back. "When Dirk fired us, he told me it was just business, that it wasn't personal . . . But *this*—"Sterling smacked the note with his hand. "This *is* personal. It's a slap in our faces."

"I'm going to blow up his precious boat! I'll bet he lied to all six of the customers he referred to us. We have to make him pay."

Sterling pondered the best course of action. "You're not wrong, but we have to be smart about it."

"Let's get into his garage," Hoyt continued. "We can key his pickup from one end to the other. Both sides."

"Will you shut up for a second and let me think? Do you have a pen?"

Hoyt patted his pants and pulled a pen from his front pocket.

"All right, here's what we do. First, we will finish our work here. Then we write on Mrs. Hansen's note and say we didn't see her letter until after we did her yard. We thank her for being a good customer, and we tell her Dirk was mistaken and that we're still in business. The note goes in her mailbox, where she can't miss it."

"Got it. Then we key his truck. I'm thinking we can slash his seats, too."

"Hoyt." Sterling put a calming hand on his brother's shoulder. "Chill and listen to me. Do you remember last Friday's bootcamp? Remember when I hit you with that uppercut at the last second?"

Hoyt rubbed his chin and nodded.

"You would have blocked it if you thought it was coming. If we're going to make Dirk pay—which I promise we will—we need to surprise him. And I don't mean surprising him by messing up his truck."

"How?"

"I'm not sure yet, but we need to plan it out. We'll do whatever it takes to make him hurt. I don't care how much work, or money, or time we need to put into it. We're going to get Pete's money back and more."

"And the boat. Don't forget the boat."

Sterling sighed. "Forget the boat. Sinking it is too risky, and I'm sure Dirk has it fully insured. It would only be a temporary inconvenience for him, not real pain. Today, we need to wrap up the other yards Dirk got for us—all five of them—as fast as we can, so we can get paid before they cut us off. What do you say?"

Hoyt gave Sterling a thumbs-up. "Sounds like a plan. Let's do it."

After Sterling and Hoyt finished the Hansen's lawn, they hurried over to the Gomez yard, which they hustled to complete in less than forty-five minutes. From there, they rushed to the next customer and repeated the process.

They tended to the next two yards without seeing the owners. But on the last lawn, Mr. Arnold met them when they arrived. He came out the front door and signaled for the boys to stop. Sterling wiped sweat from his forehead as Mr. Arnold walked over and greeted them. "I didn't expect to see you two," he said. "I heard you had moved."

"I'll bet you heard it from Dirk McCleod," Hoyt blurted. "He's such a—"

Sterling elbowed Hoyt in the side and interrupted. "He, Mr. McCleod, is such a considerate friend for reaching out on our behalf. But, unfortunately, he was wrong about us. We aren't moving, so we can continue to do your yard for you."

"How about that?" Mr. Arnold said, scratching his chin. "Dirk recommended another yard service, but I have been too busy to call them. I guess I won't need to do that after all."

"Glad to hear it. We appreciate your loyalty. I think Mr. McCleod has already caused one of our customers to switch."

"Oh? Bet that hurts the old pocketbook."

Sterling agreed, but he held back how much it hurt. "It's hard to buy school clothes and pay for school activities when you can't earn the money," he admitted. "I need to buy equipment for the science club, and Hoyt is on the football team. The fees go up every year."

"Who are your other customers?"

"Well, we lost the Hansens. The Gomezes, Pearces, LaBores, and the Franks might be on the chopping block, too."

"I know them all from the neighborhood association," Mr. Arnold explained. "I'm the treasurer. If you'd like, I can call them and let them know Dirk was mistaken about your family moving—and that you boys are still in business. What they decide to do is up to them."

"Really? You wouldn't mind?" Sterling reached out his hand and said, "Thank you, Mr. Arnold. That will help us a lot."

After Sterling and Hoyt trudged home, Hoyt texted each homeowner to tell them their yard was taken care of and that any news they heard about the Burkes moving was a rumor, and he and Sterling would continue to do their yards.

GRASS STAINS MELTED from Sterling's hands as he took a long shower back at home. While hot water massaged his back, he remembered a blog he had read a few months earlier. It was on how to install man-in-the-middle spyware between someone's computer and the Internet. Sterling wondered if that might be the perfect way to skim off Dirk's online account numbers and passwords.

Feeling refreshed and hopeful, he dried off, got dressed, and walked to his bedroom to search the internet for more information. The first article from the search results explained how to use a Raspberry Pi to host the software, which was exactly what he was looking for, and he was so engrossed reading it he did not hear Hoyt walk up behind him. Hoyt patted him on the shoulder, and Sterling practically fell out of his chair.

He sat back down and spun to face Hoyt. "Ever think of knocking before you sneak into someone's room?" he snapped.

"Take it easy," Hoyt said, giving Sterling a playful punch in the shoulder. "I didn't sneak up. You were in one of your brain-hole zones."

"Whatever."

"Anyway, I was thinking we should check out the video and see if anything is new."

"Not a bad idea."

Sterling turned back to his computer and opened the web page. He sped through the recorded video and stopped when he saw a vehicle on the screen. He moved ahead one frame at a time so he and Hoyt could see what was going on. The vehicle, a brand-new pickup truck towing an equally new trailer, had pulled up to Dirk's garage. The time stamp showed 1:42 p.m.—the same time Sterling and Hoyt were working on the Hansens' yard. Sterling pointed to the lettering on the side of the truck.

"Chelmsford Landscaping and Yard Maintenance," Hoyt read aloud. "So, that's who is taking our yard jobs?"

"Must be."

"That's a serious setup, with the trailer and everything. It probably takes at least one week of work each month just to cover the payments. It would be a real shame if they lost four or five jobs."

"Yes, a real shame," Sterling agreed.

"Hopefully, my texts and Mr. Arnold's calls to our customers will make it happen."

Sterling returned to the man-in-the-middle article and said, "You caught me in the middle of something. Can you give me another hour? Then we can plan our attack for tomorrow."

"Okay," Hoyt said, "or maybe I can make sure Chelmsford loses another job."

"What do you mean?"

Hoyt only grinned, giving Sterling a thumbs-up as he walked out the door.

ALMOST AN HOUR and a half later, Hoyt returned, and Sterling could tell he was excited about something. Before Sterling could even ask, Hoyt launched into a question of his own. "You remember those extra-strength dishwasher detergent packets Mom told us not to break open because the detergent is so strong?"

Sterling gave him a questioning look. "Yeah, why?"

"I took ten of those packets from under the sink and rode over to Dirk's. I snuck down by his house and lobbed them onto his front lawn. Detergent grenades. They're just lying there now, but when his sprinklers turn on tonight, the packages should dissolve, and I'm hoping the detergent will kill the grass. There won't be any evidence, and, fingers crossed, Dirk will blame his new yard service. If it works, I have a new strategy for dealing with any customers who don't come back to us."

Sterling laughed and shook his head. "Nice one, Hoyt. Pretty clever."

"That's all you have to say? Clever? *Genius* is more like it."

"Well, unfortunately, it doesn't help us get our money back. But it is a great prank. By the way, the universal remote I ordered came in." Sterling held it up in front of Hoyt like it was a priceless artifact. "I'll learn how to program it, and we should sneak into his garage tomorrow, pair it with his main unit, and return his remote. That will cover our tracks, and we can move forward searching for the money."

"Not as exciting as detergent grenades, but okay. While we're there, I'll be able to see if the packets dissolved."

Sixteen

LATER THAT NIGHT, Sterling's thoughts locked onto me. His mind kept replaying my flight behind the waterfall, and he asked himself where I could have gone. Did I fly out the other side unseen? Or did I find a place to nest behind the waterfall? The fact that he couldn't figure it out bothered him. And it annoyed him even more that it was distracting him from his mission against Dirk.

He was tired, but reviewed the surveillance video one more time before going to bed. A pattern had emerged. Dirk drove out of his garage most mornings around 8:15. However, one time, he returned at 9:35 and left again five minutes later. Sterling assumed Dirk had returned for something he accidentally left at home.

As Sterling planned for his operation in Dirk's garage, my image flew into his mind once more. He was torn between what he needed to do most the next morning—to set up the new remote, or to look for my nest. Sterling flipped a mental coin and decided getting inside of Dirk's house was more important than finding my nest, and I left it at that.

Having decided, Sterling walked over to Hoyt's room and knocked on the door. He heard a grunt and entered. Hoyt was lying on his bed with a sports magazine, but stopped reading to look up at Sterling. "What is it?"

"Let's try the remote tomorrow morning," Sterling answered. "We should hit the woods by eight o'clock, and Dirk will probably leave his house around 8:15. The maid service comes later in the morning, so we need to be in and out as quickly as possible. I'll need you need to stand lookout by the road, and once Dirk is gone, I'll use the opener from his truck to get into the garage. Then I'll program the new one and put the old one back in his truck. If the coast is clear and we have time to spare, I'll scout around inside the house a little."

Hoyt tossed the magazine down on his bed next to him. "Why do you get to scout inside the house? That's the fun part, and I was the one who got the remote in the first place. Not you."

"I bet we'll need to scout multiple times, so I'm going to be real quick on this first one. You can do it next time."

"Fine."

"I'm thinking we'll need to leave here at 7:45 to get there on time. Not 7:50, not 7:55. *7:45*, got it?"

"Yes, sir," Hoyt mocked.

LIKE CLOCKWORK, THE boys arrived at Dirk's property at 8:00 a.m. Hoyt took his lookout position in the trees near where Dirk's driveway met the road, and Sterling sneaked through the woods and hid in the brush behind the camera, closer to the house. He checked the camera, and it was still well hidden. At precisely 8:13, Sterling noticed the garage door opening, and Dirk drove away. A minute later, Hoyt texted Sterling to tell him Dirk's car had left the driveway and was out of sight.

8:00, 8:13, 8:14—I miss the days when sundials were man's most accurate timepiece. Back then, times such as mid-morning, midday, and dusk were close enough. People thought nothing of waiting an hour or two for a scheduled meeting. Analog clocks changed that, especially when nearly every adult could afford a wristwatch. From then on, people talked about time using terms such as half past, quarter to, and top of the hour. Sure, I've adjusted to clocks and the increased precision over the centuries, but I really prefer the old days when I could send someone a piff while they spent all that time waiting around. Digital clocks are heartless masters. And they seemed to control the Burkes' every moment—8:13 or 8:14, what's the difference? Must everything be scheduled?

At 8:15-ish, Sterling pulled on latex gloves and used the remote Hoyt had pilfered to open the garage door. Once he entered the garage and closed the door behind him, he wiped the remote with his T-shirt and returned it to its place in Dirk's truck. Now he needed to reach the opener's main unit to program his remote, but the unit was attached to the ceiling. Sterling looked for something to climb on, and a stepladder leaning against the far wall caught his eye. He set it in place and climbed up. The main unit was the same model as the one he had studied. He popped the plastic cover open and saw the button that synchronized the unit to a new remote. He pressed the button until it blinked three times and then hit the Open button on the new remote. Like magic, the door opened.

As Sterling was closing the door again, his phoned buzzed with a text from Hoyt in all caps. "HE'S BACK."

Sterling almost fell off the stepladder, but he steadied himself and hopped down. He folded the ladder and carried it halfway to the wall before remembering the main unit's plastic cover was still open. He rushed the ladder back, set it up, and closed the cover as fast as he could. As soon as he put the ladder back, something banged against the garage door, and Sterling looked for somewhere to hide. He slid underneath Dirk's truck, bumping his head on the exhaust pipe. He thought he would be out of sight unless Dirk got on his hands and knees. But that knowledge did little to calm him. His heart felt like it was beating as fast as a hummingbird's, and he held deep breaths to stay quiet. A minute passed, and Sterling's phone buzzed again. He had forgotten to silence it. When he scrambled to rip it from his pocket and turn it off, he saw another text from Hoyt. "Look out the side window."

Sterling slid over to the edge of the truck and peered up at the window. All he could see was Hoyt's nose steaming up the glass. Sterling pulled himself out from under the truck and stood to get a better look. Hoyt was on the other side of the window, doubled over and laughing. Sterling opened the garage door—Dirk's car was nowhere in sight. Sterling's anger flared, and he chased Hoyt across the yard. Hoyt kept laughing, and soon Sterling was laughing along with him. They stopped running and walked back to the garage.

"You pranked me good," Sterling said, catching his breath. "Really good."

"The best part is that I got to watch you through the window the whole time. I should have taken a video of you setting the ladder back up and diving under the truck."

"Just you wait. This isn't over."

Hoyt pulled a pair of latex gloves from his pocket and wiggled his fingers into place. "Here's an idea. Why don't you give me the remote and go stand guard? I think I've earned it. Plus, don't forget, I'm the one who got us Dirk's remote."

"Fair enough. I'll text you when I get into position." Sterling dashed off into the woods and hid toward the end of the driveway. Hoyt kept an eye out for Sterling's message, but he didn't wait around. He went straight into Dirk's house from the garage and made a beeline for the office.

Hoyt surveyed the layout of the room and opened a built-in storage compartment. It was part of the ceiling-high, wall-to-wall bookcase, a piece of expensive walnut furniture. Neatly stacked office supplies filled the compartment. Hoyt opened two other cabinets and found high school and college yearbooks and dozens of envelopes of photographs. He opened an envelope, thumbed through the pictures, and recognized several. They were copies of pictures Pete had taken during a recent fishing trip on *Leverage*. One showed Hoyt holding up two coho salmon and Sterling holding only one. Dirk stood behind them, looking like a proud father with a hand on each of the boy's shoulders. Hoyt remembered that trip well. Neither adult caught a single fish, and Hoyt won fifteen dollars for first place in the betting pool. Sterling won five dollars for second place too. Above that cabinet, in the shelves of the bookcase, Hoyt saw a larger framed version of the same photo. It was hard for Hoyt to believe that the fishing trip had happened only a few months earlier. It seemed like another life. A life when Dirk was practically family. A life when Hoyt would never have broken into Dirk's house, or needed to. A life when he would not have wanted revenge.

Meanwhile, outside, Sterling hid in the bushes near the road. He leaned with his back against a large fir tree, and the uneventful scenery was making way for boredom. Sterling passed the time recalling his last conversation with Laurel, the one in which she talked about "moving beyond the natural world." He wondered how on earth she could believe that. Maybe her palette was missing some colors, maybe even a primary one. Maybe her red was so washed out that it gave a pleasant tint to everything she saw around her. What was that transformation talk? Spiritual sensitivity to move beyond the natural world? And where would that be? Mars? Narnia? The Hogwarts School of Witchcraft and Wizardry? *Next time we should ride brooms instead of bikes. That way, I could catch that mutant dove.*

Back inside Dirk's office, Hoyt combed through the desk for more information. He found nothing unusual in the center drawer, except for the signature pad and stamp Dirk used to apply his signature at the bottom of letters and legal documents. Hanging files filled the bottom left drawer. Hoyt started with the first folder, which was labeled "Airplanes." Color brochures of small planes filled the folder—two-passenger, four-passenger, and six-passenger models. Dirk had written prices and expected monthly payments next to each plane's picture.

Sterling adjusted his back against the tree trunk and could not put me out of his mind. I didn't fit into his picture of the natural world. Maybe I was a dove crossed with a hawk or an eagle. Maybe he could become famous. Sterling imagined the news headline: *Sterling Burke Discovers a New Dove Subspecies—The Sterling Burke Fighting Dove.*

He wanted to catch me and put me in a cage. It was a bold goal, but I knew he would never succeed.

Hoyt pulled another folder from the drawer. It was labeled "Banking" and was full of monthly statements, ordered by date. Hoyt read the most recent statement and noticed a loan having a $463,000 initial balance and a $461,000 remaining balance. He let out a slow whistle at the size of the debt. As he continued to study the statement, he realized that the initial balance matched the price of a Cessna Skyline, assuming Dirk had made a 10 percent down payment. Hoyt snapped a photo of the loan's details to show Sterling later. The rest of the statements showed moderate saving and checking account balances and outstanding loans for both his car and truck. With loans for the plane, car, truck, and presumably for the house and boat, Dirk owed a lot of money.

"Wow," Hoyt muttered to himself. "He's in deep."

Hoyt's phone interrupted him with a text from Sterling. "Almost done?"

Hoyt replied, "No," and spotted a "Leverage" folder in the desk. He pulled it out and learned that Dirk owned the boat free and clear—he had made the final payment earlier that spring. A sticky note on the folder's inside flap said the title was in the safe. Hoyt replaced the "Leverage" folder and pulled out one labeled "Property Taxes."

"Bingo," Hoyt whispered.

Scanning the front page of each statement covering the past two years, he saw nothing that mentioned overdue payments. He took pictures of the most recent statements and refiled them, closed the desk drawer, and looked around to make sure Dirk's things were exactly as he had found them. When he was ready to leave, he patted his front pocket for his phone, but it was not there. And it did not seem to have fallen onto the floor either.

Hoyt hurried and reopened the desk drawers, looking in each of the folders. Finally, he heard his phone buzz and discovered it far under Dirk's desk. He got on his hands and knees to retrieve it and saw a text from Sterling, "GET OUT. DIRK'S HERE."

Hoyt jumped up and bashed his head on the underside of the desk. He returned each folder to its place, closed the drawer, and ran into the garage as the garage door opened. He saw Dirk's car backing into its spot, and he dove under Dirk's truck, as Sterling had done earlier.

As he lay petrified, he heard the car door open, and Dirk's foot landed on the floor not three feet away. Dirk was talking on the phone, and Hoyt heard him say, "I'll be there in twenty minutes. I'm getting my truck to haul the packages . . .Uh huh. Exactly . . .See you soon."

Hoyt watched Dirk take several steps and heard the truck door open. It settled lower after Dirk climbed into the driver's seat. A terrifying vision of being run over filled his mind, and he wondered if he should stay in place or run like crazy. Did the truck have enough clearance to pass over him? Would Dirk look in his mirrors when he drove away?

There was only a second to decide. As Dirk pulled the truck out, Hoyt pressed himself against the floor, hoping nothing would snag him. The moment the truck's rear wheels passed him, he rolled against the wall and froze, and the garage door closed again. He waited for Sterling to text him that the coast was clear. Once he got that message, Hoyt reopened the door, closed it, and ran to Sterling at the end of the driveway.

Sterling looked Hoyt up and down and asked, "What happened in there?"

"Man, that was close. I thought you were joking, and I barely had time to hide. I ended up under his truck like you did."

Sterling pointed at the front of Hoyt's T-shirt. "At least I didn't lie in the oil puddle."

Hoyt glanced down at his stomach. "Darn. I didn't even see it." He pulled his shirt out to inspect the mess further. "Sure hope it comes out in the wash."

During the ride home, Hoyt told Sterling what he discovered in the office, but Sterling was surprisingly uninterested after all the effort he had put into the operation. His mind was elsewhere. "Are you listening to me?" Hoyt asked, snapping Sterling back to the present.

"Sorry," Sterling replied without sincerity. "There's something that's been bugging me."

"You want to talk about it?"

"No, it's not like that. I'm fine. But there's something I need to do. Right now. Can we talk about Dirk's files later?"

"I guess . . ."

Sterling turned off the road and pedaled away from home, toward Canaan's Kitchen. He was headed for where he last saw me. If he could just get a good look, he thought he might be able to figure out a thing or two.

And, if he was lucky, he might even find my nest.

Seventeen

People are generally better persuaded by the reasons which they have themselves discovered than by those which have come into the mind of others.

—Blaise Pascal

STERLING WAS A person who wanted to control his world. He planned everything three or four steps ahead as not to run into any surprises. His peace of mind relied on the control he maintained, but I intended for him to see his control as the illusion it was. Honestly, how can anyone think he controls his world?

Pulling up to Canaan's Kitchen, Sterling leaned his bike against back of the bench where he had first talked with John and later with Laurel. The morning sun was an hour from being directly overhead, and steep rays of light slashed through the high clouds into the forest, glistening in the waterfall's mist. Droplets clung to the moss and ferns and refracted the light like miniature prisms. In the bright haze, Sterling put his hand above his eyebrows to shield his eyes and searched the area for me. He walked to the waterfall's edge, where the mist cooled the air, and peered into the small passage between the falls and the rock where I had disappeared the day before. He saw nothing. Not a flutter. Not a feather. He hoped to find a trace of my presence. Even though I'm ethereal, like the wind that blows where it wishes, I was right there with him, ever-present. Nonetheless, he could not sense me, as most people cannot.

Sterling returned to the bench and plopped down, throwing both arms over the backrest. He sat motionless for several minutes, deep in contemplation, and then slowly turned his head, reminding me of an owl searching for its prey. I could have revealed myself to him while he waited, maybe danced to another tune. But why? How would that have benefited him more than letting him learn patience, the goodness of sitting in the sanctum of silence, and spending a few minutes pondering mysteries that transcend his understanding?

A squeak from John's wheelbarrow got Sterling's attention. John was hauling a pail of red grapes and two boxes of perfect russet potatoes toward the restaurant. When John noticed Sterling, he stopped and set the wheelbarrow down next to the bench. Damp dirt speckled his boots and the knees of his blue overalls. "Mind if I join you?" he asked, taking off his gloves.

Sterling pulled his arms from the back of the bench and scooted over to make room.

John asked, "What brings you here today?"

"Bird watching," Sterling replied. "What's in your wheelbarrow?"

Grapes and potatoes. Want to take some home?"

"Thanks, but I don't have a way to carry them on my bike."

"I can give you a tote bag. You could hang it on your handlebars."

"All right." Sterling studied the produce, and something odd struck him. "John, how can you have ripe grapes and potatoes in June? Summer has barely started."

"I will tell you what, there's some history here. It was 1863 when President Lincoln set aside 3,520 acres here as a site for a lighthouse and military post. The U.S. Army Corps of Engineers was tasked with laying out what's now Port Angeles—you know, Washington D. C. is the only other city they laid out."

"Really?"

"Yes, and they copied street names from Cincinnati."

"Hmm."

"But PA was a challenge, what with the area's streams and ravines, so several of the streets are dead-ends, and others have had to have stairways and ramps built in. Follow me?"

"Yes, but I don't see what that has to do with grapes."

"We'll I'm getting to that part. As the population grew in the late 1800s, Congress agreed to sell off most of the military property to the public. During that transition, fifteen acres were inexplicably lost. That's where the grapes come in. Those missing acres are over there," he said, pointing to the other side of the waterfall and creek. "Now, that plot is not accounted for at all. The National Forest Service thinks it belongs within the Port Angeles city limits, and PA thinks it's part of the Olympic National Forest. Both are wrong. My ancestors acquired the deed for the parcel, and I own it, but it doesn't show up on any tax rolls. We call it Canaan's Garden, and it's where we grow our produce."

"That's interesting," Sterling said. "But I still don't understand how your produce ripens so early in the year. How is that possible?"

John smiled and took a handful of grapes from the pail in the wheelbarrow. He handed a few to Sterling and popped one into his own mouth. He savored it and answered, "Let's just say that Canaan's Garden's weather pattern is unique. Thermal activity keeps the ground warm year-round, and the clouds here only form during the night. They never block the sunlight—even in winter. It rains often enough, too, so the garden is always well watered. I don't have an irrigation system at all."

"And that's weird, right? That's not how farming normally works, is it?"

"No, you're right about that. The garden is mysterious."

"Yeah. Sounds like it."

John ignored Sterling's comment and asked, "So, what have you seen?" Sterling looked confused, prompting John to add, "Bird watching."

"Oh. Nothing today," Sterling replied. "But earlier, I've seen a strange dove here. I want to follow it and find its nest. You're outside most day. H*ave you seen it?*"

John scratched his chin, considering. "What do you mean when you say a strange dove?"

"It's unlike any bird I've ever seen. Once it flew right at me and knocked my hat off. It can also do aerial acrobatics—loops and dives, things like that."

"You sure it wasn't a dream?"

"I wondered about that, but then I caught it on camera. It acted strange then, too, almost like it knew I was recording it. The next time I saw it, it flew behind this waterfall and didn't come out. Is there a place for it to nest back there?"

"I have seen that dove around," John admitted. "But I'm not sure about its nesting habits. Have you had any . . . unexpected thoughts lately? What you might call *religious* thoughts?"

Sterling pondered for a moment. "I don't think so. No. But I have heard plenty of weird things from you and Laurel. No offense."

"None taken. What do you make of what you've heard?"

Sterling shrugged. "It doesn't make much sense. Laurel said it's an internal thing, that transformation you talk about, but I still don't get it. Maybe it's not for me."

"Have you ever watched a butterfly emerge from a cocoon?"

Sterling wasn't sure where John was taking the conversation, but followed along. "Yeah. We saw a video of it last year in biology."

"Tell me what happened."

"It went through a complete makeover. The larva started out as an egg, then it became a caterpillar that ate like crazy. After it reached a certain size, things got strange, and it stopped eating all together. I think became a . . . A . . ." Sterling snapped his fingers, searching for the word.

"Chrysalis?"

"Yeah, that's it. Thanks. It became a chrysalis and hung from a twig for, like, a month. Then one day, a butterfly popped out."

"Sterling, which are you more like, the caterpillar or the butterfly?"

Sterling answered without hesitation. "The butterfly. Definitely the butterfly. Why do you ask?"

"I'm just trying to see your world through your eyes."

"Which are you more like?"

"I don't think I am like either. I think I'm most like the chrysalis—somewhere in between. Not what I once was, but not yet what I will be."

"Huh. I guess that makes sense. I think."

"Actually, it reminds me of something the Master said: 'For whoever desires to save his life will lose it, but whoever loses his life for my sake will find it.'"

"What does that mean?"

"Think about it in terms of the chrysalis. If a man entered a cocoon for a month, which life would he lose? The caterpillar life or the butterfly life? And which would he find?"

"Okay, I don't mean to be blunt, but I'm even more confused. None of this is helping me. You never give me a straight answer. Instead, you answer my questions with more questions."

"It's better that you think through these things on your own. But I have something that will help you. Do you mind waiting a minute?"

"No, I'm not in any hurry. And I guess I can use some help."

Sterling watched John walk to the barn by the waterfall and enter the door. He returned carrying a canvas tote bag and a small book.

After sitting on the bench, he handed the book to Sterling. The cover was faded, and the edges worn. "It's a New Testament," John explained. "Reading it will help answer your questions, but I have to warn you, it will also raise new ones."

Sterling tilted his head, weighing his response. John obviously thought the New Testament would be useful, but Sterling did not see how it could help him—especially in his search for me. He stood and handed the book back. "Thanks, but I don't think so." His refusal to accept the New Testament did not cause me the slightest concern. I knew I would give Sterling other opportunities to learn of the life beyond.

As Sterling walked around the bench to his bike, John apologized. "I didn't mean to be pushy. I hope I didn't across that way. That book was very important to me when I first had questions, so I wanted to offer it to you. Tell you what, if you think any more about the cocoon and decide you are more like a caterpillar than a butterfly, we should talk again," he said, standing and loading two big handfuls of grapes into the tote bag. "Please take these to your father. Bethany told me he loved them."

"Will do," Sterling said. "Thanks for the chat." With that, he got on his bike.

Sterling rode away, wondering how much stranger his life could get. So far, in a week's time, a crazy dove singled him out for harassment, or for some bizarre avian communication—he was not sure which. Dirk had gone from being a good friend to a hated enemy. His family was on the brink of bankruptcy. And Laurel and John, though kind, were trying to hook him on some mumbo-jumbo about inner transformation. So many distractions. It was hard to focus on the important tasks at hand—earning more money, getting Pete's money back, and, if possible, discovering where I lived.

As Sterling cruised down the road, I flew down in front of him, just beyond his reach. Naturally, he stood up on his pedals and tried to catch me, but I maintained my speed and distance. He panted, pushing himself to catch up, and uttered a few unkind words under his breath. A piece of paper in my claws got Sterling's attention, and suddenly he was more interested in it than in grabbing me. I drifted back until the paper was within his reach. He snatched it, and I let go, spiraling upward. My delivery made, I continued my ascent, and when I was two hundred feet above of Sterling, I turned and flew back toward Canaan's Garden.

Sterling hit his brakes and skidded to a stop, watching me vanish into the distant trees. Out of breath, studied the paper in his hands. Handwritten words there read,

For whoever desires to save his life will lose it, but whoever loses his life for my sake will find it. For what profit is it to a man if he gains the whole world and loses his own soul?

— Matthew 16:25,26

Sterling read the note again. He could not pretend it was a hallucination or a dream. The note and John said the same thing. It was spooky. *How can that be? It's not possible. That dove can't write, can it? No, he must have found the note. Still, something spooky is going on.* Now Sterling wished he would have accepted John's offer for the New Testament. Maybe it would help him out. Maybe it would give him questions he didn't even know he should be asking.

Sterling carefully folded the paper, put it into his wallet, and continued thinking about its words as he biked home. *What profit is it? What am I gaining?*

Eighteen

WHEN STERLING REACHED his driveway, he found Hoyt practicing basketball drills. Hoyt was dribbling the ball between his legs when he noticed Sterling pull up. Without stopping, Hoyt asked, "So, what was so stinking important that you had to run off like that? Was it that girl?"

"No, it had nothing to do with her. It was a dead end. I don't really want to talk about it."

"Fair enough. You want to hear what I found at Dirk's?"

"Definitely."

Hoyt described the big loan that was possibly for buying a plane, the checking and savings accounts, each with less than $5,000, and the photos of the property tax statements.

"Hold on, you have pictures?" Sterling asked.

"Yeah, a bunch of them. I thought you would want to see what I found."

"Brilliant. There might be more in those documents than you realize. Send me the pics, and I'll pull them up on my laptop so we can see them clearly."

They hurried up to Sterling's room and sat on his bed. As they studied the tax statements, Hoyt pointed at the screen and said, "There. Look at that—nothing says these are past due."

"Hoyt, this is perfect. Great work."

"Still, it doesn't show us where all of Pete's money went. I'll bet Dirk is keeping it somewhere else." Hoyt clenched his fists. "We need to find it, and we need to take it. And I know what you need to do."

"What?"

"You need to hack into his computer. I bet you could find out all kinds of stuff."

Getting more money was no longer Sterling's only priority, but it was still on his short list. Not to mention, the idea of hacking into Dirk's computer was an irresistible challenge—too good for Sterling to pass up. "Actually, I was already thinking about that," he said. "A couple months ago, I read about man-in-the-middle software. I researched it more yesterday, and we can use it to spoof Dirk's computer and sniff his network traffic to capture his account numbers, user IDs, and passwords."

"And what does that mean in English?"

"Sorry. It's software that lets us watch all of Dirk's internet activity and gives us the information we need."

"You could have said that in the first place."

"I said sorry."

"So, how do we do that?"

"I need to load the software on my old Raspberry Pi, and then we need to install it between Dirk's computer and his internet."

"Back in his house?"

"Back in his house. We can sneak in tomorrow and put it in place—somewhere he won't see it. Shouldn't be too difficult."

Hoyt rubbed his neck. "I hope it's that easy."

"I still need to do more research to prepare, though."

Hoyt took that as a hint and left Sterling's room, heading back out to the driveway.

Sterling spent most of the evening poring over the blog and reviewing the steps to download, install, and configure the man-in-the-middle software. It looked like the process wouldn't take more than an hour, as long as he didn't make a mistake.

Sterling copied whole sections of computer code from the blog, pasted them into his Raspberry Pi, and configured the software to work with the Burkes' network. By eleven o'clock, he was ready to take the system for a test run, and he targeted his own Venmo account. The goal was to capture all the web addresses, usernames, and unencrypted passwords traversing the network. He looked at his Raspberry Pi's monitor, expecting to see a traffic report building up, but the screen was blank. He reread the blog while mentally checking off every step to make sure he did each one correctly. To his frustration, he could not find any mistakes, which left him with only one choice. He was forced to start from scratch, taking extra care as he moved through the process again.

It wasn't until two thirty in the morning that Sterling was ready to retest the software. He logged into his Venmo account and crossed his fingers. As he looked at his Raspberry Pi screen, he saw a record of his Venmo login, including the URL, username, and unencrypted password. Success! In an instant, Sterling went from being discouraged and exhausted to being too excited to sleep. Still, he shut down the program, turned off his screens, and crawled into bed. Tomorrow would be a big day. He tossed in bed for nearly an hour, daydreaming and flopping around like a newly caught salmon. Eventually, however, he drifted off.

AT A QUARTER past seven, noise from both garage doors opening and closing stirred Sterling from his sleep. Once he realized it was his parents leaving early for work, he rolled over and went back to sleep. An hour later, he heard another engine revving in the driveway below his window, but it was unfamiliar. At first, he pulled his pillow over his head to block out the noise, but then Hoyt barged into his room.

Sterling unburied his head from the pillow and opened one eye to look at Hoyt. "What is it?"

"The necklace girl is here," Hoyt said. "She asked if you were home. What should I tell her?"

Sterling opened his other eye. "Tell her we're closed on Fridays. She will need to come back tomorrow."

"Huh?"

"Forget it," he mumbled. " . . .Tell her I'll be there in five minutes."

Sure enough, Laurel was waiting there in the driveway when Sterling stumbled out the front door. She held a helmet on her lap while sitting crossways on the seat of a bright red Suzuki scooter. Almost everything Laurel wore was black—jeans, Converse tennis shoes, a sweatshirt, and an unzipped windbreaker. The only exception was a long red scarf, wrapped twice around her neck, that matched the scooter. When she saw Sterling, she patted the handlebars. "Not bad, eh?"

"Not bad at all," Sterling agreed. "When did you buy it?"

"I didn't. My neighbor just moved to Idaho. He tried to sell this before he left, but there were no takers, so . . ."

"He just gave it to you?"

Laurel put both fists in the air. "Yes. Totally free. It's over fifteen years old, but it has less than five thousand miles on it." She stood up, opened a storage compartment, and removed a helmet, which she handed to Sterling. "You wanna go for a spin? I got my motorcycle endorsement yesterday."

"Do you have any idea what time it is?" Sterling said. "I haven't eaten breakfast yet."

"Don't be a wuss. You won't starve."

Sterling considered telling her he had skipped dinner the night before, too.

"C'mon," she insisted. "Get your shoes and a jacket. We're going cruising."

"Fine, give me a minute." And with that, Sterling trotted into the house.

Hoyt, who had watched the interchange from the front door, stepped past Sterling and walked over to Laurel. "Hey," he said. "My name's Hoyt. I'm Sterling's brother, but I guess you know that."

Laurel fist-bumped him. "I'm Laurel. Thanks again for your help the other day." She pulled her necklace out of her sweatshirt to show him. "Who knows where this would be without your help?"

While Hoyt talked with her, Sterling returned and looked ready to go. "I only have thirty minutes," he said. "Hoyt and I have a project we need to do this morning. Could we go cruising this afternoon instead?"

Laurel shoved the spare helmet into his hands and said, "Get on." She looked at Hoyt. "We'll see you in a half hour."

They wheeled out of the driveway, and the motor's high-pitched whining sound reminded Sterling of his mother's blender. They soon reached Highway 101 and headed west, toward Forks. They exceeded fifty miles per hour, and the wind whipped Laurel's scarf into both sides of Sterling's helmet so fast his head felt like it was in a blender. He slid back on his seat and tied the ends of Laurel's scarf into double a knot, which gave him some peace. After fifteen minutes, she turned around, and Sterling texted Hoyt, "On our way back. We need to go straight to Dirk's. Be ready."

They arrived back at the Burkes' with a few minutes to spare. Sterling climbed off the scooter, unbuckled his helmet, and handed it to Laurel.

"Cool ride," he commented. "Sure beats my bike."

"Yeah, I like it," she said, returning the spare helmet to the compartment. "I love it already. The only thing is I don't know where to keep it. Bethany's garage doesn't have room, and I don't want to park it on the street. Any ideas?"

Sterling's first thought was their own garage, but he was afraid Pete would shut down that idea. "We don't have a place here, but we have a spot near the restaurant. My dad's office building has a shed in the alley behind it. It has room, and no one would bother your scooter there, either. If you want, I can text you the address and the lock's combination."

Laurel smiled. "That sounds perfect. I'll check it out."

Nineteen

AFTER STERLING RETURNED from his early morning scooter ride, he and Hoyt met in his room so they could check the surveillance video. Dirk had left his house right on schedule. They agreed the coast was clear, packed up their things, and rode over to Dirk's for a second expedition. Passing through the woods, they crept up to their hidden camera and watched to see if there was any new activity. After several uneventful minutes, Hoyt walked across the driveway and opened the garage door. Sterling followed, and they dashed inside, closing the door again behind them.

As they worked their hands into latex gloves, they listened for movement inside the house. Sterling inched open the door that led from the garage into the kitchen, and they slunk through the hallways toward Dirk's office, but Sterling stopped Hoyt at the doorway and pointed at the carpet in the room. "What do you see?" he asked.

"Nothing."

"That's right. Nothing—not a single footprint. The maid service manicured the carpet, and the tracks from the vacuum cleaner are in perfect rows, like when we mow a lawn. We'll need to vacuum the carpet the same way when we leave to remove our footprints."

"Whoa. Good catch, Sherlock."

Sterling took off his backpack and pulled out his tech equipment.

He got on his hands and knees to crawl under Dirk's desk and looked for a hidden spot to set up the Raspberry Pi. He unplugged the internet cable from Dirk's computer and plugged it into his Raspberry Pi. Next, he connected the Pi to Dirk's Wi-Fi. This channeled Dirk's internet traffic through the Pi, so the man-in-the-middle software could monitor everything, including his account numbers and credentials.

That was when a light bulb went off in Sterling's head. "Oh no," he moaned to himself.

Hoyt overheard and asked what was wrong.

"I missed something," Sterling admitted. "Something big."

Hoyt had been snooping through Dirk's office and promptly stopped. "How bad is it? Do we need to get out of here?"

"No. But I realized the only way we can see Dirk's traffic is for me to bring my laptop near enough to his router to connect to his network and download the results from the Pi. I have to be on his network."

"Well, we can make it work, right?"

"Yeah, but it'll be risky. Really risky. We'll need to do it at night."

"Piece of cake."

Sterling returned his attention to the Pi and finished taping its cords out of sight. As he was wrapping up with it, Hoyt kicked Sterling's foot to get his attention. "Hey," he said. "You've got to look at this."

Sterling backed out from under the desk, and Hoyt handed him a slip of paper. It was a cheat-sheet, written in awkward block letters—Dirk's unmistakable handwriting resulted from his mangled hand. The paper showed the PIN for Dirk's screensaver and the username and password for something called CredentialVault.

"Do you know what this is?" Hoyt asked.

"I've heard of it," Sterling replied. "I think it's a cloud-based password manager. If I'm right, this might give us everything we need. Hoyt, way to go!"

"What's a password manager?"

"It's like an electronic safe where he stores all his accounts and password information. If we have his username and password for the safe, we can access everything he keeps in the safe."

"Makes sense."

"If Dirk keeps his account information in his password manager, and I'll bet he does, it's much better than sniffing his network. We won't need to wait for him to log into each of his accounts to sniff the information. I say let's leave the man-in-the-middle system here in case this CredentialVault doesn't have what we need."

"Excellent. So, can we go?"

"Not quite." Sterling knew it was only safe to access Dirk's accounts from Dirk's own computer because his accounts could have a security feature that notified owners if someone accessed the account from an unknown device. He thought for a minute and then told Hoyt he could install remote control software on Dirk's computer so they could access and control it as if they were sitting in front of it—all from the safety of their house.

"Look, it's a lost cause trying to explain it to me," Hoyt noted. "Just do what you need to do. I'm going to find the vacuum cleaner."

As Hoyt left the office, Sterling downloaded the remote control software to Dirk's computer. It was much simpler than setting up the Pi, and Sterling was done soon after Hoyt returned. Sterling grabbed his laptop and stepped out of Dirk's office while Hoyt vacuumed the carpet back to its manicured state. When Hoyt finished, he and Sterling returned the vacuum to the kitchen closet on their way out.

As they turned to leave, they both heard the garage door closing. They locked eyes and realized that the noise from the vacuum cleaner must have masked the sound of someone pulling in.

Panic set in as they both looked around for a quick exit. Sterling pointed to the sliding door across the kitchen, but Hoyt grabbed his shirt and whispered, "No time."

Hoyt opened the closet door again and lunged inside, pushing the vacuum back as far as it would go and yanking Sterling in behind him. But the door would not shut. It was a tiny closet, and Sterling's backpack blocked the door from closing. Sterling ripped his pack off and held it above his head with both hands. He pushed closer to Hoyt, who reached around him and jerked on the door handle until the latch clicked. They stood ear-to-ear with their toes next to each other's heels. Then there was silence.

The door from the garage into the kitchen opened, and muffled footsteps entered the kitchen. There was no talking or any other sound. Hoyt's lips were right against Sterling's ear as he whispered, "If it's Dirk, he's way off schedule."

Sterling said, "Whoever it is, we have to stay here until we know for sure they're gone."

"How will we know unless we hear the garage door open?"

"I don't know. We'll just have to wait."

"This might be a bad time to mention this," Hoyt confessed. "But. I can't stand this much longer. I need to pee, and you need to shower."

"You're not the one with a backpack on top of his head. So toughen up."

"My bladder doesn't care about your backpack."

"Your bladder had better deal with it," Sterling snapped. "It could be hours. We might have to wait here until he goes to sleep."

"Okay, but in twenty minutes, this floor is going to be wet. Twenty minutes max." Hoyt shifted from one foot to the other. "Sterling, I'm going to pass out."

"Calm down. Flex your knees."

Hoyt could only bend his knees a couple of inches, but the movement helped restore his circulation. For several minutes, they didn't speak. The stale air mixed with the smell of sweaty bodies was becoming a problem, however, and Hoyt was growing nauseous. "Let me out," he whimpered. "I can't take any more."

"Hang on," Sterling said. "I have an idea to get us out of here." Sterling rested his pack on his head and held it in place with one hand. With his other hand, he eased his phone from his pocket, searched for the Port Angeles Boat Basin, and called it. He leaned away from the door until his mouth was behind Hoyt's head. When the office answered his call, Sterling whispered, "I saw someone break into a yacht. He is on board now." After a pause, he added, "The boat's name is Leverage. It's on the dock closest to the strait." Another pause. "Got it. I'll stay here until the police arrive, but my phone is dying. Please hurry." He ended the call and told Hoyt, "With any luck, they'll call Dirk to let him know."

A few more minutes passed, though to Sterling and Hoyt they felt like thirty, and they heard a phone ring across the house. Seconds later, footsteps hurried through the kitchen, and a door slammed shut. The garage door opened and soon closed again. Sterling and Hoyt busted out of the kitchen closet, gasping for fresh air. They quickly exited through the garage and ran to the trees to make their escape. Hoyt veered off behind a tree to relieve himself, and Sterling waited.

"I should have thought of this already," Sterling reflected, "but I need to buy a cheap disposable phone, a burner, in case I need to text Dirk without him recognizing my number. We were lucky the marina called him. Who knows how long we would've been stuck in there otherwise?"

"Yeah, and you should've thought of something else."

"What's that?"

"Breath mints. That was brutal. I don't think we've been that close since we were in the womb."

SAFELY BACK AT their house, Hoyt watched Sterling from bed as Sterling connected to the remote-control software on Dirk's computer. As expected, the screen loaded as if it were Dirk's own, which meant Sterling could freely operate Dirk's computer. Using the slip of paper Hoyt found, Sterling signed into Dirk's CredentialVault. It contained dozens of accounts, each with a URL, username, and password. Some were mundane, such as the Washington Department of Fish and Wildlife, where Dirk bought his fishing license. Others were clearly useful—an Ameritrade account, a Bitcoin account, and two bank accounts. There were also two email accounts, each with a cryptic username.

"How about we try the Ameritrade account," Hoyt said. "That one could be loaded."

Sterling logged in, and the account summary showed a balance of more than of a quarter million dollars. He and Hoyt's eyes widened, and they searched the transaction history, which listed monthly deposits.

"This will cover half of Pete's money," Hoyt remarked, "but we need more. Let's see the bank accounts."

Sterling nodded and opened the first account, which had a balance of $28,032. The second account's balance was $32,512.

Hoyt said, "Obviously, that statement I saw on in his office was for only one of his stashes."

"It's still not enough to pay Pete back," Sterling pointed out. "But there's a Bitcoin account yet to explore. Shall we?"

"After you."

Sterling logged in, and they saw a balance of over a $250,000. "There we go."

"I'm confused. If Dirk has this much money lying around, why would he have such a big loan for the Cessna? Couldn't he buy it outright?"

"Who knows? I need to learn about Bitcoin, though. There might be more than meets the eye." Sterling made note of the account number and the account balance. "Give me an hour, then we can decide what to do next."

Sterling found a beginner's guide online and learned enough about Bitcoin to get started. After reading it over, he went to Hoyt's room to explain what he found. "There's definitely something shady going on. Bitcoin is money that can be transferred from one person's account to another's, without a bank ever being involved. There's no official record of the transactions."

"So, why is that shady?"

"It's not necessarily, but it's used by lots of people, like drug dealers, who want to hide their money. In Dirk's case, he's probably using it to hide money from the authorities. That means when we want to empty his pockets, we'll start with his Bitcoin account, because he might not report the theft to the cops. He could get caught."

"Awesome. So, let's do it. Let's empty his pockets right now."

"Not so fast. We need to get our own Bitcoin account first. It shouldn't take long to set up. After that, we can hit Dirk where it hurts."

The words had barely left Sterling's mouth when someone knocked on the bedroom door, and Pete entered without permission. The boys whipped their attention to him like caught rats. They could not have looked more guilty. Pete stopped, suspecting he had stumbled on something not meant for him to hear. Fortunately for Sterling and Hoyt, Pete was too exhausted from work to care.

"Since we are all at home, your mom thought it would be a nice idea for us to eat dinner together tonight. That's all."

Twenty

FOR THE FIRST time in over a week, the Burke family sat at their dinner table together. During the meal, Pete updated the boys on the progress of his business and earning the money he owed. "The real estate market is slower than I hoped," he explained, cutting through a chicken breast with his knife. "Even so, we listed two new houses that should sell quickly."

"What happened with that land you had said was promising last month?" Sterling asked. "Will you build on it soon?"

"Not quite. That's going slower than expected, too." Pete caught a sideways glance from Anne, so he clarified. "Actually, it's off the table. Dirk found out about it and informed my bank that I'm having financial difficulties. So, the bank changed the loan terms, and I had to back out. Dirk might buy it and develop it himself now."

"What a friend," Hoyt scoffed. "You need to take him down. Or at least someone should."

Sterling kicked Hoyt under the table.

Pete ignored Hoyt's comment and said, "I do have some good news that you two might be interested in. Your grandpa called this afternoon, and he wants to give you his 2007 Mustang GT after you turn sixteen next month."

"What?" Sterling and Hoyt gasped in unison.

"Of course, you'll need to get your driver's licenses first, and you'll have to share the car. But the gift is certainly kind of Grandpa. I told him about the troubles we're having, too, and he even offered to pay the insurance for the first year, provided you keep clean driving records and don't get any tickets."

Sterling and Hoyt glowed like they had won a million bucks. Sterling pictured the red fastback and how awesome it would feel to drive to school in a hot car instead of riding the school bus.

"Wow," Hoyt said. "I thought, if anything, he would give us that beater pickup he still drives."

"The other part of the deal," Pete added, "is that you have to pick up the car, maybe the week after next. He offered to pay your bus fare to Spokane, but if you want to fly, you will need to pay the difference. You should also plan to spend a couple of days with your grandma and grandpa while you're out there—eat some of Grandma's home cooking and learn how to drive a stick. But first, you need to call tonight and thank him for the gift."

"Consider it done," Sterling said.

AFTER DINNER, HOYT called first to thank his grandpa, and when he finished talking, he handed the phone to Sterling. Each of their conversations took longer than expected because their grandma was chatty and had lots of question about their summer, as grandmas often do. Eventually, Sterling ended the call and gave Hoyt's phone back. Sterling stared at the floor for a moment. The car was a huge surprise, but he had something much bigger on his mind.

"You ready for this?" he asked Hoyt.

"For the Mustang? You bet."

Sterling shook his head.

"Oh. Right. The Bitcoin."

They trotted up to Sterling's room to pick up their mission where they had left off. Sterling talked Hoyt through the ground rules as he opened his laptop and opened a new Bitcoin account. "This account is top-secret," he emphasized. "No one can know about this account or Dirk's. We pretend they don't exist. Got it?"

Hoyt nodded.

"We should only access them from this laptop," Sterling continued. "And immediately after we do, I will erase my browser's history. We can't access them from our cell phones or your computer, especially not from a public computer." Sterling wrote the account numbers and passwords for both accounts on a sheet of paper and laid it on his desk. "We'll put this above the rafters in the shed behind Pete's office, in case we forget."

"Not a bad idea," Hoyt said, reading the note. "It shouldn't look suspicious if someone sees us poking around in there."

"Yes, but we each need to memorize these credentials. For both accounts. I don't want us going in and out of that shed all the time, or it *will* look suspicious."

Hoyt studied the paper and repeated each account's ID and password aloud three times. But he and Sterling both knew he would forget them by the next morning.

"All right. I've got them tucked away in my credit vault." Hoyt tapped on the side of his head. "Now, let's take everything he's got."

Sterling sighed and leaned back in his chair. "It's not that simple," he said. "Not yet. Let's wait awhile. I need time to consider the downside—"

"Ugh!" Hoyt pounded Sterling's bed with his fist. "You always chicken out!"

"Will you listen to me? This is a big step we're about to take, and once we move forward, there's no going back. I'm worried that if we take the Bitcoin now, Dirk will suspect Pete, Mom, and even us. Maybe we can make him suspect someone else instead."

"You're afraid to do it."

"No. I'm afraid it will blow up in our faces if we don't take time to consider how it could go wrong."

"Chicken."

"Back off. You know I'm right. We should go hide the paper, and while we're at it, let's buy a burner phone."

"What for?"

"Like I said—to cover our tracks. We got lucky with that break-in call to the Boat Basin."

STERLING AND HOYT coasted to a stop in the alley behind Pete's office. Sterling pulled the note from his pocket while Hoyt opened the combination lock. Hoyt's eyes ballooned as he swung open the shed door. He looked back at Sterling and gestured into the storage area. "What is *that*?"

"Oh yeah," Sterling said, looking past Hoyt. "I forgot to tell you. That's Laurel's scooter. I told her she could store it here." As Sterling went into the shed and wedged the folded paper into a tight spot above the rafters, Hoyt wheeled the scooter out into the alley to get a better look at it.

"This is sweet. Not one of those wimpy mopeds." He patted the key in the ignition, saying "Well, look at this." He straddled the seat, and turned the key. "I know what we're driving to get that phone."

Sterling walked out of the shed. "Forget it. Laurel didn't say I could use it. Besides, you don't have your license."

"Don't be lame. We both finished our driver's ed course. That's pretty much the same as having a license. How hard can it be to drive a scooter?"

"No way. I'm not doing it."

"The way I see it, you have two options. You can pedal your bike, or you can get on with me. Either way, I'm taking it."

Experience had taught Sterling that when Hoyt made up his mind on something, no logic could change it. Hoyt grinned and goosed the engine. Sterling rolled both their bikes into the shed and locked the door. He patted Hoyt on the back and told him to stand so he could get the other helmet from the storage compartment under the seat. After strapping on the helmet, he hopped on the scooter behind Hoyt.

Hoyt whipped out of the alley and sped down the road as if he were an experienced motorcyclist. Sterling was relieved when they reached the drugstore without crashing, and he told Hoyt to wait with the scooter while he went inside to buy the phone. A few minutes later, Sterling returned. Hoyt and the scooter were gone.

Sterling jabbed his phone's screen and called Hoyt, but the call went to voice mail. He sent him a flurry of texts demanding that Hoyt call him back, and ten minutes later, Hoyt responded.

His text read, "Back soon. Ran an errand."

Sterling paced the parking lot and kept checking the time on his phone. Another fifteen minutes passed, Hoyt pulled up with the scooter. He patted the seat behind him, unaware of Sterling's rage.

"What's wrong with you?" Sterling shouted. He smacked the side of Hoyt's helmet. "Where did you go?"

"Whoa, whoa, take it easy. I went to the hardware store to have another key made for the scooter."

"Another key?"

"In case of an emergency. Like the burner phone."

Sterling smacked Hoyt's helmet again and climbed onto the scooter. "Just take us back."

As they were nearing Pete's office, Sterling's phone vibrated in his pocket. He checked and saw it was a missed call from Laurel. He waited to call her back from the shed, since he figured she wouldn't be too happy if she heard the scooter's engine whirring in the background. But as the boys pulled into the alley, they saw Laurel, with her hands on her hips, standing in front of the shed's wide-open door. Hoyt slowed the scooter to a stop in front of her and killed the engine.

At first, no one spoke. Laurel's eyes glared, and her nostrils flared. Sterling dismounted from the back and removed his helmet, wishing he could crawl inside it.

Laurel walked up to him and shook a finger in his face. "Did I say you could use my scooter?" she snapped. "Did you ask me if you could use it? No, because if you did, you knew I wouldn't let you. Did you ever think that I might need it myself this evening?"

"I wasn't planning on—"

"Now I understand why you offered to let me store my scooter here. Unbelievable. Everything you do has a catch to it, huh? You know if I hadn't recognized your bikes, I would have reported it stolen. Too bad I didn't. Do guys even have your licenses?"

Color rose in Sterling's cheeks. He turned to Hoyt for backup, but Hoyt only raised his eyebrows as if to say, "You're on your own, bro. Better you than me."

Sterling looked back at Laurel. "I didn't plan to use it. I wasn't thinking."

"Yes, you *were* thinking—thinking of yourself, thinking of how to take advantage of me. Again."

"Can I talk a minute without you interrupting?"

Hoyt got off the scooter and hung the helmet from the handlebars. He stepped behind Laurel and disappeared inside the shed to fetch his bike.

Laurel took a deep breath and let Sterling continue. "You're right," he admitted. "You didn't say I could use it. I didn't ask, and I'm sorry. Again."

"You're only sorry because I caught you."

Sterling watched Hoyt wheel his bike out of the shed and catch Laurel's eye, before riding off through the alley. He shook his head. "Look. I blew it. I admit it. It won't happen again. Now, it's up to you. Can you look past this?"

"I don't think it works that way."

"You can't give me another chance?"

"I . . . I don't know."

Laurel took her phone out and texted Bethany, "I found it. Sterling took it for a joy ride." She walked over to the scooter and started it up.

"Laurel, c'mon. I'm sorry," Sterling repeated. "Please."

"Don't call me," she replied, and the revving engine drowned out all other sounds as she drove away.

AS SOON AS Sterling got home, he barged into Hoyt's room. Hoyt grinned at him and said, "Glad to see you survived."

"Thanks for manning up and telling her it was all your idea. She ripped me apart." In a strange way, thinking back on Laurel's rant made Sterling smile. He didn't know she could be so feisty. "Give me the key. This will not happen again."

"I don't have it. I hid it in the shed with the Bitcoin paper. I promise not to use it unless it's a genuine emergency."

"Yeah right. Like if you want to go to the mall?"

"No, I mean it. Look, don't we have bigger issues to deal with than that scooter? Your drama with Laurel is driving me nuts."

"I guess you're right."

"So, are we taking Dirk's Bitcoin? Or are you still chicken?"

"Well, since I had nothing else to do while I was waiting for you to come back to the drugstore, I made a plan. We need to create confusion to put Dirk on the wrong trail. After we drain his account, we'll use the burner phone to text him a red herring."

"Red herring?"

"Yeah, like a false clue."

"Okay. And then we'll steal all of it?"

"All of it," Sterling said. "Every penny."

"How about we leave $200? That will cover the severance package he gave us."

"No. That will tell him we're the ones who took his money. We might as well leave our signatures."

"I don't care. It will be hilarious. Besides, we'll be near the top of his suspect list, no matter what."

"You're right," Sterling agreed, pulling out the burner phone. "He *will* suspect us, which is why we are going to plant a false clue."

Sterling grabbed his laptop and remotely logged into Dirk's Bitcoin account. He set up the transfer from Dirk's account to theirs and pressed enter. A notification loaded, stating the entire amount was sent into their account. Sterling logged out of the session with Dirk's computer and checked his own Bitcoin account to see if it worked. Like magic, a quarter million dollars was now theirs. Sterling cleared his browser's history and high-fived Hoyt.

"There's one last thing to do," Sterling said. "Hand me the burner phone." He punched in Dirk's number and texted, "I think you are taking too much for yourself. I transferred funds to cover my risk. Stay cool. You are in way over your head." He set the phone down and exhaled.

"What happens now?" Hoyt asked.

"We just lit a fuse. It's only a matter of time until the bomb goes off."

Twenty-One

All men's miseries derive from not being able to sit in a quiet room alone.

—Blaise Pascal

ON SATURDAY MORNING, Laurel and Bethany sat on the bench outside the restaurant an hour before work. They planned to meet John, and while they waited, Laurel related her encounter with Sterling from the previous night. Bethany was disgusted and said Laurel should tell Sterling he owes her money for gas. John arrived in the middle of their discussion and sat between them. The girls grew quiet.

"Ladies," John greeted. "Perhaps we should begin by talking about the time you spent last week in Canaan's Garden. Was it worthwhile?"

Bethany looked at her hands. "Well, Stella quit, so we were short a server. I needed extra money and picked up two of her shifts. After working long days, I was too tired to go."

"Yeah," Laurel said. "I got busy with other things and forgot."

John replied, "I understand. It's easy to miss, especially since you are both still trying to get in the habit."

"I meant to go, and I feel guilty," Laurel confessed.

"I get it. Not going makes you feel guilty. When I feel guilty, I'm even less likely to do those things I know I should. Spending time in the garden makes me want to spend more time there. At first, I did it because I knew I should, but now I look forward to it. I go to the garden because I want to spend time there, to quiet myself, to rest, to contemplate, and to hear." Both girls nodded in agreement, and John continued, "Why don't we skip our discussion for this morning? It is more important for each of us to get a fresh taste of time in the garden."

John stood, and Laurel and Bethany followed him to the barn beside the waterfall. Soon, they were standing in a patch of ripe strawberries, and John sauntered to the orchard, where branches sagged beneath the weight of ripe fruit. Bethany sat in a lounge chair. Laurel removed her shoes and socks and walked across the lawn, her feet massaged by the forest green grass. Several other people were in the garden along with them, but it was serene, and everyone kept to themselves.

Laurel found a perfect patch of grass and laid on her back facing the rising sun. She closed her eyes, and the light turned her eyelids a translucent pink. I let her quiet herself, and she reflected on her week—the highs and the lows, the times she responded to my piffs and the times she went her own way. She thought about what she had said to Sterling and how had she said it. A smile crossed her face. She was pleased that she defended her position as the scooter's owner and had let Sterling know who was boss. So, I piffed her, *Forgive our debts as we forgive our debtors.*

In the garden's stillness, this penetrated her now quiet heart like a seed in good soil. She considered her own debts, how she had hurt others, and now her self-righteousness wasn't so appealing. She wondered if she would have been so forceful with Sterling if she had truly forgiven him for taking her necklace. Probably not. A single tear inched along the side of her face. I piffed her again. *Love your enemies, treat them as you would treat close friends.* Tears flowed, and it pleased me to know she had listened. She showed signs of true understanding. Hopefully, Laurel will look back on this hour in the garden as a time of cleansing and inner transformation. She will always need it.

Laurel contemplated my piffs and was humbled by the idea that she might need to apologize to Sterling. She stood and wiped her eyes with the back of her hands. Across the garden was a book exchange box that sat on top of a fence post. It resembled a bird house, except for a hinged glass door on its front. John, who had crafted it, patterned it after Canaan's Kitchen and had attached a layer of small granite fragments on its exterior walls to mimic the restaurant's stonework. Laurel walked over to the box and opened its little glass door, removing a well-worn Bible from within. She took the Bible back to her patch of grass, where she sat and read the sixth chapter of Luke. On those pages, the Master's words were written:

But to you who are listening, I say: love your enemies, do good to those who hate you, bless those who curse you, pray for those who mistreat you. If someone slaps you on one cheek, turn to them the other also. If someone takes your coat, do not withhold your shirt from them. Give to everyone who asks you, and if anyone takes what belongs to you, do not demand it back. Do to others as you would have them do to you.

If you love those who love you, what credit is that to you? Even sinners love those who love them. And if you do good to those who are good to you, what credit is that to you? Even sinners do that. And if you lend to those from whom you expect repayment, what credit is that to you? Even sinners lend to sinners, expecting to be repaid in full. But love your enemies, do good to them, and lend to them without expecting to get anything back. Then your reward will be great, and you will be children of the Most High, because He is kind to the ungrateful and wicked. Be merciful, just as your Father is merciful.

She focused on a particular passage: "From him who takes your goods, do not ask them back. And if you lend to those from whom you hope to receive back, what credit is that to you? Love your enemies, do good and lend . . ." Despite their rocky start, Laurel did not consider Sterling to be her enemy. He was a friend—not a good friend—but certainly not an enemy. If she could not love Sterling as a friend, how could she ever expect to love an enemy? But their fight about the scooter still bothered her. He should have asked permission. But if he had, she knew she wouldn't have let him borrow it. He didn't have a driver's license, let alone a motorcycle endorsement. I piffed her, *Be merciful.* She pondered this and returned the Bible to the book box on her way out of the garden.

As she closed the barn door behind her, Laurel wondered why she so often did things she regretted and didn't do many of the things she should. Was her behavior getting worse, or was she becoming more aware of it? She knew if she didn't apologize to Sterling as soon as possible, she might put it off indefinitely. She had to make things right.

AT HIS DESK that morning, Sterling reviewed the surveillance video of the front of Dirk's house and noted that Dirk had driven away two hours earlier than usual. And he had not returned. Sterling thought that was odd, so he kept the video window open to see right away if Dirk pulled into his driveway. In another window, he launched the remote control software to access Dirk's desktop. He searched Dirk's emails for messages containing words like "payment," "Bitcoin," and "tax." Then he found a folder labeled Property Taxes.

When he started reading, he got a text from Laurel. She asked to meet at the shed at one o'clock. Sterling stared at the message, unsure of Laurel's intentions. He was not in the mood for another round of rantings, so he ignored the text and put his phone on the desk. As he turned his attention back to Dirk's emails, his phone chirped again. This time Laurel texted a smiley face and another message saying, "Let's go for a ride on the scooter." Sterling didn't realize he had been holding his breath. He exhaled, leaned back in his chair, and replied that he would meet her.

With a new boost of confidence, Sterling returned to the property tax folder. It contained several messages from an obscure email account, and the account looked strangely familiar. He tried to recall where he had seen it. After eliminating a few possibilities—school, science club, yard care customers—he was almost certain where he had seen it. He opened the photo gallery on his phone and scrolled back until he found the picture of the business card Laurel had showed him at the restaurant.

"That's the one," Sterling said to himself. The emails on Dirk's computer matched the handwritten address on the back of the business. The first email had arrived almost two months earlier, and someone who referred to himself as "the Mole" had signed each one. One email said the Mole could create *counterfeit tax statements* for specific properties. Sterling did not believe what he was seeing. It made no sense.

Sterling was reading Dirk's reply when movement in the video window caught his attention. Dirk's Tesla had pulled into his driveway. Sterling knew that because Dirk's desktop monitor was displaying the same thing that Sterling was seeing on his laptop, he needed to disconnect fast. He scrambled to pull up Dirk's screen saver and ended the remote control session.

Sterling tried to comprehend what he had just read. *Counterfeit tax statements.* Had Pete's real property taxes been paid? Did Dirk ask the Mole to create phony tax notices? Was this whole financial mess a scam? Sterling was blown away. It wasn't exactly good news. If any of that was true, he and Hoyt couldn't prove it without revealing they had broken into Dirk's house and his computer. Or could they?

Sterling charged into Hoyt's room. He heard panting, but no one seemed to be there. He walked around the bed and found Hoyt on the floor doing push-ups. "What's up?" Hoyt grunted, finishing his set.

"I found emails on Dirk's computer from someone who offered to alter the property tax statements on Pete's properties."

"What does that mean?"

"The statements Pete showed us might be bogus. But I don't know for sure. Dirk came home, and I had to disconnect before I could read everything. We need to figure out what's happened."

"Fake property tax bills?"

"It looks that way."

"Yes! If that's true, we're going to crush him like a bug! I can feel it."

Twenty-Two

Truly, it is evil to be full of faults; but it is a still greater evil to be full of them and to be unwilling to recognize them, since that is to add the further fault of a voluntary illusion.

—Blaise Pascal

STERLING LEFT HOME at quarter to one, which he knew from experience would give him enough time to meet Laurel at the shed by one o'clock. But after walking for only a few minutes, he shivered. A marine fog had recently rolled in and shrouded the area with a cool dampness. Sterling turned back and grab his black, long-sleeved fleece to wear over his T-shirt. By the time he made it to the alley, he was five minutes late. When he saw the scooter already parked outside the shed, he winced and buckled up for another one of Laurel's scathing lectures.

Instead, as Sterling approached her, Laurel pulled the spare helmet out of the scooter's storage compartment and handed it to him. "I was afraid you had decided not to come," she said. "Not that I blame you, after yesterday."

"Sorry I'm late. Had to go back to the house for something." He put on the helmet and wondered why he and Laurel always seemed to be telling each other they were sorry. "Thanks for waiting."

"No worries. You arrived just in time. Hop on, and we can head over to the City Pier. I was thinking about coffee and a walk along the waterfront. You good with that?"

"Sounds great."

THEY PARKED THE scooter in a motorcycle space near the ferry terminal and stowed their helmets. Each of them took a turn looking into the scooter's side mirror to finger comb their flattened hair. With the imprint of their helmets mostly gone, they walked to the coffee kiosk between the terminal and the Olympic Discovery Trail. "My treat," Laurel insisted.

Sterling thanked her and ordered a salted caramel latte. She ordered her coffee black. After getting their drinks, they walked east along the ODT. The overhead sun had broken through the fog and was now steaming moisture from the paved pathway. Sterling handed Laurel his latte and removed his fleece, tying it around his waist.

As they resumed their walk, Laurel said, "I want to tell you something. I can't get yesterday out of my mind. You and Hoyt were wrong to take—"

"Wait. Are we really doing this again?" Sterling protested.

"Doing what?"

"Arguing."

"No, that's not what I mean. You were wrong to take my scooter, but my reaction was wrong, too. Honestly, my reaction might have been worse. You told me you were sorry, but I didn't back off. I didn't even consider forgiving you."

Sterling took a sip from his drink and watched the trail ahead.

Laurel cleared her throat and added, "It was Hoyt's idea, wasn't it?"

"How did you know?"

"I was replaying the situation in my head this morning and realized that he smirked at me as he rode away on his bike. He was the one I should have been talking to."

"I still didn't try hard enough to stop him."

"The only reason I'm bringing up all this again is because I need to ask you to forgive me for how I yelled at you. Can you do that?"

Sterling let out a groan. "What's with the endless apologizing and forgiveness talk? We hardly know each other, but every time we talk, at least one of us is apologizing. It's not normal. Maybe we each should go our own way. It's like we bring out the worst in each other."

"With that logic, I should stop seeing everyone I know. I can't speak for you, but I am a mess. I'm always doing what I don't want to do, and I don't do what I know I should. Then, I apologize and try over, only to blow it again. The way I see it, you aren't causing my problems, you're are just getting hit by them. Like everybody else."

Sterling considered this. "I guess I see your point. But enough with the endless apologies. My skin is thick. I can handle it. I'll bet you can too. When Hoyt and I tick off each other, we let it go. A few days later, everything is fine."

"I can't just let it go. I need to be forgiven, and I need to change, to transform."

Sterling nearly choked on a sip of his latte. "What's with you? If it isn't forgiveness, it's transformation. Do you live in another world?"

Laurel paused. "Is that a rhetorical question? Or do you honestly want to know?"

"A little of both, I guess."

"I can try to explain where I'm coming from, if that would help you understand. But I'm not going to pour out my soul so you can make fun of me."

"Try me."

"Okay. I first started hearing this kind of talk when I moved in with Bethany and her parents about two years ago. I'd known Uncle John already, but after I moved in, he spent more time with me. I think he was trying to fill in for Dad—you know, make sure I had a father figure in my life. So, John would talk about things like transformation and forgiveness, which you've probably heard for yourself by now. I thought it was weird at first, too. But then I noticed that John's not like most people. It's like he lives in this world, but he's truly a citizen of a different world."

"Too much substance abuse in his younger days?"

"I used to wonder that, too, but that's not it. He's the real deal. He might seem spacey, or like his mind is somewhere else, but he is completely here, in the present. And he likes everyone he meets. Doesn't matter who they are or what they've done—good, bad, or awful—he loves them. He's always calm and peaceful, even when things go sideways. So, when he talks about transformation and a right way of living, he backs it up with his actions."

"Sounds like he put a spell on you. Does he walk on water, too?"

"Hey." Laurel cut in front of Sterling and faced him. "You can tease me. But please don't be cynical. I was skeptical at first myself. Skeptical is okay, but cynical . . ." She shook her head. "It will blind you. Now, do you want me to explain this or not?"

"Yes. I'll chill. Go on."

She took a deep breath, and they kept walking. "Anyway, I thought John might be a fair-weather phony—someone who always smiles and says everything is going great, even when it isn't. But I've watched him closely for two years now. He's solid. Consistent. Well, you must know what I mean. You've met him."

"Yeah. he was nice to me."

"And you've only spent a couple minutes with him, not years."

Sterling might have been holding back his cynicism, but his skepticism was on full alert. He thought John was nice enough, but not super special. Definitely not the being of pure light that Laurel seemed to think he was.

Laurel took Sterling's hand and led him to a bench that faced the strait. The fog had lifted, and sunlight played on the water's surface. They sat and enjoyed the view before Laurel continued. She turned to face Sterling and had his full attention. "This may sound crazy to you," she said, "but Bethany and I couldn't resist the life that John always talked about, so we asked him to guide us in the way of the Master."

"The way of the Master?"

"It's like this—there's a world, a kingdom, that's always nearby, but it's hidden, unless you know to seek it. You can't see it, touch it, smell it, hear it, or taste it. But once you search for it in the right way, you know it exists. John says when you spend time in the kingdom, it becomes more real—and more mysterious—a place of unending surprise and wonder, a place to seek life.

"It's ruled by Jesus, the Master, who is as mysterious as the kingdom itself. He is hidden, too, but he endlessly seeks us, to help us grow. He has supreme power, but he lets people act on their own choices. He's the one who created that mysterious world, along with this one." She patted her forearm. "The one we experience every day with our senses. He was once in this world, like us, physically, a long time ago, but now he can be found in the kingdom I'm talking about. The Master speaks to those who rest and listen in solitude, and once we find him, he promises to never leave us. He offers a rich life beyond money and material things. He replaces our restlessness and striving with peace. John says that if we let the Master's kingdom touch our selfish lives, we will be transformed.

"I know, it's a lot to comprehend. And the path is hard to follow. That's why I need a guide, like John, to show me the way. I lose my cool, rant and rave, and spew judgment—"

Sterling nodded in agreement, and Laurel added, "Yeah, you already know that. But it's not the Master's way. He wants me to love and forgive. Even those who take my scooter without permission." She smiled and waited for Sterling to respond, but he sat there with his arms crossed.

"Sterling, if you taste the kingdom, you will understand what I mean."

"Taste? You said we can't taste it or touch it or see it."

"I guess I did." She laughed. "But you know what I mean. You'll have a hard time tasting the kingdom if you take everything so literally."

"I always take things literally. It's foolish not to. I don't mean that you are foolish. I'm sure you're sincere. Misguided possibly, but I wouldn't call you a fool."

"Is there a difference between misguided and foolish?"

Sterling grinned. "Literally, there is. At least a small one. All I'm trying to say is that I think you really are sincere, and I don't want to hurt your feelings. Honestly, I probably shouldn't say much more than that."

"No, I want to know what you are thinking. I bared my inner life to you, after all."

"Okay. I think a lot of what you said sounds pretty woo-woo, but I've gone through some weird stuff myself lately, so there might be a grain of truth in it. For instance, I was talking to John, and he told me that if someone wants to save his life, he must lose it."

"I believe that."

"Well, you won't believe this—it gets crazier. Right after he told me that, a dove delivered a note to me. A dove. And the note said the same thing John did." Sterling removed the note from his wallet, unfolded it, and handed it to Laurel. She studied it and handed it back. "If I didn't have the note," he said, "I wouldn't believe it."

"It is hard to believe. Are you messing with me?"

"Not at all. And I'm sure it was a dove that made the delivery, not an owl."

Laurel laughed at the Hedwig reference. "I guess it's not any wilder than what I was saying. Maybe we both need to give each other room to walk on the fringe."

"Maybe so."

Laurel stretched her arm out across the back of the bench and looked up at the clouds. "So, other than special deliveries and fights over scooters, what's going on with you?"

Sterling stared out at the water, watching the waves pulse slowly against the shore. "Mom and Pete are gone from sunup to sundown every day, doing whatever realtors do. You know, searching for clients, getting new listings, showing houses, and sitting on open houses—that kind of stuff. I'm getting tired of grazing on PB and J sandwiches. But if I didn't eat them, I'd starve."

"So, are the PB and Js the worst of it?"

"No. I have another problem, too. Remember what I told you about Pete's business partner ripping us off? Hoyt and I are trying to get our money back."

"How's that going?"

Sterling continued to stare at the water as if he was waiting for a submarine to surface from the deep. "It's too early to say. We may have found a way to get part of it back. But keeping it may be tricky. Dirk is totally going to bring the heat if he suspects we took the money."

"Took the money? Like, you stole it?"

"Uh, not exactly . . . it's a gray area."

"When I said I would give you room to walk on the fringe, I didn't mean you should cross the line."

"No, it's not like that. It's complicated. Basically, Hoyt and I are in a tight spot. We can't tell the police what Dirk has done because they might do nothing. And even if they did something, they might drag their investigation out for months and then decide not to take any action. Not to mention, the police would want to know how Hoyt and I uncovered Dirk's crime, and . . . we may not have followed the most legally upright procedures along the way."

"That doesn't sound like a tight spot. It sounds illegal. Maybe you should care more about doing the right thing and not so much about getting the money back. Especially if Dirk will come after you. He's slimy."

"I'll be careful."

Sterling knew his reasons for going after Dirk went deeper than getting Pete's money back. He wanted to make Dirk hurt, and when he did, he wanted Dirk to know who was responsible for it. But those desires made Sterling increasingly uneasy. There was a good chance Laurel was right, and he should be more concerned about doing the right thing.

They hung out near the beach for a little longer, delving into easier conversations and commenting on the sights of the strait. From there, they walked back to the scooter and left, returning to the shed in the alley. Laurel opened scooter's storage compartment again and pulled out a small, gift-wrapped package. She handed it to Sterling, who unwrapped it.

"John told me he offered you a Bible, but you didn't take it. Will you take one from me?"

Sterling turned the Bible over in his hands, shrugged, and said, "I guess it can't hurt. Thanks."

"You need to let it speak to you. Go to a quiet place and read a little at a time. Listen to the Master's voice and let it come alive."

I could sense Sterling's hesitation, but I was not worried. Laurel's small gift was like a seed, and seeds are patient, sometimes waiting for decades before taking root. This seed won't be the last to cross Sterling's path. I will sow countless others before him, and each will whisper an invitation to an abundant life.

Twenty-Three

IN THAT AFTERNOON sun, I flew high above Sterling as he walked home from the storage shed. He looked down at the Bible in his hands, reflecting on his talk with Laurel. Sterling thought she was an unusual girl, if not downright odd. She was unlike any of his other friends, who would never give a moment's thought to things like *forgiveness* or *transformation.* And if they did, they would be too self-conscious to mention it. Sterling admitted he would be as well. What was it that attracted him to her? Laurel had something more than her good looks. She had something deeper, something Sterling didn't see in his other friends. At the very least, she had guts to give him a Bible, knowing he had refused one from John. Sterling concluded she must have thought he needed to learn the rules of good behavior. "Do this, don't do that."

He reached home, and I landed on a branch outside his bedroom window in time to watch him set the Bible on his nightstand, go to his desk, and open his laptop. He scanned through the surveillance videos of Dirk's house, as had become his habit, working his way from the most recent footage to the oldest. Dirk had driven off in his Tesla about three hours earlier and had yet not returned.

Seeing that the coast was clear, Sterling remote-controlled into Dirk's email account and went directly to the property tax folder. He read each message from oldest to newest, and the emails revealed the truth. Sure enough, Dirk had an accomplice, the Mole, who had full access to the county's property tax records. Every penny of the taxes for Pete's commercial properties had been paid, but the Mole had created fake notices and sent them to Pete to scam him.

Sterling realized Pete was in a no-win predicament, and Dirk was in a no-lose position. If Pete repaid the taxes, he would lose $550,937.23, and the Mole would redirect the money from the county's treasury and into an account he shared with Dirk. On the other hand, if Pete did not repay the taxes, the Mole would raise a false red flag in the county records, and Pete would lose his properties, unless he could find a buyer who would take responsibility for the back taxes. According to the emails, Dirk was planning to make a low-ball offer to buy the properties from Pete and pay the taxes himself. Of course, Dirk would not actually have to pay any taxes, since they technically were not owed. Instead, he would purchase the properties for a fraction of their market value and walk away much richer. Either way, the bottom line was simple—Pete would lose, and Dirk would win.

Sterling also knew the email messages were not merely information. If he involved the police, the messages were potential evidence to be used against Dirk and his accomplice. But if Sterling copied the messages and reported Dirk to the police, Dirk would swear that Sterling fabricated them using a word processor. Sterling tried to think if there was any way around it.

After pacing his room for several minutes, he recalled a guest speaker Mr. K. had once invited to the science club. The talk was about how to recognize spam and malicious email messages. At the time, Sterling found the subject boring and had almost snuck out the back door to escape. Now, he was glad he had suffered through it. The speaker had explained every email message contained detailed routing information that was not displayed by default. She said the information included IP addresses for each stop the email made en route to the recipient, date and time stamps, and checks to make sure the message did not get corrupted during transmission. In short, every email had a hidden record that could prove its origin, and the speaker showed the science club members how to view it.

Sterling rushed back to his laptop to pull up the information for Dirk's messages. Once he could make copies of them, those emails could be used as solid evidence in the eyes of the law. He downloaded the messages, including the routing information, put Dirk's computer into sleep-mode, and disconnected from it.

Sterling then copied Dirk's messages onto two different USB thumb drives and deleted the messages from his laptop. He took both USB drives to Hoyt's room to tell him the good news. But Hoyt was not there. Sterling texted him, and Hoyt responded that he was playing pickup basketball at the park. Sterling asked him to come home right away, saying he had something important to show him, and Hoyt replied that he would be home in ten minutes.

Thirty minutes later, Hoyt walked into Sterling's room eating a hamburger. Sterling turned from his desk and heard his own stomach growl. "Ooh. That looks good. Did you get one for me?"

Hoyt wiped a dab of mustard from his lip with the back of his hand. "Didn't think of it. You can stop at a burger joint whenever you want, so don't blame me if you're hungry."

"That's fair. Still, you could have asked me if I wanted something."

"C'mon, I stopped playing ball when you asked. Don't expect me to do everything for you. Now, do you have something important to show me or not?"

Sterling held up the USB drives and waved them in the air. "You'd better believe it. I've got proof."

"Proof of what?"

"Proof that our good ol' friend Dirk is cheating Pete. Those property tax notices were fake. The taxes *have* been paid, like Pete thought. Now we need to figure out how to get the rest of Pete's money back."

"Let's turn Dirk in to the cops. They'll settle everything else for us."

"And admit that we broke into his house and hacked into his computer? I don't think so. Do you have any idea how much trouble we'd be in?"

"Yeah, but can't Dirk find out what we did, anyway? Couldn't he report *us* to the cops? We could end up in juvie even if we don't bust him."

"Hmm. I suppose that's possible. Good point." Sterling rubbed the scar on the side of his head. "If he's smart, he can get as much dirt on us as we have on him."

"Plus, he's an upstanding adult, and we're just a couple of dumb kids. Who do you think the cops will believe?"

Sterling sighed. "Dirk."

"Obviously."

Sterling tried to think how Dirk could feasibly catch them. Had they left any tracks? Sure, their equipment was on his property, but they could easily pack it up. Then Sterling remembered the science club speaker again. She said something about how deleting files from a hard disk did not actually remove them. Instead, the computer marked the file's storage space as being available for use by new files. So, old files would only be destroyed if new files overwrote them. That meant that both Sterling's laptop and Dirk's computer could be storehouses of incriminating evidence.

"Hoyt," Sterling said, "we've got to cover our tracks. As soon as it gets dark, you need to sneak into Dirk's yard and remove my surveillance gear. Everything has to go—the camera, Pi, cables, and extension cord. And on your way, stop and hide this USB stick in Pete's shed. I'm going to connect to Dirk's computer and reformat his hard disk, and then I'm going to reformat mine and rebuild it."

"You're going to do what?"

"Never mind. I'm going to destroy every trace of information on the disks."

"Got it. But why wait until dark to get the gear? I can grab it now. I'll be careful."

Sterling hesitated, but he ultimately remembered how stubborn Hoyt could be. Besides, they had practically become professionals at sneaking around Dirk's house.

While Hoyt went to the garage to get his bike, Sterling reconnected to Dirk's computer to reformat its hard disk. In his excitement, however, he failed to check the surveillance video after talking with Hoyt, and in that window of time, Dirk had returned home. In fact, Dirk was checking his email at the same time Sterling had remotely connected to his computer. Dirk scratched his head as he saw a new window open on his screen. He looked at the keyboard, wondering if he had bumped some key. Up on the monitor, characters appeared as if he were typing them himself, but his hands were on the armrest of his chair. A message popped up asking for confirmation before reformatting the hard disk. It warned him that the action was non-recoverable. Dirk stared at his screen in confusion, and confirmation was given, as if by a phantom. His hard disk whirred in a frenzy, like a hamster racing on an exercise wheel.

Dirk assaulted his keyboard as if he could enter a random command to halt what was happening. But the electric hamster was not easily silenced. Dirk shouted and smashed his left hand on top of his desk, jolting the keyboard and the mouse. He then pressed the control-alt-delete combo, hoping to interrupt the process. When nothing happened, he pressed it again and again, with more force each time. The unstoppable whir continued. In desperation, he got on his hands and knees—not to pray, but to yank the power cord from the outlet. The whir faded to silence, and the computer's lights went out.

Frazzled, Dirk climbed back to his feet and grunted, "Whoever did this is going to pay!"

HOYT WALKED INTO Sterling's room with an armload of surveillance gear. Sterling looked it over to make sure Hoyt retrieved everything. "Looks good. Thanks."

"No problem. By the way, I took ten more detergent grenades to

Dirk's. The first batch worked great. His lawn looks like a pack of dogs went crazy, marking their territory. I bet the grenades I just lobbed will drive him nuts."

"Nice. Did you run by the shed?"

"Yep. The USB drive is up in the rafters with the scooter key and Bitcoin paper. Where did you put the other USB drive?"

"I took the seat post out of my bike, taped the drive inside, and then put the seat post back on. Nobody will ever look there."

"Man. You're not messing around." Hoyt flopped onto Sterling's bed and stared up at the ceiling fan. "Oh yeah. I wanted to ask you something."

"Shoot."

"I mean, you must have thought this through, but I'm missing something—if the property tax notices Pete showed us were fake, then that means the real property taxes were paid."

"Right."

"And Pete hasn't paid the fake ones yet?"

"Nope."

"Then did Dirk even steal from Pete? And if he didn't, then was taking the Bitcoin necessary?" Hoyt watched Sterling wrinkle his forehead before continuing. "Because if the Bitcoin wasn't really making up for anything stolen . . . then we're the only thieves in this scenario. You gotta clear this up for me. I know you have an answer."

Sterling sat in silence. His only response was, "I oopsed."

Hoyt shot up from the bed. "What? That's all you can say?"

"I never thought about that."

THAT NIGHT, AS Sterling lay awake in bed, Hoyt's conundrum haunted him. He could not sort out what to do. One minute, he wished he hadn't stolen the Bitcoin at all. Or at least that he would have waited longer to do it so Hoyt had time to put two plus two together. The next minute, he thought Dirk deserved to lose his Bitcoin, if not more, after lying to Pete and betraying him like he did.

And that wasn't to mention how Dirk had cost them a few yard customers.

At half past two, Sterling fell asleep after reaching his decision. Right and wrong didn't matter anymore. Vengeance was the only way. He would keep the Bitcoin and search for hard evidence to make Dirk pay for what he had done to Pete. This was Sterling's chance to prove to Pete that he would stand up for himself and for his family, at any cost. Even if it meant risking being grounded and dealing with the cops.

Twenty-Four

THE FOLLOWING MORNING, Dirk packed a small overnight bag and drove his Tesla to *Leverage*. He planned to corner his accomplice, the Mole, at the basin and interrogate him about his stolen Bitcoin. Dirk knew the Mole moored his boat right across from his own, and Dirk was prepared to spend the night on *Leverage*, if needed, to wait until the Mole showed up. On the way to his slip, Dirk spotted an enormous man grinding barnacles and paint off a fishing trawler's hull. He recognized him—Bert King, a six foot-eight fisherman with linebacker shoulders. Bert dressed like a person who had not glanced at his reflection in a mirror for days. The elbows and knees of his coveralls were worn through, and paint dust stuck to every inch of him, especially to his goggles and sweat-stained do-rag. Dirk walked over and stood beside him, unnoticed.

"Hey, Bert. It's been a long time."

Bert stopped the grinder and removed his respirator mask. He looked up in confusion, trying to tell who was there through the muck on his goggles. When he perceived it was Dirk who greeted him, Bert's mouth hung agape. He and Dirk had an unfortunate history. As a result, they rarely spoke. It had been over twenty years since they worked together on a commercial fishing boat in Alaska. And back then, Dirk had all ten fingers.

The accident had happened one day when Dirk was reaching over the side of the boat to free a sea lion that was tangled in the fishing net. At the very moment Dirk snagged the net with the gaff hook, Bert rushed next to him and fired a shotgun at the sea lion's nose. The blast killed the sea lion and maimed Dirk's thumb and two fingers in the process. The captain bandaged Dirk's hand and radioed for a helicopter to evacuate him to a hospital in Anchorage. There, a doctor cleaned and closed the wound, but the fingers could not be saved. Dirk ended up rejoining the boat when it docked in Anchorage ten days later. Bert apologized again and again, and each time, Dirk told him not to worry about it. But Bert's regret overwhelmed him, and he deserted the fishing boat before it left port to resume fishing.

Over twenty years later, the memory was still fresh for Bert. His remorse was unchanged, like Dirk's hand. Now, as Dirk stood next to him, Bert removed his goggles and wiped them with his handkerchief, looking around like he wanted to disappear.

"If it isn't Dirk McCleod," he said in his deep, gravelly voice. "I heard you were doing real well, and it's obvious just looking at you."

"You always were a charmer. Say, what are you doing with your boat out of the water during fishing season?"

"Oh, the driveshaft seal started leaking. It's going to take five or six days to get the replacement part and install it. Rather than wasting the time, I took her out of the water to clean and paint her hull." Bert's eyes wandered down to Dirk's hand, and he couldn't hold back yet another apology. "I've got to tell you, even after all these years, I still feel terrible about your hand."

"Look, I told you not to worry about it."

"I know, I know, but if there's anything I can do to make it up to you, I'll do it. I mean that. You say the word."

Dirk nodded, and standing in Bert's shadow, he seemed to notice anew how massive he was. "Now that you mention it, there might be something I could use your help with."

"Name it. Anything."

"There's a guy who keeps his boat across from mine. He could help me find out who took a bit of money from me, but I don't know if I can trust him. Things might go south when I confront him, and I'd like to have you nearby, just in case."

"No problem. My place is only five minutes away, and I'll be here at the dry dock for the next couple of days. Give me a call."

Dirk got Bert's number, and they chatted about old times for a while before Dirk continued to his boat. From *Leverage*, Dirk saw that the Mole's boat was not in its slip, so he made himself comfortable in the cabin and waited. He read a book on how to make a fortune in the stock market, and after finishing the first chapter, he stood to see if the Mole had returned. The boat was still nowhere in sight. Dirk checked the tide on his phone and saw that slack tide had occurred only an hour earlier and wondered if the Mole was out fishing for halibut. If that were the case, he would return shortly. Dirk was halfway through the second chapter of his book when he heard a motor approaching and saw the flying bridge of a boat as it idled into its slip. Dirk texted Bert to meet him at *Leverage.*

Walking across the dock to the bow of the Mole's boat, Dirk waited for the Mole to see him. When he did, the Mole waved and tossed the bow line. "Give me a hand with that, will ya?"

Dirk tied the line to the cleat, and the Mole called out, "You want some halibut?"

Dirk shook his head. "No thanks. Techs, we need to talk."

When not engaged in illegal schemes and covert communications, Dirk's accomplice was a man who went by the name *Techs*—an apt nickname, given his vast and detailed knowledge of computers.

Techs shut down his engine and stepped onto the dock, where he secured the stern line. He turned back toward Dirk. "Got a new project for us?"

Dirk pulled out his phone and showed him the text message Sterling had sent as a red herring. Dirk waited for Techs to read it and asked, "What do you know about this?"

"Nothing."

"Nothing, huh? Hard to believe." From the corner of his eye, he saw Bert lumbering toward them. Dirk motioned for him to wait by *Leverage* and turned back to Techs. "Who else might have sent me that?"

"How should I know? You think I sent it?"

"All I know is somebody did, and that same somebody hacked into my Bitcoin account and emptied it. You're the only person I know with the skills to do that."

"I'm flattered you thought of me," Techs responded, "but that kind of thing is below me. Bitcoin accounts are a punk hacker's favorite target, not mine. Have you ever logged into your account from a public computer or on public Wi-Fi? Maybe at a coffee shop?"

"No, and it's not that simple. Whoever took my money knows my cell number. I think that narrows it down. It's got to be someone I know."

"Not necessarily. But I see your point. It's unlikely for a random hacker to send a text like that. But it wasn't me." Techs glanced across the dock and nodded toward Bert. "Who's your friend? I didn't know you were hiring thugs these days."

Dirk waved Bert over, who approached and reached out his hand. "Name's Bert. Dirk and I go way back."

Techs shook his hand and introduced himself. "The pleasure's all mine."

"Let me ask you this," Dirk interrupted. "Do you know how to recover data from a partially reformatted hard disk?"

"You kidding me? I worked in cybersecurity for ten years before developing apps for the county. So, yes, I understand computer forensics. Why?"

"Yesterday afternoon, I was checking my email, and a window popped up on my screen. It showed a message about formatting my hard disk. Without touching my keyboard, the action was confirmed, and a warning popped up, saying I couldn't undo it. Before I could even back out, the action was confirmed again, and my disk light came on and stayed on. I tried to stop it, but couldn't. I finally had to pull the power cord to kill it."

"Hmm. Sounds like someone was remotely controlling your computer. That person must have issued the format command and then confirmed it. Any idea who that could be?"

"Why do you think I'm standing here?"

"I'm telling you, it wasn't me. I know I can't prove it, but you have my word. There's really no one else you could think of who could do that?"

Dirk thought. "Hard to say. My former partner might want to, but that's impossible—he's less computer savvy than I am. I don't see how he could be the one."

"Odds are, whoever did it is the same person who took your Bitcoin. And you definitely need to find out who it is." Techs mulled it over and added, "Please tell me you regularly backup your computer."

Dirk rubbed his forehead. "I think I made a copy of my financial files six months ago. Since then, I haven't made any."

"Do you store your files on the cloud?"

"The cloud? What's do you mean?"

"Forget it. You would know it if you're using it. It might be possible to recover data from your hard drive because it stopped when you pulled the plug. Formatting can take an hour or more, depending on the size of the drive. So, your disk may still hold useful data. That said, you'll need special analysis software to find out. Not only that, but you'll also need to know how to run the software and interpret the results. It all depends on what data got reformatted. You may recover a lot, or you may get nothing."

"I'm a businessman, not a geek. Is there someone who can analyze it for me?"

"Sure. There's a shop in Seattle and several in the Bay Area. It will cost you at least twice what you paid for your computer, and they usually have at least two months' backlog. Otherwise, the FBI has a lab that is great at recovering data, but they only work on criminal cases."

"What about you? Can you do it?"

"Wait a sec. You come out here, interrogate me, accuse me of theft, and then ask me to help you deal with your sensitive information. What am I missing? Do you trust me or not?"

"I'm in a bind, and I'm thinking you're probably clean. If you really did steal from me and crash my computer, I don't think you would point me to places that can recover data. The reality is that I need to recover that data right away, not in two months, and I can't trust a stranger to do it. So, I'll ask again, can you do it?"

"Sure, I can do it, but it's been several years since I worked on something like that. I can probably get a free evaluation copy of the disk recovery software to save you some money. It would take a few days." Techs's expression hardened, and he added, "But, I don't know. If you're not convinced we're good with this whole Bitcoin situation, I'm not sure I want to get involved."

Bert made a move toward Techs, but Dirk put his arm out and cut him off. He motioned Bert back behind him. "I have to be cautious," Dirk said to Techs. "I may never trust you one hundred percent, but we're good. I'll make another promise to you. If I find out it *was* you who ripped me off, I can blow the whistle on you with the county, and I will. Got it?"

"I hear you."

"Okay then. Now, the thing that is bothering me in all this is that whoever sent that text saying I got more than my fair share . . . he must have inside information."

"Well, whoever was remotely controlling your computer could have easily read the emails we sent to each other."

"I suppose so. How much are you going to charge me to fix my computer and catch this rat?"

"Hmm. This is a short-term gig. I normally don't take on work for less than eight weeks, but since we're such trusting friends, I'll give you my long-term rate. Two hundred an hour, plus expenses."

Bert mumbled, "Boy, am I in the wrong business."

Techs added, "But you need more than your hard disk analyzed. You need to beef up your physical security, too. I'm talking about infrared cameras, motion detectors, audio recorders—all with the ability to notify your phone in real time. Top-of-the-line gear will run you several thousand, but I'll keep it under three grand and can install it all in one day for a flat fifteen hundred."

Bert interjected and said to Dirk, "If you don't want to install cameras on your boat, I can keep an eye on it, at least until my gasket gets installed. I can even sleep in the cabin, free of charge. It will save me rent at the boarding house."

Dirk looked Bert up and down, undoubtedly repulsed by his dirty appearance. "How about you just keep an eye out? I keep the cabin locked up anyway, so it's always secure."

"What's the plan if we see someone acting suspicious?" Bert asked.

Dirk replied, "Call me. Get a complete description and his license plate. Stay with him if you can, but don't spook him. I need to grab him and make him talk, persuade him to return my money."

"And no cops," Techs clarified. "We'll take care of this ourselves."

Twenty-Five

AT THE SAME moment Dirk and Tech struck their deal at the Boat Basin and shook hands, Sterling awoke in his bed. As he lay there, adjusting to the new day, I piffed him to read his Bible. He looked over at it curiously and reached for it. After clicking on the lamp beside his bed and fluffing his pillow, Sterling turned to the fifth chapter of Matthew and read the words:

"You have heard that it was said, 'An eye for an eye and a tooth for a tooth.' But I tell you do not resist an evil person. If anyone slaps you on your right cheek, turn to them the other cheek also."

Sterling was confused, and I piffed him to read the verse again, which he did. Three times. His stomach clenched tighter with each reading as he considered the cowardly idea of not resisting an evil person. The thought of turning the other cheek brought back the shame of the incident in the second grade when he didn't have the guts to stand up and fight the bully who had knocked him into the mud puddle. He *had* turned the other cheek, and everyone in his class thought he was a wimp for it.

The command of the Master continued to trouble Sterling, so he crawled out of bed and went to the kitchen to devour two bowls of cereal while pondering the words. After breakfast, he met Hoyt in the driveway to set out for their three yard jobs. Each of them had dressed well for the weather, wearing shorts, a T-shirt, and a baseball cap. The temperature was already in the mid-seventies. Hoyt and Sterling normally started their yard jobs closer to nine, but many customers liked to sleep in on Sundays, and waking them with a roaring lawn mower was not good for tips. Fortunately, all three of the jobs lined up for the day were on the same block, a block which somehow evaded Dirk's attempt to poison the boys' customer base. Sterling figured Dirk simply lacked the contacts on that street.

During their walk to the shed to retrieve the mower and edger, Hoyt asked Sterling about the property taxes again. He wanted to know how certain Sterling was that the notices were bogus.

"I guess I can't be 100 percent sure," Sterling conceded, "but it sure looks that way. The emails spelled out the scam in black and white."

"So, what's our next step? Do we give Dirk his Bitcoin back?"

"Yeah, I spent a long time thinking about that last night. If we don't tell Pete the tax notices are fake, he'll keep trying to slash expenses. And if we tell him he doesn't owe those taxes, life goes back to normal—allowances, new school clothes, and you get to play football in the fall. The problem is that if we tell Pete, he can't know how we found out. We can't mention sneaking into Dirk's house or hacking into his computer. Or stealing a quarter of a million dollars in Bitcoin."

"For sure. If he knew that, we'd be worse off than we are now. Probably grounded for life with no allowance."

"So, we need to figure out another way to tell Pete. As far as the Bitcoin goes, I think we should keep it. At least for now."

"Really? I don't think that's a good idea."

"Hear me out. We can always give it back later, but if we give it back now, we'll never be able to get it again. Dirk's been spooked, so he would certainly change his password and maybe even transfer everything to a different account. We couldn't get it a second time if we wanted to." When Sterling saw Hoyt was still unsure about keeping the Bitcoin, he added, "Think it over. We don't have to decide right away."

Before the heat of the afternoon, Sterling and Hoyt had finished their three jobs, stowed their equipment back in the shed, and walked home. As they entered their driveway, Pete was pulling his SUV out of the garage. He stopped and lowered his window. "Glad to catch you. Our yard could use some attention. Please take care of at least the front lawn today and finish the rest by tomorrow. Understood?"

The boys nodded.

"Good. I also wanted to tell you that your mom is at an open house now, and I have a showing in thirty minutes that could be a quick sale. The buyers are well qualified and like what they saw on the internet. And if they buy it, I'll give you each two weeks' allowance after it closes."

"Awesome," Hoyt said. "How soon will that be?"

"Average closing time is two months."

"At least it's before school starts. That's good news, huh?" Hoyt glanced at Sterling, who suddenly had a weird expression on his face. Hoyt couldn't tell if it was fear or excitement.

"Yes it is," Pete said. "I'll let you know how it pans out. But I'd better get going. I'll see you boys later."

Pete started to put up his window, but Sterling stepped forward and grabbed the top of it. "Wait. There's something I have to tell you."

Pete lowered the window again, surprised at the urgency in Sterling's voice.

"What is it? Is everything alright?"

"It's fine. I just . . ." Sterling paused, realizing that whatever he said next could not be taken back. "I wanted to tell you something I overheard at the ATM this morning. A man and a lady ahead of me were talking to each other, and I heard the lady say that a friend of hers told her the county had a glitch with some of the property tax bills. She said a couple of tax payments were recorded multiple times and others weren't recorded at all. I thought you should check with the county. It's a long shot, but who knows? They could have made a mistake with yours."

Pete readjusted his hands on the steering wheel. "Huh. I never considered it could be a mistake. It couldn't hurt to check it out. I'll do that first thing tomorrow. Thanks for telling me."

Sterling stepped back as Pete drove away.

"Good thing we agreed on how we were going to tell him," Hoyt said sarcastically. "Where did that come from? You could have ruined our entire operation."

"I was thinking about it while we were working. It seemed like a safe story to tell him, so I went for it."

"Yeah, I guess it was kind of slick. You think Pete will actually check with the county?"

"The odds are good. We can check with him tomorrow."

Sterling did not feel great about lying to Pete, but he thought it served the greater good. Tipping Pete off would be worth it if it helped their lives return to normal, and if it helped the Burkes get revenge against Dirk. After all, this was Sterling's chance to show Pete he could fight back.

I WAS DISAPPOINTED, but not surprised, by Sterling's compulsion to get even with Dirk and keep his Bitcoin. Sterling, like so many people who had yet to be transformed, balanced life's equations in his own favor, without giving a thought to love or mercy. It grieved me that the words Sterling had read a few hours earlier, words about turning the other cheek and not demanding an eye for an eye or a tooth for a tooth, had fallen among thorns and were choked out. Sterling's heart was not yet ready to nurture such seeds.

The Master commands people to turn the other cheek when they are wronged. But turning the other cheek is rarely done. To Sterling's credit, turning the other cheek in love before one has been transformed is impossible. The Master commands it—not so people *will* do it, but precisely because they *cannot* do it. It is like many of the Master's other teachings. Love your neighbor as yourself. Do not look at a woman with lust. Do not call someone else a fool. And, the hardest of all, be perfect. These commands can only be performed by transformed people. The purpose is to show people their need for transformation, to see their need to live according to a higher standard than their earthly abilities can achieve.

Twenty-Six

THE FOLLOWING DAY, Sterling and Hoyt were finishing eating sandwiches in the kitchen when their parents walked in from the garage. Without so much as a greeting, Pete said, "Family meeting in the living room. Five minutes. Bring your food if you have to."

Sterling looked at Hoyt, who shrugged his shoulders. Neither knew what the meeting could be about. To prepare themselves for any upcoming lecture, they each shoveled generous scoops of mint chocolate chip ice cream into a bowl and smothered it with chocolate syrup. When they entered the living room, Pete was already sitting in his chair, and Anne sat on the armrest next to him.

Pete was stoic until the boys took their seats. Then he smiled. He waved a batch of papers in the air. "First, the good news. I went to the county office this morning and checked the last five years of my property taxes. Everything was paid on time, with no penalties. I spoke with a supervisor and showed her my tax notices. She studied them and said they looked authentic, but she assured me they weren't. She gave me these receipts proving that I owe nothing, and she kept copies of the delinquent notices so she could look into the situation. In short, that's $550,000 we don't owe."

Sterling fist-bumped Hoyt and said, "Good thing we overheard that lady at the ATM."

"Funny you should mention that. The county said nothing like this has ever happened before. I told her about the people you overheard at the ATM, but she said no one has contacted their office about other mix-ups. I must admit I was somewhat confused, and I hope you will clear things up for me. Especially since I know you wouldn't lie to me. Care to explain?"

"Um, well . . ." Sterling began and abruptly ate a spoonful of ice cream to buy himself time. "I think the woman was from another county, and she happened to give me a good idea."

"Is that your final answer? Because I suspect you didn't hear about the billing mistake at an ATM. You certainly seemed nervous yesterday when you fed me that story about waiting in line, which was a big red flag. Given what I learned at the county and their surprise at our situation, I think you owe me another explanation. And make sure it's the truth this time. How did you really find out about this?"

Sterling shared a pained glance with Hoyt. The game was up. He considered how to break things to Pete and hoped the good news about the property taxes would take a little of the sting out of the bad news about their surveillance activities. "It was early last week. Monday, I think. Hoyt and I went to see Dirk at his house . . ." And Sterling recounted to Pete the steps they had taken to investigate Dirk's emails and accounts—recording his router information, borrowing the garage remote, sorting through his file cabinet. He conveniently left out the part about siphoning thousands of dollars of Bitcoin. Sterling saw no reason Pete needed to know about that just yet. "So, that's when I knew you needed to double check your property tax records." Sterling concluded, "And it's a good thing I did. Think about all the stress and suffering you avoided."

Pete nodded, trying to process the load of information Sterling had dropped on him. "I'm certainly glad to know about the taxes. But what you and Hoyt did to get the information is insane. Spying on someone's financial records? Their emails? Your mother and I did not raise our sons to be criminals. You know, I was going to restore your allowances, but that deal is off the table now."

Anne agreed. "You two broke the law. Breaking and entering is a serious offense. Right now, you could easily be living in detention with some real creeps."

"But we didn't *break in*," Sterling said.

"That's a technicality. You certainly didn't have permission to enter his house."

"What choice did we have?" Hoyt interjected. "Besides the scam with the taxes, Dirk drove some of our best yard customers away. And he did it just to be mean. He messed with our whole family. We needed to know why."

"Dirk clearly has unresolved issues," Anne replied. "There are things he needs to change and things he needs to accept. But that doesn't excuse what you two did. Personally, I think getting off with only losing your allowance is too lenient. I would have grounded you for a month for this type of behavior."

"Sterling," Pete said. "You mentioned writing down Dirk's router information. What did you need that for?"

Sterling stared down into his bowl of ice cream and stirred until the chocolate syrup completely blended into the melted ice cream. "We needed to know when Dirk was away from home," he answered quietly. "So, we installed a webcam to watch the front of his house. We used his internet connection to send us the video."

Hoyt volunteered, "And we used his internet to remotely control his computer so we could look through his files."

Sterling glared at Hoyt and added, "But . . . we realized that what we were doing was wrong. We have already removed everything—the webcam and the remote control software."

"You both got lucky this time, but now it's over. I want you to drop it. No more digging into Dirk's business. Our family needs to put Dirk and everything about him behind us."

Anne added, "And if you don't, there will be much more serious consequences. Losing your allowance will seem like a gentle slap on the wrist."

EVEN AFTER PETE insisted that Sterling and Hoyt let go of the situation with Dirk, Sterling would not. Although he considered doing the right thing and even recalled the verse that spoke about turning the other cheek, he still felt the need for revenge. The idea of an eye for an eye and a tooth for a tooth sat well with him, and he calculated that the scales of injustice remained tipped too far in Dirk's favor to leave it alone. Sterling grew more determined to even the score, and make Dirk pay.

I can't say Sterling's response shocked me. Humans never surprise me anymore. I have seen it all—righteous people committing evil and evil people acting righteously. Although they rarely see it in themselves, people are a fusion of contradictions, and Sterling was no different. I had hoped he would let it go like Pete wanted, but when he refused, my hope for him did not lessen. Nor would it ever.

There are certain things you must know to understand what was going on inside Sterling's head at that time, even if Sterling did not understand them himself. His real motivations were to stay in control and to convince Pete he was tough and gain his approval. You can imagine then why turning the other cheek was not appealing. To Sterling, it was a total loss of control, and it was not the action of someone tough. That was why he did not seriously consider it.

Up in Hoyt's room, he and Hoyt regrouped. "Wow." Hoyt laughed. "We got off easy. Yesterday, we didn't have money for football and your science club, and I was afraid we would be wearing clothes that didn't fit. Today, we have everything back. Minus our allowance, I guess. But that's not so bad, all things considered. Plus, it's nice to have to have that whole mess with Dirk behind us."

Sterling snapped, "Oh, it's behind you, is it? Because it shouldn't be! It's certainly not behind me. Do you think Dirk will magically stop sabotaging us if we ignore him? Or if we give his Bitcoin back? We can't trust him. He could find another way to hurt Pete's business, and he could keep bugging Mom. I say if he messes with the Burkes, he needs to know it's going to hurt. Now, you can back down if you want, but I'm not going to stop looking out for our family."

"Whoa, whoa, I never said anything about backing down. Sure, I think we should let it go. But we're a team, and if you think there's more to be done, I won't let you do it alone. I'll always have your back."

Twenty-Seven

Men despise religion. They hate it and are afraid it may be true.
                                                            —Blaise Pascal

LATER THAT DAY, Sterling had worked himself into a fit and was taking out his malicious energy on making a sandwich. With gritted teeth, he slapped down and layered mayo, mustard, ham, cheddar, jack cheese, dill pickles, and potato chips between two slices of trimmed whole wheat bread. A sound from his phone interrupted his wrathful thoughts. Sterling looked down at it and saw a text from Laurel. "Dad's boat needs exercise. Wanna go fishing with me? Right away?"

Naturally, Sterling jumped at the chance to hang out with Laurel. Something about her mysterious, sometimes spacey mindset drew him to her. She was an enigma he wanted to solve. He accepted her invitation right away, but that only left him with fifteen minutes to finish his lunch. Sterling scarfed his sandwich and inhaled five Oreo cookies along with a glass of milk before sprinting upstairs to grab an old sweatshirt and a baseball cap, which he crammed into his rear pocket. Then he got another text that Laurel was waiting outside. Sterling met her in the driveway, where she sat on her scooter wearing suitable fishing clothes—a baggy, dark gray sweater, paint-stained sweatpants, and ratty tennis shoes. She smiled at Sterling and handed him a helmet.

AT THE BOAT Basin, where Laurel's father moored his boat, Laurel breathed in the sea air and said, "It's a great day to catch fish. Let's stop at the bait shack and buy a bucket of fish guts and a dozen herring. Maybe we'll get lucky and catch something worthwhile."

"Fine by me, but don't expect me to bait your hook," Sterling teased.

Laurel took a step back and looked down at her outfit. "Don't let this beauty fool you. I've been baiting my own hooks since Dad bought the boat. I can pull-start the motor, too."

"All right, I'm impressed." Sterling tipped his cap and added, "Too bad you won't catch as many fish as I will. Bet mine will be bigger, too."

"You want a fishing derby, huh?" Laurel shook her head and laughed. "Bring it on."

They kept trash-talking as they bought their bait and walked past the dry dock to the area where the smaller boats moored. "This is it." Laurel pointed as she approached a boat and stepped over its side. "Dad bought her three years ago. Along with the motor and the trailer. He got a good price, but everything was in rough shape. The boat had spent forty years collecting cobwebs in a barn near Sequim before we picked her up. It took Dad at least a month to clean the hull, refinish the woodwork inside the cabin, and paint the outside."

"Cool. It looks like he knew what he was doing."

"Thanks. Dad really got into it and even rebuilt the motor. The major addition was a second-hand radar unit that cost half as much as the boat itself. He claimed it was necessary in case he ever got caught in a surprise fog, but I think it was a cool gadget that caught his eye. But the boat looks much better now, even though she's nothing fancy or very big compared to the other boats out here." She grinned and added, "He named her *Meryl*, after moi."

"Anyway, Dad made me promise to run the motor while he's gone—at least once a month. He says it isn't good for it to sit for long periods. And he made me promise not to take the boat out of the basin by myself. Without you, I'd be stuck here listening to the motor idle at the dock for half an hour or so. So, I'm glad you could come."

"Happy to be your deckhand."

Sterling watched as Laurel retrieved the boat's keys and unlocked the door to the cabin, where she pulled out two crab pots and two sets of fishing gear. She then went to the controls, pushed the accelerator lever all the way forward, and turned the key to start the motor. It groaned and turned over a few times before stopping and clicking. The battery was dead.

"That doesn't sound good," Sterling commented.

Laurel removed the motor's cover to expose the pull cord. "It's been two months since I ran it. I guess that's why Dad asked me to come out here more often." She grabbed the starter cord handle with both hands, braced her foot against the transom, and pushed off with her leg. The motor turned over again but didn't start. "Sometimes it takes a couple of tries." She pulled twice more, and Sterling offered to help. "Not yet," she said. "I've got this." She walked to the helm and moved the accelerator lever back to half throttle. Returning to the motor, she braced her foot again, tightened her jaw, and launched herself backward. The motor coughed twice and then roared to life. Laurel looked at Sterling and flexed her biceps. "Told you I had it."

Sterling chuckled. "I never doubted you."

"Good. Now help me cast off these lines."

Sterling did as she asked, and they soon were puttering into the basin.

As they neared the exit, Sterling scanned the docks and locked his eyes on one boat in particular. It was *Leverage*. Dirk was onboard, too, and he turned and spotted Sterling watching him. The two locked eyes for a moment. Neither of them waved or acknowledged the other. They both turned away as *Meryl* cleared the marina and cruised into the strait.

After fifteen minutes, Laurel killed the motor, and the boat coasted to a stop. "Okay, here's my plan. We bait the two crab pots and throw them in here—one for you, and one for me. Then, while huge crabs are fighting with each other to see who can fill our pots, we'll fish for salmon. After we catch our limit of lunkers, we can pull in these pots and head back. Sound good?"

"Sounds a little too good. How do you plan to carry our haul on your scooter? Drag the fish behind us?"

"I'll call John. He'll bring his truck."

"Nice. Wouldn't want anything to hold me back from the mountain of fish I'm about to catch."

They each baited a crab pot with fish guts and made sure the ropes were securely fastened to the floats before lowering the pots over the side. Laurel grabbed the salmon poles and handed one to Sterling. They were nice, Sterling thought, but not as nice as the ones Dirk had bought for him and Hoyt. He tried to forget about that as they baited their hooks with herring and let out their lines. They put their poles into holders and sat, watching for signs of biting fish.

It was calm out on the water, and Laurel broke the silence. "So, that man, Dirk . . . I saw you two looking at each other back at the basin. Didn't seem too thrilled to see each other."

"No, I don't think either of us were."

"You hate each other, don't you?"

"I can't speak for Dirk, but he's sure done bad things to us. I suppose he hates me. And, I guess I hate him, too." Sterling kept his eyes on the tip of his fishing pole. "Dirk used to be like a second father to me."

"That must be weird."

"It is. Honestly, it's hard to believe. I even had a dream about him last night. He was chasing me, and I was trying to get away, only I was running in slow-motion and couldn't escape."

"Ugh, I hate that feeling."

"Same here. Dirk was moving fast, and when he caught up with me, I turned to fight him. I won't tell you all the gory details, but it was brutal. We were knocking out each other's teeth and things like that."

"Man, are your dreams always that violent?"

"No. The strange thing was after I woke up, I read that Bible you gave me and found some verse about an eye for an eye and a tooth for a tooth."

"That's the one about turning the other cheek?"

"Yeah, that's it."

"Huh. There could be a lesson in there for you."

"There might be, but it's summer break. No lessons until the fall."

"I'm serious. Don't you wonder why unusual things are happening to you? Did you already forget that a dove delivered a note to you, a note that repeated what John had said? I don't think they're coincidences. Something's definitely happening, but you don't seem to care. You only joke about it."

"That's not true. I *have* been thinking. A lot. And it puzzles me, maybe even freaks me out a little. I'm trying to make sense of the transformation and world-beyond talk, but it's going to take more time. Not to mention, I have other problems to deal with, you know."

"Well, as long as you are thinking about it."

"I can't get it out of my mind."

At the same time, each of their pole tips dipped toward the water. Sterling and Laurel jumped up in unison and set their hooks. Laurel's fish dove, and the line frantically spooled from her reel, making a whistling sound. Sterling's fish did the same, but didn't dive as far. Sterling kept the drag on, and the fish began to tire. It neared the surface, and Sterling could see it was a good size Chinook salmon. Then it dove again, but not as deep as its first dive, and Sterling reeled it back toward the boat. The process repeated itself before Sterling got him next to the boat. Sterling gently lifted its head out of the water. He had never netted his own fish, but as he turned to Laurel for help, he could tell she was completely occupied trying to reel hers in. He picked up the net with his left hand, eased the basket under the fish, and pulled the net up. He lifted his catch into the boat and gloated, "Mark it down—Sterling Burke for Most Fish and Biggest Fish awards."

Laurel nodded to the cabin. "Get the scales from the cupboard. I want facts, not whatever tales your imagination dreams up."

Sterling retrieved the scales and weighed his fish. "Twenty-two pounds!" he shouted.

"The only reason you have the first fish"—Laurel groaned, fighting the one on her line—"is because your minnow was so easy to land. Wait 'til I bring this baby in." Sweat beaded her brow, and she continued the slow rhythm of lifting the pole's tip above her head and then spinning the reel's handle as she lowered the tip. Each hoist pulled the fish a couple of feet closer. After another twenty minutes, Laurel's salmon broke the surface twenty yards away. "Finally." Laurel gasped. But her relief vanished as the salmon dove again and spooled out all the line she had worked so hard to reel in.

"I could take over for you," Sterling offered.

"Just hold my pole while I take my sweater off. And keep the tip up." Sweat drenched the pirate mascot on Laurel's red Peninsula College T-shirt. Laurel took the pole back and continued the fight, working the fish up to the surface. The salmon made its last run, and Laurel pulled it alongside the boat.

Sterling dipped the net and hoisted it into the cockpit, where he hooked it onto the scale.

"Oh," Sterling muttered as he looked at the scale. At forty-eight pounds, Laurel's salmon dwarfed his catch. "You win the Biggest Fish award. At least for now."

He took her behemoth to the fish box at the back of the boat. They each baited their hooks once more to try their luck again. With the poles returned to their holders, Laurel and Sterling sat on the fish box and rested.

After a moment of enjoying the sunshine, Sterling said, "Thanks for bringing me out. I haven't been fishing in a while. Not since . . ."

"Since what?"

"Well, since I went fishing with Dirk. Hoyt and I used to go out on his boat with him—more times than I can count. But those days are long gone. Good riddance, I say."

Laurel said, "I can see why you hate him, but you mentioned that verse earlier. The one about turning the other cheek".

"Yeah, what about it?"

"Have you tried it?"

Sterling's pole dipped toward the water once again, and he jumped up to grab it. As he reeled, he could tell the fish on the line felt like his first one, so he relaxed and cranked slower. Why rush when he needed time to think of an answer to Laurel's question? I might add that it was not the first time a fish saved someone. My old friend Jonah, of course, comes to mind.

Sterling landed his salmon after about ten minutes of reeling, and it was virtually the twin of his first one. Not the monster he was hoping for. Laurel scooped it up and added it to the fish box.

"I win the Most Fish award."

Immediately, Laurel's pole dipped sharply, and the line sung off the reel. She fought the catch for a few minutes, but the struggle was intense and seemed to be wearing her out. "Sterling, you might have to help me with this one." She groaned. "Your arms haven't worked much, and mine haven't recovered from landing my whale."

He reluctantly agreed, and they took turns reeling the fish toward the boat.

"Back to my question," Laurel said, as Sterling shot her a nervous look. "That's right," she continued. "I'm not letting you off the hook. Pun intended. Have you tried turning the other cheek with Dirk?"

The distraction of landing the fish slowed their conversation and gave Sterling time to contemplate his response.

"I've thought about it," he said. "But I can't find the justice in it. Dirk deserves to pay, and turning the other cheek is too good for him. I want him to go to jail."

"Is that how you hope things will end?"

"Ideally? No. But what I really want is impossible."

"What do you want?"

"I wish everything could go back to normal. With Dirk, I mean. I want things to be the way they were two weeks ago."

Laurel took the pole from Sterling to give him a break. She steadily reeled. "How did you feel then?"

"Everything was fine."

"But how did you feel?"

"I wasn't upset. I never had trouble sleeping. I didn't hate anyone."

"Do you want that back?"

"Sure. But I don't see that happening."

"It can happen, but it's up to you. You have to turn the other cheek."

"That's easy for you to say. But it isn't easy for me."

"I didn't say it would be easy, but I have done it. Some guy wouldn't give my necklace back, and the very thought of that person made me angry. Then I turned the other cheek, and it turns out he's a decent guy. Not much of a fisherman, though."

Sterling smiled and took the fishing pole back. He thought about what Laurel said, but he did not respond. He focused instead on landing the fish.

When they finally reeled in Laurel's second fish, they were exhausted and clearly saw why. The fish was at least as big as Laurel's first. "I guess that means you win the Most Room for Improvement award, huh?" she joked.

"I guess so." Sterling laughed, wiping the sweat from his forehead.

"I don't know about you, but I'm beat. Why don't we check those crab pots and head back?"

After they motored over to Laurel's pot, Sterling reached over the side and pulled Laurel's float into the boat. He tried to pull the pot toward the surface, but it was too heavy. "Man. What's going on down there?"

"Hang on." Laurel disappeared into the cabin and returned with an electric pot-puller winch. She set it up and turned it on, and its motor groaned under the load as it steadily cranked the pot toward the surface. Sterling and Laurel watched as the pot emerged with two large Dungeness crabs clinging to the outside of the pot. Laurel pulled the pot into the boat to see what else was inside. It was stuffed with three more similar crabs.

"Wow, nice catch," Sterling said, and he tossed the two freeloader crabs into the fish box, leaving the other three in the pot. Laurel motored over to Sterling's float, and Sterling winched it to the surface. His pot contained five medium-sized Dungeness, notably smaller than Laurel's.

"Pretty good!" Laurel congratulated him. "And don't look so sad. They might not be as big as my haul, but they're not runts either."

"Whatever," Sterling replied. "Your old-timers are probably as tough as railroad spikes."

Laurel ignored him and started the motor to return to the marina. But before she put it in gear, Sterling glanced over the side of the boat and saw a nice halibut floating right on the surface. "Wait! Hand me that," he said, pointing to the gaff hook stowed under Laurel's seat. She did as he asked, and he hauled the halibut onboard and lifted it up for her to see. "Well, well, well! Look who has the most fish now."

Laurel looked at the water on her side of the boat and saw another halibut, which was much larger than Sterling's. She took the hook from Sterling and gaffed the fish. As she tried to lift it, she stopped. "Quick— I need some help here." Sterling joined her, and together they pulled the halibut onboard. They panted, looking down at it. "Not a bad haul for a few hours of fishing," Laurel noted. "We both have our limits of salmon, crab, and halibut. I'll call John to see if he can meet us at the dock with his truck."

"Ask him to bring ice, too," Sterling added, marveling at all their fish. "Lots of it."

When Laurel ended her call, Sterling said to her, "This is the weirdest fishing trip I've ever heard of. I can't believe how much we caught, and I can't believe how big yours are. I expected to pull in at least one of the big ones."

"Maybe you care too much about competition. Yours are fine. You should be satisfied."

"No way, mine are puny. And I don't believe in that 'less is more' idea. More is always better. Anyway, I am still amazed. Did you think we would have this kind of luck when we set out?"

"No, I'm as surprised as you are. But I probably shouldn't be—life with the Master is always an adventure. You never know what might happen or how He will provide."

I had been soaring high above Laurel and Sterling as they motored in, and I floated down, almost to sea level, and hovered ahead of the boat. I vocalized my oowoo-woo-woo call and landed on the prow, perched like a figurehead. Sterling and Laurel both locked their attention on me. Sterling even picked up the net and stepped toward me. He seemed to change his mind, however, because he stopped, set the net down, and was content to watch me. I looked at him over my shoulder, winked, and then flew off.

Sterling kept his eyes on me as long as he could, and he thought about how it was a curious ending to an already strange afternoon. It gave him a funny feeling, and he wondered what other coincidences might come his way.

Twenty-Eight

MONDAY MORNING, TECHS took the early ferry to Seattle to buy the surveillance equipment for Dirk's property. Everything he purchased was state-of-the-art, including a doorbell camera and two military-grade remote cameras, each with infrared detection. The analytics software cost as much as the surveillance equipment, but it was worth it to Techs, especially since it wasn't his money. The software provided both license plate and facial recognition, with automatic zoom when it detected an object in motion.

Back in Port Angeles, Techs installed the cameras to give complete day and night visibility of Dirk's front yard and house. He configured them to send video both to a mobile app and to the analysis software on his own server. Then Techs drove home with Dirk's partially reformatted hard drive to inspect it for damage, as well as for any clues a hacker might have left behind. He connected it to his laptop and sorted through the data using the disk recovery software.

When Techs had spoken with Dirk about it initially, Techs had made it sound like recovering data was very difficult and highly uncertain. But he knew otherwise. Reformatting a disk was like deleting the table of contents from a book—the book might look empty to a novice, but an expert knew how to turn the pages and could reconstruct the table of contents from scratch. Once the disk recovery software finished analyzing Dirk's data, it reconstructed it all into files, and Techs had full visibility of the contents. Much of which Dirk likely would not want him to see.

Techs made a copy of the reconstructed files, in case he would need them for his own purposes later. He then overwrote the Dirk's disk with random data to erase the original, so he could tell Dirk it couldn't be recovered. As he reviewed his copy, Techs noted two suspicious applications that had been downloaded and deleted at some point. They didn't seem to belong to Dirk. Right when Techs was about to inspect the files, however, his phone buzzed.

Techs recognized the number. It was Susan, his old boss from the county. He thought about ignoring it, but as he turned his phone over, he realized there was a slight chance Susan had found out about the fake property tax notices. If so, he would need to know. He answered the call. "Hello, Susan. What a pleasant surprise."

Susan skipped the social niceties. "Techs, we have a problem here and need your expertise. But I don't want to discuss it over the phone. Can you come into the office?"

"Ooh, sorry. Today is packed. Tomorrow, too. The next day might work. I'll have to check my calendar."

"This can't wait. How about four thirty today? You can bill us for a full day."

"This must be important. What does it concern?"

"I'll tell you at four-thirty."

"Okay . . . See you then."

TECHS KNOCKED ON Susan's office door right on time. She opened it and motioned him toward the guest chair across from her. A fast food container lay open on her desk, and Susan held up a finger as she finished chewing a bite of food. "No time for lunch," she said. "It's been one of those days. Thanks for coming in on short notice. How are you?"

"I'm landing on my feet. Things are coming together. So, what's got your hair on fire? A system crash?"

"No, our property tax software has been acting odd. It issued several inaccurate notices—notices that listed multiple years of non-payment and associated interest and penalties. Enough to cause panic." She slid copies of Pete's paperwork across her desk as she continued. "These statements threatened to send the properties to auction if the taxes weren't paid promptly. But the taxes had already been paid. As you can see, the notices look like they came from our system. I don't know if it's a bug or malware or other malicious activity. We need help to figure that out."

"Hmm. That's serious."

"It is, and you're the only one who knows the system inside and out."

Techs picked up the papers to examine them and eased back into his chair. "I don't know about this. I would like to help, but don't see how I can fit it in. I landed a new contract that pays super well, and I don't want to work eighty hours a week. That's what it would take to do both jobs."

Susan leaned forward, setting her elbows on the desk. "Look. I know your contract here ended abruptly. I blame the bean counters for that. You have a right to be sore, but please don't take it out on me. There's no one else I can trust with something this serious. We need you."

Techs glanced out the office window. When he did not respond, Susan added, "We can increase your hourly rate by 25 percent, and you can work part time."

"I'll do it. But I can only give you twenty hours a week until the end of next month. After that, we can talk about increasing it to thirty. Deal?"

"Deal. Now, the first thing I want you to determine is how many taxpayers are affected. I don't want this to blow up in our faces with the elections coming in the fall. Right now, we only know of one property owner—this Peter Burke." She tapped on the papers. "But he said his son heard others mention the same problem. If that's the case, we need to know about it as soon as possible. So, how soon can you start?"

"Well, we're looking at a messy process ahead of us. I'll need to conduct a complete root-cause analysis, which could take as little as a few hours, but a couple of weeks or months is more likely."

"We don't have weeks or months."

"Here's the rub. The better I perform or the luckier I am, the less time I take, and the fewer hours I can bill. Plus, while I'm working on this, I'll be forced to turn down the new business I already have in my sights. So, to make this worthwhile for me, I'll need a non-cancelable work order for four weeks. If I finish this as early as you want, you can put me on other projects—things I can work on part-time so I can manage my other business. If I don't resolve your problem, you can cut me loose after the four weeks, or not. It's up to you."

"Consider it done. We can have that work order ready by tomorrow morning. So, like I said, when can you start?"

"I can make tomorrow morning work."

Susan and Techs shook hands, and Techs stood to leave the office. On the way down to his car, he texted Dirk and told him they needed to meet as soon as possible. He said it was urgent. Dirk replied right away, and they agreed to meet at Techs's boat.

DIRK AND TECHS reached the parking lot at the same time and walked to the docks together. Once they got onboard Techs's boat and entered the privacy of the cabin, Techs said, "Okay. A lot has happened today, and I need to bring you up to speed on several things. First, let me see your phone."

Dirk pulled out his phone and started to hand it over, but he hesitated. "Wait, what's this about?"

"I need to install the surveillance app so you can see the videos and receive the alarms. That okay with you?" Dirk let go of his phone, and Techs explained what he had done. "I installed the cameras at your house and the analysis software on one of my servers. Everything is top-notch, commercial grade, much better than the typical household gear. You've got precision optics, zoom, tilt, audio, and anomaly detection. When something unusual happens, we will each get an alarm, and we can watch the video in real time. Look." He returned Dirk's phone, and two thumbnail pictures scrolled across the screen, one from each camera. Techs reached over and tapped one of them, expanding it to full screen. "You can rewind the feed as well."

"Nice," Dirk noted as he explored the app. "What's the price tag?"

"The gear cost $4,000 and change. I have the receipt. Plus $1,500 for my services."

Dirk looked up from his phone. "Sounds awfully steep."

"Do you want to save a couple of pennies when you have so much at stake?"

Dirk shook his head.

"I didn't think so. Speaking of stakes, there's something else we need to discuss. There's been a complication. With the property taxes."

"Complication?" Dirk frowned. "Is that a delicate way of saying you screwed up?"

"Hey, this isn't on me. It's a fluke."

"What happened?"

"Burke discovered those notices were fake, and he's not going to give another dime to the county."

"A complication, huh?" Dirk's rage bubbled up and exploded. "Don't tell me that! Our plan was perfectly clear. If Pete paid the taxes, we'd pull the money out of the county's purse and split it fifty-fifty. Or, if Pete didn't pay, I would offer to buy up his properties for next to nothing, and we would turn around and sell them for a fortune. Now you're telling me both those options are off the table? That's no *complication*. It's a disaster!"

"I know it's not ideal," Techs said, trying to calm Dirk. "But I can control the blowback. No one will know we did it. I met with someone at the county office, and they're hiring me to figure out what 'went wrong with the system.' They're hiring *me*. For a disaster, I'd say thing are working out well for us. Don't you see? I'm going to deliver preliminary results soon. I'll take the full length of the contract to provide a complete report. I will 'discover' that the new, hot-shot IT guy messed up. His career at the county will be over, and we'll be safe. I have it under control."

"So you say. I still don't feel safe. How did Burke find out?"

"I don't know yet. Susan told me Burke's son heard of other people with the same problem, so Burke double-checked his taxes. But you and I both know no one else had that problem. My guess is that Burke's son stumbled onto something that tipped him off."

"You said this was foolproof, that you knew how to hide your tracks. Obviously, you overrated yourself."

"Not so fast. Remember your whole Bitcoin fiasco? Whoever stole it probably hacked into your computer, and if they did, they could have read our emails discussing the bogus bills."

Dirk sighed and rubbed the side of his face, thinking. "You might be right. But Pete can barely check his own email, let alone hack into mine. His wife is smarter, but she isn't devious enough to think of it."

"What about the son?"

"Sons. They're twins. But they're not even old enough to drive."

"Doesn't matter. Everything they would need to know is on the internet just waiting for them to use it—especially if there are two of them."

"Only one of them has the brains to do this. The other is a jock."

"I'll bet the smart one did it. And my analysis of your hard drive showed me how he pulled it off." Techs explained what he found— evidence of a remote control program. "That's how he reformatted your disk."

"Sterling Burke," Dirk exclaimed. "You're sure it was him?"

"I can't identify the person, but their IP address is located close to your house. Where do the Burkes live?"

"A couple blocks away."

"There you go. We have our target."

Twenty-Nine

The last proceeding of reason is to recognize that there is an infinity of things which are beyond it.

—Blaise Pascal

THE NIGHT BEFORE, Sterling had finished reading the book of Matthew and had also read John from beginning to end. When he woke up the following morning, he reflected on the stories about fish. What was the deal with the Master and fish? Jesus made them multiply like rabbits. It didn't matter if they were dead or alive, or how many they started with—there were always more fish at the end of the story than at the beginning. Once, Jesus started out with two fish and five loaves, and then he fed five thousand men, not counting women and children, and ended up with twelve baskets of leftovers. That was a lot of fish. Another time, when he started out with seven loaves and a few small fish, he fed over four thousand people and ended up with seven large baskets to spare. If that weren't enough, in yet another story, he told the disciples, who had fished all night and caught nothing, to cast their nets out one more time. They listened to him and hauled in 153 large fish.

Sterling thought the fishing episode with Laurel was just as strange. He wondered how her salmon were so much bigger than his. And how her crabs were giants. Two of them hung onto the outside of the pot, practically begging to be caught. Then there were the halibut who conveniently forgot they were bottom dwellers and swam right up to the boat, happy to be gaffed. *That's not to mention that crazy dove,* Sterling thought. *I'll bet he showed up just to bug me. The events of that afternoon seemed to be beyond reason.*

Sterling had forgotten one other instance where the Master spoke about fish, in the thirteenth chapter of Matthew, so I piffed Sterling the passage as a reminder.

"Once again, the kingdom of heaven is like a net that was let down into the lake and caught all kinds of fish. When it was full, the fishermen pulled it up on the shore. Then they sat down and collected the good fish in baskets but threw the bad away. This is how it will be at the end of the age. The angels will come and separate the wicked from the righteous and throw them into the blazing furnace, where there will be weeping and gnashing of teeth."

SOON AFTER BREAKFAST, Sterling got a text from Laurel: "Forgot to tell you. Appt with the director at ten. Can you meet me at the shed in forty mins?"

Sterling responded, "Director?"

"Running Start."

It seemed to Sterling that everything with Laurel was a last-minute fire drill. He was tempted to tell her he was busy. But he was available, and honestly, he wanted to know if he could get into the program a year early. "OK," he replied. "See you in 40."

Sterling dressed in a solid blue polo and gray denim pants, and he tied a gray sweatshirt around his waist. He pulled on his newest tennis shoes and trotted to his bike. Arriving at the shed early, he unlocked the door and stepped inside to make sure the paper with the Bitcoin information was out of sight. With that taken care of, he wheeled the scooter out and was putting on his helmet when Laurel walked up. She wore a collage of mismatched colors that shouted insults at each other. Sterling handed a helmet to her. "That's weird . . ."

"What?"

"I didn't know an art student could be color blind."

She laughed. "Well, for your information art should never be boring. Oh, I wanted to tell you that John said thanks for giving the restaurant your minnows and baby crabs yesterday. The customers loved them."

They hopped on the scooter and left for the college. About a mile and a half from the campus, the scooter's motor sputtered and died. Laurel coasted to the curb and inspected the dashboard. She leaned to the right so Sterling could see over her shoulder and tapped the gas gauge. "I thought it would flash when it got near empty," she said.

"You mean like your helmet is flashing now?"

"Huh? Oh, I get it. Aren't you the funny boy today? So, I'm thinking we can walk to the college or walk the scooter to the gas station. Either way, we're probably going to be late."

"Makes sense to get the gas first."

After wheeling the scooter down the road and filling the gas tank, Laurel and Sterling sped to the campus. They arrived half an hour late, jogged to the Student Services Center, and went straight into the Running Start office. The receptionist looked up, and Laurel explained their delay and apologized for being late. The receptionist gave Laurel a stern look and informed her that the director would be busy until one o'clock. Laurel said that was fine, and she led Sterling back out of the office.

As they left, Laurel suggested, "While we wait, why don't I give you a campus tour? Afterward, we can get takeout at the deli and eat by the reflecting pool. It's a nice place to pass the time."

The college covered about seventy-five acres of land and sat in the foothills of the Olympic Mountains, which stood guard to the south. The northern view took in the harbor, hook, and the strait. Sterling stretched up onto his toes so he could see far enough out onto the water to spot where they had fished the day before. The incident still amazed him.

As they walked, Laurel pointed out the athletic facilities, classrooms, and the combination bookstore and market. They ended their tour at the deli, where Laurel ordered a teriyaki rice bowl, and Sterling chose the build-your-own-sandwich menu and paid for everything. By that point, they had an hour to kill until their appointment, so they went to the arboretum on the east edge of the campus and sat on the lawn to eat.

Sterling took a swig of his Pepsi and asked, "What does it take to be righteous?"

Laurel coughed on her bite of rice. "Where did that come from?"

"I was thinking about it. I read something in the Bible you gave me about the righteous and the wicked. The wicked end up like flaming marshmallows. Lots of wailing, gnashing of teeth, the stench of burning hair. That sort of thing. Obviously, being righteous is the better choice. So, what does it take? How good is good enough? How bad is too bad?"

"Um, where to begin?" she said, caught off guard by Sterling's heavy question. "Actually, John talked to Bethany and me about this a few months ago. I'm pretty sure I remember most of it. The bar for being righteous is set very high. Being righteous means you are innocent, blameless on all accounts—one hundred percent."

"I'm feeling hot already."

"Yeah. Everyone messes up."

"Sure, but I have messed up *a lot.*" He took another bite and spoke with a mouthful of sandwich. "I've done some bad stuff."

"Me too. But that's only the surface. It's the inside that matters most. The real problem is what goes on inside your head, or, I guess, your heart. What we think, what we value, what we're willing to do to get what we want."

"So, hate would count as an inside problem?"

"Exactly. Heart issues are always the hardest to deal with."

"If you only knew."

"I know you hate Dirk. And I'll say it again. You need to forgive him."

"That's not possible. Besides, I'm in the middle of getting even."

"You can always stop. Maybe you should think about backing off and apologize to him."

Sterling looked at Laurel's compassionate smile and wondered what her expression would be if she knew he had broken into Dirk's house and hacked into his computer. Not to mention stealing the Bitcoin. Especially stealing the Bitcoin. Then a new and sobering thought grabbed his attention. *Why hide it? Why not find out what she'll do? Get it over with.* He finished chewing and cleared his throat. "Will you promise to keep a secret?"

She nodded.

"Say it out loud."

"Yes, I promise to keep a secret."

"You can't tell anyone. Not even Bethany."

"Not even Bethany."

"Okay. I broke into Dirk's house. More than once. I hacked into his computer and spied on his emails. And I stole all his cryptocurrency."

After a moment of silence, Laurel mumbled, "And I thought the necklace was bad." She looked up at Sterling. "Even after all that, the Master will forgive you if you ask him. He can make you innocent, despite what you've done."

"Really? It's that easy? Sounds weird to me." Sterling thought it sounded too good to be true. He was convinced he was headed for the fire.

"I know how it sounds at first, but it'll make sense if you keep reading. Believe me. I was in your place not too long ago."

Sterling stared down at the rest of his sandwich. "I guess I'm not as hungry as I thought." He stood and walked over to a trash can to dump his lunch. He stopped and turned around, noticing that Laurel had not moved. He returned and extended his hand down to her. "Want to head back to the director's office?" She took his hand without saying a word, and he pulled her up. "Sorry to disappoint you," he added. "I'll understand if you want nothing to do with me."

"That's not what I'm thinking," she said. "You need a friend now more than ever."

Back at the Running Start office, they sat in silence as they waited for their appointment. The receptionist was gone from her desk, and when she returned, she said, "Mr. Chris got back early from lunch. I told him you were here, and he said you're welcome to head to his office down the hall. He's expecting you."

Laurel knocked on the door, and Mr. Chris called them in. Laurel greeted him warmly and reminded him that Sterling was the friend who was interested in early admission into Running Start.

"Oh, yes," Mr. Chris noted, motioning toward his two guest chairs. "Please, have a seat." After the three of them sat, and Sterling and Mr. Chris got acquainted, Mr. Chris asked, "So, Sterling, why do you want into this program? And why do you think we should admit you in your sophomore year?"

Sterling corrected his posture and looked directly into Mr. Chris's hazel eyes. "I am an excellent student, and I love working with computers. I have taught myself how to program, and I never miss my school's science club meetings. But there's only so much I can do on my own. I want to learn more, like advanced programming and cybersecurity. Mr. Keller, the science club adviser at my school, would agree that I'm ready for the challenge, and that's what I hope Running Start can offer."

Mr. Chris leaned back in his chair. "I know Mr. Keller—and his '67 Goat. He and I go way back. I'll touch base with him about this. If he says you can walk on water and everything else checks out, we can admit you for two afternoon classes."

Sterling tried to hide his excitement, but it was obvious on his face. Mr. Chris smiled and continued, "The way it works is that you'd attend your high school in the morning and take two classes here in the afternoon. Only one can be technical—the other must be English or psychology or something from our humanities department. Understand, you would be on probation for the first term, which means we'll be monitoring your progress to make sure you have what it takes to stay afloat."

"I understand," Sterling replied. "I promise I won't disappoint you."

"Glad to hear it. I'll speak with Mr. K., and then I'll get hold of your high school counselor and your transcript to ensure everything is in order. You should hear from me in a couple of weeks. These things move slowly during the summer. By the way, I believe you need to thank Ms. Mercury here. She gave you a glowing recommendation that convinced me to meet with you today." Mr. Chris took a long look at Laurel and added, "You know, Meryl, I can't help but think how much you look like your mother did when we were in high school. Please, tell her hello for me."

Sterling and Laurel thanked Mr. Chris and exited his office. As they walked back to Laurel's scooter, Sterling said, "Thanks for setting this up for me. And for putting in a good word. I owe you."

"You're welcome. You can pay me back by not blowing this. Wouldn't want me to look like a dummy for praising you, now would we?"

"Definitely not." Sterling laughed, but his excitement about Running Start faded as his thoughts returned to righteousness and flaming marshmallows. How could he be forgiven? Could he forgive Dirk? He and Laurel both grew quiet as they walked toward the parking lot.

"You're right," Sterling said finally, pulling them both from their thoughts. "About me needing a friend. Thanks for sticking with me."

"Maybe my colorblindness extents to people," she teased, "and I don't see how badly you and I clash. Or maybe I like our friendship, and that's why I'm sticking around."

"Well, I hope it's the second reason."

"Don't worry. I think it is."

Thirty

TECHS'S ALARM BLASTED him out of bed at half past six. He showered, dressed, and drove to the café he had frequented when he worked for the county. He had his usual—black coffee and the three-egg scramble with whole wheat toast—and left a generous tip before driving to the county offices five minutes before eight.

By force of habit, he walked into his old office, oblivious to the new name on the nameplate. He startled the young man seated at the desk there. "My bad," Techs apologized. "Wrong office."

"Wait, you must be Techs," the young man said. "Come on in, I figured this was your old spot." He stood up and shook Techs's hand. "Josh Parnell. I'm the new IT Supervisor. Susan told me you're going to investigate that property tax issue for us. We'll take all the help we can get."

"It's my pleasure." Techs forced a smile and backed his way through the office doorway. "I better get to work—"

"Just a sec," Josh called out. "I'm sure you know your way around here, but I need to update you on a couple of changes, namely the centralized access management system I installed. Now, instead of using separate usernames and passwords to log into each system, we all log in once to the access manager, and provided we have permission, it logs us into the individual business systems we need." Josh reached for a stack of papers on his desk and handed one to Techs. "This single set of credentials will get you into the access manager, and it will let you access the property tax system. And our centralized log management system. That is the second change I implemented."

Techs read over the information. "You've certainly been busy, haven't you?"

Josh thanked him, though it wasn't a compliment. "Security was lacking when I stepped in, hence the changes. Speaking of the log management system, each of our business systems now forwards a record of all activity to the central system. Every log in, every command a user enters is recorded there. So, if someone here created those tax statements you're investigating, that would be the place to look."

Techs nodded and maintained a strong poker face. "Convenient."

"You can use the cubicle at the end of the hall." Josh pointed. "It's the one farthest from the windows. Let me know if you need anything."

Techs walked to his desk and set up his laptop. He logged into the new access manager and spent the rest of the morning familiarizing himself with the log records, especially looking for activity that pointed to him. At noon, he returned to his favorite café and texted Dirk to meet him at the dock at 5:15. After taking a full hour for lunch, Techs returned to his cubicle, slipped off his loafers, and stuffed earbuds into his ears. He reopened the activity records and searched for any trace of the fake tax notices he had created. The system pinpointed the statements and, after several hours, confirmed their origin—a phantom user account. Techs breathed a sigh of relief. As he had planned, the tax notices could not be linked to him. He knew he was safe. Still, he tried to delete the record so no one else could inspect it. But his account did not have permission for him to perform that action. Instead, he spent the rest of the day combing through files for any other evidence that might be used against him. That task was as boring as reading through pages of phone book entries. Shortly after five, Techs decided he had done enough for one day and packed his things, went to his car, and drove across to the Boat Basin.

IT WAS FIVE thirty by the time Techs arrived at the docks. He found Dirk sitting in a chair on *Leverage*'s rear deck, and Dirk waved him over. As Techs stepped aboard and took a seat next to him, Dirk said, "I've been thinking about our talk yesterday. About the possibility that Sterling Burke hacked into my computer. If that's true, we have no idea what he found, what he knows. Sterling's a genius, at least for a kid his age, and I'm uneasy at the thought of certain information being in his hands."

"You tell me where he lives. I can easily convince them to answer some questions. I can be very persuasive, if you get my drift."

Dirk dismissed the idea with a wave of his hand. "Not yet. If you shake him up, and he's not involved, it'll stir up a hornet's nest. He could go to the cops. I need hard evidence, something solid that shows his involvement. His brother's, too."

"I'm okay with waiting for a couple of days. Three at the most. After that, we need to move in on them before they involve the law."

Dirk pulled a picture from his pocket and handed it to Techs. "Here's a photo of the boys. The hacker is probably the one on the left, the one with the scar. That's Sterling. Those cameras you installed should catch them if they come near my house. Beyond that, we'll just have to keep our eyes open."

"How about a car?" Techs asked. "Do they drive? I could hide a homing device under their vehicle."

"No. I told you, they're too young. They ride bikes." Dirk reached down and grabbed a paper bag that sat between his feet. He pulled out two burner phones. "I already gave one of these to Bert. I showed him their picture, and he'll keep watch around here. I programmed each phone with our numbers. If you see either boy, call me. Don't take action on your own."

Techs took the phone. "Suit yourself. You know, while we're on the subject of working together, there's something else we need to discuss."

"What is it?"

Techs looked around, and although no one was near, he lowered his voice. "I recovered the data from your hard disk and found more than evidence of the remote control software. You were foolish not to have encrypted your data, especially since you're involved in an illegal smuggling operation."

Dirk scoffed, "What on earth are you talking about?"

"Your attempt to hide it was amateurish. Laughable, actually. I first got suspicious when I saw that big deck crane over there. When I asked about it, your answer was lame. You said you wanted to help a friend salvage relics from an old shipwreck. Please—you'd never put such an ugly monstrosity on your pride and joy, so I knew you were up to something. When I found emails sent to you from a cryptic email address, I got curious. The content was gibberish at first, but I went back and analyzed them."

"This is ridiculous. You're dreaming."

"Really? Let's see if I can refresh your memory. Each message contained scrambled GPS coordinates and times and an attached audio file. I deciphered the coordinates pretty easily and found they were locations in the strait. The dates and times were trickier to solve, but I noticed they always coincided with low tides during moonless nights. The audio almost stumped me—I thought they were recordings of whale sounds at first. But then I remembered a news story I read a few years ago. It was about a group of local crab fishermen caught up in an illegal operation to double their haul. They just so happened to collect their extra, unlicensed crab pots in the strait, at low tide, on moonless nights. Isn't that a funny coincidence?"

"Hilarious," Dirk grumbled.

"Well, what really got me was how they recovered their pots, since their marker buoys were hidden beneath the surface. As it turns out, each buoy was attached to a remotely controlled motor that responded to specific sounds. When the fishermen were above the pots, they used speakers beneath their boats to play a certain audio file, and the crab pot motors would recognize the sound and let out line until the buoys rose to the surface. The crabbers could then haul in the pots, using a deck winch similar to yours. Does this ring any bells for you?"

"I didn't see the news article."

"I see. I'm not sure why I thought you would have known about it. . . Oh, that's right! When the crabbers were busted, your friend, Bert, was named as a person of interest. But the police couldn't prove his involvement, so they let him go."

Dirk stood up to leave. "I don't have time for this."

"Make time," Techs snapped. "Sit down."

Dirk exhaled and took his seat. "Go on."

"Thank you. Here's the situation. I suspected you were using that crane for smuggling, so last night I followed you on my boat, lights off and from a distance. I got close enough to film you with an infrared camera I picked up in Seattle. I'm sure the cops would be interested if someone anonymously sent them the video."

Dirk looked over his shoulder at the winch and then turned back to Techs with an expression of both respect and resentment. "Well, well. You have done your homework, haven't you? When you first asked me about the winch, I was afraid you were suspicious. I worried you might try to hack into my computer to find out more. That's why I suspected you of stealing my Bitcoin."

"Anyone with an ounce of technical smarts could have hacked into your computer. Your security is pathetic. The Burke boys probably stole your Bitcoin. They'll admit it when we question them."

"Skip the lecture. How much do you want to keep quiet?"

"I want in on your smuggling operation. Your lousy security wiped out my income from the fake taxes Burke should have paid to us, so you owe me. It looks like you are clearing $40,000 a month from your little transportation business. I'll settle for 25 percent of that."

"And what will you do to earn it?"

"I'll keep quiet. Plus, I'll provide proper security, and I am sure I can think of some ways to expand your operation. You could end up pulling in more than before."

"It's an interesting idea. I'll think about it."

"Fair enough." Techs nodded. "But the way I see it, you don't really have a choice."

Thirty-One

LATE ONE LAZY afternoon, Sterling pulled the Xbox console and car racing cockpit from his closet, where they had been gathering dust for over three months. He hooked them up to his external monitor, loaded his racing game, and took a 2007 Mustang GT for a spin. Roaring through the city streets, he leaned into each turn and smoked the tires at every chance. He was having fun until he remembered the mess he was in with Dirk. If Pete caught him going after Dirk, Sterling knew the video game would be as near as he got to driving a real Mustang for a long time. He tried to push it out of his mind and slammed through the gears on the simulated streets, blowing by a Camaro and driving on the sidewalk.

As Sterling raced through traffic, Laurel texted him. "Found old pics of your mom and Dirk."

Sterling read the message twice. This would not help him forget about things. He replied, "Can you talk?" Laurel sent a thumbs-up, so Sterling called her.

"What pictures?"

Laurel explained that after Mr. Chris told her how much she and her mother looked alike, she dug out her mother's high school yearbook from the closet. "That's how I found pictures of a young Dirk McCleod and Anne Baker. Looked like they were named

Homecoming King and Queen." She described another picture of them smiling googly-eyed at each other and holding hands. "The senior class voted them the school's cutest couple."

"How is that possible?" Sterling felt deceived. He had always assumed his parents met Dirk around the time Pete and Dirk formed their partnership. "Laurel, I need to see those pictures. Please send them to me."

"Sure. Give me a few minutes. I already put the yearbook away."

"Thanks . . . I guess. Are they going to make me sick?"

"I can't say."

They disconnected, and three minutes later, Sterling was cringing at the pictures on his phone. He emailed the pics to his laptop so he could enlarge them. The pictures were every bit as disturbing as Sterling had imagined. He charged out to the driveway, where Hoyt was shooting baskets. Hoyt made a free throw, got the rebound, and then passed the ball to Sterling. Sterling caught it with one hand and put it on the ground.

"Hey," Hoyt complained, "what gives?"

Sterling held out his phone. "Look at these pictures."

Hoyt glanced at the phone, and, when he realized what he was looking at, pulled it closer and enlarged the picture. "That's Mom? And Dirk?" He swiped to the next picture.

"It gets worse. Read the captions."

"The *cutest couple?* "He gasped.

Sterling took his phone back. "I never would have believed it, but this is no Photoshop scam. It's real."

"Do you think Pete knows? And why didn't Mom tell us when she was talking about Dirk hitting on her?"

"I don't know. They owe us an explanation." He picked up the ball and clanged a shot off the back of the rim. As the shadows lengthened, he and Hoyt took turns shooting. Neither of them spoke for some time, as they were consumed by their thoughts. Nearly an hour later, Pete's SUV drove up to the house, and his headlights sliced into the driveway, blinding the boys.

They stepped out of the way as Pete pulled into the garage, and no sooner had he parked than Anne's car turned into the driveway. Pete's garage door shut, and Anne's opened, as if the two doors were winking at the boys. Both parents walked out to greet them.

Anne smiled and gave each one a hug and peck on the cheek. "Isn't this a nice surprise? All of us are at home and awake at the same time. We should spend the evening together since your dad and I are leaving for that real estate seminar tomorrow. We need to be out the door by five o'clock to get a spot on the 7:05 ferry."

"Ugh, don't remind me." Pete groaned.

"Why don't you come inside for dessert?" Anne asked the boys. "Let's meet in the kitchen. I bought a dozen cookies, and the last time I looked, we had a carton of ice cream in the freezer."

Sterling and Hoyt's lack of enthusiasm was evident on their faces.

"Something the matter?" Anne asked.

"We really need to talk," Sterling said. "About . . . something. Meet us in the living meeting room. Five minutes."

"Oh. All right." Pete and Anne gave each other a puzzled look and walked into the house.

STERLING AND HOYT were already in the living room, sitting on either end of the couch, when their parents entered. Pete relaxed into his armchair, leaned back, and kicked his feet up on the footstool. Anne sat on the armrest next to him and put an arm around his shoulders. Pete asked, "So, what's going on? What's so important that it can't wait until after cookies and ice cream? Another confession?"

Sterling looked over at Hoyt and back to Pete. "Possibly." He cleared his throat, and his eyes shifted to Anne. "Mom, we want to know how long you have known Dirk."

She replied, "Well, we knew each other back in high school. We met during our junior year and became friends the next year. Your father, too. Why do you ask?"

Hoyt started to speak, but Sterling cut him off and took out his phone. Sterling showed her the pictures from the yearbook and said, "It looks like you were more than friends."

Anne looked at the picture and nodded. "Yes, that's true. It must be a surprise to you, but Dirk and I were more than casual friends. He was my boyfriend during our senior year."

"A surprise to us?" Hoyt blurted. "How about a shock? Or electrocution?"

Sterling asked, "Do you think your past *friendship* might have had something to do with Dirk betraying us?"

"It could have. I think he wanted to rekindle the old flame. But that fire turned to ashes a long time ago. At least mine has."

"Dirk broke it off right after graduation. He found a new girlfriend, some hot girl who had moved to town," Pete added. "Err, not that your mother wasn't hot herself."

"Ew." Sterling and Hoyt moaned in unison.

Anne squeezed Pete's neck lovingly. "Nice save, honey. Anyway, Dirk went away to college in Bellingham, and your father and I started seeing each other. Plus, Dirk fished during the summers, so I didn't see him for several years. After college, he worked in Seattle until moving back to PA, and that was nine years ago. Pete and Dirk's paths crossed in the real estate world, and they renewed their acquaintance."

Sterling asked, "Do you really think that explains why he turned on us?"

"Relationships are complicated," Pete explained. "Unresolved issues might disappear for a while, but then something can trigger them again."

"What unresolved issues, exactly?"

Pete and Anne paused and shared an uncomfortable look. Anne said, "We didn't want to tell you this until you were older—"

"But," Pete interjected, "Dirk finally realized he had made a mistake when he dumped your mother for Miss Hottie. Of course, *I've* known that for years. He wanted to pick up where he left off in high school. When your mother put him in his place, he went off the deep end."

Anne agreed. "I think he became increasingly resentful of Pete over the years. Pete not only wound up with me, but he was also the brains of their partnership. The visionary, the deal-maker. Yes, Dirk was charismatic and useful, but he was the roadie for the rock star, necessary, but he knew he could be replaced. I think he felt threatened, and he let bitterness take root. And I know bitterness can start out small, like a pebble in your shoe. But it doesn't stay that way. You can't get it out of your mind, and it grows into something much worse.

"I experienced that after Dirk dumped me—deserted me, really. At first, I felt abandoned, but that feeling turned into a deep-rooted hatred. I couldn't think of anything else. I quit enjoying the things I used to love. One day, I finally realized I needed to forgive him. It was a long process, but each day I hated him less and less. Pete and other friends helped me move past Dirk. Soon, I realized I got a much better man than Dirk would ever be."

Hoyt asked, "So, you're saying Dirk has always been jealous of Pete and couldn't take it anymore?"

"In a nutshell, yes," Pete answered. "And he can be ruthless. Fortunately, we caught him in his scheme before things got worse. Now, our finances are looking better, and with your mother working, the future looks bright." Pete patted Anne on the knee, then looked back at Sterling and Hoyt. "Does this answer your questions? Is the family meeting over?"

Both boys nodded, but Sterling wasn't sure he and Hoyt knew the whole story.

Thirty-Two

In faith, there is enough light for those who believe and enough shadows to blind those who don't.

—Blaise Pascal

WITH HIS LIFE hopefully returning to normal, Sterling decided to revisit his UROV project and make some extra money. He called the manager at the Boat Basin and pitched his business idea, explaining how UROV could inspect boat hulls so owners would know when they needed to pull their boats out of the water to hydro-wash them. He talked about how it could even boost the Basin's hydro-washing business, and he concluded by asking for permission to post fliers on the message boards at the entrance to each dock. The idea intrigued the manager, and he gave Sterling the go-ahead. Sterling thanked him and offered an hour of free services to inspect the pilings under one dock.

Sterling designed the fliers, which described the service and listed his rates and phone number. When he finished, he texted Laurel on a whim. "Want to help me with something at the marina this morning?"

She replied, "Sure. Can I pick you up in 30?"

He agreed and hurried to get ready. He printed ten fliers, slid each into a waterproof plastic sleeve that he borrowed from Pete's desk, and put his fliers and a box of thumbtacks, also borrowed from Pete, into his backpack. Then he rushed to eat a bowl of cereal before Laurel arrived with her scooter.

Twenty minutes later, Sterling and Laurel were tacking up fliers across the docks. They spread out to get the job done faster, and when they met up again, Laurel brought a man Sterling didn't recognize with her. Laurel introduced him. "This is Mr. Watanabe," she said. "He saw me putting up your poster and wants to know more about you inspecting his boat."

Sterling explained his process, and Mr. Watanabe apparently liked what he heard. After Sterling finished his spiel, Mr. Watanabe hired Sterling on the spot to inspect his boat. He took a business card from his wallet and wrote his slip number on it. Sterling took the card and promised to email a link to the UROV video in two or three days.

When Mr. Watanabe returned to his boat, Sterling turned and high-fived Laurel. "How about I buy you brunch to celebrate landing my first inspection job?"

AS THEY STOOD just inside the restaurant door and waited to be seated, Bethany waved at them. She signaled for Laurel over to her. "Sam called in sick again," Bethany said. "I know you aren't scheduled until noon, but is there any chance you can start now?"

Laurel shook her head. "Sorry, Sterling is buying me brunch."

"Oh? Lucky girl."

"Quit it—it's not like that. I can take Sam's shift whenever we're done. Maybe around eleven?"

Sterling watched the exchange from across the room, and he saw Laurel whisper something to Bethany. Bethany nodded in agreement. She picked up a menu and motioned for Sterling to follow her and Laurel to a table.

They sat by the window again. When Bethany took their orders, Laurel said, "I'll have the omelet, egg whites only, with avocado, tomatoes, and goat cheese. Nine-grain toast, dry. And coffee to drink, black."

Sterling ordered a short stack of pancakes topped with an over-easy egg and two extras, peanut butter and strawberries. He asked for coffee to wash it down.

"Woof," Laurel said, crinkling her nose. "Are you really going to eat that combo?"

Sterling grinned. "It may look bad, like the colors you throw together, but it'll taste great. I hope. Even if it doesn't, I'll never tell you."

"Be that way," Laurel teased. After Bethany poured their coffees and walked back to the kitchen, Laurel said, "So, I've been thinking about the question you asked me. About how to be righteous."

"And?"

"And I don't think it's possible—"

"Yup. I thought it was too good to be true."

"Wait, I wasn't finished." Laurel laughed. "I was going to say it's not possible unless you let the Master take control of your life. He's our only shot at righteousness. I know he will forgive you, transform you, and lead you into the life of the kingdom beyond. He'll show you how to live and what to do with the kleptocurrency you stole."

"*Crypto*currency."

"Whatever. *Klepto*currency. *Crypto*currency. In this case, either works, but that's not my point. I think you need to figure out how important that money is to you. If it is too important, you need to reconsider what you're doing. Did you read where the Master says, 'Anyone who loves their life will lose it, while anyone who hates their life in this world will keep it for eternal life?'"

"Sounds vaguely familiar, but it's more mumbo-jumbo to me."

"I get that, but John explained it to Bethany and me a while back. It's technical, but enlightening."

"I like technical."

"Not like computer technical. It's Greek technical. It involves understanding the verse as it was written in the Greek."

"Got it. It's all Greek to me anyway," Sterling said with a smirk.

"That word *life* the Master uses refers to our soul life."

"Huh?"

"It's our selfish will, our untransformed mind and emotions. So, if we love our soul life as it is now, we will miss out on transformation. Because we're afraid to lose our current soul life. But if we hate our soul life, we will gain a new one for eternal life, because it's been transformed. We all need to be transformed, to be made new. Does that make sense?"

Sterling thought about it, but the transformation talk was still a foreign language to him, especially when Greek was added to the lingo. "I think so," he said. "It's like installing a major update on my computer."

"Well . . ."

But before Laurel could respond further, Bethany brought out their food, to Sterling's relief. She put their meals on the table and said to Sterling, "That is an unusual combination. Hope you enjoy it."

"Believe me, I will," Sterling said, giving her a thumbs-up. "I am going to savor every bite." He sat still while Laurel prayed quietly. After she looked up, he evenly spread the peanut butter on the top pancake until it looked like a professionally iced cake. Then he slid the egg off its plate onto the stack of pancakes without breaking the yolk. Finally, he added the sliced strawberries and drizzled syrup over the absurd mountain of food. He leaned back to appreciate his work. Laurel snapped a picture as Sterling sliced out his first bite. He and smiled, lifting the forkful of food up to his mouth to pose for another picture.

After he savored his first bite, he said, "Have you noticed how weird our conversations are?"

"What do you mean?"

"I was thinking about how we keep circling back to this *transformation* thing. Do you have any idea how strange that sounds? How unusual you are? None of my other friends try to change each other. And they accept me the way I am. They think that I'm an okay guy. Not perfect, but good enough."

"Change isn't a bad thing, Sterling. That's what I'm getting at. Besides, I'm not trying to change you for my sake. I'm trying to change you for your sake." She took a sip of coffee and shook her head. "Wait, no. No, that's not right. What I mean is that I want you to let the Master change you. So you let go of your selfish soul life and pursue a new spiritual life. We all need to do that, especially me."

"All right then. So, tell me, how are you doing with that?"

Laurel stopped cutting into her omelet. She leaned toward Sterling and asked, "Are you asking me this so you will have a few minutes to eat in peace while I explain, or do you really want to know?"

"Both. But mostly I want to eat this thing before it gets cold."

She resumed carving a bite out of her omelet. "I guess I'm learning a lot. I don't think people can transform themselves, at least not on the inside where it counts. They can temporarily change what's on the outside. You know, what they let other people see. But they can't transform hatred into love. I know I can't. I've tried, and although I made temporary headway, it didn't last. That's why I go into the garden to read, to listen, to meditate, to pray. Something happens whenever I'm there."

Laurel stopped talking when Bethany approached to refill their coffees.

Sterling put his hand over his cup to signal he had enough. After Bethany stepped away, Sterling said, "The garden sounds interesting. I want to see it for myself."

"You would like it, but you need faith to enter it and experience what I'm talking about."

"Hang on. If it's real, and not imaginary, I can visit it without faith. Faith is for things that aren't real."

"Oh, it's real. And it's transforming."

"All the more reason to see it." Sterling poked a stray strawberry with his fork. "Where is it?"

"It's close." She gestured to the window. "Just across the pool below the waterfall."

"Okay. And how does it transform?"

"Well, that's where faith plays a big part. Let me explain it this way.

When you found my necklace and refused to give it back, I despised you. Even after Hoyt paid for it and gave my necklace back, I still despised you. I fantasized you died a slow, painful death. My inner response was much worse than what you did, and I realized that soon after I walked away. I knew I was wrong and wanted to change. But I couldn't—at least not on the inside. Then you told me you were sorry. That confirmed to me that I needed to forgive you. I wanted to forgive you, but inside, I couldn't replace my bitterness with love and forgiveness." She took another sip of her coffee and paused, hoping Sterling would say something, anything. But he held his stoic expression.

"I went into the garden that night," Laurel continued, "and read about the Master forgiving me as I forgave others. I asked Him to help me. A few days later, I went back to the garden a second time and did the same thing. It helped. It's like my bitterness was an ugly sandcastle on the beach that held resentment in and kept forgiveness out. Each visit to the garden was like a wave from the incoming tide, and each one removed more of the castle, washing it away a little at a time. That was almost two weeks ago, and now it's gone. Compassion has replaced my bitterness, and that compassion is making me want your transformation and not your slow, excruciating death."

Sterling scowled. "How do you think that makes me feel? Am I such a loser that you struggled for days to get to where you no longer wanted to see me tortured and dead?"

Laurel wanted to answer, but she didn't know what to say.

Sterling stood, pulled a twenty and a ten out of his wallet, and slapped them onto the table. "I'm out of here. You can finish your breakfast in peace." With that, he strode out the front door and texted Hoyt that he was on his way.

Bethany walked over to the table with the check and asked, "What got into him?"

"I messed up. I was trying to explain transformation, but it all went wrong. I thought if I could show him how much the Master changed me, it would give him hope for himself."

"That boy is unstable. And I prayed for him like you asked."

"He's confused." Laurel handed Bethany the money from the table. "I'm going to stop by the garden after work. I need to pray about how to patch things up with Sterling. He could always use our prayers."

IN EXCEPTIONAL TIMES, it has not been unknown for the kingdom beyond to converge with specific places in the material world. Canaan's Garden is such a place. It is physical ground where people can move beyond to commune with the Master and get a glimpse of the future kingdom, a kingdom where the wolf will live with the lamb and plants will bring forth bountiful fruit. Despite its serenity, Canaan's Garden is only a small instance of such convergence. The greatest one happened somewhere else for three brief years, over two thousand years ago.

Thirty-Three

STERLING ARRIVED AT the shed sweaty, irritated, and late. Hoyt had already taken out the lawnmower and edger and was leaning against the locked shed door by the time Sterling showed up. As Sterling walked his bike to the door to store it inside, he mumbled, "Sorry I'm late. Couldn't be helped."

Hoyt responded, "Let's get moving." He pointed at the edger and started pushing the mower. "At two o'clock, I'm meeting some guys from the team at the park for conditioning drills."

Sterling locked up the shed again and picked up the edger. "No worries, we'll be done by then. If not, I'll finish up by myself."

As they walked to do their first yard, Hoyt said, "I've been thinking. Since Pete and Mom are away for the whole week, do you want to do something fun? Like, something crazy? Now's our big chance."

"No. I think I might steal a few necklaces, kick a dog or two. Maybe hijack someone's identity."

Hoyt stopped pushing the mower. "Whoa. You're in bad shape, aren't you? Girl troubles?"

"More like the girl is having boy troubles—with me. Turns out I'm not good enough for her."

"Ouch. What happened?"

"Eh, I don't want to talk about it. It's not worth it."

Hoyt continued with the mower as Sterling pushed in his earbuds and blasted his brain with one of his favorite playlists. Later, the boys finished the first yard without talking, except for when Hoyt pointed out two small strips of grass Sterling had missed. They worked the other two jobs in the same way. When they returned to that shed shortly after 1:00 p.m., Sterling broke his silence by saying, "I'm going for a ride," and he left Hoyt to lock up.

STERLING WONDERED IF Hoyt had a good idea about doing something fun while their parents were away, especially since their shared sixteenth birthday was the next day. Sterling continued cruising on his bike until he reached the ferry terminal, and he sat on an empty bench there to consider the possibilities. He watched the ferry fade into the distance as it cruised toward Victoria, and for a moment, he considered taking the evening ferry himself. At least that would be fun and out of the ordinary. But he dropped the idea when he remembered his family was planning to take that very trip the following week to celebrate his and Hoyt's birthday. *Might as well let Pete pay the forty bucks*, Sterling decided.

A breeze blew off the water, and the smell of the salty air reminded him of sitting nearby with Laurel. It's remarkable how a simple smell can trigger a memory, though in this case, it was a memory Sterling was not eager to recall. He wanted to get out of town to clear his head and think, at least for a night or two. But with no car and not much money, his options were limited. After thinking for a while, he realized an overnight backpacking trip would be perfect. It could be a mini vacation from his computer, yard work, and Laurel.

Sterling remembered Hoyt would be starting his conditioning drills soon and texted him. "Great idea. Backpack into PJ Lake? Want to join me for our birthday?"

"Can't," Hoyt replied. "I'm going to be wiped out after training."

"Suit yourself. I'm going anyway. See you tomorrow."

Sterling rode home and loaded up his backpack. In addition to the basic camping gear, he grabbed two freeze-dried meals from the camping bin and a water bottle. After patting his pockets and taking one last look around, he decided he had everything he needed to set out, so he strapped on his backpack and walked to Mount Angeles Road. As the occasional car came up behind Sterling, he stuck his thumb out, hoping for a lift. The third vehicle kindly pulled over—a pickup driven by a middle-aged man who looked like he belonged in the outdoors. He lowered the passenger window and called out for Sterling to toss his pack in the back of the truck and climb in.

Sterling did as the man instructed and told him where he was headed. "You can drop me at the Obstruction Point Road intersection. I can walk to the trailhead from there."

"Don't worry about it," the driver said. "I can take you to right the trailhead. It's only a few miles out of my way, and I'm in no rush." At the intersection, the man turned onto the unpaved road and asked Sterling, "Hiking out to the lake?"

"That's the plan."

"How many nights are you roughing it?"

"Just one. I'll hike out in the morning."

"Should be a fine evening for it."

Before Sterling could say anything else about it, the truck's bouncing over one pothole and then another interrupted him. After nearly three more bone-jarring miles, they stopped at the empty parking area, and Sterling climbed out. He grabbed his pack, thanked the man, and started hiking.

His destination was only a mile away, but the trail to get there was difficult—either descending or ascending for nine hundred feet of elevation gain. Sterling's legs burned as he climbed past the waterfall up to the lake. He paused to catch his breath and gaze over the tranquil water. As far as Sterling could tell, no other campers were at the lake, so he had his pick of campsites. He followed a fisherman's trail around the edge of the lake to the far side, where he chose a secluded lake-front spot. Sterling pitched his tent, inflated his sleeping pad, and unstuffed his sleeping bag before taking a leisurely stroll by the water while it was still light. He walked around the entire lake, exploring a few side trails here and there, and was back where he started in less than an hour. Back at his camp, Sterling filled some time by skipping stones across the water and sitting on a log to watch small trout leap after bugs. Sterling looked at his phone, but it didn't have coverage and the battery was at 50 percent.

The great outdoors now seemed less than great, and Sterling had a sinking feeling he might be in for a boring night. He regretted not bringing a fishing pole, a book, or his earbuds. He set up his small stove on the log and boiled water to rehydrate his beef stew. Eating dinner occupied him for a few minutes, but he wished there was time to pack everything up and hike out before the sun set behind the mountains. But the shadow crawling up the mountain to his right warned him that dark comes early in the mountains, and he hunkered down for the night.

Sterling looked around as he heard voices coming from across the lake. Three older boys—likely home from college, he guessed—stepped out from the trail. They made their camp directly across the lake from Sterling, and one of them started a campfire, despite the rules against it. Then came the blast of rap music, and the bass rumbled across the small lake and into Sterling's ears. He had forgotten how much he disliked rap, and he hoped they had forgotten to charge the speaker's battery.

Occasionally, the boys' laughter traveled over the lake with the music, which made Sterling more and more aware of his boredom, and he wondered why he did not ask a friend to join him camping. With a few texts, Hoyt could have gathered at least five friends from the football team. But Sterling's friends from the science club were loners who acted lost without a computer in front of them. They probably would not have enjoyed backpacking, but Sterling figured one or two of them might have been desperate enough for friendship to try it out. In his solitude, without his screens around to distract him,

Sterling regretted lost friendships with Dirk and Laurel. Not to mention the coldness he had shown to his own brother. It didn't surprise Sterling that he found himself alone on the edge of the wilderness.

When dusk reached his campsite, it brought cooler air and swarms of mosquitoes. Sterling retreated into his tent, zipped the entrance shut, and clapped three buzzing mosquitoes that had chased him inside. He flopped onto his sleeping bag and played an old video game on his phone that didn't require the internet. He kept an eye on his phone's battery to save enough charge for the morning and his long walk to town. When the battery level dropped to 10 percent, Sterling powered off his phone and reached into his pack for the one luxury he had thought to bring from home—his Bible. In the waning light, he turned to the book of John, and as he read, he noticed the line, "To the Jews who had believed him, Jesus said, 'If you hold to my teaching, you are really my disciples. Then you will know the truth, and the truth will set you free.'" Sterling wondered what that meant, so I piffed him. *Seek the truth.* He read the verse again, and it made him ponder the nature of truth itself.

What is truth? He thought. *Can anyone know it? I guess there are scientific truths and laws of nature that can be proven. But beliefs? How can anyone know which belief is right? Look at all the religions: Buddhism, Islam, Hinduism, Christianity? They all claim 'the truth,' and yet they have different beliefs and disagree, even among themselves. Buddhists against Buddhists, and Christians against Christians. Yeah, some truth that must be.*

He returned to his Bible and kept reading. Several chapters further, Sterling stopped at the part where Jesus said, "I am the way and the truth and the life." He stared off at the side of his tent. *How could a person claim to be the truth?* Speaking of the truth, Sterling wondered if what Laurel had told him about the garden was true. She seemed sincere about it, but he realized he must find out for himself.

Outside the tent, full darkness had fallen, and Sterling braved the mosquitoes and stuck his head outside the tent to watch the stars illuminate the nearly moonless night. The dying fire from across the lake offered the only other illumination. Screeches and howls from distant coyotes echoed over the lake and into the mountains. The pack of animals sounded closer than Sterling would have liked, and he noticed the fire across the lake had grown brighter. He went back into the shelter of his tent.

Hoping to read further, Sterling scavenged around in his supplies and pulled out a headlamp. He pushed the switch, but it was already turned on, and the battery was dead. Disappointed, he crawled into his sleeping bag and zipped it up to his shoulders. As he lay there, he listened to the frenzied howls fading into the distance, but the night did not yet become silent. Among other nocturnal creaks and scampers, he flinched at the sound of wings flapping close to his tent. "Probably an owl," he told himself. What would be next? A cougar? A bear? He remembered seeing the bear spray in the camping bin, next to the freeze-dried food. Like several other items Sterling now wanted, however, it sat safely at home.

It was a rough night for sleeping, and Sterling tossed and turned. At the faintest dawn, he emerged from his tent and packed things up. He skipped breakfast and was on the trail an hour before sunlight would even touch the lake. He took a wide detour around the boys' now quiet camp and hiked to the parking lot, seeing a lone Jeep he thought must belong to one of the boys. The sun crested the horizon and fell on Sterling as he trekked along the rutted dirt road toward Mount Angeles Road. As soon as Sterling's feet hit the pavement again, he listened for a vehicle headed to Port Angeles. But the traffic was heading up the road in the opposite direction, to Hurricane Ridge, not down to PA. As he waited, Sterling thought again about how he had left things with Hoyt, and he turned on his phone and texted him, "Sorry for being a jerk yesterday. I'm heading home now. Happy birthday, bro!"

He looked up the road. There were still no cars driving toward town, so he began to walk. An hour passed without a single car going his way. But he didn't mind. He had time to think, which was what he left town to do. He spent a long time replaying what Laurel had said about the garden and their transformation discussion. He realized their disagreement would trigger another round of apologies. *Why wait to deal with it?* He stopped and texted Laurel. "I overreacted. My skin's not as thick as I thought. Sorry."

He hoped she would reply right away, but his phone was silent. After all, she was probably still asleep—Hoyt, too. When he heard a car approaching from behind, he stuck his thumb out and waved it so the driver would be sure to notice. The car slowed to a stop, and the driver welcomed him inside. Sterling loaded his pack into the backseat and joined the driver up front.

"Thank goodness," Sterling exclaimed. "Everyone was going the other way. I was afraid I was going to have to walk the entire fifteen miles back to town."

"Were you up at Mount Angeles? the driver asked.

"No. I camped at PJ Lake."

"I see. I was up at Hurricane Ridge, before daylight, to take pictures of the sunrise. Lucky for you, I need to be at work by nine. No one else in their right mind would be driving this direction at this hour."

"You're the only car I saw. Thanks again for stopping."

After they arrived in town, Sterling continued walking home and checked his phone, hoping to see a message from Laurel or Hoyt. But there was nothing.

It was time to move ahead, time to see if Canaan's Garden was real or not. To find out if Laurel was right.

Thirty-Four

Nothing gives rest but the sincere search for truth.

—Blaise Pascal

WHEN STERLING ARRIVED home and checked the time, it was still early in the morning. He suspected Hoyt was still in bed, so he went around the house quietly—unpacking his camping gear, eating a bowl of cereal, and getting his bike out of the garage. He pedaled toward the waterfall at Canaan's Creek. When he reached the bench at the foot of the falls, Sterling sat, looking for the entrance to the garden. Laurel had said it was right across the pool. He searched for any entry points. There was the barn on the right side of the restaurant, the rock wall next to the barn, the waterfall, the pool, and the creek below the pool. Sterling remembered seeing John come out of the barn with a wheelbarrow full of produce from the garden, so he thought he might enter the garden by going through the barn, but he could see the barn door was padlocked. That left only one option—crossing the pool.

Sterling stood and walked to the edge of the pool to examine it. He could not see the bottom. How deep was it? What was the bottom like? Was it lined with sand or pebbles, or covered with stones? Was it jagged, flat, or slippery? How fast was the water flowing? He noticed something strange about the speed of the current, like it was rushing too fast for the volume of water coming from the waterfall. The pool looked calm on its surface, but as Sterling studied it, he realized it flowed almost as fast as the stream below it. It was only fifteen feet across, but he knew if he dove in and tried to swim to the other side, the current would thrust him into the chute and wash him down to the strait. He tested the water temperature with his hand. It was ice—snowmelt from the Olympic Mountains.

Sterling sat on a stone at pool's edge to develop a plan. Was he crazy for even considering getting in that water? Possibly. Was he still curious? Absolutely. Was crossing the pool worth the risk? He spent a moment considering the answer as he watched the water rush by. He clenched his fists, determined. He needed to know the truth.

There was a small nook in the rock wall next to the barn, a gap just big enough for Sterling to stash his T-shirt, wallet, and phone. He stored his things in the crevice, walked back to the pool, and looked down at the stone he had been sitting on. *That's it*, he thought. *A ballast. If a heavy weight keeps a ship stable, it should work for me.* He tried to pick it up, but it was too heavy. He searched for a smaller one, but the next stone was too light. The third one he hefted was perfect—small enough to hold on to but heavy enough to keep the current from washing him down the chute. Or so he hoped. He held the stone close to his stomach and proceeded to the water.

Sterling's first step into the creek was easy. His left foot landed on a smooth surface, and the water was only halfway up to his knee. His following step scared him since it was into roiling water that obscured the bottom. He breathed deeply and took a big step, plunging to his thighs. The current was stronger, and Sterling teetered and nearly fell. Once he regained his balance, he turned to face upstream, leaned into the flow, and bent his knees to lower his center of gravity. He slid out his right foot to feel for his next step and discovered a large rock he would need to step over.

Sterling took another deep breath and put one foot on the rock to lift himself over. As he was mid-step, balancing on one leg, he hurried to plant his step on the other side. But as he stepped over the rock, his foot landed in a hole, and he sunk in the icy water up to his armpits.

Sterling gasped from the shock of the cold and tried to determine his next move. The water was obviously getting deeper, and he feared his next step would take him all the way under.

He stole a glance over his shoulder to where he first stepped into the pool and was briefly tempted to back out. But he gritted his chattering teeth and pushed onward. He slowed his breathing to calm himself and took another big step into the unknown depths, then vanished beneath the surface. Instinctively, Sterling's eyes shot open under the water, but he could see nothing through the turbulent bubbles. The rumble of the current combined with the nearby waterfall to overwhelm his ears with noise.

There was no time to lose. Sterling's next step landed on smooth bottom, but it took him even deeper. His ballast stone slipped from his grasp, but he caught it at his knees. He pulled it up to his chest again, clinging to it for dear life. Curiously, the water felt warmer at the new depths, especially near his ankles. Sterling realized he had stepped near a hot spring, which explained the larger than expected volume of water flowing from the pool. But the warmth was little comfort. Sterling was past the point of no return.

He took another long step, and the current raged against him. Any misstep would send him hurtling down the chute. His lungs burned, and the current pushed against him harder. His fingers cramped as he struggled to grip the stone, but he pushed forward. Bubbles rose from his face, and he could hold his breath no longer. His ears rang, his heart hammered, his hands shook. He was seconds away from inhaling water.

As he kicked his foot out in front of him, it bumped into a vertical rock wall. Sterling wondered if he had reached the other side. He pinned the ballast stone against the wall with one hand while reaching up to with the other. Thankfully, he felt a ledge a foot above his head, and in one quick motion, he dropped the stone and grabbed the wall with both hands. He gripped the ledge and pulled himself up out of the water, where he rolled onto his back.

Sterling gagged and sputtered and rested there until his breathing returned to normal. He wiped the water from his eyes and looked up at the wall behind him. If the garden was real, the entrance would have to be there, like Laurel said. But the longer Sterling's eyes searched, the more he was filled with a painful sense of disappointment. The entrance he had hoped for did not exist. That made Laurel a liar or a lunatic. Or some sick blend of the two. Sterling did not even bother sitting up. He stayed on his back and felt his eyes well with tears. He had almost drowned to find the garden, and now that he knew it didn't exist, he realized how badly he had hoped it did.

To make matters worse, he was stranded by the waterfall and would have to cross back through the pool. And this time without a ballast stone.

Thirty-Five

The supreme function of reason is to show man that some things are beyond reason.

—Blaise Pascal

STERLING SHOUTED ACROSS the pool for help, but the waterfall's roar smothered his cries. He yelled until his voice became hoarse. Still, there was no response. His cell phone was safely stowed next to the barn, and no one had a clue where he was. His parents were in Seattle, and Hoyt knew he wanted to be left alone. And Sterling *was* alone. He had no choice but to rescue himself. The sheer cliff above him offered no way out, and going down the creek promised being swept away by the current and hurtling through the narrow, rocky chute. Sterling stared at the pool and prepared himself for his only option—going back into the frigid depths.

He shuffled to the edge of the water and inhaled three breaths, each one deeper than the one before. Finally, he squatted, inhaled once more, and dove from the ledge. After torpedoing into the water and rising to the surface, Sterling was already halfway across the pool. He swam as hard as he could for three strokes, and his right hand touched the far side. But the current was fierce, and it pulled him downstream feet first before he got a handhold. His knees and stomach scraped across the pool's lower lip like riding a water park slide down a jagged washboard. An eddy spun him around, sending him speeding headfirst. Sterling yelped and crossed his arms over the top of his head as he slammed into one rock after another.

Suddenly, his body jerked to a stop, face up, in the middle of the stream. His left foot was wedged between two rocks, and water rushed over his face. Sterling coughed and tried to twist his foot free, but the water's force kept it tightly wedged between the rocks. He lunged forward into a sit-up position so his face was out of the water. With frantic gasps, he caught his breath, but he couldn't hold the upright position for long. His abs burned, so he had to take a deep breath and lay back under the water. He exhaled and pulled himself into a sitting position again. Trying to buy himself more time, he wrapped his arms under his left knee for support. He breathed deeply and looked up—I was circling above him, and he hoped I would deliver a note to someone for help. I tipped my wing and flew off to the garden.

When Sterling's abs and arms needed a break, he lowered himself into the water to rest before sitting up again to breathe. He was getting tired, and each retreat out of the water grew shorter. Fifteen minutes passed, and he could only hold his face out of the water long enough to take one quick breath.

AS I SOARED into the garden, John was picking strawberries. I landed beside him and grabbed a berry in my claws. He watched me take flight again and fly toward the cliff above Sterling. I piffed John to follow me, knowing he would recognize my voice. He knew something was wrong, and less than a minute later, he and I were at the stream's edge, looking into the chute to where Sterling struggled for his life.

John raced back to the barn and returned with a coil of rope. He made a lasso and tossed it to Sterling, who held it as tight as he could with his numb fingers. John shouted, "Loop it under your arms!" But Sterling could no longer hold himself out of the water and fell back. John could only see Sterling's foot sticking out of the rushing water and feared he was too late. As he tried to think of another way to rescue Sterling, two hard tugs came from Sterling's end of the rope. John pulled Sterling upright and tied his end of the rope around a cedar tree. Sterling was still stuck, but the rope at least held his head above water.

"Hang on!" John hollered. "I'll get you out!"

John ran behind the barn and pulled a ladder out from under the leaves. He carried it downstream to Sterling and laid it flat across the creek, like a bridge, where he crawled across it on his hands and knees. John stopped directly above the rocks that trapped Sterling's left foot.

Sterling shivered and said, "I was ready to give up and stay underwater."

"You're going to be fine," John assured him. He reached between two rungs to feel Sterling's foot and ankle. "I don't think anything's broken. I'm going to see if I can lift it out—holler if it hurts." John reached under Sterling's foot with both hands and pulled. It didn't budge, and Sterling hollered that it hurt. John ignored him and jerked hard. It popped free. John let go, and the rope kept Sterling from being washed away. "Now," John said, "we have to get you out of there before you freeze. Can you pull yourself up to the ladder?"

"I think so."

"Great, but wait until I get off the ladder. I don't think it will hold both of us."

Once John was back on solid ground, Sterling pulled himself upstream with the rope to the ladder. He grabbed two rungs and hooked a leg over the top to hoist himself up. He laid prone across the rungs and wondered if I had led John to rescue him. He untied the rope from under his arms and crawled across the ladder to the stream's bank. John helped him to his feet, and together they carried the ladder to the nearby bench, where Sterling collapsed, shivering.

"You wait here," John said, and he carried the ladder back to the barn and returned with an old blanket. He draped it over Sterling and sat beside him. "What happened? Did you fall in?"

"No. I was looking for the garden Laurel told me about. I needed to know if it's real or . . . something she made up. Or if she was totally delusional. She told me it was across the pool, but it wasn't there."

"How do you know it wasn't?"

Sterling wrapped the blanket tighter and said, "I crossed the pool and looked for it. It wasn't there."

"Crossed the pool? How?"

Sterling explained how he crossed, climbed on the ledge to look around, and tried to swim back.

"My goodness," John said. "I don't know whether you are very foolish or extremely daring."

"Mostly foolish, especially since I bought Laurel's story. Anyway, it's over now. I can't believe you saved me. Thank you, by the way. How did you find me?"

"A little birdy told me you were in trouble."

"The dove?"

"That's right. The dove led me to you."

Sterling reflected on that for a moment, but then his thoughts returned to the garden. "Why did Laurel lie to me?"

"About what?"

"The garden."

John chuckled. "She didn't lie to you. It really does exist, and it *is* across the pool. I was there before I came to help you. You have to understand something." John shifted to look directly into Sterling's eyes. "You can't find the garden through your own effort. You must trust the Master, and he will lead you there."

"Let me guess—*I must follow the Master so he can take me beyond.*"

"Maybe you are less foolish than you think. You may be beginning to understand. But it takes faith, not your own strength, to find what you're looking for. Not one big leap of faith, either. Many small steps, one in front of the other. Each step might be uncomfortable, but each will also be an adventure, and your faith will increase."

"If that garden is real, it doesn't need faith to be seen. Am I wrong?"

"Not entirely, but I'm not sure you've understood things yet. Keep seeking."

Sterling stood and folded John's blanket. "I'll try. Thanks again. And for talking with me."

"You are welcome," John answered. "I enjoy our talks." He looked up at the darkening sky and then at Sterling, who still looked cold. "Looks like rain. Can I give you a lift?"

"No thanks. I'll ride fast. It'll warm me up." He walked to the nook next to the barn and retrieved his phone, wallet, and T-shirt before walking to his bike.

I made my oowoo-woo-woo call to get Sterling's attention, and as he looked up at the waterfall, I flew out from behind it, performing huge loops and landing on the barn's roof. I held an olive branch in my beak and shook it at him. Sterling focused on the three black olives, each as large as a robin's egg, that dangled from the branch. He laughed, dumbfounded, and I swooped from the roof and dropped the olive branch into his hands. I flew to the birdhouse above the barn door and squeezed myself through the entry, waving my tail feathers at Sterling as I disappeared.

Sterling considered the branch in his hands, looked back up at the birdhouse, and started pedaling home.

On his ride back, Sterling's ankle was sore, but it was loosening up. Still, his attention was more on the low, bass rumble of distant thunder that was growing closer and prompting him to pedal faster. Despite his speed, he could not out ride the downpour, and he arrived home cold and soaked. He ran into the house, took a hot shower, and put on dry jeans and a warm sweatshirt. He went downstairs to the kitchen and made two tuna melt sandwiches, each with cheese on both sides of the tuna. They were delicious. But after he finished, somehow Sterling felt strangely empty.

Thirty-Six

JUST AS STERLING washed down his tuna melt sandwich with a glass of cold milk, he heard a cheer from upstairs. He went to Hoyt's room and knocked on the door. A TV was blaring, and Hoyt yelled, "Come in!" A pile of dirty clothes blocked the door, and Sterling slowly bumped it open with his shoulder, rattling the trophies on his brother's 'I'm a Winner' shelf. Hoyt sat on his bed watching a recording of the 2020 Super Bowl. He pointed at the screen. "Did you see that touchdown pass? Mahomes nailed it."

"What are you doing?"

"Studying. Preseason practices are right around the corner."

Sterling stepped between Hoyt and the screen. "Could you pause that for a second?"

Hoyt frowned and stopped the game. "Yeah, happy birthday to you too. You still down in the dumps?"

"No. I'm okay. We need to talk. I'm worried about that Bitcoin."

"C'mon, do we have to talk about that now? I was just forgetting about it."

"It's important, and I haven't forgotten about it. Will you help me?"

"What are you thinking?"

"We need to make a decision. We know the tax bills were phony, so Dirk didn't con Pete out of any money. And we think Dirk did something illegal to get the money, but we don't know for sure. If it's legal money, and if Dirk tells the police it's been stolen, we could get caught. I don't know if the police could track the Bitcoin to us, but they probably have ways I don't know about. The bottom line is, I don't know what the cops would do to us, and I don't want to find out. It could be bad. So, I say we transfer the money back."

Hoyt started to answer when a flash of light illuminated his room. One second later, thunder rattled his window. "Huh, the forecast was clear for tonight."

"The weatherman must have forgotten it's Port Angeles. What do you think about returning the Bitcoin?"

"I don't know." Hoyt groaned. "It's not so much that I want the money. We couldn't spend it, not without raising suspicion. But I don't want Dirk to have it. I hate him."

"Do you want to go to jail for it?"

"Of course not. But the *ifs* are in our favor, right? *If* the money is legal, which it most likely isn't. *If* he calls the police, which he probably won't. *If* the cops trace it to us, which . . . is possible. Look, you're the smart one, and you said yourself that Bitcoin accounts are secret. So, let's keep it. We won't spend any of it until we go away to college. Then, we'll only spend small amounts. Keep it under the radar."

Sterling shook his head. "No way. Even if Dirk doesn't call the cops, he's smart. Smart enough to suspect Pete, or us. He may come after us, even if he doesn't know for sure we did it."

"We can deal with that. He attacked Pete. He hit on Mom. He tried to ruin our stupid yard business. I hate him, and he should pay. For all of it. It needs to cost him. And I still want to sink his boat."

"It's too risky. I don't think we can keep the Bitcoin. As a matter of fact, since I'm the one who took it, I'm going to give it back."

"You're going to overrule me just like that?"

"Sorry, but I don't see any choice."

"Sissy."

"You know I have to do this."

"Whatever." Hoyt looked out his window at the sheets of rain pelting their house. "You know what this weather is good for?"

"Hibernating?"

"Detergent grenades. The rain will dissolve the granules by morning."

"You already did that. Let it go."

"What? You can give the Bitcoin back, and you can keep trying to talk me out of sinking his boat, but I gotta have a little revenge."

"Fine," Sterling said, turning to leave the room. "Don't get caught."

HOYT TOOK A large umbrella from the hall closet and walked to the grocery store to buy a bucket of detergent pods. As he neared Dirk's driveway, he noticed two fresh signs posted on the edge of his yard—one asked people to keep their dog on a leash, and the other reminded people to pick up after their pets. Hoyt smiled as he closed the umbrella and walked into the woods, working his way between the trees, toward the house. Once he was in a prime position to attack Dirk's entire front lawn, he leaned the umbrella against a tree and opened the bucket. Seventy-five pods waited to be lobbed. Hoyt took a handful and threw one pod after the other onto the lawn, spacing them ten feet apart. He had to step out from the trees to reach the far corners. Five minutes later, the bucket was empty, and Hoyt took it, along with the umbrella, to leave.

STERLING ANXIOUSLY LOGGED into his Bitcoin account to check on Dirk's stockpile. He saw that the value of Dirk's Bitcoin had increased by nearly ten thousand dollars since he had taken it. For a second, he considered keeping the gain and splitting it with Hoyt, but he talked himself out of it, transferred everything back to Dirk, and closed his own account. He breathed a sigh of relief and walked to Hoyt's room to tell him it was done, but Hoyt was not back yet. Sterling wondered if Hoyt was still at Dirk's, and he opened the 'Find My Fam' app on his phone to see. The map displayed Hoyt's phone in

Dirk's front yard. Sterling zoomed in and watched Hoyt's location move to the street and toward home.

HOYT WAS A block from home when a Porsche Boxster skidded to a stop right next to him. Hoyt found that odd, but kept walking. A man with a ponytail and a neatly trimmed beard got out of the driver's door and hurried around the front of the car toward Hoyt. When Hoyt saw the man approaching, he dropped his empty bucket and threw the umbrella at him, point first. Hoyt ran as if he were trying to elude a tackler, and the man pursued. Hoyt faked left, cut right, and hurdled over a fire hydrant, but the man ran faster than Hoyt expected and was not far behind him. Hoyt made a hard right into a driveway and ran into the backyard. He vaulted over a fence and onto a cement basketball court that he had used many times.

Knowing the neighborhood gave Hoyt a home-court advantage, and the man was losing ground. Hoyt scaled another fence and heard a thud behind him as his pursuer landed awkwardly. Hoyt ran up to a gate and opened it to the front yard. He quietly closed the gate behind him and sprinted to the sidewalk. When he looked over his shoulder, he saw his pursuer about ten yards behind him, and the uneven clomp of the man's footsteps on the sidewalk faded as Hoyt increased his lead.

Hoyt looked up the street and saw a large man with broad shoulders and a Fu Manchu mustache standing on the sidewalk. Hoyt hurried up to him and said, "Thank goodness—you gotta help me. There's someone chasing me, and I don't know what to do."

The large man nodded and motioned for Hoyt to stand behind him. As Hoyt stood there, he noticed the man stunk like sweat, motor oil, fish scales, and cigarettes, all brewed together in a spittoon. He took a step away. They waited in the drenching rain to see what the pursuer would do as he drew closer.

The running man slowed to a limping walk, reached them, and stopped, his chest heaving from the chase. He said, "Nice catch," and the tall man spun around and clamped his huge hand around Hoyt's wrist. Hoyt tried to pull away, but the man's iron grip held him tight.

The tall man said to the other, "I started over as soon as you called. Then I saw him running and figured he might be the kid we've been watching for."

"Good thinking. I sent a text to Dirk but haven't heard back."

"So, what should we do with him, Techs?"

"Uh, that's problematic, *Bert*. Now he knows both our names."

"So? Why don't I take him to my boat? I can take him to the middle of the strait, where the sharks are."

Hoyt froze fearfully still.

Techs's phone buzzed. "Nice. Now he answers." Techs stepped aside from Hoyt and Bert to answer Dirk's call. "Hey. We got one . . . Hold on, let me check." Techs walked over to Hoyt and grabbed his face, turning it to one side and then the other. Techs returned to his call. "Yeah, it's the one without the scar. I saw him on camera in your front yard and took off to catch him." Techs listened and then said, "Both of us. Bert's here, too. The kid can identify us. We're going to the basin, and then Bert is taking him out fishing on the strait, if you catch my drift." He turned away from Hoyt and Bert and listened again. "I don't like that," he responded. "Sounds risky. He knows our names." He paced up and down the sidewalk. "All right, if you insist. We'll see you there."

Techs walked over to Bert. "Dirk wants us to take the kid to his boat so he can question him. Says he'll take care of him after that. I don't like it, but I guess he's the boss. At least for now."

Bert clubbed his right paw into the side of Hoyt's head, and Hoyt dropped to the ground. "That'll make him easier to transport. My truck is right over there." Bert nodded toward an old, dented Dodge pickup.

Bert threw Hoyt over his shoulder, carried him across the street, and dropped him onto the grass strip between the sidewalk and his truck. Then Bert gagged him with a greasy rag, pulled a length of wire out from his truck bed, and rolled Hoyt onto his stomach. He tied Hoyt's hands and legs together behind his back. Hoyt resembled a skydiver in freefall.

Techs watched Bert with some discomfort. "Awfully natural at that, aren't you?"

Bert did not appreciate Techs's sense of humor and gave him a grim look.

Techs quickly added, "Good job. I'll meet you at Dirk's boat," and jogged off to retrieve his car from the other street.

Bert picked up Hoyt and dropped him into the bed of his pickup. He drove off toward the basin.

STERLING WAS PUZZLED watching his tracking app. Hoyt's phone had zigzagged through a nearby neighborhood and stopped only a block from home. After a minute or two, Hoyt's phone moved fast across town and then ended up at the Boat Basin. Sterling texted Hoyt, "What you up to?" Suddenly, Hoyt's phone disappeared from the app altogether. Sterling waited to see if it would reappear, and when it did not, he mentally retraced Hoyt's path and remembered Hoyt's comments about detergent grenades. *What if Dirk saw him?* Sterling worried. *Maybe Dirk caught him, but why couldn't Hoyt get away? Or did Hoyt get into a car with somebody else and ride to the marina? That would explain the higher speed. Still, if it was Dirk, Hoyt could be on Leverage.*

Sterling considered riding his bike to the marina, but thought it would take too long. By the time he would arrive, Hoyt could be somewhere else, and it would be hard to track him while riding in the dark. He wondered if he should he call the police, or if he was totally overreacting. He decided to watch his app for a few minutes to see if Hoyt popped up again.

TECHS HAD MET Bert in the parking lot five minutes earlier, and before Techs had time to get out of his car, Dirk had emerged nearby from the darkness like an apparition, wearing black. Techs pointed to Bert's truck bed, and Dirk looked inside. In a hushed voice, Techs said, "After you question him, he needs to disappear. Permanently."

"Just get him onto my boat," Dirk said. "We can talk there."

Dirk retrieved one of the marina's carts and pushed it next to Bert's truck. Bert scanned the parking lot to make sure nobody was watching before lugging Hoyt out of the pickup and dropping him into the cart. Dirk walked ahead while Bert pushed the cart and Techs followed. They reached *Leverage* unnoticed. As Dirk unlocked the cabin door, Techs took Hoyt's phone out of his pocket and tossed it into the water. Bert carried Hoyt into the cabin and dumped him onto a berth.

Dirk asked Techs, "What was he doing in my front yard?"

"The cameras showed him throwing something, lots of something, all around your grass. He kept pulling things out of a bucket and tossing them onto the lawn."

"Huh. Something's been killing my lawn, but I thought it was neighborhood dogs or spilled gas. I even chewed out my new yard man and threatened to fire him. Never thought about Hoyt. Maybe I shouldn't have messed with their yard business."

Techs said, "I vote to let Bert take the kid out on his boat. Nobody will suspect Bert, and he can return without the kid. Problem solved."

"First," Dirk clarified, "this isn't a democracy. We don't vote, because I'm in charge. Second, I need to question him. Then I will take care of him."

"But what if he talks you out of it?" Bert asked.

Dirk raised his maimed hand. "Bert, you told me you wanted to make this up to me. So shut up and let me do it my way."

Thirty-Seven

TWO WEEKS EARLIER, a small tropical disturbance had formed 300 miles northwest of the Marshall Islands, one-third of the way between Australia and Port Angeles. The disturbance was hardly noticeable in its early stage, but over four days, it strengthened considerably. The low-pressure area took another week to reach the coast of Washington State and enter the Strait of Juan de Fuca, only sixty miles west of the Boat Basin.

On the evening that Hoyt lay unconscious on *Leverage*'s berth, the storm tracked east through the strait, until it was due north of Port Angeles, and then it did the unexplainable. The system exploded from a micro-storm into a full-fledged blow, filling the entire strait with high seas. Clouds darkened the sky and blocked the sun. Rain poured from the heavens. Winds increased to fifty miles per hour, with gusts to eighty. That, combined with the incoming tide, created swells twenty feet from trough to crest.

In short, it was not a good time to leave the safety of the marina.

STERLING CLOSED HIS tracking app and rebooted it, as if that would make Hoyt magically reappear. Unfortunately, it did not, and the unknown was driving Sterling nuts. *Is Hoyt in danger? Did he get into a friend's car to get out of the rain? Did he decide to sink Dirk's boat?* Sterling hated insufficient data—it paralyzed him. He tried to calm himself. *Don't over think this. You need more information. Go to the basin and look for Hoyt. That way, you'll know for sure if he needs help.*

Sterling strapped on his helmet and pulled his bike out of the garage. Before he even left the driveway, the wind was blowing a fierce waterfall of rain across his face, but he pressed on. As he reached the Olympic Discovery Trail, he was soaked, and he closed his eyes to slits, open barely enough for him to keep on the trail and watch for cross-traffic at intersections. The headwind was brutal and slowed Sterling to a jogger's pace, even though his quads burned with effort. He turned off the ODT onto the Boat Basin's entrance road and winced in pain as a cramp seized his left calf. He crossed the parking lot and let his bike fall to the ground between his legs before running along the pier toward Dirk's slip. A minute too late, he recognized *Leverage*'s profile as it powered into the churning dark of the harbor. Sterling had a bad feeling that Hoyt was onboard.

He called Laurel, and she picked up right away. "What's up?"

"I need to use your dad's boat," he said. "I know where you hide the keys, but after the scooter joyride, I thought I'd better get your permission."

"Sorry, I can't let you. Dad loves that boat, and made me promise not to let anyone else take it out."

"It's an emergency. I think Dirk took Hoyt on his boat. I'm worried, and Mom and Pete are out of town. Please?"

"You should call the police. Or the Coast Guard."

"No, I . . . I can't. I could get in trouble. I'm counting on you."

Laurel paused for so long that Sterling looked at his phone to see if she was still on the call.

"Okay," she answered at last. "I can be there in ten minutes."

"Great. Dress warm. And hurry."

Sterling walked to the nearby fish cleaning station, seeking shelter from the storm. The shack was better than standing out in the open and offered a little protection from the wind. A single light bulb mounted on the ceiling flickered and shook in the wind as Sterling watched the gale over the water for any sign of *Leverage*'s return. He checked the time on his phone frequently until it had been fifteen minutes. He peered around the station's wall to see if he missed Laurel's arrival. She was nowhere in sight, but Sterling saw a man walking up from one of the wharfs. He strode up the steep ramp, his ponytail swinging back and forth, and passed the fish cleaning station.

The man briefly noticed Sterling, did a double take, and halted. He and Sterling made eye contact, and the man slowly reached behind his back. He pulled a small pistol from his waistband. "Keep quiet," he said. "You're coming with me."

"What?" Sterling stammered as he looked at the gun. "Who are you?"

"I think you know who I am. Just call me the Mole."

Sterling's heart raced, and he knew he was in an entirely new depth of trouble.

Techs marched Sterling down the ramp and to the dock, pushing him forward with the pistol at his back. He prodded Sterling to get onto his boat. "Climb the ladder to the flying bridge. And then don't move."

Sterling had no choice but to do exactly as Techs ordered. Up on the flying bridge, the wind and rain whipped him, and he shielded his face with his arm. When he peered out to the strait, he could see only the outline of the basin's exit and the flickering whitecaps of the waves beyond.

Techs disappeared into the cabin and returned wearing orange rain gear. While he untied the lines and readied the boat for departure, Sterling texted Laurel, "On a boat. Kidnapped."

The boat drifted away from the dock, and Techs climbed the ladder, looking like an over-sized traffic cone in his poncho. Without warning, he punched Sterling in the stomach. "I saw the light from your phone," Techs snapped. "Give it to me." Sterling handed it to

246

him, and Techs tossed it overboard. "You pull a stunt like that again, and you're the next thing going over." He started the engine and motored toward the harbor, just as Dirk had done minutes earlier.

As the boat bucked in the storm, Techs pulled out the burner phone Dirk had given him and made a call. "Dirk, Techs here. I got the other one. We're on my boat, and we're going fishing."

"Forget the fishing," Dirk ordered. "Keep him at the basin, and I'll meet you there in a few hours. I need to talk to him. After that, I'll take care of him."

"Whatever."

Sterling overheard the call and realized that because Techs had used his real name, there was not much hope of getting back to shore alive. Sterling said a silent prayer for his safety and for Hoyt's. It was an awkward prayer, but awkwardness did not matter. The Master heard it nonetheless. I was pleased with Sterling, too. Though he could not see me, I was circling above him, keeping him always in my sight. The storm did not bother me in the slightest.

When Techs fully cleared the basin, he opened the throttle and roared into the waves. Ediz Hook offered little protection from the wind, and the water became more treacherous every minute. The bow slammed into the chop. Each wave temporarily slowed the boat like a speed bump.

Techs was on alert, cycling his attention from Sterling, to the radar, to the GPS display, and to the blackness that loomed beyond the bow. Once he felt in control of all four, he said to Sterling, "So, which one are you? The brain or the brawn? I don't remember."

"Huh?"

"You and your brother."

"Oh, uh, I guess I'm the brain . . . What about you and Dirk? You the brain?"

Techs chuckled. "Definitely. But Dirk's not much for brawn."

"Are you two partners or something?"

"You could say that. I'm helping him with his *import* business."

"More like smuggling business."

"Can't say I'm surprised that you know. You must have seen his emails, you little punk. Where's his Bitcoin, by the way?"

"In his account."

"That's not what I heard."

"Well, that's where it is. Maybe Dirk isn't the best partner."

"Yeah, you're telling me." Techs pulled out his phone again and opened his email. He copied coordinates from a message into his boat's GPS. "I read Dirk's emails, too, so I know all about this pickup. I don't trust him to send me his coordinates. Good thing I already have them."

Entering the strait's open water, the boat left the choppy waves behind them and traded them for deep swells, which forced Techs to reduce speed to avoid burying the bow into walls of water. As soon as a swell lifted the bow, Techs increased power and climbed it. When he reached the windblown crest, he eased the throttle off and surfed down the backside into another trough. Sterling had never been on such rough seas. He licked salt water from his lips, and his stomach tightened at the bottom of each trough, when all he could see around them were mountains of water.

Techs said, "You were clever with your hacking setup. But not quite clever enough. You were the one who reformatted the hard disk, weren't you?" he asked, but did not wait for a reply. "Thought so. You know reformatting doesn't remove the data. A pro with the right tools can recover it, which is exactly what I did. Dirk asked me to analyze the disk, and I recovered everything, including evidence of all the fingerprints you left behind in his system. Don't play dumb. I know about the remote control software you installed."

"That *I* installed? What makes you think I installed it?"

"The IP address pointed right to your neighborhood. It was you. No doubt."

"Man, I thought I had covered by tracks."

"Yeah, you did—like an amateur."

Lightning flashed across the sky and illuminated the whitecaps like silver flags in the wind. Thunder cracked two seconds later. Sterling wondered if the storm could get any worse.

"Were you involved with the bogus tax bills?" he asked. "The ones the county sent to my dad?"

"I was more than involved," Techs answered proudly. "Those statements were my brainchild. I programmed the system to issue the notices from the county. That's why they looked exactly like the official ones."

"They fooled Pete."

"They should have. It was a perfect plan. Dirk was going to buy the properties for cheap. Either that, or your dad was going to pay all those taxes, which I was going to reroute into a hidden account, and Dirk and I were going to split the haul."

"Too bad someone blew the whistle on your scam."

Techs smirked. "It is too bad, isn't it? But that someone is going to pay. Big time. And I'm still benefiting from the fallout. The county hired *me* to investigate the problem. Me! I'll pin the whole thing on the stooge who took my position. They'll fire him, and I'll get my old job back. Maybe even get a raise."

"Nice. You're a dishonest worker and a smuggler. Congrats."

"Bold words coming from a kidnapped nerd," Techs hissed. "You can't even imagine how much money I'm making between the two." He powered the boat up the face of a large swell and backed off to surf down.

"So, what's your setup?" Sterling asked. "You pass the goods from one boat to another? I saw Dirk's emails, but I don't understand how it works."

Techs looked Sterling up and down with curiosity. "I guess it won't hurt to tell you. It's not like you'll get a chance to tell anyone. Our operation moves illegal goods between Canada and the States—Cuban cigars and drugs come in, pistols and ammo go out. But the real money is in pharmaceuticals. They're compact and high-value. But Dirk doesn't really care what the goods are. He charges $20,000 per run, and he makes a couple of runs each week. Most of the money goes into his pocket, but my cut isn't bad."

"What about the plane? Is that for smuggling, too?"

"Not yet, Sherlock. But it will be. Dirk plans to grow the business by delivering up to 600 miles from here. I'm talking Seattle, Portland, Spokane, even Boise."

Sterling noted they were only two miles from the waypoint Techs had entered into his GPS. "We're not on our way to a drop now, are we?" he asked. "It's got to be too dangerous to transfer the stuff in these seas."

"That's the genius of it," Techs replied. "There isn't another boat. The stash is waiting for us on the bottom of the strait. Dirk sends an audio signal, and a buoy rises to the surface, and then he pulls the stash in like a crab pot. Didn't you notice that big winch he installed on *Leverage?*"

"He said it was for helping scuba divers salvage relics from shipwrecks."

"Please. You believed that?" Techs squinted at his radar and then at the GPS. "All right. They're just ahead. He has your brother, the brawn... and I just realized how touching it will be. You boys can tell each other goodbye."

Thirty-Eight

WHEN *LEVERAGE* NEARED the shipping lanes out in the strait, Dirk shifted the boat into neutral and went to the cabin to check on Hoyt. Hoyt was still unconscious, but he was breathing normally and appeared to be unhurt except for a very swollen eye. Dirk untied the wires from Hoyt's hands and feet, seeing as they were no longer necessary, and went back to the helm. Five minutes later, the boat crossed into the shipping lanes, without running lights. Dirk maneuvered the throttle to ride over the swell, just as Techs had done.

Hoyt jostled in the cabin. He had been dreaming he was riding a mechanical bull in a cowboy bar, and he had stayed on the beast for eight seconds before being thrown to the ground. His waking reality was not much different. The floor was rising and falling, and the flash of a lightning bolt illuminated the cabin through the starboard portholes. Hoyt sat up to look, but he saw only blackness. It didn't help that one eye was swollen shut.

Without any light, Hoyt was uncertain whose boat he was on. He struggled to his feet, nauseous and concussed as he was, and sidled toward the cabin door. Along the way, he felt the wall for a light switch. When he flipped on the lights, he was even more confused. How did he get on *Leverage*? Did those men steal it? Hoyt staggered to the tool drawer, which he knew well from having helped Dirk in the old days, and located a utility knife to slip into his pocket. He grabbed one of Dirk's jackets from the closet, put it on, and approached the cabin door. When he tried the knob, he was surprised to find it unlocked, and he peeked his head out from the door. There was no one on the deck. Seasick, he rushed to the nearest rail and puked over the side. He looked up a moment later, letting the rain revive him.

Hoyt took the utility knife from his pocket and turned to find where the men were. He climbed the ladder to the flying bridge, and as his hands were at the top rung, a wave slammed into *Leverage* broadside. Hoyt's feet slipped from the ladder, and the knife clanged against the metal rungs as it fell to the deck.

Dirk turned from the helm and ripped his pistol from its holster. He brandished the gun at Hoyt. "Don't try anything. Stand over there," he said, motioning to the far side of the bridge. Dirk kept an eye on Hoyt as he managed the swells. "Listen to me. If you want to get out of this storm alive, you won't try anything foolish. Now, I'm going to put my gun away because I need both hands here on the bridge. Without me at the wheel, you'll never make it back. You'll either get lost or, more likely, capsize the boat. So. no funny business, got it?"

The next swell lifted the bow nearly straight up, and Hoyt hollered, "We'll be lucky to make it back at all!"

"I can handle this!" Dirk slowed *Leverage* to a crawl and scrutinized his GPS display. He turned the bow toward the west, into the wind, pushed the throttle forward to one-quarter speed, and told Hoyt to take the wheel and keep a due-west heading.

Dirk descended the ladder to the cabin and returned to the deck carrying an object the size and shape of a shoe box. Hoyt watched him push a button on the side of the box. A red light on the top flashed, and the box sounded a loud noise like an out-of-tune violin playing a whale's song. Dirk then hooked the box onto the end of his winch cable, swung the winch arm over the side, and lowered it into the water. After a minute, he pulled it back to the deck, disconnected the box from the cable, and powered it off.

Dirk scanned the water's angry surface, apparently waiting for something to appear.

"What's that?" Hoyt shouted, pointing in front of the boat. A glowing fluorescent orange buoy that resembled a crab pot marker had surfaced a short distance away.

Dirk climbed the ladder and piloted *Leverage* forward until its bow was only ten feet from the buoy. He hustled down to the deck and retrieved a pole with a hook on its end to snag it. After he caught the buoy and pulled it out of the water, he attached it to the winch cable.

Hoyt watched as the winch slowly reeled in the line and smirked at Dirk. "Pulling up sunken treasure, huh?"

"Could be anything. I don't know the details, and I don't want to know. My job is just to make the swap on time, even if it means weathering a storm like this."

"Even if it means doing something shady?"

"Don't get all high and mighty with me. I'm still waiting to get my Bitcoin back from a certain someone. My investigator is sure either you or Sterling stole it. Either way, I expect it back immediately."

"You'll have to talk to Sterling. He's the one who pulled that off. He promised to share it with me, but he's the only one who can access the account."

"I assumed he was the only one capable of stealing it, between the two of you. Still, you need to convince him to return what it rightfully mine."

"I tried, but he thinks it's a great insurance policy. If either of us disappears, you'll never get it back. And a quarter of a mil is a lot of money, especially for someone who owes so much on an airplane."

"How about that?" Dirk smiled. "I believe I underestimated you boys."

"*Sterling.* You underestimated Sterling—I had nothing to do with it. But if you let me go, I'll convince him to give it back."

"Fine. You're safe with me."

"Like I said, the Bitcoin was Sterling's idea. My only genius was killing your lawn with dishwasher detergent.

"Somehow, I'm not surprised it was your handiwork. I thought my new yard guy's mower leaked gas. When he denied it, I fired him."

"Mission accomplished." Hoyt grinned, and he paused. "It was low, what you did to our yard business. What happened? You were our family's best friend."

"Ask Pete. This is all more his fault than mine."

"How?"

"It started with our partnership. While I did the heavy lifting and worked in the background—dealing with loan officers, re-zoning, getting permits, lining the contractors up, inspecting their work, paying them—Pete smiled that oily smile of his, and people lined up to make deals. Which only made more work for me."

"But you were partners. You both made the same money. Right?"

"Yes, but I was afraid he would cut me out. He could hire a decent business manager for much less money than I was getting. I'd be out on the curb while he was earning even more and more."

"He wouldn't do that."

"I couldn't chance it. I needed more money, not less."

"But you're already rich. What could you possibly need all that money for?"

"I needed it to impress your mother."

"Ugh!"

"You need to understand—I wanted to offer Anne more than Pete could give her. And I would have taken good care of you boys once we were together."

"All I know is that you hit on Mom, and that makes me sick."

"You make it sound so crass. I wasn't *hitting* on her. We were simply talking. I want her back, I'll admit it, and I realize I never should have let her go. She's a wonderful woman and was kind enough to keep me in the picture when I came back to town all those years ago, when you and Sterling were babies. That was when I met Pete, and we all became close friends."

"And you pay back that friendship by hitting on her at Canaan's Kitchen?"

"I told you I wasn't hitting on her. I was only asking her to leave Pete. We could have made it work. You and Sterling get along well with me. Pete could have had visitation rights."

"Are you out of your mind?"

"Enough!"

An object the size of a refrigerator broke the water's surface. Dirk hoisted it up and pulled the cable to swing the winch arm over the deck. Hoyt offered to help. But as he stepped behind Dirk, he smashed Dirk into the railing instead. Hoyt snatched the pistol from Dirk's holster and stepped away, pointing the gun at Dirk's chest. "You underestimated me, too. Finish pulling that thing in. It'll be useful evidence."

Dirk glared at Hoyt. "You're in over your head." Dirk lowered the object onto the deck and unhooked the cable. He opened ten latches and slid the lid off to the side. There were twelve identical cubes within. Hoyt watched carefully as Dirk opened *Leverage*'s fish box and withdrew twelve more packages. He exchanged the two sets, replaced the lids, and pushed a button on the side of the orange buoy. He then lowered the container and the buoy back into the depths.

"What did you put into it?" Hoyt asked.

"I couldn't say for certain. Pretty sure it was pistols, though. Canada really restricts handguns, so helping people protect themselves is very profitable on my end. Speaking of which"—Dirk nodded to the gun in Hoyt's hands—"the one you are holding isn't loaded.

"I don't believe you."

"Check the cylinder. Go ahead. You won't see any bullets."

Hoyt took a couple of steps back and peered into the cylinder's chambers. All empty. He spun the cylinder to make sure.

Dirk added, "You didn't think I would shoot you, did you?"

"After what you've done to our family, I think you could do anything."

"I can't shoot with my right hand, and I can't hit anything with my left. You overestimate me. Besides, even if I *could* shoot, I never would shoot you."

"So, the gun is just for intimidation?"

"No. I may need it later. I have bullets for it."

"Need it for what?"

Dirk looked at Hoyt uneasily. "You know that investigator I mentioned?"

"Yeah."

"He's bringing Sterling out to me, but he's not as nice as I am. He wants you both dead, and I'm not sure I can talk him out of it. Now, can I have my gun back?"

Hoyt figured it was best to surrender the pistol, so he did.

"Thanks," Dirk said. "Go into the cabin and stay out of sight."

Thirty-Nine

LAUREL HAD ARRIVED at the Boat Basin's parking lot minutes after Sterling was forced onto Techs's boat. She ran through the pouring rain to the slip where her dad moored *Meryl,* expecting to find Sterling impatiently waiting. But he wasn't there. Laurel stepped aboard, removed the keys from their hiding spot, and started the motor. She unlocked the cabin and went inside to put on a life vest and her dad's bright yellow rain gear. Laurel looked back toward the wharf for Sterling, but the lights on the dock only illuminated arrows of sideways rain. She checked her phone and saw Sterling's message from earlier, saying he was on a boat, kidnapped.

Laurel could hardly believe it, and she wondered what had happened. Helping Sterling rescue Hoyt during the storm was scary enough, but the thought of rescuing Hoyt *and* Sterling by herself was terrifying. As she panicked, she realized Sterling wasn't the only one who needed more faith. She stopped and prayed a quick prayer for safety—for Sterling, for Hoyt, and for herself.

As *Meryl's* motor idled, Laurel ran to *Leverage's* slip, passing other boats whose masts swayed like drunken sailors. Each boat was dark, except for the one moored across from *Leverage's* slip, and it was pulling away by the time Laurel reached that end of the dock. She feared Sterling was onboard, so she rushed back *Meryl* to cast off the lines and set out in pursuit. Laurel did not know for sure if Sterling was on the boat she was chasing, but she was unwilling to bet he wasn't. If she could catch sight of Sterling to prove he was on the boat, she would call 911, even if he didn't want to involve the authorities. But first she had to catch up to the boat. She steered for the harbor, driving fast and ignoring the marina's speed limit.

Techs had a few minutes' head start and sped up once he entered the harbor, so even when Laurel pushed the throttle all the way forward, she could not gain on him. However, when Techs hit the swells past the hook and slowed for safety, Laurel did not. Pulsating gusts and the roar of the outboard motor sounded like kettledrums. Rain soaked Laurel's bushy hair until it drooped into limp ringlets, and bow spray salted her lips. She was cruising full tilt, and she was determined to catch up and help Sterling.

Laurel's gallant mission was quickly becoming a daunting ordeal, for which she was horribly unprepared. Laurel had never taken *Meryl* out by herself, let alone in the dark, and especially not in the middle of a gale. What was worse, Laurel was losing sight of Techs's boat in the storm. At least her father had taught her to use the fancy radar he had installed, so she powered it up spotted her target not far ahead.

The sea grew even more tempestuous, and Techs's larger boat plowed through the swells while *Meryl* bounced and lurched as Laurel did her best to match his speed. Laurel widened her stance and dared to steer with one hand while she called John with the other. As soon as he answered, she yelled, "I'm in Dad's boat in the strait! I think Sterling's in trouble in another boat I'm following. He needs help! Actually, *we* need help!"

"Go back to the basin!" John ordered. "This storm is getting worse, and it's no time to be out on the strait."

Laurel struggled to pilot the boat and hold her phone at the same time, so she reduced her speed. "I'm following Sterling, and even if I turn around, I'm not sure I could find my way back in the dark. Can you help us?"

"I got called to fill in for a boat pilot. There was a lot of shipping traffic tonight, unfortunately. I'm nested against a tanker right now, just waiting for the pilot to jump onto the ladder."

"Can you see me on your radar?"

"Not if you are on the other side of the tanker. Wait . . . I see two small craft, one not far behind the other, both headed west-northwest. Is that you?"

"It has to be."

"Give me twenty minutes, and I'll come find you. Until then, stay safe!"

Laurel returned her phone to her pocket, gripped the wheel with both hands, and resumed her full-throttle chase. On top of one swell, she could see the running lights on Techs's boat flickering in the distance as he crested a wave. She slapped her forehead when she realized *Meryl*'s running lights were off and toggled the switch to turn them on. With a bit more visibility, she could tell that John was right—the storm was getting worse. Laurel struggled to keep the bow facing into the windblown waves. She climbed the face of a big swell and saw Techs's boat closer, about two hundred yards ahead. She pulled back on the throttle and slid down the back of the swell, but when she reached the bottom and rammed the throttle forward again, the motor did not respond. Laurel's attention snapped to the tachometer and the fuel gauge. Both were pegged to zero.

Without power, Laurel could not steer *Meryl*, and the wind blew the boat sideways. Relentless swells hit *Meryl* broadside, threatening to swamp her, or worse, flip her over. Laurel frantically called John to tell him she was dead in the water.

He said, "Listen carefully—get the sea anchor from the storage compartment under the vee berth. Take it to the bow and call me back."

As Laurel staggered into the cabin looking for the sea anchor, a wave threw *Meryl* sideways, and Laurel banged her head against the wall. Dazed for a moment, she rubbed her hand against her temple.

Even though it was too dark to see, Laurel knew she was bleeding. But she ignored that and opened the storage compartment under the mattress. She felt a coil of rope that was attached to a canvas device, pulled it out, and staggered out of the cabin up to the bow, dragging the canvas anchor behind her.

When she called John again, he told her, "Tie the loose end of the rope securely onto the bow cleat and then throw the rest overboard. The canvas cone will float and create enough drag to point the bow into the storm."

"Are you sure?"

"Positive. Pray that it keeps you from capsizing. I'm on my way."

Laurel did as John instructed and felt the line connecting the sea anchor to the boat grow taut as the bow turned toward the wind. Still, large swells lifted and dropped *Meryl* like a car on a roller coaster. Laurel clung to the helm and looked at her phone. She would have to wait another ten minutes for John to arrive.

The boat rose on another crest, and Laurel saw the dim shape of two different swells rushing toward her like two sides of a wedge. She was right between them.

The waves intersected as they passed the sea anchor, and their combined energy jerked *Meryl* upward and tore the cleat from the bow. Laurel stared up at the looming wall of water, took a deep breath, and gripped the steering wheel with all her strength. The giant wave teetered and crashed upon the boat, flooding the cockpit and the cabin.

Though slammed by more than a ton of water, Laurel clung to the wheel. Waves continued to bury the boat so only Laurel's head and *Meryl*'s windshield rose above the water. Laurel pulled out her phone, which—amazingly, still worked—and called John.

He answered and shouted, "Are you all right? You dropped off my radar."

"Hurry! I'm sinking!"

"Don't worry," John reassured her. "The boat won't sink. Just stay with it. I'm not far, and I'll find you. Call me back as soon as you see me."

After the call, John said a quick prayer and radioed the Coast Guard to report a boat in need of rescue. He gave them *Meryl's* coordinates, along with his position. The Coast Guard personnel, already on their highest alert, leaped to their stations, and in less than two minutes, an eighty-seven-foot cutter with a ten-person crew launched into the strait from Ediz Hook. The cutter, designed for emergency search and rescue, had surface-search radar to detect swamped boats and other unusual objects in the water.

As Laurel waited, she shivered from head to toe and could barely feel her fingers. It was increasingly difficult to grasp the wheel, and her grip on her phone was slipping. She squinted out at the darkness behind her, desperately watching for John's arrival. With her attention on the horizon, she did not notice the second sneaker wave towering before her. When it collapsed upon *Meryl,* it tore Laurel's hands from the wheel and swept her overboard. For a terrifying twenty seconds, Laurel struggled under the water and thought her life was over, and then her life vest popped her to the surface. She spewed out a mouthful of saltwater and cried out, "Thank you!"

She remembered she needed to stay with *Meryl,* but, as she spun around looking, she could not locate the boat. It wasn't until she rose to the top of a swell that she spotted *Meryl* drifting only twenty yards away. Laurel swam toward it, but the wind swept her farther away. She pulled harder with each stroke, fighting her way, but the storm was against her.

The cutter reached *Meryl* ahead of John and deployed three seamen in a small boat to conduct the rescue. Each wore an orange, insulated immersion suit to protect him from the frigid waters, and the cutter behind them shone a spotlight to aid their search. Laurel saw the light and the rescue team in the distance, and she yelled and waved her arms to get their attention. But the noise of the gale swallowed Laurel's frantic yells, and her arms were so weak from the cold that they barely reached above her head. The inflatable boat pulled alongside *Meryl,* but the searchers found no one aboard. They affixed a location transponder to *Meryl's* rail to locate the boat later and radioed the cutter to announce the beginning of their search for a person in the water.

The searchlight scanned the dark waves, and after passing near her twice, the beam finally located Laurel, practically blinding her. The sailors raced to reach Laurel and pulled her into the small boat. As they sped back to the cutter, they caught air at the top of each swell, and they did not slow down again until they docked at the rear of the cutter.

Other personnel rushed Laurel to the safety and warmth of the cutter's cabin. A female sailor met her there and introduced herself as Seaman Duran. The woman took Laurel's temperature and walked her to the galley, which doubled as a medical station. Duran motioned for Laurel to sit on a bench, where she covered her with two blankets and gave her a cup of hot tea. Laurel's shivering hands sloshed the tea in its mug, spilling it onto the table. Duran told Laurel to hold still as she bandaged the gash on the side of her head, but Laurel stopped her.

"Have you rescued Sterling or Hoyt?"

"Who?"

"Friends who need my help."

"What are you talking about?"

"They've been kidnapped on two different boats. That's why I went out."

"Wait here."

Duran returned with a man who introduced himself as Chief Petty Officer Taylor. "What's this about your friends?"

Laurel explained what she knew and how she was on her way to rescue Sterling when the wave swamped her boat.

Taylor trotted to the helm and radioed the Coast Guard Office to send all available units to search for the two other boats. Laurel overheard Taylor shouting commands to the sailors and saw search lights illuminating the water in multiple directions. It was clear to Laurel, even from inside the cabin, that the crew had practiced this drill many times.

Duran turned her attention back to Laurel's cut, but Laurel interrupted her again. "Can you ask that man to contact John Mercury? He should be on a pilot boat. Tell him I'm safe and ask him if he has rescued Sterling or Hoyt."

Duran agreed and left to speak with CPO Taylor again. When she returned, she said, "Any other surprises? Or can I bandage you up now?"

Laurel said, "That's it."

"Good. This is a nasty wound that needs treatment. You'll need a doctor to look at it when we get you to shore."

"I will, but right now, I just want to find my friends before something bad happens."

Forty

EVERYTHING AROUND STERLING spelled doom. His kidnapper, the gun, the raging storm that tossed Techs's boat. To Sterling, it was not a question of whether he would survive. It was a question of how he would die. Would Techs make it quick and shoot him? Would Techs throw him overboard and let the cold strait finish the job? Would the boat sink and take them both down with it?

Whatever happened, Sterling suspected he would be going *beyond* much sooner than he had hoped. He regretted his decision to push Laurel away when she tried to tell him about life in the kingdom, and right now, he could use more information. *I am about to lose my life,* Sterling thought. *And for what? I wanted to get Pete's money back? To have nicer clothes? To get even with Dirk? I hacked, lied, and stole— look where that's got me. It's worthless now. None of it helped me gain true life.*

Sterling was losing all hope, but at that very moment, both Laurel and John were praying for him and Hoyt. Sterling was unaware, too, that I hovered high above him, keeping watch in perfect calm. I piffed him to jump overboard into the turbulent waters and escape. But in his fear and sorrow, he did not notice, so I piffed again. Sterling looked over the side of the boat, but drew back at the sight of the churning water. In his defense, sometimes a step of faith and a leap of faith look the same.

Techs shouted at Sterling and ordered him to step to the railing. Techs cocked his gun and pointed it at Sterling's chest. "I've changed my mind," he said. "The longer I keep you around, the longer you'll be a pain in my neck. Besides, I can't trust Dirk to do the right thing. No hard feelings, kid. It's just business."

As Techs was about to pull the trigger, he saw a sleeper wave loom in front of his boat. He quickly yanked the throttle back and braced for the wall of water charging at them. The maverick breaker smashed onto the deck, and tons of seawater poured to the stern and washed off into the strait again.

While Techs ran to the bow, inspecting it for damage, I descended from above and plunged toward Sterling's chest. I rolled onto my back, like when I crashed into Dirk's window, and rammed him with the force of a lineman. Sterling let out a brief yelp, and he catapulted over the rail and splashed into the strait.

Sometimes faith needs a little nudge.

When Techs found his boat was unharmed, he drew the pistol again and walked back to the helm to face Sterling. But Sterling was gone. Techs searched in the cabin, looked over the transom at the swim platform, and even looked in the fish box. Figuring Sterling fell into the water, Techs looked at his wake but spotted nothing. He turned the boat around and backtracked for five minutes, and still there was no sign of Sterling. Techs was pleasantly surprised—the rogue wave had saved him the trouble of shooting Sterling, removed the possibility of him being charged for murder, and best of all, got rid of the boy. Techs returned his course to Dirk's rendezvous point and left the matter of Sterling behind him.

Despite eluding his captor, Sterling was not exactly happy to be in the strait. Waves from the west pounded him like he was a punching bag, and he tried to keep them at his back as they lifted him to the heavens and dropped him into the depths. He gasped for air between each swell, went under, and surfaced, spitting water and gasping again.

Struggling to keep himself afloat, Sterling's legs and arms cramped from nonstop use. He sank and stayed underwater longer each time. He had flashbacks of being stuck in Canaan's Creek earlier that day. There was something strangely comforting about being underwater. The deep seemed to beckon him with the peace and silence of a tomb. Sterling had the answer to his previous question—he was bound for a watery grave.

In his despair, Sterling prayed another awkward prayer. He felt hopeful and foolish at the same time. Hopeful because there was a spark of faith, and foolish because he was not sure he believed in prayer. He asked for forgiveness from the Master for breaking into Dirk's house, for hacking into his computer, and for stealing his Bitcoin. But most of all, he asked forgiveness for hating Dirk. As Sterling became comfortable praying, he asked the Master to help him out of his trouble, and he promised to seek him—if he survived.

Back on Techs' boat, while Techs focused on locating *Leverage*, I swooped and landed in his cockpit. Strutting inside the cabin, I grabbed a life jacket with my beak and dragged it toward the door. The bulky jacket caught on the doorframe, so I put all my strength into a combination tug, crow-hop, and flap of my wings. The vest popped free and landed on the cockpit deck, and I plopped onto my tail feathers. Admittedly, it was not my most graceful move, but it was effective. I grasped a strap in my claws and flew off the boat with it, speeding to Sterling. As I approached him, I circled just overhead to get his attention.

He reached for a strap of the life jacket, but the falling swell pulled him away. I piffed him to recall when he was riding his bike, and I delivered the note from the book of Matthew. He recited the words to himself:

For whoever desires to save his life will lose it, but whoever loses his life for my sake will find it. For what profit is it to a man if he gains the whole world and loses his own soul?

Sterling stared up at me, marveling, and remembered when we danced. He chuckled, and the chuckle grew into a laugh, which turned into a cough as sea water surged into his mouth. When Sterling rose on the next swell, I dropped the vest, and it fell perfectly over his shoulders. He secured the straps under his legs and across his chest.

"I'm ready!" he shouted. "I'm ready to lose my life for the Master's sake!"

At his words, the storm instantly calmed. The winds ceased, Sterling's hatred of Dirk evaporated, and he suddenly understood how the Master had lifted Laurel's bitterness toward him.

I tipped my right wing and flew into the cloudless sky, recalling the words of the psalmist:

They cried out to the Lord in their trouble, and he brought them out of their distress.

He stilled the storm to a whisper; the waves of the sea were hushed.

They were glad when it grew calm, and he guided them to their desired haven.

Sterling was astounded that his prayer stilled the storm to a whisper and hushed the waves of the sea. But Sterling's prayers were only part of the picture. He did not know that the seas grew calm, not only in answer to his prayer, but also in response to the cries of Laurel and John.

Great joy erupted in heaven when Sterling asked to be forgiven and decided to surrender his life for a better one. He had been moving toward this moment since his first encounter with Laurel and his first encounter with me. At any point, he could have denied my wooing and continued to control his own life. But when he said, "I'm ready to lose my life for the Master's sake," he embarked on his sojourn. He became a resident foreigner in this world and a citizen of the hidden kingdom. Although he would not take up permanent residence in that place for many years, I knew he would become increasingly comfortable with its ways.

So, as the storm dissipated, Sterling contemplated the impact of losing his life, and all the while failed to notice that the current was pulling him farther from land and headlong into the shipping lanes.

Forty-One

DIRK CALLED TECHS and said, "I'll be heading back to the basin soon. Meet me there."

"Don't bother," Techs replied. "I'm nearly at your drop location. Have you taken care of the twin?"

"Wait, what do you mean? You're nearly at the drop?"

"I'm almost at the drop coordinates right now."

"I told you to meet me at the basin."

"Yes, you did. I said, 'Whatever.' And now I'm here. I deciphered the coordinates from your email. Have you taken care of your twin?"

"From my email? That's impossible. I just received the message about this drop late last night."

"Did you really think I couldn't recover all the data on your disk, including your email password?"

Dirk grimaced and shifted his phone from one ear to the other. "I knew I shouldn't have trusted you."

"It's a little late for that. Have you taken care of the kid?"

"Of course." Dirk bluffed. "I knocked him out with the fish club, tied a weight to his ankles, and tossed him overboard. What about yours?"

"Mine was a piece of cake. He fell overboard when a sneaker wave smashed into us. I turned around and searched for him, but no luck.

He's gotta be at the bottom by now."

Dirk struggled to hold his composure at the news of Sterling's death. "I told you I needed to question him about the Bitcoin."

"Relax. I asked him for you. He said he returned it to your account."

"It was empty last time I looked."

"Check it again."

"I can't right now. Techs, you knew I needed to talk to him. What if he lied to you?"

"Too bad. You won't be seeing him again. He's fish food."

"Really comforting. Thanks." Dirk sneered. "You know what? I don't think he fell in at all. You probably threw him over. I know you wanted to get rid of him."

"Save your breath. He fell overboard. That's all there is to it. And it was a good thing he did, because you wouldn't have had the guts to do it yourself. As a matter of fact, I bet you haven't taken care of his brother."

"You're delusional."

"Oh, yeah? Well, I'm only a few minutes away, and when I get there, I'll look for myself."

Dirk ended the call and hurried down from the flying bridge to the cabin. He loaded six bullets into his revolver, spun the cylinder, and handed the gun to Hoyt.

"What's this for?"

"My aim is terrible."

"And mine isn't much better."

"Last year, I remember you hit four out of six targets at the range."

"You call that good aim?"

"Better than mine," Dirk said. "My new partner turned against me, which honestly, I might have deserved. But he's almost here, and he's going to be looking for you. I told him I tossed you overboard, but he's not buying it. I think I can talk him down when he gets here. But I'm warning you, you need to stay out of sight. If he sees you, shoot him."

"What? I can't shoot anybody."

"Hoyt, listen to me. It's your only chance to survive. This guy, he"—Dirk hesitated, seeing the fear in Hoyt's eyes—"He threw Sterling overboard."

"Sterling! Then what are we waiting for? We have to go get him!"

"No." Dirk shook his head. "It's too late for that. He's gone."

"Gone."

Hoyt tried to wrap his brain around the news. Sterling was dead, and all because of his stupid detergent prank. Hoyt stammered, searching for a solution, and his shock quickly turned to rage. He was not planning to hide from Techs. He was going to make him pay.

At the sound of a motor revving in the distance, Dirk turned to look over his shoulder and saw the incoming boat. Hoyt retreated to the cabin and peered out a porthole to watch Techs's movements. Dirk waved Techs over, and Techs's boat slowed and drifted to within twenty yards of *Leverage*. When it stopped, the two boats faced each other, bow to bow, like gunfighters in a shootout.

Techs walked to the front rail and hollered, "Did you pick up our goods?"

"They aren't *our* goods," Dirk answered, "but yes, they're on board. I'll deliver them to the drop-off location later this morning."

"McCleod." Techs snickered. "You are such a sucker." He pulled out his own pistol and aimed at Dirk. "You have delivered the goods far enough. I'm taking them from here. Why would I settle for a mere delivery fee when I can get so much more? I'll bet I can sell whatever you pulled up on the black market for far more than my cut would have been."

"You're making a huge mistake." Dirk raised his hands cautiously. "If I miss this delivery, they'll come after me . . . after us."

"I don't doubt that. But I'll make sure they never find you, and they don't even know I exist."

While the two men talked, Hoyt exited the cabin on the far side of the boat and snuck up the ladder to the flying bridge, where he crawled to the helm. Because he laid low, he could not see either man, but he could hear their conversation. He heard Techs say, "Prepare to be boarded," and then his ears rang with the report of a gunshot.

Hoyt rose to his knees to see what happened, and he spotted Dirk collapsed on the deck below. Without hesitating, Hoyt shifted *Leverage* into gear and slammed the throttle forward, charging toward Techs's boat. Techs scrambled to his own helm, but by the time he reached the wheel, *Leverage* had rammed into his bow and knocked him headfirst into the dashboard. He struggled to his feet and fired four shots at *Leverage*, but missed Hoyt entirely.

Hoyt stood and fired five shots back, sending Techs ducking behind the cabin for cover. Hoyt shifted *Leverage* into reverse and then pushed the throttle forward. He jerked the wheel from left to right while backing up to make himself harder to hit.

Techs stood and emptied his pistol at Hoyt before he tucked it into his waistband and ran up to his flying bridge.

Hoyt saw his opportunity. He jammed *Leverage* into forward and opened the throttle. Before Techs could move his boat, Hoyt scored his second hit. As the boats jostled in the water, Hoyt circled to the stern of Techs's boat, eyeing the two Yamaha outboards. He rammed into the port engine, and it dangled from its mount. Techs shifted his boat into gear and moved away, but with only one outboard motor working, half speed was as fast as he could go. Hoyt repeated the assault and nailed the starboard engine, snapping its steering mechanism. The motor roared, but with no steering, the boat spun in circles until Techs cut power and let his boat drift.

Leaving Techs with an empty gun and a disabled boat, Hoyt motored far enough away to get out of pistol range, and then he turned his attention to Dirk. He unclipped a flashlight from under the dashboard and shined it down on the deck.

Dirk had pulled himself up enough to lean against the cabin, and blood seeped from his left shoulder. Through clenched teeth, he called up to Hoyt, "Did you hit Techs?"

271

"Not with the gun, but his engines are out, and I moved us away from him. I don't think he can hurt us now."

"Okay . . . I need you . . . I need you to help me stop the bleeding. And activate the Automatic Identification System transponder."

Hoyt ran inside the cabin and switched on the transponder. He took the radio's microphone from its hook, announced an SOS and that the captain had been shot, and retrieved the first aid kit to take to Dirk. Once Dirk was stable, Hoyt returned to the cabin to wait by the radio for any response.

Meanwhile, across the strait on the Coast Guard cutter, CPO Taylor had received the distress call and picked up his mic to respond. "*Leverage*, your AIS tag popped up on my radar. We are currently engaged in a rescue, but I have your position. Standby." Taylor radioed the Coast Guard station and asked them to send backup to *Leverage*, but all units were deployed with other emergencies. A minute later, his radar showed a small blip on the surface, 300 yards ahead and 100 yards to the port. "That's him," he yelled, and after alerting the crew, he altered course. A seaman scanned the waters with a spotlight until he located Sterling bobbing in his life jacket, and he signaled CPO Taylor, who announced it to the rest of the boat.

"Man in the water!" the officer called over the speakers. "Prepare to rescue." The cutter's search light remained focused on Sterling, blinding him. The same three crew members who had rescued Laurel earlier pulled Sterling from the calm waters and transported him to the cutter, where Seaman Duran wrapped a blanket around his shoulders.

As Duran escorted him to the cabin, Sterling stopped and asked anxiously, "Have you found my brother? They're planning to kill him."

Duran said, "I've heard some talk about that. Why don't I take you to CPO Taylor?"

Sterling let the blanket fall to the floor, and they trotted to the pilothouse, where Duran introduced Sterling to CPO Taylor. Sterling skipped the formalities and blurted, "A man, Dirk McCleod, took my brother on his boat, *Leverage*. It can't be far from here. I think Dirk plans to kill him."

Taylor pointed to a chair next to him. "Sit down and tell me what's going on."

Forty-Two

STERLING TOLD CPO Taylor everything he knew about Hoyt's abduction, including what he learned from Techs. He skipped over his own adventure because, at that moment, Hoyt's safety was the only thing on his mind. Taylor listened carefully, and Seaman Duran stood by. They both let Sterling finish without interruption.

When Sterling concluded, Taylor responded, "We just got an SOS call from *Leverage,* so that's where we're headed. The captain has been shot, and unless someone else is on the boat, it was your brother who called us. He didn't mention being hurt himself, so you can rest assured." The officer took off his cap and wiped his forehead. "I'll tell you, this is the craziest night I've ever seen. A sudden storm rages and then disappears as fast as it showed up, and now three kids are in danger in three different boats. Is there anything else you need to tell me before we get to *Leverage?*"

Sterling looked down at his hands and replied, "Just one more thing—there's a guy named Techs. I was on his boat when I went into the water. He's out there, too, and I think he's smuggling something with Dirk."

"Can this night get any stranger?" Taylor asked. "Thank you for telling me." He grabbed the intercom mic and announced, "All hands at full enforcement readiness." Taylor then waved Duran over to the navigation screen and pointed to the icon labeled *Leverage.* "The radar shows another craft next to her," Taylor noted. "This could be dangerous. Take the boy to the galley, where the girl is."

As soon as Seaman Duran took Sterling to where Laurel was being kept, Laurel jumped from the booth and hugged Sterling. "Thank goodness!" she cried. "I haven't stopped praying since you told me you had been kidnapped."

"Wait a sec. What are you doing here? Did you come out with the Coast Guard?"

"No, I tried to follow you on *Meryl.* I saw a boat leave the basin and thought you must be on it. But it was a disaster out in the storm, and Dad's boat got swamped. I called John, and he must have called the Coast Guard. I'm lucky to be alive . . . too bad Dad's going to kill me."

Sterling and Laurel sat down in the booth, and Seaman Duran excused herself to report to Taylor. Sterling and Laurel sat in stunned silence for several moments, and Sterling said, "You shouldn't have tried to rescue me. But thank you for doing it. And for praying."

"What are friends for?"

Sterling smiled. "I guess you're right . . . I wanted to tell you, I prayed too. Dirk's partner was going to kill me, but then that crazy dove came out of nowhere—the one that has been showing up all over the place."

"Really?"

Sterling nodded. "He rammed me so hard I fell overboard, which is probably how I survived. It was a strange answer to my prayer. At first, I thought he tried to kill me, since I was struggling in the water and thought I would drown. But just when I was about to give up, the dove dropped a life vest right onto my shoulders. That kept me afloat while I waited and prayed. It wasn't long before the Coast Guard showed up and pulled me out of the water."

"I don't think that dove's intervention was a coincidence."

"I finally figured that out," Sterling said, pulling his blanket tighter around his shoulders. "Now, I want to follow the Master and let him transform me, whatever that will bring."

"You've got a long and exciting road ahead of you, but for now, you can sit back and relax."

"Not yet. I can't relax while Hoyt is out there somewhere with Dirk."

Up in the wheelhouse, Taylor slammed both throttles all the way forward, and the cutter roared at full speed toward Dirk and Techs's boats. As they approached, a sailor shined the cutter's spotlight on *Leverage.*

Duran walked to the bow to contact the boat. She held up a megaphone and called out, "Anyone aboard?"

Hoyt stepped out from the cabin into the bright spotlight and waved. "Me and one other!" he shouted. "He's been shot." In the distance, Hoyt saw Techs stumble out of his cabin and aim his pistol toward *Leverage.* Hoyt ducked for cover barely a second before Techs fired three quick shots. One shot hit the cabin, and the other two missed altogether.

Duran dropped to the deck, and the spotlight swung to Techs. Two sailors ran to the two fifty-caliber machine guns mounted on the cutter, and Taylor yelled into the intercom, "Fire warning salvos!"

Immediately, each gunner fired a brief burst, and muzzle flashes stabbed out of the barrels like electric daggers. The machine gunners then aimed directly at Techs, ready to shoot if he posed a threat. Techs dropped his pistol into the water and put both hands in the air.

Four seamen launched from the cutter in the inflatable boat. The small inflatable dropped off one sailor at *Leverage,* and the other three motored over to secure Tech's and his boat. Hoyt escorted the lone seaman on *Leverage* to Dirk, and the man shined his flashlight on Dirk's wound to examine it.

"Will he be all right?"

"I'm not an EMT, so I can't diagnose him or treat him," the seaman answered. "But we'll get a helicopter out here right away." He wrapped a bandage around Dirk's shoulder and radioed the Coast Guard station for evacuation.

A few minutes later, thumping rotors punctuated the night and announced the helicopter's arrival. As the chopper hovered over *Leverage,* its crewmen lowered a rescue basket onto the deck, and the seaman loaded Dirk into it. Once Dirk was secured in the basket like a cocoon, the winch lifted him up to the helicopter, and it sped to the hospital in Port Angeles, taking the thumping sounds of its blades into the distance.

Meanwhile, on Techs's boat, one of the crewmen handcuffed Techs and hauled him to the inflatable. Another crewman stayed onboard to protect Techs's boat as potential evidence, while the others transported Techs to *Leverage,* collected Hoyt and the first sailor, and returned to the cutter. As the crewmen escorted Techs to a room below deck, they passed the galley, and Techs met eyes with Sterling.

Sterling approached him and said, "Who's the clever one now, big guy?"

Techs lunged forward and bashed Sterling's face with his shoulder before being yanked back by his captors.

Sterling held his nose as blood dripped onto the floor. Laurel handed him two napkins from the table, and Sterling hoped she would attribute the redness in his face to his injury and not to his embarrassment.

Soon after Techs was taken away, another group came down the hallway, and Sterling recognized a voice. "Hoyt?" he yelled, and then ran to the door to see. When Hoyt turned the corner, Sterling rushed to him and gave him a hug.

"Sterling?" Hoyt stammered. "Dirk told me you were dead."

"Me? I thought *you* were dead. Techs told me that Dirk killed you." Sterling hugged Hoyt tighter.

Hoyt said, "Whoa. Let's not get carried away."

Sterling stepped back and looked Hoyt over. "Are you okay? What happened to your eye?"

"It's nothing. I'm fine. Somehow."

"We prayed for you," Laurel interjected. "Sterling and me."

Hoyt raised an eyebrow at Sterling. "*You* prayed?"

"Yes, and it looks like it worked."

"Don't get carried away. This all could have been a coincidence."

"That's possible, but . . . I'm finding some of these 'coincidences' too coincidental to believe."

"Wait a minute," Hoyt redirected. "How did you get here?"

"I came to help you and—"

"Excuse me," Seaman Duran interrupted, walking into the galley with clipboards and pens. "Each of you needs to fill out one of these forms before we can release you. They're essential to our report of what happened tonight." She set the materials on the table in front of the boys and Laurel. "Be thorough and take your time. Write down every detail. And don't forget to sign and date them when you're finished."

The three of them did as Duran asked, although Hoyt rushed through all eight pages to get it over with. He clapped his clipboard back down on the table and said, "I almost got away."

"What do you mean?" Sterling asked, looking up from his paperwork.

"I mean, when those guys caught me back by our house. I outran the ponytail guy, but I trusted the wrong partner, and it turned out they were working together. The big one sucker punched me, knocked me out, and I woke up on *Leverage* with Dirk. I watched Dirk, by the way. He's definitely up to something shady—smuggling, like you suspected. After he pulled in his haul, Techs showed up, and he and Dirk started arguing. Oh, and Dirk got shot."

"What? Is he okay?"

"Dunno. A helicopter had to take him from the boat. Anyway, what was I saying? Right, the gunfight! Techs and I were shooting at each other, and I crashed Leverage into his stupid boat—at least three times. *Leverage* didn't take on water, though, which was too bad. That was my chance to sink her."

"Hoyt—"

"What a night. And it turns out Dirk fired the new yard guys. He said that—"

"Hoyt! Will you chill and let us finish these forms?"

"Who cares about paperwork? I can't wait to tell my friends about this."

Sterling set down his pen and glared. "I wish it never happened. No one won tonight. Do you understand that?"

"Well, we kind of did—"

"No, we all lost. We lost a lot. Dirk did, too, assuming he survives. It wasn't so long ago that we were tight with Dirk, and we shouldn't be so quick to forget it. He was a good friend to Pete and Mom, not to mention his partnership with Pete. Now, we'll never hang out with Dirk again. Never go fishing with him, never groan at his bad jokes. And that's not just bad for us—it's terrible for Dirk. He lost the most in this. Sure, he's rich, but he has no real friends, and he has no family now that we're out of the picture. On top of that, he'll probably do hard time for smuggling. Think about it this way, Hoyt. Even after Dirk recovers, his life is over."

Hoyt said nothing in response and looked at Sterling like he was from outer space.

Duran walked through the doorway again asked, "All done?" Hoyt nodded, but Sterling and Laurel shook their heads and continued writing. "All right. Hurry if you can. We'll be at the station in five minutes. Wait here until someone comes for you."

As Duran turned to walk out of the galley, Laurel said, "Wait! I need to tell my uncle I'm safe. Can I borrow a phone?"

"I forgot to tell you. He radioed the captain. He knows you are safe. I'm supposed to tell you he had to make another pilot run and he'll meet up with you as soon as he can."

Forty-Three

DAWNING SUNLIGHT BRIGHTENED the underside of a cumulus cloud layer, making the clouds look like cotton balls soaked in crimson. But everyone on board the Coast Guard cutter was too busy or too tired to appreciate the beauty of the sunrise.

CPO Taylor steered his vessel into its slip at the station and held it in position until two seamen secured the lines and put the boarding steps in place. On the dock, four uniformed police officers waited, and they were joined by two detectives wearing slacks, sport jackets, and ties. As the cutter unloaded, Seaman Duran walked copies of Sterling, Hoyt, and Laurel's paperwork directly to one of the detectives. Techs shuffled off the boat behind her, escorted by two crew members, and was delivered to the uniformed officers. A detective and an officer led Techs to a patrol car to drive him to the police station.

When Sterling, Hoyt, and Laurel stepped onto the dock, still wrapped in their blankets, Laurel said, "We can walk from here to the basin, and I can give you a ride home on my scooter. We might have to take two trips, though."

"Whatever it takes," Sterling said. "I can't wait to get home and crash onto my bed."

As they turned to leave the dock, however, three police officers and the second detective stepped in front of them. The detective extended his badge and said, "I'm Detective Bloch. I am investigating this case, and I need you all need to come down to the station for some questions."

"We're beat," Sterling said. "We've been up all night. Can't we go home and get some sleep first?"

Detective Bloch smirked. "Sorry, kid. That's not how it works when there's been a shooting."

AT THE POLICE station, Bloch took the three into a holding room and handed them each a piece of paper to record their contact information along with their guardians'. They followed his instruction, and after collecting their papers, Bloch abruptly left the room. As soon as the detective closed the door behind him, Hoyt walked to the doorknob to test it. It was locked. Laurel shivered and went over to the wall thermostat, where she wedged a skinny finger through a gap in the protective cage and turned the heat to a toasty seventy-seven degrees.

At his desk, Detective Bloch called Pete to tell him about the storm, his sons' perilous encounters, and the Coast Guard rescues. Pete asked Bloch if the boys were under suspicion of committing a crime, and when Bloch assured him they were not, Pete agreed to let Bloch question the boys without being present. Pete explained that both he and his wife were in Seattle and couldn't be back in less than three or four hours, so Bloch offered to take all three teenagers home once he finished questioning them. After ending the call with Pete, Bloch tried to reach John, but the call went to voice mail. He left a message asking John to call him back.

After nearly an hour had passed, Bloch returned to the holding room. He collected Sterling for questioning and dropped him off in a smaller room to wait. As Sterling entered, he observed the stark, cold room, which was furnished with only a metal table and four metal chairs. He shivered as he tried to pick a seat close to a heat vent. The ten-by-twelve room had four vents near the ceiling, one on each wall, and Sterling guessed each one hid a camera and microphone. One wall was completely reflective, fitted with one-way glass. Sterling wondered if anyone would observe the questioning. He felt like a fish in an aquarium and sat with his back to the glass wall while he waited. Bloch returned to the room and flipped on additional lights. Sterling squinted under the brightness, and Bloch pointed to the chair facing the glass.

"Please," he said, "sit here and tell me what happened."

As Sterling summarized the events of the past ten hours, Bloch frequently interrupted him for clarification and further details. Bloch's questioning was direct and thorough, and he wrote extensive notes in a spiral notebook. Most of the questions probed the kidnapping, Dirk's shooting, and the smuggling. Sterling provided details about going to the marina to meet Laurel and trying to find Hoyt. Bloch scribbled quickly as Sterling described how Techs kidnapped him and threatened to kill him. But when Sterling reached the part about me saving him by knocking him into the strait, he didn't think Bloch would believe the truth. To be fair, Sterling wouldn't have believed it had he not experienced it himself. Instead, he told Bloch he fell overboard and implied he was already wearing the life jacket.

The nature and tone of Bloch's questions grew more intense when they discussed Dirk's smuggling operation. Sterling felt uncomfortably pressured, like Bloch was an aquarium keeper closing in with a net, trying to scoop him up. Besides investigating the big fish—Techs and Dirk—Bloch apparently wanted to build a case against the small fish, too. Sterling answered Bloch's questions honestly and told him he was not involved in the smuggling. He was careful not to volunteer information about his surveillance, hacking, or stealing. The way Sterling saw it, if Bloch was going to chase small fish, he was going to need to do it without being given any bait.

After scribbling ten pages of notes in just under an hour, Bloch returned Sterling to the holding room and took Hoyt next for questioning. An hour later, he repeated the process with Laurel. Afterward, Bloch thanked them for their cooperation and told them not to be surprised if he had follow-up questions later. They said they understood, and Bloch offered to take them all home.

Back at the Burke house, Sterling staggered up to his room, changed into dry clothes, and collapsed onto his bed. As he lay there, exhausted, he smiled. He was looking forward to what he would do with the second chance he had been given.

Forty-Four

AS IT TURNED out, Sterling was too wired to fall asleep right away. Drifting on the edge of consciousness, he put the storm and rescue out of his mind, but the thought of a certain Mustang GT kept him awake. Sterling was scheduled to take his driving test in a few days, and he searched his mind, double-checking that he was fully prepared. He had quizzed his friends who had already passed their driver's tests, so he knew what skills the examination covered and the route he would likely need to navigate. After more than an hour of rehearsing, his weary body fell into such a deep sleep that he did not hear his parents come into the house after they returned from Seattle. He didn't hear it when his dad knocked on his bedroom door, either.

"Sterling?" Pete waited a moment before entering.

Sterling didn't move, so Pete walked to the bed and nudged Sterling's elbow. Sterling jolted awake. "Rise and shine.," Pete said. "We need to talk. Everyone is waiting in the living room.

They walked downstairs together, and Hoyt was already sitting on the couch and appeared to be half asleep.

Anne ran to Sterling and hugged him as if he had returned from the dead. "Happy birthday," she whimpered into his shoulder. "I'm so happy you lived to see it. The detective said you nearly drowned in a freak storm." Sniffling, she pulled back from him. "What happened?"

"It was pretty scary for a few minutes, but it's all right. I'm okay now."

Pete sat in his favorite chair, and Sterling waited until his mother let go of him before sitting in the rocking chair at the far end of the room. Pete shook his head and pointed to the nearby spot at the end of the couch. Sterling slowly stood again and walked over next to Hoyt to take a seat, but his mother intercepted him and gave him another hug.

"You should have called to tell us you were all right," she said.

"I lost my phone."

"I'm sure you could've borrowed one."

"Hoyt lost his, too."

"Well," Pete interrupted, "while we are both relieved that you boys are safe, you have a lot of explaining to do. Do you have any idea how worried we were when the police called to tell us there had been serious trouble? A shooting, boat wrecks, near drownings? Any of those by itself is alarming—the combination of all three is a cardiac arrest. Couldn't you two stay out of trouble for a couple of days?" Pete gestured to Hoyt. "You first. What happened?"

Hoyt yawned and launched into his story. He summarized how Dirk sabotaged their yard business, how he got caught after poisoning Dirk's lawn, how he was kidnapped, and how Dirk wanted to protect him from Techs and got shot. Hoyt paused and concluded by saying, "And to think Dirk did all that because he wanted Mom back. Strange, huh?"

Pete ignored Hoyt's comment. "Detective Bloch told me you tried to sink *Leverage.*"

"Not entirely true. Mostly I wanted to get away from Techs, so I rammed his boat to disable it. I wanted to get even with Dirk, and I definitely wouldn't have minded if *Leverage* sunk. But really, it was in self-defense."

Sterling shook his head at Hoyt and said, "Brilliant. Risk sinking the boat that was keeping you from drowning."

"Hey." Hoyt sneered. "I knew the Coast Guard was on the way."

Pete held up a hand. "Enough." He looked at Sterling. "Your turn."

When Sterling started to answer, his mother's phone rang. Not recognizing the number, she let the call go to voice mail. Sterling looked back at Pete and took a deep breath. "I wondered where Hoyt was and looked up his location on my phone. When I saw him speed to the marina, I got worried and decided to meet up with him to make sure he was all right."

"That was good thinking. Gutsy, too," Pete interjected.

"Whatever," Hoyt said.

Sterling shook his head at Hoyt. "Right after—"

His mother's phone rang again. It was the same caller, and this time, she answered it. After listening for a moment and muttering several, *uh huhs*, she looked at her watch and said, "Sure. That's no problem. See you then."

Anne ended the call and apologized to the family for the interruption. She told Pete, "That was Dirk's attorney. She claims to have urgent information for us, and she's on her way." Anne turned back to Sterling and said, "Please continue."

"As I was saying, right after I got there, I saw *Leverage* heading out of the basin. Dirk's new partner, that man named Techs that Hoyt mentioned, saw me and forced me onto his boat at gunpoint. We went out into the storm, which kept getting worse, and he threatened to shoot me. But right before he did, a dove flew into me and knocked me overboard. I was about to drown in the waves when the dove dropped a life jacket to me, which saved me until the Coast Guard showed up."

"I was believing you until the part about the dove," Pete said. "Did something hit you in the head?"

Hoyt snickered. "That girl, Laurel. She has him spinning in circles."

"You're just jealous," Sterling replied before continuing. "The dove is a whole other story. I'll tell you about it, but then you'll think I'm crazy for sure."

Before Sterling could tell them about me, Hoyt interrupted,

"Sterling, did you ever tell them about the Bitcoin you stole?"

"Bitcoin?" Anne asked.

"I'll explain that later."

"Stealing Bitcoin?" his mother said. "I want to hear about that now."

Sterling glared at Hoyt and sighed. "It's cryptocurrency. It's like money, but it's often used on the dark web, completely under the government's radar. Dirk had around a quarter of a million in his account. The worst part is . . ." Sterling stopped, realizing he could never take his next words back. "I did steal it. I opened my own Bitcoin account and transferred everything from Dirk's account into mine." Sterling gave Pete a pleading look and said, "Please, wait. I know it was wrong, and I already transferred everything back to his account. Every penny."

Before Pete could respond, the doorbell rang.

Pete answered the door and ushered a woman into the living room. She was about fifty years old and wore a red sweater and blue jeans. Pete said, "This is Ms. Scott, Dirk's attorney."

Anne and the boys stood up and introduced themselves. Pete pulled the rocking chair nearer to the family for Ms. Scott, and everyone took a seat.

"You can call me Diane," she said. "And excuse my casual clothes—I was relaxing at home this morning when Mr. McCleod called. I've been going nonstop ever since."

"You spoke with Dirk?" Sterling asked. "Is he going to be all right?"

Diane started to answer and paused. She leaned forward and solemnly folded her hands. With a quiet voice, she said, "There's no easy way to say this. Mr. McCleod passed away as we finished speaking this morning. The doctors think a blood clot went to his heart."

A shocked hush fell on the Burkes. Anne sniffled on her way out of the room and returned with a box of tissues and red eyes. Diane waited for Anne to settle herself and then continued. "Just before Mr. McCleod passed, he instructed me to inform you immediately of his will. He didn't say why he wanted it done so quickly, and I didn't have a chance to ask him. I am merely carrying out his last wish."

Diane asked Sterling and Hoyt to tell her their full names and birth dates. They did so, each with a puzzled look on his face. She nodded. "I drafted his will nearly two months ago. Rather than waiting for you to read the entire document, why don't I tell you the main points? I'll leave a copy for you, and I'll be happy to answer questions."

Diane turned to Anne and continued, "Mrs. Burke, Mr. McCleod named you the successor trustee. That means you are responsible for administering his estate. Sterling and Hoyt are the sole beneficiaries. Mr. McCleod left everything to them—to be shared equally. The trust stipulates that the boys cannot access the assets until their eighteenth birthday, which I see is exactly two years from now. I am sorry to bring such sad news on your birthdays. But happy birthday, anyway."

"I can hardly believe this," Anne exclaimed. "In the past few years, Dirk spent more and more time with the boys, but he never gave them anything of value."

"He didn't explain why he left everything to your sons, and although I was curious, it wasn't my place to ask. I assumed he had a special relationship with them. Mrs. Burke, I suggest you hire your own estate attorney and tax accountant. They can provide valuable counsel, and the trust can reimburse you for those expenses." She paused and asked the family, "Any questions at this time?"

All four of the Burkes shook their heads, too stunned to think.

Ms. Scott stood and said, "I'll leave you alone to process your loss. Again, I'm very sorry."

Pete walked her to the door and came back to his chair.

The Burke family sat without speaking for several minutes, though no one was more bewildered than Sterling. He was trying to put the jigsaw of information together in a way that made sense. But the pieces would not fit, especially not his emotions. As soon as Ms. Scott announced Dirk's death, he was consoled by knowing he had already forgiven Dirk. He realized the hatred that once controlled him was a bondage that had promised to satisfy him, but never could. Now, instead of being pleased with Dirk's death, he felt genuine sorrow. Would the grief he now felt be any easier to deal with than hatred? And what about confusion? Why would Dirk betray them and treat them so cruelly, only to leave everything to Hoyt and him? Sterling feared he would never know.

Pete broke the silence. "In all the bad news, I forgot to say something very important to you boys—happy birthday. Unfortunately, we had planned to pick up your gifts in Seattle, but that was cut short. So, we will try to shop for gifts today. And we still plan to go to Victoria next week. In the meantime, you each need to get new phones. You can charge them to our mobile plan. Sound good?"

"Pete," Sterling asked, "who will arrange a funeral for Dirk?"

Before Pete could answer, the doorbell rang again.

Forty-Five

PETE RETURNED TO the living room with a middle-aged man who wore a dark blue business suit. Pete introduced him, saying, "This is Agent Carter with the Drug Enforcement Agency. He has some questions for you boys."

Carter greeted everyone, unbuttoned his suit jacket, and sat in the rocking chair. He pulled a recording device from his jacket and asked, "Do you mind if I record this?"

Pete nodded and took out his own phone. He said, "You can record it, and I will, too. Just to make sure we stay on the same page."

"I have no problem with that." Carter cleared his throat and turned to the boys. "First, Sterling and Hoyt, let me give you the background information. We have suspected Dirk McCleod of drug trafficking for over three months now. Four weeks ago, we opened a temporary field office here in Port Angeles solely to put McCleod under 24-7 surveillance. We deployed high-tech hidden cameras, microphones, and GPS trackers—the works. Last week, we obtained a search warrant for his house, office, and boat, and we are currently gathering the evidence we need to prosecute him. If he is convicted, we'll seize any and all assets he purchased with his drug money.

"With that being said, in the process of monitoring McCleod, we inevitably recorded you boys sneaking into the garage, setting up your camera, and trashing his lawn." Agent Carter chuckled and added, "You had us pretty confused at first, then we realized there are two of you. And you were lucky McCleod never caught you setting up your camera—without that freak accident with the bird hitting the window, you wouldn't have gotten away with it. Yes, we saw quite a lot of activity on that property, including McCleod's associate installing *his* cameras, and I'd wager there isn't another home in PA with more cameras observing it. But I digress.

"Besides video surveillance, we installed our own remote control and spyware software on McCleod's computer. Ours was much more difficult to detect than yours, as you might imagine. Still, when you reformatted McCleod's hard disk, you made a lot of trouble for us, and our technical expert wanted me to arrest you. We lost an unknown amount of data and are considering charging you with destroying evidence. However, our tech should have copied the disk by that point, which is his mistake, but he wants to hang it on you."

Pete interrupted, "Boys, it certainly sounds like you left out some key details when you told us what happened. You're both in trouble."

Carter reiterated, "To be clear, this is a serious offense. We're talking about multiple accounts of breaking and entering, destroying evidence, and interfering with an investigation. It's hard to say what your sentences will be if you are found guilty at trial. It largely depends on whether you will be tried as minors or as adults. Could go either way. But I'll warn you, the federal district attorney always pushes for trying minors as adults. He wants the most severe sentence he can get."

Sterling and Hoyt went pale and sank into the couch as Agent Carter continued.

"It's a good thing you removed your surveillance gear when you did and didn't interfere any further with our investigation. Otherwise, my supervisor would never have approved the deal I am going to offer you. It's pretty simple—if *you* help us, *we* will help you. If you give us a lot of help, we will help you a lot. Now we know McCleod was smuggling. This morning, we recovered more than half a million dollars' worth of illegal pharmaceuticals from his boat. We think the drugs originated in Asia, and we know they came into the U.S. from Canada. We also know he transferred the drugs to his boat, but we don't know how he did it. We had a GPS tracker on his boat and have been working with the Coast Guard to watch for a rendezvous with the supplier. But even with its high-tech surface radar, the Coast Guard hasn't seen McCleod rendezvous with another boat. Until last night, when *Leverage* smashed into Lorimer Niblick's boat, McCleod has never been near enough to anyone's vessel to transfer anything. Bottom line, we don't think there was another boat in the smuggling operation, and the Mounties agree. That's where you boys can help us out.

"Hoyt, we know you were on *Leverage* last night when McCleod transferred the drugs. We need you to tell us how he did it, and if you do, the District Attorney will not file charges against you or your brother. So, first off, did you see the transfer?"

"Yeah," Hoyt said, "I saw it firsthand."

Pete interrupted, "Hoyt, wait. The deal needs to be in writing, signed by the proper authorities."

Agent Carter reached inside his jacket and pulled out a folded paper. He handed it to Pete, and Pete studied it.

Hoyt asked, "Who is Lattimer Numlick?"

"Lorimer Niblick," Carter corrected. "He goes by Techs."

"This looks good," Pete said, folding the paper again. "Go ahead, Hoyt. Tell Mr. Cater what happened."

"Okay," Hoyt said, casting a sly glance at Sterling. "You're right, Mr. Carter. There wasn't another boat. Or a raft . . ."

The man leaned forward on his knees, listening intently as Hoyt explained. "A giant dove flew over the boat over and dropped the package right into the middle of *Leverage*'s deck."

Sterling tried to stifle a laugh, but it burst out of him.

"A dove?" Carter asked. "What do you mean?"

"Nothing. I'm just messin' with Sterling."

"Look," Carter admonished. "If you get cute with me, the deal is off."

"Sorry, I'm so tired that I can barely stay awake. Here's what really happened." Hoyt told Carter how Dirk navigated to a specific location, put the speaker under the water, and used his winch to recover the pod and the drugs. As an afterthought, he added, "After removing the drugs, Dirk put new packages into the pod and lowered it again. He thought they were pistols."

"Are you sure about that?"

"Absolutely. Well, not about the pistols. That was Dirk's guess."

"Do you know the coordinates McCleod used to reach the drop?"

"No, but he used *Leverage*'s GPS to get there."

"They are probably still there," Sterling offered. "I know how to find the waypoints he stored on his system. But why don't you use the tracker you hid on his boat?"

"We don't have it. It must have fallen off in the storm."

"Or in the ramming." Sterling smirked at Hoyt. "I'll bet somebody from the Canadian side of the strait will pick up the guns Dirk loaded into the pod. They will wait until it's dark, maybe tonight. You should be able to catch them with your advanced equipment and expert technical staff. You know—the works."

Agent Carter laughed. "I'll give your regards to my team."

Pete looked at Carter and said, "I'd say the boys fulfilled their part of the deal, especially telling you about the two-way transfer. Do you agree?"

Carter nodded.

"Please say it out loud for the recording," Pete said.

"Yes. I believe they did their part. I think my superiors will agree."

"Good. Could you tell us more about seizing Dirk's assets?"

"Sure. If McCleod is convicted, the law gives us the right to confiscate any assets that were found to have been purchased with drug money. Our financial experts will piece together a trail of his drug activity and the money he made from it."

Sterling asked, "How do you convict a dead person?"

"I'm not sure I follow—"

"Dirk died early this morning."

"Oh. I wasn't told."

"So, if you can't convict him, you can't take his stuff, right?"

"That's a good question. Unfortunately, I don't know the answer. That's up to the legal team."

Carter stood and asked Pete, "Is there a private room where I can call my superior?"

Pete led him into the den. When Pete returned and sat again, he said to Sterling and Hoyt, "I know I said you're both in trouble, but on the second thought, I think you two have probably learned your lesson. Plus, you helped the DEA solve a tough case. I have a deal for you. Unless I learn of something else you shouldn't have done, I won't punish you."

Having finished his call, Agent Carter walked back from the den and announced, "No more questions for now. But this remains an open investigation. Please don't discuss it with anyone."

Pete showed Carter the door. When he joined Sterling and Hoyt in the living room again, he stood quietly for a moment with his hands in his pockets. "There's one more thing I'd like to tell you two. I know we discussed how trying to get our money back wouldn't work, but you both proved me wrong. Discovering the property tax scam completely turned things around for us, and for that, I need to thank you. Obviously, destroying Dirk's lawn was not a good idea, and it nearly got you killed. But I applaud your courage, especially how you handled yourselves on the boats in the storm. I'm proud of you." Pete looked Sterling and then Hoyt in the eye. "After everything that's happened, I've done some thinking. And from now on, I would like you to call me Dad."

Sterling and Hoyt looked at other—Hoyt with anger in his eyes, and Sterling with uncertainty in his. Pete stepped to the couch and leaned over to hug each of them.

After Pete left the room, Hoyt turned to Sterling and said, "What the heck? Fifteen years of him being a drill sergeant, and *now* we've finally earned the right to call him Dad? I don't think so. He's still Pete to me."

Sterling considered it and said, "When you say it that way, it makes me mad, too. But Pete could be trying to tell us he wants to soften up. You know, show us he cares about us. It wouldn't hurt you to give him a chance. I'm going to try calling him Dad."

"Whatever. I'm going to see if Mom will take me driving. I want to ace my driver's test."

Forty-Six

THE BOYS HAD completed their driver's ed course at the end of the last school year, and as soon as they had their certificates in hand, they had scheduled their license tests for the day after their sixteenth birthday. Sterling signed up for the first slot in the morning at 9:00 a.m., and Hoyt took the second at 9:30. But now that the day had come, Sterling was nervous, and his stomach twisted so that he could eat only two pieces of dry toast for breakfast.

When Hoyt walked into the kitchen and poured a large bowl of Frosted Flakes cereal, he glanced at Sterling's plate. "With that wimpy breakfast, you'll crash halfway through your test. Pun intended."

"I'll be fine."

"Is your stomach bothering you or something? Like before big math tests?"

"I told you. I'm fine."

"Wanna bet?"

"I'm fine."

"Wanna bet? I'll bet you two-week's of mowing our lawn that I get a better score than you."

"This isn't a game of HORSE."

"No, but it's not math or science either, and I think you're scared."

"Why don't you just eat your cereal before it gets soggy, Tiger?"

"C'mon. Four weeks of mowing our lawn—edging included."

"No, thanks."

"Four weeks. Plus, if I lose, I'll let you drive the Mustang on the first day of school."

Sterling tapped a piece of toast on his plate as he thought. "Deal. But only if you agree to ride in the back seat like a dweeb."

"That's more like it."

Their mom walked into the kitchen and asked, "What are you two betting on this time?"

Sterling answered, "Who's going to get the best score on our driving test."

"What does that matter as long as you both pass? And I'm sure both of you will."

"I don't know about Sterling," Hoyt said, "but I'm ready."

Anne looked at her watch. "We'll need to leave in ten minutes."

Sterling nodded, set down his toast, and went to his room. Anne and Hoyt watched him go, and Anne asked, "Why do you boys bet on things like that? Does everything need to be a competition?"

"Sterling's good at everything. And most of the time, he keeps all his smarts neatly ordered inside his brain. So, when the opportunity is right, I try to get inside his head. To psyche him out."

"That's terrible."

"It's only when he has a big test, and it's just for fun. I want him to pass—I just don't want him to outscore me. I practiced more than he did."

Sterling returned to the kitchen, and the three of them went into the garage to leave. Sterling climbed into the driver's seat of his mother's black X5. He slid the seat back, adjusted the mirrors, and entered the DMV's location into the GPS. His mom sat in the passenger seat, and Hoyt sat behind her, watching Sterling. The SUV's 360-degree cameras helped Sterling back into the street without a problem.

At the DMV, he parked in a space reserved for test takers. Inside the office, Sterling and Hoyt checked in with the receptionist and sat to wait for an examiner. A gray-haired, grandfatherly gentleman with a clipboard stepped into the lobby and called Sterling's name.

Sterling and his examiner got into the X5, and the man told Sterling where to drive. The test included the procedures Sterling's friends had told him to expect—lane changes, a left turn onto a one-way street, and parallel parking on a hill. Sterling drove below the speed limit the entire test, checking his mirrors frequently and signaling well ahead of every turn. After returning to the DMV parking lot, Sterling cut the ignition, and the SUV filled with an uncomfortable quiet as the examiner scribbled down his final notes. The man turned to Sterling and handed him the worksheet.

"Congratulations," he said with a smile. "Now go inside, and they'll give you your license."

Sterling looked over the worksheet and saw he lost seven points for hesitating while merging onto Highway 101. Sterling shrugged it off. He was going to get his license, and that was what mattered. So what if he had to mow their lawn four weeks in a row?

While Sterling waited in line to get his picture taken, a very attractive young woman called Hoyt's name, and Sterling turned to watch the two of them walk out to the parking lot. In his distraction, Sterling did not notice the clerk calling for him until the man had to repeat himself. "Next!" the clerk called louder, and Sterling scrambled to the kiosk to have his photo taken.

Fifteen minutes passed as Sterling and his mother waited for Hoyt to return. When he did, he stood in the doorway, dejected, and motioned for them to leave with him. Anne put her hand on Hoyt's shoulder as the three of them walked to the car.

Sterling let his mom drive, and while Hoyt rode shotgun, he sat in the back seat. After several minutes of stiff silence, Hoyt explained what had happened. "I was doing great until the parallel parking. It was a tight spot, and the backup beepers started beeping right away, so I knew the truck behind me was close. I should have looked at the cameras."

"So, you couldn't get the car into the spot?" Sterling asked.

"That's the thing. I did, but I think I touched the truck's bumper. Barely. I did great for the rest of the test. But, according to the examiner, touching another vehicle is an automatic fail. She said I would have scored a ninety-seven otherwise."

Anne said, "I'm sorry to hear that. But you can take it again. This time, checking the cameras."

"The lady said I have to wait at least a week." Hoyt groaned. "And I won't be able to drive the Mustang back from Spokane."

Sterling tried to offer some consolation. "If it makes you feel any better, you would have beaten my score by four points."

"It doesn't."

"If that babe had been sitting next to me, I wouldn't have looked at the cameras, either."

"Yeah. She did make me a little nervous."

"You can still drive the Mustang while we're in Spokane. Grandpa can supervise."

"Oh wow," Hoyt said sarcastically. "What fun."

Forty-Seven

Faith embraces many truths which seem to contradict each other.
                                        —Blaise Pascal

STERLING HOPED THAT if his family could put the Dirk disaster behind them, their world would soon return to normal—or even better than normal. For starters, Sterling and Hoyt had their allowances and enough yard jobs to pay for their school activities, not to mention the inheritance coming their way, however much it would be. On top of that, Pete was giving them a second chance, and the harmony of the Burke household was being restored. Still, not everything had fallen into place. The dove was a bigger mystery than ever to Sterling, and he wanted to understand it. On a more tangible note, he needed to buy a new phone.

As Sterling rode his bike to the store, he thought about taking advantage of his dad's generosity and upgrading to a premium phone. After all, Sterling did just narrowly escape death. But, as he reconsidered, Sterling settled for the latest version of the basic iPhone, along with a screen guard, protective case, and wireless charger. Instead of riding home from the store, he went to Canaan's Kitchen, hoping to catch up with Laurel and ask about her dad's boat.

When Sterling reached the restaurant, he passed through the front door and nearly ran into Bethany. "Back so soon?" she asked, smiling. "Would you like a table?"

"Actually, I was hoping to catch Laurel on her break."

"You're in luck. Her break starts in ten minutes."

"Honestly?"

"Would I lie to you?" She giggled and added, "Forget I asked that."

"Will you please tell her I'll be waiting on the bench?"

"Sure thing."

As Sterling waited outside, he pulled his phone from his pocket and explored its new features. A few minutes later, he heard a voice say, "I'll have to get a new one, too." He looked up as Laurel sat down next to him. Sterling greeted her and said, "I wanted to check in, now that things have settled down. Have you dried out and warmed up yet?" Noticing the bandage on her head, he added, "And how's your head?"

"I'm fine." She touched her bandage. "This cut is the worst of it, but it only took a few stitches, and the doctor says it will heal without a scar."

"Lucky you."

"How about you? How are you doing?"

"I'm still tired, but I can't complain. You know, I don't think I can thank you enough for trying to rescue me in the storm."

"You are welcome—again. I hope you would have done the same for me."

"Definitely. How did your dad take the news about his boat?"

"Oh, man." Laurel sighed. "He wanted to kill me when he heard I took *Meryl* out in the storm and swamped her. He expects me to pay half of whatever it costs to get her back in shape. And he wants it done by the time he comes home in August."

"Ouch."

"I know. The good news is that John offered to do some of the work, so that should cut costs a little."

"I can help, too. I think it's fair to say I owe you."

"Really? Well, if you're serious, John plans to pick her up this afternoon so long as he can get someone to help him." Laurel nodded toward Sterling's phone in his lap. "I could give you his number to text him."

Sterling agreed and sent John a message. John replied at once and offered to pick him up in ten minutes.

"Speaking of dads," Sterling said. "Pete did something strange. He told Hoyt and me he was proud of us. He offered to pay for our new phones, and he even asked us to call him Dad, not Pete."

"Whoa. That's a change."

"Exactly. I suspect aliens reprogrammed him. I hope it will last."

Laurel laughed. "What made all that happen?"

"No idea. The fact that Hoyt and I nearly checked out probably had something to do with it. Who knows?"

Laurel asked for the time, and when Sterling told her, she stood. "I need to get back to work," she said. "But I'm glad you stopped by. Let's get together early next week, okay?"

"Sounds good. I'll text you."

"How about I text you? Since my phone is at the bottom of the strait."

Sterling waved goodbye as Laurel returned to work, and he was thankful for second chances—yes, for his dad giving him and Hoyt a break, but most of all, for surviving the storm. Sterling felt like he received a second life, and he did not want to mess up his opportunity.

John's pickup pulled into the parking lot, towing an empty trailer, and John tooted the horn to get Sterling's attention. John lowered the window and invited Sterling into the truck, telling him to put his bike in the bed.

Sterling climbed into the passenger seat and said, "Pretty scary storm the other night, wasn't it?"

John reached over and patted Sterling's shoulder. "I can't tell you how thankful I am that you boys and Laurel are safe. It's too bad about Mr. McCleod, though."

"Sure is." Sterling turned his face away from John and rubbed the tears that welled in his eyes. He added, "I'm not sure if Laurel told you, but Dirk—uh, Mr. McCleod—cheated our family."

"Oh?"

"Yep, he did, and I hated him for it. I thought I had quit caring what happened to him, but it turns out I hadn't. I still care about him, even though it's too late. That second chance is gone."

"I'm sorry to hear that. But you can learn a lot from this. It's important to take each opportunity when it comes and never assume you'll have a second chance."

They continued their ride in silence until they passed the marina's entrance. Sterling watched the sign come and go. "Where are we going?"

"The Coast Guard tied up Meryl in one of their berths down a ways. It's a good thing you're helping me because they want it removed today."

"What are you going to do with her?"

"When a boat and its motor drown like *Meryl* and her outboard did, every hour you delay fixing it causes more damage. Saltwater corrodes the inside of the motors. It's easy enough to rinse off the outsides, but the insides are what's important."

"I didn't know corrosion would start so quickly. And Laurel said you are going to do the repairs?"

"Well, not quite. A friend of mine has offered to rebuild the outboard. He'll spray oil into the cylinders first and then disassemble the motor to clean every part that the seawater touched. When he puts them back together, they should be as good as new. The sooner that can get done, the better. Especially since Laurel's parents will be here in August. They'll want to fish while they're here, no doubt. Although I don't understand why they don't do their fishing in Alaska. Anyway, Laurel's dad wants *Meryl* to be in pristine condition. Or at least as good as it was."

"Laurel said her dad expects her to pay half."

"That's right. But my friend, Charlie, owes me one. I can get the boat back in shape while he's working on the motor. Together, that will save a fortune. The electronics are certainly ruined, though, and they are expensive."

"Maybe I can help with that."

"I could use your muscle to help me load the outboard into Charlie's garage. It's a two-man job. You up for it?"

"Sure. But I was thinking I could help pay for part of the electronics. After all, Laurel was trying to save me."

"I suppose she was. That would be awfully nice of you."

When they arrived at the Coast Guard station and walked to where *Meryl* was docked, they discovered she had several inches of water in her bilge, which complicated matters. The water added a lot of weight, so it took ten minutes of hard work for John and Sterling to pull the boat from the berth to the boat ramp. From there, John backed the trailer into the water, clipped *Meryl*'s to the winch, and started cranking the handle. He strained to pull Meryl onto the trailer, but once her stern was out of the water, John removed the drain plug to release the trapped water. After the bilge was empty, Sterling cranked the boat the rest of the way onto the trailer, and John secured it. All that was left was to deliver the motor to John's friend Charlie.

During the drive, Sterling said, "You remember that dove I mentioned the other day? While I was on Techs's boat, I sensed I was supposed to jump into the water, but I was afraid to do it. Then the dove came out of nowhere and knocked me into the strait."

"It knocked you off the boat?"

"Like a freight train, clean over the railing. But that's not the strangest part. I couldn't keep myself up in the waves, and that same dove dropped a life jacket for me. It saved my life."

John rubbed his chin as he listened. "That's quite a story," he said, "but I can't say it surprises me. Laurel and I were praying for you. I think the dove was an answer to our prayers."

"Could've been. That night, I decided to lose my old life and seek a new one, but now I'm not sure I'm really ready to do that."

John asked, "What are you thinking?"

"It sounds so . . . well, weird and unreal. I'm into math and science.

Math is real, and science is too. This faith and transformation and going beyond stuff is contrary to science. I can't abandon science or reason."

"Are you sure you need to abandon science and reason to experience the higher world?"

"I don't see how science and reason are compatible with it."

"So, the laws of science govern everything in this world, and because the world beyond can't be explained by these laws, it can't be real. Is that what you are saying?"

"Pretty much."

"Why do you think spiritual realities are limited to conforming to science? Why can't each world be governed by its own rules?"

"Hmm. I haven't thought about it that way. I need to consider it."

"I admit it is strange when the two worlds overlap."

"Overlap?"

"Like when a dove saves your life."

"Sure. Still, I don't know what to make of it. I'll need to think about it more."

"You should, and take your time. While you do, I suggest you pursue the world beyond. You have seen powerful evidence for it, and I'm sure you will find more if you look."

"Sounds reasonable."

AT CHARLIE'S HOUSE, Sterling jumped out of the truck and walked over to the open garage door, where he found a note tacked to the door-jamb. Charlie had left instructions to load the motor into the garage and close the door afterward. John walked up beside Sterling, and they both peered inside the garage.

Sterling noticed an engine hoist, like the one Mr. K had in his garage, and pointed to it. "Do you think we could use that?"

John shrugged. "I don't see why not."

Sterling pushed the hoist to the pickup, and its four wheels squeaked like oil had never been discovered. He wondered if Charlie really knew how to maintain mechanical things. John wrapped the chain around the motor, and they lifted it out of the bed and pushed it into the garage.

After the motor was stowed away, John and Sterling got into the pickup to drive back to Canaan's Kitchen. Along the way, John said, "When you mentioned science earlier, it got me thinking. I'm all for science, like you, but I don't think science is the answer to everything in life. There are things science can't measure."

"Maybe not right now," Sterling replied, "but we're making advancements every day."

"True. But can science measure love? Can it measure forgiveness?"

Sterling sat in silence, thinking for a minute, and then said, "That wasn't a rhetorical question, was it?"

"No, it wasn't. But you don't need to answer it right away. Consider it. Keep in mind you don't need to get rid of all your doubts and questions at once. That is part of transformation. It is a lifelong process, venturing into a mysterious reality."

Forty-Eight

WHEN STERLING WAS half a block from home, noticed a news van parked on the street in front of his house. He remembered that several days before there was a news story about Dirk's murder and smuggling operation, and it mentioned that 'unnamed minors' had been involved. Someone must have leaked their names to the television station, but Sterling didn't want to talk. He knew nothing good could come of it. Besides, he and Hoyt were on a tight schedule to take care of some yards, and he was hungry. Sterling pedaled fast around the van and into the driveway, dropped his bike in the driveway, and ran into the house. He went straight to the kitchen and ate two quick bowls of granola for lunch.

Just as he spooned up his last bite, Hoyt walked in and said, "Time to leave."

Sterling shook his head. "It won't be easy. There are reporters outside. I think they want to interview us."

"Cool."

"No, it's not cool. We shouldn't talk with them."

"Why not?"

"Just trust me. It's a bad idea."

Hoyt relented and went to the garage to grab his bike. He met Sterling in the driveway, but before they could even ride out of the driveway, a reporter from the van stepped in front of them. "Are you the Burke boys?" she asked hopefully.

Hoyt stopped and said, "In the flesh."

"Great! We'd love to interview you about the smuggling and shooting."

Hoyt began to answer, but Sterling smacked him on the arm and said, "No comment—*right?* Let's go!"

The boys peeled around the other side of the reporter and raced away, ignoring her fading plea to answer questions. The reporter turned and hollered at the cameraman to get into the van, and the chase was on. The van's tires squealed as the news team sped off in pursuit.

Over his shoulder, Sterling saw the van approaching, and he yelled to Hoyt, "Follow me!"

He turned down a narrow side street that was lined with parked cars, and the boys veered around an Amazon delivery truck parked on the road. The news team hooked the turn and rumbled down the street after them, but the delivery truck blocked their path, and the boys reached the Olympic Discovery Trail before the van could pass. Sterling and Hoyt had escaped, and they panted to catch their breath as they pulled up to the shed for their yard equipment.

"I think we should have talked with them," Hoyt said. "We could have been on TV. What's the worst that could have happened?"

"Do you want the world to know we broke into Dirk's house, stole his Bitcoin, and nearly sunk his boat?"

"Okay. When you put it that way . . ."

THAT AFTERNOON, WHEN Sterling and Hoyt returned home after their yard jobs, they were relieved to see an empty street in front of their house. The news team had apparently given up, or they were called to a more important story. Sterling was glad he had escaped his five minutes of infamy and was ready to resume a normal life. To celebrate, he went to his room and took out a box from his closet. It held an old robot project he had set aside back in the spring.

At his computer, Sterling downloaded the software that would allow him to control the robot. More specifically, he was most interested in the robot's arm. If he could make it work as he hoped, he would adapt an underwater version and attach it to UROV so he could salvage small items from the marina floor. When Sterling moved the controller, however, the robot's arm was clumsy and jerked around like a fast-forwarded video. Sterling cut the power and tried programming a delay loop into the code, experimenting with it until the arm moved slowly and with much more precision. He was sure he could make an arm work on UROV, and he ordered a waterproof robotic arm from the internet.

To relax, Sterling played Minecraft until Anne called the family for dinner. She had bought a family-sized pizza, half pepperoni and half Canadian bacon with pineapple. Sterling took a slice of each and laid them together face-to-face like a sandwich. He smiled as his family watched with curiosity and relished taking a big bite from it.

Mrs. Burke said, "While you boys were working, I went into the office and got some good news. We have offers on both of our new listings—at full price. Plus, I picked up an additional listing."

"You mother is doing well," Pete added. "The clients love working with her, and I have more time to spend on commercial business. Because of that, things don't seem like they'll be slowing down soon, so I'm going to set up an account for you boys to order meal deliveries whenever your mother and I can't make it for dinner."

"All right!" Hoyt cheered.

"Don't go overboard," Pete warned. "And you're on your own for breakfast and lunch."

"Also," Anne said, "I studied the will Ms. Scott left. It included a list of Dirk's accounts, so I took a quick look at them. It looks like you will have money to pay for all your college expenses."

The boys nodded soberly. After what seemed like a sufficient pause, Sterling asked, "Any chance we can use some of it for school stuff this year?"

"No. You need to earn your own money for that."

Pete's buzzing phone interrupted the conversation, and Pete left the room to answer in private. Five minutes later, he returned, shaking his head.

"Is something wrong?" Anne asked.

"That was Detective Bloch. He wanted to come by tonight with more questions, but I convinced him to meet at my office at nine tomorrow morning instead. I have a bad feeling about this, so I'm going to have Gerry sit in on the meeting."

"Who's Gerry?" Hoyt asked.

"He's an attorney who leases space in my office building. He's a month behind on his rent, so I have a feeling he'll jump at the opportunity to help. In the meantime, you boys need to rest up tonight. You still look tired."

THE FOLLOWING MORNING, Pete, Sterling, and Hoyt arrived at the office ten minutes before nine. They climbed the stairs and entered a door marked Gerald Erickson, Attorney at Law, and Pete introduced the boys to Gerry. From there, the four of them walked down the hall to the offices of Burke & McCleod Properties to wait for the meeting. Sterling glanced at Dirk's vacant office and felt a stab of sorrow. Pete brewed a pot of coffee and checked his watch, expecting the detective any moment.

Right at 9:00 a.m., Bloch walked in. He wore the same slacks and sport jacket as before, but with a fresh white shirt and red tie.

Pete greeted him and stood, saying, "This is Gerald Erickson. He'll be representing us legally."

"I see," Bloch replied, and he shook Gerald's hand. "Well, as I said on the phone, I have a few more questions. Shall we begin?"

Pete gestured to the table where the carafe of coffee sat, and the men and boys took their seats. Gerry switched on a small tape recorder and laid it on the table. Bloch poured himself a cup of coffee, took a sip, and said, "First, I have questions for Hoyt. The District Attorney thinks you willfully attempted to destroy evidence that was on McCleod's boat, given that significant damage occurred. Would you like to explain how that happened?"

"Sure. Right before Techs shot Dirk, I heard him yell, 'Prepare to be boarded,' and I was afraid he would board *Leverage* and kill me. So, I hid up on the flying bridge near the helm, and when I saw Techs moving his boat toward *Leverage,* I acted in self-defense."

"How so?"

"I, uh, floored it and I rammed his boat with *Leverage,* and Techs fell and hit his head, so to make sure he couldn't follow me, I circled behind his boat and smashed into his outboards—to disable his boat. I was going to take off after that, but the Coast Guard showed up and took things from there."

"To be clear, are you telling me you weren't trying to sink Dirk's boat?"

"No, sir. I never wanted to sink his boat."

Listening to Hoyt's feigned innocence was almost too much for Sterling, and a smile curled at the corners of his mouth. He forced himself to look straight ahead, his eyes as still as a statue's. He did not even dare to take a sip of his coffee, knowing if he made the slightest movement, his facade would crumble and laughter would come pouring out. But maybe Hoyt was telling the truth. Maybe he really had given up on his obsession to sink *Leverage,* but Sterling doubted it.

"As a clarification," Gerry asked, "will you be charging my clients with trying to damage or sink either vessel or to destroy evidence?"

"Not at this time," Bloch answered, looking down at his notepad. "We don't have any hard proof of that."

"I'm glad that's settled," Gerry said.

Bloch looked at the boys. "As you know, we have Lorimer Niblick in custody, but he has lawyered up, so now his lips are sealed." Bloch glanced at Gerry and added, "No offense—you know how some lawyers are." Erickson waved off the comment, and Bloch continued, "I'm trying to understand Techs's involvement in the smuggling operation, and I'm wondering if either of you boys can provide any insight into that."

Sterling looked at Hoyt. Seeing that Hoyt had nothing to comment, Sterling said, "When Techs forced me onto his boat, we talked about the operation. He told me he found out Dirk was smuggling, and he wanted to force his way in to get a cut."

"How did he know Dirk was smuggling?"

"Dirk had a problem with the hard disk on his computer. Techs was helping him recover lost data, and in the process, he found evidence of what Dirk was up to."

"How long ago was that?"

"Not long. Earlier this week, I think."

"Okay. Regardless, it looks like the only case we can build against him at the moment is for first degree murder, probably not for smuggling."

"That sounds like it should be enough," Pete commented.

"No case is foolproof. We prefer multiple charges in the event that one falls through. A solid plan B, if you will."

"What about the property tax scam?" Sterling asked. "Can't you bust him on that?"

"I heard someone talking with another detective about a property tax issue, but I'm not familiar with it. It's not my case."

Pete asked, "Was it Ms. Richards from the County Treasurer's Office?"

"Could have been. It was a woman." Bloch looked at Sterling and asked, "Would you be willing to answer questions from the other detective about that case?"

"I guess so."

"Very good. I just have one more question. Hoyt, who was the man you said helped Dirk abduct you?"

"Techs called him Bert, but I don't know him."

"Can you describe him?"

"It was dark, but yeah, I can tell you a couple of things. He was a giant. Like six-foot-ten. Broad shoulders, scruffy face with one of those mustaches, with hair like black caterpillars hanging down each side of his mouth. Dirty clothes, and he stank like fish. I think he knew both Techs and Dirk."

Sterling leaned forward and said, "I'm pretty sure I've seen him. I was walking with a friend at the marina once, and there was a big guy working on his boat at the dry dock."

"That gives me something to work with. Thank you both."

"Is that everything?" Gerry asked.

Bloch nodded and stood up. "I believe so. If not, I will get back to the Burkes."

Forty-Nine

THE DAY STERLING and Hoyt were scheduled to travel to Spokane and pick up the Mustang finally arrived, and it arrived at the crack of dawn. They awoke at 5:00 a.m., dressed, ate a quick breakfast, and grabbed their packed bags to load into Anne's car. Their mom dropped them off at the Bainbridge ferry terminal five minutes before the 7:05 boarding, and thirty-minutes later they were in Seattle walking to the Amtrak station, which doubled as the bus station. They had bus tickets for Spokane, and the trek ahead of them wasn't scheduled to end until 5:00 that evening.

Sterling and Hoyt took seats next to each other near the back of the bus and were sleeping soundly before they reached Everett. They snoozed through the towns of Monroe and Leavenworth and stirred when the bus made a twenty-five-minute stop in Wenatchee. They exited the bus to stretch their legs, and each bought a couple of candy bars and a can of pop from the vending machines. Hoyt also bought the most recent issues of *Sports Illustrated* and *Muscle & Fitness Magazine* to help pass the time.

Back on the bus, the remaining three hours crawled as Sterling anticipated driving the Mustang. He knew he was too eager, so he distracted himself by playing video games on his new phone, and Hoyt appeared to be trying the same with his magazines.

At 5:00 p.m., after nearly twelve hours of sitting and waiting, they arrived in Spokane and exited the depot to find their grandparents. They found their grandpa waiting in his Ford Explorer, and after the boys hopped in the backseat, he drove them to their mini-farm, twenty miles north. At the homestead, their grandma served generous portions of chicken and dumplings, which had been one of the boys' favorite meals since they were five years old, and the food reminded Sterling of the many meals his grandmother had cooked for them throughout the years.

After dinner, Sterling was eager to see the Mustang and take it for a spin, but he figured it would be rude to ask to see it, so he endured chit chat with a polite smile. When their grandpa asked what was new, the boys mentioned nothing about Dirk or the storm. Sterling, especially, was tired of the recent events and did not want to relive the drama again. Instead, they talked about playing basketball and building science projects. Stories that did not raise uncomfortable questions.

It was not until breakfast the next morning that their grandpa said, "I'm sure you want to learn to drive your Mustang."

Sterling and Hoyt's attention snapped up from their waffles, and they said in unison, "Yes, please!" They jumped up from the table, took their dishes to the sink, and waited by the front door while their grandpa went to get the keys.

On the way to the barn, their grandpa told them about restoring the car. "I didn't remind your father that it is a Shelby Cobra GT500, not a vanilla GT. I was afraid that if he knew how fast it was, he might not let you have it. This baby has 500 horsepower and requires your utmost respect."

"You're right," Sterling said. "Dad doesn't need to know that."

Their grandpa opened the barn door, and as the morning light fell on the shining beast, and the boys nearly drooled on the floor. Sterling thought the car's black paint and silver racing stripe looked better than Mr. K.'s GTO, and he could hardly wait to show it off to him.

"Grandpa," Sterling said. "This is sick!"

"Sick? Oh, I thought you would like it."

"No, no—sick means *excellent.*"

Their grandpa lifted his eyebrows and said, "Okay. I think I get it. Well, this sick baby is as fast as a Corvette, so you boys had better be careful with it. You'll do fine once you learn how to shift its six-speed manual transmission. Why talk about it? I'll show you how." Their grandpa demonstrated using the clutch and how to shift through gears, and after he explained the basics, he asked Hoyt to get behind the wheel.

Hoyt hopped in the driver's seat, pushed in the clutch, and shifted into first gear. He let out the clutch and promptly killed the engine. He restarted it and, giving it more gas this time, spun the tires. After that, he drove flawlessly, shifting like an experienced driver. Sterling was not surprised.

"All right," their grandpa said. "We ought to let Sterling have a turn with it."

Sterling's attempts were more painful to watch. He killed the engine on his first three starts, forgot to push the clutch in when he came to a stop, and needed help to find reverse. Despite the struggle, his grandpa was patient, and after two hours of practice, Sterling was able to drive without killing the engine. But he wasn't as smooth as Hoyt, and he was thankful that the drive home would not require many shifts.

The boys spent the rest of the day helping their grandfather with chores around the farm—mending broken fences and changing the oil in his tractor. By evening, their thoughts were back on the Mustang, and they looked forward to driving it home the next day.

AFTER BREAKFAST, THE boys said goodbye to their grandparents and left for home, with Sterling at the wheel and Hoyt at the radio. Their route was a 400-mile straight shot, almost due west. Sterling was extremely cautious and always kept under the speed limit. After four hours of nonstop driving, he pulled into a mini-mart to stretch his legs and get gas. Sterling went inside the store, and when he returned to the car, Hoyt snatched the keys from his hand.

"My turn," he said, walking to the driver's side. "I need the practice."

"No way. Give me the keys." Sterling followed him and held out his hand.

"Nope."

"You know you're not allowed. I'm the only legal driver."

"C'mon, it'll be fine. I'm a better driver than you, anyway."

Hoyt climbed into the driver's seat and started the car. He pointed Sterling to the passenger seat, but Sterling did not leave the driver's door. Hoyt lowered the window a few inches and said, "It's a long walk." He revved the engine, put the car in first gear, and started rolling.

Sterling panicked and ran around to the passenger door. He jumped into the moving car and buckled up. "Just because I'm in the car with you doesn't mean you have my permission. If anything goes wrong, you're on your own, bro."

"Chill. Oh, and please, shut up," Hoyt said as he cranked the radio volume.

Back on the highway, Hoyt smoothly shifted through the gears until he was cruising in sixth gear at ten miles above the speed limit. The road climbed as they entered the Cascade Mountains, and the Mustang's motor kept pace with no trouble. With the sun shining and the car roaring, Sterling had started to relax. He and Hoyt were even singing along with the radio.

Then Hoyt noticed something in his side mirror—a Washington State Patrol car came out of the curve behind him. "There's a WASP behind us," he said, slowing to the speed limit. "If he pulls me over, I'm dead."

"How unfortunate. You knew what you were getting into."

"What should I do?"

"Drive carefully, like you have a cop watching your every move."

"Should I pull over?"

Sterling looked out the rear window and saw the patrol car was still far off. "That would look suspicious. I say keep driving unless you see a business or rest area to pull into."

"He's getting closer. Give me your license."

"Yeah, right. Just keep cool. He'll probably pass us."

They reached a long straight section with no oncoming traffic, but the patrol car did not pass them. Then the flashing lights kicked on. Hoyt down shifted to fourth gear and revved the engine. "We can outrun him. I'm gonna do it."

"Are you crazy? You can't outrun his radio."

"So?"

"He'll radio ahead for reinforcements." Sterling pointed to the side of the road ahead and said, "Signal and gently pull over at that wide spot."

Hoyt groaned and stopped at the pullout, turning off the engine and rolling down his window. After a minute, the officer walked up to the driver's side.

"License, proof of insurance, and registration, please."

Hoyt opened the glove compartment and found his grandpa's insurance card and registration. He handed them to the officer and said, "It's my grandfather's car. He's letting us take it to Port Angeles."

"License, please."

Hoyt retrieved his wallet from his rear pocket and opened it to show the officer his learner's permit. But, before he removed it, Sterling reached to the floor by Hoyt's feet and said, "Sterling, I think you dropped this." He handed his own license to Hoyt. "Here."

I did not condone what Sterling had done—substituting his license for Hoyt's permit. However, it reminded me of the Master's merciful substitution for mankind.

Hoyt handed the license to the officer, who examined it and said, "Less than a week old, huh? Quite a car for a new driver."

"Yes, sir."

"Do you know how fast you were driving?"

"Five over?"

"More like ten over."

"Okay. I'm sorry."

"Tell you what, I'm going to give you a late birthday present and skip the ticket. But keep it under the limit from now on. Besides, I wanted to get a better look at your wheels. Would you mind popping the hood?"

"No problem." Hoyt pulled the hood release and got out to lift the hood so the officer could see the supercharged engine.

The officer studied it and whistled. "You're a lucky man. Thanks for the look." On his way back to his patrol car, he called over his shoulder. "Take it slow, Sterling."

Hoyt got back in the driver's seat and handed the license back to Sterling. "Thanks."

"Sure," Sterling said. "Honestly, I don't know why I did that."

"Do you want to drive the rest of the way?"

"You think?"

They waited for the patrolman to drive off and then switched seats. The radio kept them company as they continued the road trip without speaking and let their heart rates return to normal. Eventually, Hoyt turned the radio down and said, "Tell me about the dove."

"The dove? What do you want to know?"

"What really happened on Techs' boat?"

"I told you. The dove knocked me into the water and then dropped a life jacket."

"You expect me to believe that?"

"I guess. That's what happened."

Hoyt shook his head and looked out the window.

Sterling turned off the radio and added, "I know it's weird, but strange things keep happening. I'm beginning to believe there is more to life than what we see."

"Sounds spooky."

"I agree. But I think it's worth looking into. I need to find some answers."

"Well, let me know when you get that figured out. Then all this crazy talk can stop."

The rest of the drive to Port Angeles was smooth and uneventful. The boys arrived home late that afternoon, parked the car proudly on the street for all the neighbors to see, and took their packs inside. Hoyt suggested they order pizza, but Sterling said, "Why have a delivery when we can drive ourselves?"

An hour later, the boys' stomachs were full, and they were cruising through PA with the windows down and the radio up. They drove until sundown and returned home. Soon after they parked, Pete and Anne arrived and asked for a recap of the trip. The boys glanced at each other and talked a great deal about their grandparent's farm and how much they enjoyed the home cooking. Funny, they never mentioned anything about the patrolman.

Fifty

AT SIX O'CLOCK the next morning, the Burkes' doorbell shattered the silence of the house, and it rang repeatedly. Pete rubbed his eyes slowly rolled out of bed. Pulling on his plush Calvin Klein bathrobe and tying the belt around his waist, he pattered down the stairs and peered through the door's peephole. On the other side stood Agent Carter and two others, wearing blue Drug Enforcement Agency windbreakers. Behind them, blue lights flashed from two Clallam County patrol cars, and several police officers watched from the street. Pete ripped the door open with a look of bewilderment.

"What's going on here?"

"Mr. Burke," Agent Carter said. "We are taking Sterling and Hoyt with us."

"What about our agreement? You and the boys had a deal. Remember?"

"My supervisor and the district attorney overruled me. If you recall, I said, 'I think they did their part.' But I couldn't sell it upstairs. Somebody needs to go to jail in a high-profile smuggling case like this one. I wish I could tell you otherwise, but my hands are tied."

"This is an outrage," Pete snapped. "I trusted you. By the way, your subtle approach is considerate." He nodded toward the patrol cars and flashing lights. "Thanks for not ramming the door down."

"Sarcasm doesn't help anyone."

"Look, what do you need my boys for, anyway?"

"Questioning and likely to charge them for destroying evidence."

"That's absurd."

"May we come in?"

"No. Where are you taking them?"

"We have a temporary field office in town. In fact, it's just one door down from yours—which we are searching, by the way. We have a warrant, and an agent is combing through Dirk's things as we speak."

"I see," Pete said. "Wait here, and I'll get Sterling and Hoyt. But don't question them without both me and our attorney present. They're minors, after all."

"The attorney is permitted to be with them, but you aren't. We plan to charge your sons as adults, so a guardian isn't required."

Pete closed the door and went upstairs to wake the boys. He told them to get dressed right away, and once they stepped downstairs, Sterling and Hoyt found their father on the phone with Gerry Erickson. After he ended the call, Pete explained what was happening. He forbade Sterling and Hoyt from answering questions without Gerry being present. Carter thanked Pete for his cooperation, and the DEA agents escorted the boys to separate patrol cars. Pete grimaced as he watched the cars drive off, and he hurried inside to get dressed, wake Anne, and catch up with the caravan.

Gerry was waiting outside the DEA office when the others arrived. While the officers took the boys out of the patrol cars, Pete parked and trotted over to Gerry to discuss their plan. Everyone converged at the front door, and Gerry introduced himself to the three agents as the Burkes' attorney. "I'd like to be present for questioning."

"I'm sorry," Agent Carter responded. "We plan to question them separately."

"I must not have been clear. I *demand* to be present with each of them during questioning. And you need to keep them together."

"Fine," Carter said. "But the father can't be present." He led everyone but Pete into the building, and they walked down a hallway to a bare room with only a plastic table and folding chairs. The agents sat on one side of the table, and Gerry and the boys sat on the other. "I would offer you coffee," Carter said, sorting through a small stack of papers on the table, "but we don't have a coffee maker." He looked up at Hoyt and Sterling. "So, we might as well get to the point. We are investigating you both—Hoyt for attempting to destroy evidence, and Sterling for actual destruction of evidence. Both crimes are felonies, and because they are related to drug charges, we will charge each of you as adults. Understood?"

The boys nodded.

"All right," Carter continued. "Hoyt, let's start with you."

Gerry held up his hand to halt the questioning and reached down to his briefcase. He set up a tape recorder on the table and said, "I'm sure you have hidden microphones in here, but if you don't mind, I'll be making a copy for myself."

Agent Carter frowned, but he said nothing to stop Gerry and proceeded with the interrogation. "Dirk's boat, *Leverage*, was used in the commission of a crime. The boat itself and articles onboard are evidence. Now, Hoyt, Seaman Duran told us she overheard you say you rammed Niblick's boat in an attempt to sink *Leverage*. That constitutes attempted destruction of evidence. What do you have to say for yourself?"

Hoyt said, "I rammed Techs's boat with *Leverage* because I needed to disable it to get away from Techs. I was afraid that if I didn't, he would chase me and shoot me."

"Are you saying Seaman Duran lied to us?"

"No. I probably did say I was trying to sink *Leverage*. But I was just saying that to sound tough for Laurel and Sterling. It was just trash talk. I didn't mean anything by it."

"Perhaps," Carter said, folding his hands upon the table. "Given that you used *Leverage* to hit Niblick's boat multiple times and were going to hit it again when the Coast Guard arrived, the Attorney

General plans to charge you with attempted destruction of evidence and with obstruction of justice."

"No wonder you three are stuck in a temporary office in the great metropolis of Port Angeles. With portable furniture and no coffeemaker."

"Excuse me?"

"You must be bottom feeders at the DEA. Keep up this excellent work, hassling victims of a kidnapping, and you'll be transferred to Forks to chase drug-running vampires and werewolves."

"What's that supposed to mean?"

"Never mind. Apparently, you've been so busy charging the wrong people that you didn't have time to read *Twilight*."

Sterling laughed. "See? He does it all the time. He gets scared, and his mouth goes off by itself—no thinking required. I was there on the Coast Guard cutter when he talked about sinking *Leverage*, and I will testify that he was only talking a big game. He didn't mean it. And I was in the room when he said it, not passing by as Seaman Duran probably was. I saw Hoyt's expression, and I know him better than anyone. I know how to interpret what he means, not just what he says."

Agent Carter ignored Sterling's commentary and said, "Sterling, since you've volunteered to enter the spotlight, let's discuss your destroying data on Dirk's hard disk. That is *actual* destruction of evidence, and Niblick told us you did it. Care to explain your actions?"

Across town, I was in the birdhouse, above the barn door at Canaan's Garden, but I knew exactly what Sterling was thinking—every thought that crossed his mind, every word before it was on his tongue. There was nowhere he could go to be away from my presence. He was precious to me, and I was standing by to piff him in case he needed a nudge to tell the truth, even if it put him at risk with the DEA.

When Sterling started to respond to Carter's accusation, Gerry interrupted and leaned over to Sterling, whispering, "Don't admit to anything. And don't get lippy. They can make you regret it."

Sterling nodded and turned back to the agents. "It's true. I reformatted Dirk's hard disk to destroy evidence of the remote control software I had installed on his computer. I thought I had succeeded, but Techs bragged he could recover the data from the drive, which he did, and he analyzed it. That's how he learned about Dirk's smuggling operation. After getting what he wanted from the disk, Techs overwrote the contents, and that destroyed any evidence your team was after. If you search Techs's computers, I think you'll find the software he used to do it. I didn't destroy the data, Techs did. I'll bet he made a copy of Dirk's disk, too."

"Even if we cannot prove you overwrote the data," Carter clarified, "you confessed to attempting to destroy evidence. We can at least charge you for that."

Sterling grabbed Gerry's arm and whispered something.

Gerry shook his head and said to the agents, "I need to confer with my clients. My office is right next door. If you think it's necessary, one of you can stand guard outside to prevent an escape." He picked up his briefcase and motioned for Sterling and Hoyt to follow. An agent joined them and paced the hallway outside the office while the three conferred in Gerry's office.

Sterling told Gerry about Dirk's Bitcoin and asked if they could trade that information for immunity.

"We can try," Gerry said. "Hopefully, they haven't talked with Detective Bloch yet. Wait here while I write an affidavit."

"A what?" Hoyt asked.

"It's like a contract for an agreement. I'll make it tough for them to break, unlike the oral agreement they make with you the other day." Gerry sat at his desk, edited a document, and printed two copies.

After Gerry called Pete and brought him up to speed, the three returned to the DEA's meeting room. Gerry pulled his chair close to the table and said, "My clients learned that Mr. McCleod has approximately $250,000 in Bitcoin, likely from his smuggling operation, and they have the account credentials. I realize that information may be valuable to the DEA, especially as the Bitcoin may be seized by your agents. So, here's my proposition—if Sterling and Hoyt can provide information leading to the recovery of the money, then you will grant full immunity to both of them. What do you say?"

Agent Carter nodded, intrigued. "We suspected McCleod was getting paid in Bitcoin, but we couldn't find evidence of it. Give me a minute to make a phone call." Carter stepped out of the conference room, and a few minutes later, returned. "Gentlemen," he said. "We have a deal."

Gerry set two copies of the affidavit on the table and slid them across to the agents. "It's going to be in writing this time. One copy for you, and one for me. Please sign and date them both."

"Fair enough." Agent Carter signed both copies and asked the boys when they could provide the account credentials.

Without hesitation, Sterling reached across the table, grabbed Carter's affidavit, and borrowed Gerry's pen. He printed the 24-digit account number and 18-character scrambled password on the paper—all from memory—and said, "There you have it. Can we leave now?"

Agent Carter smiled. "Yes. And just so you know, we wouldn't have charged either of you. The DA only wanted to scare you enough to ensure that you told us everything."

"Well, just so *you* know. I would have given you the Bitcoin information even if you didn't make the deal."

I was proud of Sterling.

Fifty-One

We run carelessly to the precipice, after we have put something before us to prevent us from seeing it.

—Blaise Pascal

AFTER RETURNING HOME from the DEA interrogation, Sterling went to his room, laid on his bed, and closed his eyes, hoping to catch up on the sleep the agents had interrupted. Not surprisingly, he was much too wired to fall asleep, and he instead let his thoughts wander to pass the time. As he lay there, he was reminded of his fiasco at Canaan's Creek and his failure to find the garden. Perhaps it was worth seeking out again, but logic told Sterling to forget about it, to push the whole idea out of his mind. After being given a second chance, however, the garden appealed to him more than ever. Laurel had described it as a place of renewal, and Sterling's longing for such an experience had grown like a hunger, a yearning deep within him. He got up from his bed, knowing he had to try again to cross over and experience the garden.

This time, Sterling's goal was different. He no longer wanted to learn if the garden was real. Now, he hoped it was real, even though it was difficult to believe, and he wanted to explore it. He pushed forward despite his doubts. Little did he realize a flicker of faith can make a world of difference.

IN THE PARKING lot at Canaan's Kitchen, Sterling stepped out of the Mustang and looked up as a shadow flashed over his head. He laughed. I soared past him, glided to the ledge above the barn door, and beckoned him to follow me. Sterling chuckled to himself and walked over, remembering the days when he thought about capturing me. It seemed so strange and long ago. As he approached, I clutched a key in my claws—it was a gold skeleton key, ornate like ones used to unlock treasure chests and secret chambers. A ruby, sapphire, and diamond adorned the handle, and three gold prongs held each jewel in place. I hung the key from my perch, and when Sterling was beneath me, he noticed it and extended his hand. The time for teasing was gone, and I dropped the key into his palm. He turned it over in his hands and squinted at four small letters stamped into the gold—I-N-R-I. Unbeknownst to him, the markings were in Latin and matched the inscription written upon on Jesus's cross, "Jesus of Nazareth, the King of the Jews."

Sterling sensed the key was extraordinary, and he hoped it would lead him to an equally extraordinary place. He took the padlock from the barn door in one hand and held the key with the other. The style of both matched, and he fit the key into the lock. Taking a deep breath, he closed his eyes and turned the key. The padlock clicked open.

He removed the dangling lock, opened the door, and peered inside. I dropped from my ledge and flew ahead of him into the darkness of the barn, piffing him to follow. Sterling trembled with anticipation and recalled the Master's words about losing one's old life to gain new life. He stepped inside the barn and, while letting his eyes adjust to the dim light, he inhaled moist air and heard the cascading waterfall. To his right, through an opening in the barn's side, muddy wheel ruts marked a path between the rock wall and the curtain of falling water. It was undoubtedly the passage to Canaan's Garden.

Sterling carefully followed the path, and with each tentative step, he felt as if he was being washed on the inside. A new life grew within him like a seed freshly planted, softening and thirsting to spring up.

Mist from the waterfall covered him with tiny droplets, and he shielded his eyes as he proceeded behind it. Although his clothes were damp from the mist, Sterling felt relaxed and snuggly warm, as if he was sitting on a log next to a campfire on a fall night. He blinked the moisture from his eyelashes and noticed a curious change in the path at his feet. The mud had become lush grass. Sterling looked ahead and saw Canaan's Garden for the first time.

A verdant pasture sloped down before him, and on three sides, the foothills of the Olympic Mountains protected the garden. In the center of the garden, a crystal-clear river sprang from the ground and divided into four brooks that flowed to the garden's four corners. Each stream was small enough to leap across, though each grew wider as it flowed onward.

Sterling marveled at the expanse, and only afterward did he notice the garden itself. The crops were organized into many small sections separated by grass walkways, and each teemed with unique plant life. As Sterling ventured deeper into the garden, he saw bees and hummingbirds gathering nectar from blueberry and marionberry blossoms, and the berries ripened in front of Sterling's eyes like time-lapse photography. When the berries were ready to harvest, a team of robins gently picked them and transported them to an array of baskets lined up on a row of wagons hitched to a garden tractor. Labels such as blueberries, walnuts, and olives identified each basket and seemed to guide the robins as if they could read.

In a nearby orchard of lush apple, pear, and plum trees, more bees and hummingbirds flew from blossom to blossom. The newly pollinated blooms grew to full size and completely ripened within minutes. Deer approached the trees and stood on their rear legs, gently picking the fruit with their mouths. They pranced to a row of buckets and delivered it, each according to its kind. Sterling walked over to the baskets, took a yellow Jonagold apple, and twirled it in his hand. There was not a tooth mark or bruise anywhere. As he observed in wonder, a squirrel darted between his feet to drop a walnut into another basket.

Two doves swooped past him, carrying green and black olives to their baskets, and as Sterling watched them go, he started to comprehend the symbiotic collaboration throughout the garden. Rabbits gathered lettuce and tomatoes, crows delivered corn, and moles teamed up to drag onions to a group of raccoons who sorted them into proper baskets.

Sterling continued to explore, and he stumbled upon a patch of forest where he followed a shaded path that wended between gigantic cedars and hemlocks. Thick moss and lichen draped from every branch. Ferns grew from the forest floor and from the upper side of the moss-covered tree limbs. Eventually, the path led Sterling out from the trees and into an open acre of lawn that was scattered with mossy cabanas and benches. To Sterling's surprise, a few of the shelters were occupied by people who were talking quietly, kneeling, or reading. Not wanting to disturb them, he turned to explore the other side of the garden.

Sterling passed back through the patch of blueberries, marionberries, wild blackberries, and strawberries and was struck by how their sweet aromas filled the air. He picked four plump blackberries, and their juice ran down his fingers as he slowly savored them. He was reminded of Pete when he tasted the fresh olive bread at Canaan's Kitchen. He wiped a drop of juice from his chin with the back of his sleeve and let out a contented sigh.

Sterling looked around again and spotted a familiar person walking several rows ahead of him. It was Laurel, heading toward the cabanas. He did not call out to her for fear of disturbing her peace, but once she was farther along the path, I piffed him to follow. He hesitated for a moment, but then sensed it was the right thing to do. By the time he caught up with Laurel, she was sitting on a bench in a cabana, eating a handful of blueberries.

Sterling stepped to the doorway and sheepishly said, "Hello?"

Laurel stopped eating mid-bite. "Sterling?" She got up and stepped out into the sunlight where Sterling stood. She shielded her eyes with her hands and smiled. "I can't say I expected to see you here this morning."

"It's a surprise to me, too. But I couldn't get the garden out of my mind. I was going to explore the other side of it when I saw you."

"How did you find the way in?"

"It's . . . hard to explain. There was a dove, and it wouldn't leave me alone. Somehow, I knew I needed to follow it, and it gave me a key."

"Ahh, it's always something like that. Everyone gets piffs, but they are easy to miss. I'm glad you paid attention."

"Piffs?"

"Yeah, that's what John calls them. They're nudges from God. Sometimes they're dreams or unexpected encounters. Sometimes they're passing thoughts. Piffs make you wonder if there might be more to life than what our five senses can detect."

"Huh. I guess I've been piffed."

Laurel nodded. "There are more to come."

Sterling's eyes wandered to the beauty surrounding them. "This place is amazing. It's unlike anything I imagined."

"Told you," Laurel said, delighted. "Canaan's Garden has it all. It's a land of brooks, fountains and springs, a land of fruit trees and every kind of vegetable, a land in which we lack nothing. Springs below and the rain above water it every night." She took hold of Sterling's arm. "Come with me. There's someone you should see."

Laurel led Sterling to a grove of fruit trees, and John was pruning unproductive branches there. Laurel got his attention, saying, "Look who I found enjoying the garden."

John turned and broke into a huge grin. "I can't say I'm surprised. How do you like the place so far, Sterling?"

"It's almost unbelievable. Did you grow all this?"

"Well, I can't take credit for that—I'm just the caretaker. I try to ensure the fruit grows to maturity and ripens right here in the garden."

Sterling asked, "So, this garden is here to provide food for you and the restaurant?"

"That's partially true, but that's not all. The garden has a higher purpose. It is an oasis for the spirit, soul, and even the body. A place of transformation. Without transformation, we can never transcend our material world. We keep stumbling over, struggling, doing the things we really don't want to do, and neglecting the good. This garden is an ideal place to overcome, to cultivate our inner life. To grow."

"Man, I wish I had a garden like this," Sterling said. "I could sure use it."

"You do have one," John replied. "This is your garden now, too. You're welcome to come here whenever you want."

Sterling looked at Laurel, who nodded in agreement. He thanked them both and said, "I see why this place means so much to you two. It's perfect."

"You'll enjoy it even more as you learn to wait and listen," John said.

Sterling patted at his pocket and pulled out his phone. "Speaking of listening, I forgot I silenced my phone. Hoyt's been trying to call me. We have to work this afternoon."

"You better take care of that," John said. "The garden will always be waiting whenever you're free to return."

"I'll come back as soon as I can. I want to learn about new life."

Laurel said, "Bethany and I plan to meet here with John this evening after work. Would you like to join us?"

"What time?"

"Around 7:30."

"Can I meet you earlier? Say, 7:00?"

"Sure."

Sterling waved goodbye to Laurel and John and retraced his steps along the muddy path behind the waterfall to exit the barn. As he locked the door and returned the key to its place above the door, he was astonished at how easily he entered the garden. He shook his head and returned to his normal world, already looking forward to that evening.

Fifty-Two

It is the heart which perceives God and not the reason. That is what faith is: God perceived by the heart, not by reason.

—Blaise Pascal

AFTER DINNER, STERLING drove the Mustang to meet with John, Bethany, and Laurel. He arrived at the restaurant half an hour early, so he could have time alone to think before returning to the garden. He parked the car in the spot closest to the waterfall, where Laurel couldn't miss it, and sat on the bench to wait for her. In the quiet, Sterling was reminded how crazy the past few weeks had been. From the storm to Dirk's shootout, to the interrogations with the cops and the DEA. Now there was a whole world beyond to reckon with.

Sterling was eager to catch up with Laurel. He had yet to tell her about his inheritance, being accepted into Running Start, getting his driver's license, and his trip to Spokane to get the car. But he knew there might not be time to discuss all of it before the meeting. The more Sterling thought about talking with everyone in the garden, the more he became nervous about saying something stupid. John, Bethany, and Laurel understood so much more about transformation than he did. Sure, John had said transformation was a lifelong process, but Sterling's had just begun. He felt like an outsider looking in, and he had many questions. *What does God expect from me? What if I keep doing the wrong thing? Is it a sin? Will God give up on me? Is doubting wrong? Should I go to church? So many things inside me need to change—hatred, unforgiveness, loving money—things I am powerless to change. And there are so many things I need to become—loving, forgiving, and generous.*

Sterling ran his fingers through his hair and took a deep breath. *Good thing it's a lifelong process.* Laurel walked out of the restaurant and had changed after work. She was wearing faded, torn blue jeans, a red T-shirt, matching red shoes, and a frown. When she approached the bench, Sterling asked what was wrong.

"Dad called," she said. "He's still pretty sore about *Meryl*. Mostly that I took it out by myself in such a storm. I can't say he's happy that I swamped it either, though." She sat next to Sterling and continued, "By the way, he asked me to thank you for helping John take *Meryl* to Charlie's. Sounds like they restored everything except the radio, radar, and depth finder—too much salt water. So, I'll have to replace them before Mom and Dad get here next month. It'll take all my savings and then some. And that's if I can buy at least one of them used."

"I'll help. Hoyt and I have enough yard jobs, and my parents said they'll pay for my school clothes."

"I can't let you do that."

"Why not? If I remember correctly, you wrecked the boat trying to help *me*. Oh, and Dirk's insurance will pay to repair *Leverage,* so it will belong to Hoyt and me and me in a couple of weeks. If *Meryl* isn't ready when your dad comes back, he can use our boat when he wants to go fishing."

Laurel stared at Sterling as if he were a new person. Such effortless generosity seemed to come out of the blue, but it suited him.

"I was wrong about you, Sterling Burke," Laurel said. "You're all right."

WHEN STERLING AND Laurel stood to walk into the garden, I soared over them. My form as a dove in Sterling's life had served its purpose, and now I can interact with him anew. A material body will no longer be necessary, and as a spirit, I will never leave him. He understands he is a sojourner in this world, a temporary resident, and his permanent citizenship is in the world beyond. I will continue to piff him, and his ability to hear me will increase, especially as he spends time in the garden, reading the Bible, and listening. I will make the Master's words come alive to him, and I will remind him of the truth he has read. He will become more familiar with Jesus, and I will reveal the Master's will to him. Steadily, Sterling's faith will increase, and he will transform on the inside. He will always have questions, but his questions will change and develop as he grows. There are many things he will not understand until the day he goes beyond Canaan's Garden and enters to the ultimate garden for eternity.

Sterling can look forward to a long journey ahead.

Author's Notes

I hope you enjoyed reading *Sterling's Sojourn*. My website has information about Port Angeles and the Raspberry Pi. Plus, it offers a Discussion Guide for your use. Please visit www.tedgary.com/freebies to access this information.

Blaise Pascal (June 19, 1623 - August 19, 1662) was a French scientist, mathematician, and religious philosopher. His accomplishments include laying the foundation for probability theory, developing Pascal's Law which describes fluid mechanics in a closed container, and inventing the first computer—a mechanical calculator. In addition to his scientific contributions, Pascal wrote *The Province Letters* to express the idea that people experience God through the heart and not through reason, which was a controversial thought in his day.

Since then, science has advanced, is advancing, and will continue to advance. However, the principle of faith has not changed, and Pascal's belief is still true—God may be appreciated through reason, but the experience of Him transcends all rational thought.

Sterling's Sojourn is a work of fiction. Except for public places in or around Port Angeles, all the names, characters, businesses, places, events, and incidents in this book are either the product of the author's imagination or used in a fictitious manner. Any resemblance to actual persons, living or dead, or actual events is purely coincidental.

www.ingramcontent.com/pod-product-compliance
Lightning Source LLC
Chambersburg PA
CBHW051331250626
47155CB00007B/2550